Constance Fenimore Woolson

Horace Chase

A Novel

Constance Fenimore Woolson

Horace Chase
A Novel

ISBN/EAN: 9783743334380

Manufactured in Europe, USA, Canada, Australia, Japa

Cover: Foto ©Andreas Hilbeck / pixelio.de

Manufactured and distributed by brebook publishing software
(www.brebook.com)

Constance Fenimore Woolson

Horace Chase

HORACE CHASE

𝔄 𝔑𝔬𝔳𝔢𝔩

BY

CONSTANCE FENIMORE WOOLSON
AUTHOR OF "JUPITER LIGHTS" "EAST ANGELS" ETC.

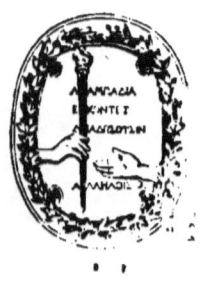

NEW YORK
HARPER & BROTHERS PUBLISHERS
1894

HORACE CHASE

CHAPTER I

In a mountain village of North Carolina, in the
year 1873, the spring had opened with its accustomed beauty. But one day there came a pure cold
wind which swept through the high valley at tremendous speed from dawn to midnight. People
who never succumb to mere comfort did not relight
their fires. But to the Franklin family comfort was
a goddess, they would never have thought of calling
her." mere "; " delightful " was their word, and Ruth
would probably have said " delicious." The fire in
Mrs. Franklin's parlor, therefore, having been piled
with fresh logs at two o'clock as an offering to this
deity, was now, at four, sending out a ruddy glow.
It was a fire which called forth Ruth's highest ap-
probation when she came in, followed by her dog,
Petie Trone, Esq. Not that Ruth had been facing
the blast ; she never went out from a sense of duty,
and for her there was no pleasure in doing battle
with things that were disagreeable for the sake merely of conquering them. Ruth had come from her

1

own room, where there was a fire also, but one not so generous as this, for here the old-fashioned hearth was broad and deep. The girl sat down on the rug before the blaze, and then, after a moment, she stretched herself out at full length there, with her head resting on her arm thrown back behind it.

"It's a pity, Ruth, that with all your little ways, you are not little yourself," remarked Dolly Franklin, the elder sister. "Such a whalelike creature sprawled on the floor isn't endearing; it looks like something out of Gulliver."

"It's always so," observed Mrs. Franklin, drowsily. "It's the oddest thing in the world—but people never will stay in character; they want to be something different. Don't you remember that whenever poor Sue Inness was asked to sing, the wee little creature invariably chanted, 'Here's a health to King Charles,' in as martial a voice as she could summon? Whereas Lucia Lewis, who is as big as a grenadier, always warbles softly some such thing as 'Call me pet names, dearest. Call me a bird.' Bird! Mastodon would do better."

"Mastodon?" Ruth commented. "It is evident, His Grand, that you have seen Miss Billy to-day!"

Ruth was not a whale, in spite of Dolly's assertion. But she was tall, her shoulders had a marked breadth, and her arms were long. She was very slender and supple, and this slenderness, together with her small hands and feet, took away all idea of majesty in connection with her, tall though she was; one did not think of majesty, but rather of girlish merriment and girlish activity. And girlish indolence as well. Mrs. Franklin had once said: "Ruth is either running, or jumping, or doing something in such haste that she is breathless; or else she is stretched out at full length on the carpet or the sofa, looking as though she never intended to move again!"

The girl had a dark complexion with a rich color, and hair that was almost black; her face was lighted by blue eyes, with long thick black lashes which made a dark fringe round the blue. The persons who liked Ruth thought her beautiful; they asserted that her countenance had in it something which was captivating. But others replied that though her friends might call her captivating if they pleased, since that word denotes merely a personal charm, they had no right to say that she was beautiful; for as regards beauty, there are well-defined rules, and, with the exception of her wonderful eyes, the face of the second Miss Franklin transgressed every one of these canons. Ruth's features were without doubt irregular. And especially was it true that her mouth was large. But the lips were exquisitely cut, and the teeth very white. Regarding her appearance as a whole, there was a fact which had not as yet been noticed, namely, that no man ever found fault with it; the criticism came always from feminine lips. And these critics spoke the truth; but they forgot, or rather they did not see, some of the compensations. There were people not a few, even in her own small circle, who did not look

with favor upon Ruth Franklin; it was not merely, so
they asserted, that she was heedless and frivolous,
caring only for her own amusement, and sacrificing
everything to that, for of many young persons this
could be said; but they maintained in addition
that hers was a disposition in its essence self-in-
dulgent; she was indolent; she was fond of luxu-
ries; she was even fond of "good eating"—an odd
accusation to be brought against a girl of that age.
In this case also the charges were made by feminine lips. And again it may be added that while
these critics spoke the truth, or part of the truth,
they did not, on the other hand, see some of the
compensations.

"Why do you say '*poor* Sue Inness,' His Grand?"
inquired Dolly, in an expostulating tone. "Why do
people always say '*poor*' so-and-so, of any one who
is dead? It is an alarmingly pitying word; as
though the unfortunate departed must certainly be
in a very bad place!"

"Here is something about the bishop," said Mrs.
Franklin, who was reading a Raleigh newspaper in
the intervals of conversation. Her tone was now
animated. "He has been in Washington, and one
of his sermons was—"

But she was interrupted by her daughters, who
united their voices in a chant as follows:

"Mother Franklin thinks,
That General Jackson,
Jared the Sixth,

> Macaroon custards,
> And Bishop Carew,
> Are per-*fec*-tion !"

Mrs. Franklin made no reply to these Gregorian assertions (which she had often heard before), save the remark, "You have torn your skirt, Ruth."

"Oh, please don't look at me over your glasses, His Grand. It spoils your profile so," answered Ruth; for Mrs. Franklin was surveying the skirt with her head bent forward and her chin drawn sharply in, so that her eyes could be brought to bear upon the rent over her spectacles.

She now drew off these aids to vision impatiently. "Whether I look through them or over them doesn't matter; you and Dolly are never satisfied. I cannot read the paper without my glasses; do you wish me to know nothing of the news of the world?"

"We'll *tell* you," responded Dolly, going on busily with her knitting. "For instance, to-day: Genevieve has had *all* the paint cleaned and *all* the windows washed; she is now breathing that righteous atmosphere of cold, fireless bleakness and soap which she adores. Miss Billy Breeze has admired everything that she can think of, because admiration is so uplifting. And she has written another page about the primeval world; now she—"

Here the door which led to the entrance-hall was opened with a jerk by Linda, a plump negro girl, who bounced in, ejaculated "Lady !" in a congratulatory tone, and then bounced out to act as usher for the incoming guest.

"Billy herself, probably," said Mrs. Franklin. "Ruth, are you stretched out there under the plea that you are not yet fully grown?"

But Ruth did not deem it necessary to leave her couch for Miss Billy Breeze. "Hail, Billy!" she said, as the visitor entered. "Mother thinks that I ought to be seated politely on the sofa; will you please imagine that I am there?"

"Oh, certainly," replied Miss Breeze, in a conciliatory tone. Miss Breeze lived under the impression that the members of this family quarrelled with each other almost incessantly; when she was present, therefore, she did her best to smooth over their asperities. "It is rather good for her, you know," she said reassuringly to Mrs. Franklin; "for it is a windy day, and Ruth is not robust." Then to Ruth: "Your mother naturally wishes you to look your best, my dear."

"Do you, His Grand?" inquired Ruth. "Because if you do, I must certainly stay where I am, so that I can tuck under me, very neatly, this rip in my skirt, which Miss Billy has not yet seen. Petie Trone, Esq., shake hands with the lady." The dog, a small black-and-tan terrier, was reposing on the rug beside Ruth; upon hearing her command, he trotted across to the visitor, and offered a tiny paw.

"Dear little fellow," said Miss Breeze, bending,

and shaking it gently. " His Grand must allow that
he looks extremely well?"

For the circle of friends had ended by accepting
the legend (invented by Ruth) that Mrs. Franklin
was Petie Trone's grandmother, or " His Grand."
The only person who still held out against this title
was Genevieve, the daughter-in-law; Mrs. Franklin
the younger thought that the name was ridiculous.
Her husband's family seemed to her incomprehensi-
bly silly about their pets.

Miss Wilhelmina Breeze was thirty-five; but no
one would have thought so from her fair pink-and-
white complexion, and young, innocent eyes. From
her earliest years she had longed to hear herself
called " Wilhelmina." But the longing was almost
never gratified; the boyish name given to her in
joke when she was a baby had clung to her with
the usual fatal tenacity.

" Miss Billy, have you seen mother to-day?" Dolly
inquired.

" Not until now," answered the visitor, surprised.

" Well, then, have you thought of mastodons?"

" Certainly I have; and if you yourself, Dolly,
would think more seriously of the whole subject, the
primeval world — you would soon be as fascinated
with it as I am. Imagine one of those vast extinct
animals, Dolly, lifting his neck up a hill to nibble
the trees on its top!" said Miss Breeze with enthusiasm. " And birds as large as chapels flying through
the air! Probably they sang, those birds. What

sort of voices do you suppose they had? The cave-lion was twenty-nine feet high. The horned tryceratops was seventy-five feet long! It elevates the mind even to think of them."

"You see, His Grand, that she *has* thought of mastodons," commented Dolly. "Your unexpected mention of them, therefore, is plainly the influence of her mind acting upon yours from a distance—the distance of the Old North Hotel."

"Have you really thought of them, dear Mrs. Franklin? And do you believe there can be such a thing as the conscious—I mean, of course, *uncon*-scious—influence of one mind upon another?" inquired Miss Billy, her face betraying a delighted excitement.

"No, no; it's only Dolly's nonsense," answered Mrs. Franklin.

"It's easy to say nonsense, His Grand. But how, then, do you account for the utterances of my planchette?" demanded Dolly, wagging her head triumphantly.

Dolly, the second of Mrs. Franklin's three children, was an invalid. The Franklins, as a family, were tall and dark, and Dolly was tall and dark also; her face, owing to the pain which frequently assailed her, was thin, worn, and wrinkled. She sat in a low easy-chair, and beside her was her own especial table, which held what she called her "jibs." These were numerous, for Dolly occupied herself in many ways. She sketched, she carved little knick-knacks,

she played the violin ; she made lace, she worked
out chess problems, and she knitted ; she also scribbled rhymes which her family called poetry. The
mantel-piece of this parlor was adorned with a hanging which bore one of her verses, stitched in old
English text, the work of her mother's needle :

> "O Fire ! in these dark frozen days
> So gracious is thy red,
> So warm thy comfort, we forget
> The violets are dead."

The family thought this beautiful. Dolly's verses,
her drawing and wood-carving, her lace-making and
chess, were amateurish ; her violin - playing was at
times spirited, and that was the utmost that could be
said of it. But her knitting was remarkable. She
knitted nothing but silk stockings, and these, when
finished, had a wonderful perfection. Dolly was
accustomed to say of herself that in the heels of her
stockings was to be found the only bit of conscience
which she possessed.

When she mentioned planchette, her mother
frowned. "I do not approve of such things."

"Yes, because you are afraid !" chuckled Dolly.

"Oh, anything that dear Mrs. Franklin does not
approve of—" murmured Miss Billy.

Mrs. Franklin rose.

"His Grand is fleeing !" Dolly announced, gleefully.

"I must make the salad-dressing, mustn't I ? Ruth

will not touch Zoe's dressing. Billy, Mr. Chase is to dine with us to - day, informally; don't you want to stay and help us entertain him?" added the mistress of the house as she left the room.

"Dolly," suggested Ruth, from her place on the rug, "set planchette to work, and make it tell us secrets; make it tell us whether Miss Billy understands the *true* character of Achilles Larue!"

"She does not; I can tell her that without planchette," replied Dolly. "Only one person in the world has ever fully understood Achilles—had the strength to do it; and *he* died!"

"Yes, I know; I have heard Mr. Larue speak of that one friend," said Miss Billy, regretfully. "How unfortunate that he lost him!"

"Yes, baddish. And the term is quite in his own line," commented Dolly. "With him it is never warm, but warmish; the bluest sky is bluish; a June day, fairish; a twenty-mile walk, longish. In this way he is not committed to extravagant statements. When he is dead, he won't be more than deadish. But he's that now."

Mrs. Franklin, having made the salad-dressing (when she made it, it was always perfection), returned to the parlor. "Ruth, go and change your dress. Take Miss Billy with you, but take her to my room, not yours. For of course you will stay, Billy?"

"I don't think I'd better; I'm not dressed for the evening; and I said I should be back," answered Miss Breeze, hesitatingly.

"To whom did you say it? To the Old North? Run along," said Mrs. Franklin, smiling. "If it is shoes you are thinking of, as yours are muddy, Ruth can lend you a pair."

"That she cannot," remarked Dolly. "Buy Ruth six pairs of new shoes, and in six days all will be shabby. But you can have a pair of mine, Miss Billy."

When she was left alone with her elder daughter, Mrs. Franklin said: "Poor Billy! She is always haunted by the idea that she may possibly meet Achilles Larue here. She certainly will not meet him at the Old North, for he never goes near the place, in spite of her gentle invitations. But here there is always a chance, and I never can resist giving it to her, although in reality it is folly; he has never looked at her, and he never will."

"No. But you need not be anxious about her," replied Dolly; "she has the happy faculty of living in illusions, day after day. She can go on hopefully admiring Achilles to the last moment of her life, and I dare say she even thinks that he has a liking for her, little as he shows it. She has occult reasons for this belief; she would find them in a kick."

"Goose!" said Mrs. Franklin, dismissing Billy's virginal dreams with the matron's disillusioned knowledge. "Aren't you going to change your dress, Dolly?"

"Why? Am I not tidy as I am? I thought you considered me too tidy?" And it was true that the elder Miss Franklin was always a personification of rigid neatness; from the dark hair that shaded her tired face, to the shoes on her feet, all was severely orderly and severely plain.

"Oh, go, go!" answered her mother, impatiently.

Dolly screwed up her mouth, shook her head slowly, and laid her work aside; then she rose, and with her cane walked towards the door. On her way she stopped, and, bending, kissed her mother's forehead. "Some of these days, mother, I shall be beautiful. It will be during one of our future existences somewhere. It must be so, dear; you have earned it for me by your loving pity here." Nothing could exceed the tenderness of her tone as she said this.

Mrs. Franklin made no response beyond a little toss of her head, as though repudiating this account of herself. But after Dolly had left the room, a moisture gathered in the mother's eyes.

Ruth, meanwhile, had conducted Miss Billy to her own chamber.

"But Mrs. Franklin said I was to go to *her* room?" suggested the guest.

"She doesn't mind; she only meant that Bob is probably here," answered Ruth, as she opened the windows and threw back the blinds; for the afternoon was drawing towards its close.

Miss Billy took off her bonnet, and, after a moment's thought, hung it by its crown on a peg; in that position it did not seem possible that even Bob

could make a resting-place within it. Bob was young
and very small. He was beautiful or devilish according to one's view of flying-squirrels. But whether
you liked him or whether you hated him, there was
always a certain amount of interest in connection
with the creature, because you could never be sure
where he was. Miss Billy, who was greatly afraid
of him, had given a quick look towards the tops of
the windows and doors. There was no squirrel visible. But that was small comfort; Bob could hide
himself behind a curtain-ring when he chose. One of
the blinds came swinging to with a bang, and Ruth,
reopening the window, struggled with it again.
"There is Mr. Hill coming along the back street on
Daniel," she said, pausing. "He is beckoning to me!
What can he want? You will find shoes in the
closet, Miss Billy, and don't wait for me; I am going down to speak to him." Away she flew, running
lightly at full speed through the upper hall and down
the back stairs, closely followed by Petie Trone, Esq.

Miss Billy closed the window and stood there for
a moment looking out. Presently she saw Ruth at
the stone wall at the end of the garden. She also
recognized (with disapproving eyes) the unclerical hat
of the Rev. Malachi Hill, who had stopped his horse
in the road outside. He was talking to Ruth, who
listened with her chin resting on her hands on the
top of the wall, while the wind roughened her hair
wildly, and blew out her skirts like a balloon. Miss
Billy watched her for a while; then, after making

her own preparations for the evening, she seated herself by the fire to wait. For no one could make Ruth come in one moment before she chose to do so; it seemed better, therefore, not to call attention to her absence by returning to the parlor alone, lest Mrs. Franklin should be made uneasy by knowing that the girl was out, bareheaded, in the cold wind. Having made her decision (Billy was always troubled, even upon the smallest occasion, by four or five different theories as to the best course to pursue), she looked about the room with the same wonder and gentle dislike which she had often felt before. The necessary articles of furniture were all set closely back against the wall, in order that the central space of the large chamber should be left entirely free. For Ruth did not like little things—small objects of any kind which required dusting, and which could be easily upset. Miss Billy, who adored little things, and who lived in a grove of them, thought the place dreadfully bare. There were no souvenirs; no photographs of friends in velvet frames; there were no small tables, brackets, screens, hanging shelves, little chairs, little boxes, little baskets, fans, and knickknacks; there was not even a wall-calendar. With Miss Billy, the removal of the old leaf from her poetical calendar, and the reading of the new one each morning, was a solemn rite. And when her glance reached the toilet-table, her non-comprehension reached its usual climax. The table itself was plain and unadorned, but on its top was spread out a profuse array of toilet articles, all of ivory or crystal. That a girl so wholly careless about everything else should insist upon having so many costly and dainty objects for her personal use in the privacy of her own room seemed remarkable. "Give Ruth her bath in scented water, and all these ivory and crystal things to use when she dresses, and she is perfectly willing to go about in a faded, torn old skirt, a hat entirely out of fashion, shabby gloves, and worn-out shoes; in short, looking anyhow!" mused Billy, perplexed.

Down-stairs Mrs. Franklin was receiving another visitor. After Dolly's departure, Rinda had made a second irruptive entrance, with the announcement, "Gen'lem!" and Mr. Anthony Etheridge came in. Etheridge was a strikingly handsome man, who appeared to be about fifty-eight. He entered with light step and smiling face, and a flower in his coat.

"Ah, commodore, when did you return?" said Mrs. Franklin, giving him her hand.

"Two hours ago," answered Etheridge, bowing over it gallantly. "You are looking remarkably well, my dear madam. Hum-ha!" These last syllables were not distinct; Etheridge often made this little sound, which was not an ahem; it seemed intended to express merely a general enjoyment of existence—a sort of overflow of health and vitality.

"Only two hours ago? You have been all day in that horrible stage, and yet you have strength to pay visits?"

"Not visits; a visit. You are alone?"

"Only for the moment; Dolly and Ruth are dressing. We are expecting some one to dine with us— a new acquaintance, by-the-way, since you left; a Mr. Chase."

"Yes, Horace Chase; I knew he was here. I should like to kick him out!"

"Why so fierce?" said Mrs. Franklin, going on with her lamplighters. For the making of lamplighters from old newspapers was one of her pastimes.

"Of course I am fierce. We don't want fellows of that sort here; he will upset the whole place! What brought him?"

"He has not been well, I believe" ("That's one comfort! They never are," interpolated Etheridge), "and he was advised to try mountain air. In addition, he is said to be looking into the railroad project."

"Good heavens! Already? The one solace I got out of the war was the check it gave to the advance of those horrible rails westward; I have been in hopes that the locomotives would not get beyond Old Fort in my time, at any rate. Why, Dora, this strip of mountain country is the most splendid bit of natural forest, of nature undraped, which exists to-day between the Atlantic Ocean and the Rockies!"

"Save your eloquence for Genevieve, commodore."

"Hum-ha! Mrs. Jared, eh?"

"Yes; she knew Mr. Chase when he was a little boy; she says she used to call him Horrie. As soon

as she heard that he was here, she revived the acquaintance; and then she introduced him to us."

"Does she *like* him?" asked Etheridge, with annoyance in his tone.

"I don't know whether she likes him or not; but
she is hoping that he will do something that will increase the value of property here."

"It is intelligent of Mrs. Jared to be thinking of
that already," said Etheridge, softening a little. "Perhaps if I owned land here, I should take another view
of the subject myself! You too, Dora—you might
make something?"

"No; we have no land save the garden, and the
house is dreadfully dilapidated. Personally, I may
as well confess that I should be glad to see the railroad arrive; I am mortally tired of that long jolting
stage-drive from Old Fort; it nearly kills me each
time I take it. And I am afraid I don't care for nature undraped so much as you do, commodore; I
think I like draperies."

"Of course you do! But when you—and by you
I mean the nation at large—when you perceive that
your last acre of primitive forest is forever gone, then
you will repent. And you will begin to cultivate wildness as they do abroad, poor creatures—plant forests
and guard 'em with stone walls and keepers, by Jove!
Horace Chase appears here as the pioneer of spolia-
tion. He may not mean it; he does not come with
an axe on his shoulder exactly; he comes, in fact,
with baking-powder; but that's how it will end.

2

Haven't you heard that it was baking-powder? At
least you have heard of the powder itself—the Bubble? I thought so. Well, that's where he made his
first money — the Bubble Baking-Powder; and he
made a lot of it, too! Now he is in no end of other
things. One of them is steamships; some of the
Willoughbys of New York have gone in with him,
and together they have set up a new company, with
steamers running south—the Columbian Line."

"Yes, Genevieve explained it to us. But as he
does not travel with his steamers round his neck, there
remains for us, inland people as we are, only what he
happens to be himself. And that is nothing interesting."

"Not interesting, eh?" said Etheridge, rather gratified.

"To my mind he is not. He is ordinary in appearance and manners; he says 'yes, ma'am,' and 'no,
ma'am,' to me, as though I were a great-grandmother!
In short, I don't care for him, and it is solely on Genevieve's account that I have invited him. For she
keeps urging me to do it; she is very anxious to have
him like Asheville. He has already dined with us
twice, to meet her. But to-day he comes informally
—a chance invitation given only this morning (and
again given solely to please *her*), when I happened
to meet him at the Cottage."

"How old is the wretch?"

"I don't know. Forty-four or forty-five."

"Quite impossible, then, that Mrs. Jared should

have known him when he was a boy; she was not born at that time," commented Etheridge. "What she means, of course, is that she, as a child herself, called him 'Horrie.'"

Mrs. Franklin did not answer, and at this moment Dolly came in.

"Yes, I am well," she said, in reply to the visitor's greeting; "we are all well, and lazy. The world at large will never be helped much by us, I fear; we are too contented. Have you ever noticed, commodore, that the women who sacrifice their lives so nobly to help humanity seldom sacrifice one small thing, and that is a happy home? Either they do not possess such an article, or else they have spoiled it by quarrelling with every individual member of their families."

"Now, Dolly, no more of your sarcasms. Tell me rather about this new acquaintance of yours, this bubbling capitalist whom you have invented and set up in your midst during my unsuspecting absence," said Etheridge.

"You need not think, commodore, that you can make me say one word about him," answered Dolly, solemnly; "for I read in a book only the other day that a tendency to talk about other persons, instead of one's self, was a sure sign of advancing age. Young people, the book goes on to say, are at heart interested in nothing on earth but themselves and their own affairs; they have not the least curiosity about character or traits in general. As I wish to be considered young, I have made a vow to talk of nothing but myself hereafter. Anything you may wish to hear about *me* I am ready to tell you." Dolly was now attired in a velvet dress of dark russet hue, like the color of autumn oak leaves; this tint took the eye away somewhat from the worn look of her plain thin face. The dress, however, was eight years old, and the fashion in which it had been made originally had never been altered.

"The being interested in nothing but themselves, and their own doings and feelings, is not confined to young people," said Mrs. Franklin, laughing. "I have known a goodly number of their elders who were quite as bad. When these gentry hold forth, by the hour, about their convictions and their theories, their beliefs and disbeliefs, their likings and dislikings, their tastes and their principles, their souls, their minds, and their bodies—if, in despair, you at last, by way of a change, turn the conversation towards some one else, they become loftily silent. And they go away and tell everybody, with regret of course, that you are hopelessly given to gossip! Gossip, in fact, has become very valuable to me; I keep it on hand, and pour it forth in floods, to drown those egotists out."

"When you gossip, then, I shall know that *I* bore you," said Etheridge, rising, "I mustn't do so now; I leave you to your Bubble. Mrs. Jared, I suppose, will be with you this evening? I ask because I had thought of paying her a how-do-you-do visit, later."

"Pay it here, commodore," suggested Mrs. Franklin. "Perhaps you would like to see her 'Horrie' yourself?"

"Greatly, greatly. I am always glad to meet any of these driving speculators who come within my reach. For it makes me contented for a month afterwards—contented with my own small means—to see how yellow they are! Not a man jack of them who hasn't a skin like guinea gold." Upon this point the commodore could enlarge safely, for no color could be fresher and finer than his own.

After he had gone, Mrs. Franklin said: "Imagine what he has just told me—that Genevieve could not possibly have known Horace Chase when he was a boy, because she is far too young!" And then mother and daughter joined in a merry laugh.

"It would be fun to tell him that she was forty on her last birthday," said Dolly.

"He would never believe you; he would think that you fibbed from jealousy," answered Mrs. Franklin. "As you are dressed, I may as well go and make ready myself," she added, rising. "I have been waiting for Ruth; I cannot imagine what she is about."

This is what Ruth was about—she was rushing up the back stairs in the dark, breathless. When she reached her room, she lit the candles hastily. "You still here, Miss Billy? I supposed you had gone down long ago." She stirred the fire into a blaze, and knelt to warm her cold hands. "Such fun! I have made an engagement for us all, this evening. You can never think what it is. Nothing less than a fancy-dress procession at the rink for the benefit of the Mission. A man is carrying costumes across the mountains for some tableaux for a soldiers' monument at Knoxville; his wagon has broken down, and he is obliged to stay here until it is mended. Mr. Hill has made use of this for the Mission. Isn't it a splendid idea? He has been rushing about all the afternoon, and he has found twenty persons who are willing to appear in fancy dress, and he himself is to be an Indian chief, in war-paint and feathers."

"In war-paint and feathers? *Oh !*"

"Yes. It seems that he has a costume of his own. He had it when he was an insurance agent, you know, before he entered the ministry; he was always fond of such things, he says, and the costume is a very handsome one; when he wore it, he called himself Big Moose."

"Big Moose! It must be stopped," said Miss Billy, in a horrified voice. For Miss Billy had the strictest ideas regarding the dignity of the clergy.

"On the contrary, I told him that it would be a great attraction, and that it was his duty to do all he could," declared Ruth, breaking into one of her intense laughs. Her laugh was not loud, but when it had once begun it seemed sometimes as if it would never stop. At present, as soon as she could speak, she announced, "We'll *all* go."

"Do not include me," said Miss Billy, with dignity. "I think it shocking, Ruth. I do indeed."

"Oh, you'll be there," said Ruth, springing up,

and drawing Miss Billy to her feet. "You'll put on roller-skates yourself, and go wheeling off first this way, then that way, with Achilles Larue." And, as she said this, she gleefully forced her visitor across the floor, now in a long sweep to the right, now to the left, with as close an imitation of skating as the circumstances permitted.

While they were thus engaged, Mrs. Franklin opened the door. "What are you doing? Ruth — not dressed yet?"

"I'm all ready, His Grand," responded Ruth, running across the room and pouring water into the basin in a great hurry. "I have only to wash my hands" (here she dashed lavender into the water); "I'll be down directly."

"And we shall all admire you in that torn dress," said her mother.

"Never mind, I'll pin it up. Nobody will see it at dinner, under the table. And after dinner my cloak will cover it—for we are all going out."

"Going out this windy evening? Never! Are you ready, Billy? And Ruth, you must come as you are, for Mr. Chase is already here, and Rinda is bringing in the soup."

"Never fear, His Grand. I'll come."

And come she did, two minutes later, just as she was, save that her wind-roughened hair had been vaguely smoothed, and fastened down hastily with large hair-pins placed at random. Owing to her hurry, she had a brilliant color; and seeing, as she entered, the disapproving expression in her mother's eyes, she was seized with the idea of making, for her own amusement, a stately sweeping courtesy to Horace Chase; this she accordingly did, carrying it off very well, with an air of majesty just tempered at the edges with burlesque.

Chase, who had risen, watched this salutation with great interest. When it was over, he felt it incumbent upon him, however, to go through, in addition, the more commonplace greeting. "How do you do, Miss Ruth?" he said, extending his hand. And he gave the tips of her fingers (all she yielded to him) three careful distinct shakes.

Then they went to dinner.

CHAPTER II

THE meal which followed was good; for Zoe, the cook, was skilful in her old-fashioned way. But the dinner service was ordinary; the only wine was Dry Catawba; Rinda's ideas of waiting, too, were primitive. The Franklins, however, had learned to wait upon themselves. They had the habit of remaining long at the table; for, whether they were alone or whether they had a guest, there was always a soup, there was always a salad, there were always nuts and fruit, followed by coffee—four courses, therefore, in addition to the two which the younger Mrs. Franklin, whose household was managed in a very different way, considered all that was necessary "for the body."

"A serious rice pudding, Genevieve, no doubt *is* enough for the body, as you call it," Dolly had once said. "But *we* think of the mind also; we aim at brilliancy. And no one ever scintillated yet on codfish and stewed prunes!"

"Mrs. Jared Franklin is well, I hope?" Chase asked, when the last course was reached. He was not fond of nuts or figs, but he was playing his part, according to his conception of it, by eating at intervals one raisin.

"Quite well; thanks. I have never known her to be ill," replied Dolly.

"Mr. Chase, I am going to suggest something: as mother and my sister-in-law are both Mrs. Jared, and as mother has no burning desire to be called 'old Mrs. Franklin' just yet, why don't you say 'Mrs. G. B.' when you mean the younger matron?"

Chase would never have thought of calling either the one or the other a matron, his idea of the word being the female superintendent of a public institution. "G. B.—are those her initials?" he said. "Yes, of course; G. for Genevieve, or Gen, as I used to call her."

"And B. for Beatrice; isn't that lovely? Our own names, unfortunately, are very plain — Ruth, Dolly, and Jared; Genevieve has taken pity upon the Jared, and changed it to Jay. Mother, however, actually likes the name Jared. She is weak enough to be proud of the fact that there have been six Jared Franklins in the direct line, from eldest son to father, going back to colonial days. People are *very* sorry for this delusion of hers; they have told her repeatedly that the colonial period was unimportant. Genevieve, in particular, has often explained to her that modern times are far more interesting."

"I guess there isn't much question about that, is there?" said Chase. "No doubt they did the best they could in those old days. But they couldn't do much, you see, because they had nothing to work with, no machinery, no capital, no combinations;

they couldn't hear anything until long after it had happened, and they couldn't go anywhere except on horseback. I've always been glad *I* didn't serve my time then. I guess I should have found it slow."

"You must find Asheville rather slow? remarked Dolly.

"It is more than slow, Miss Franklin; it has stopped entirely. But it has great natural advantages—I have been surprised to see how many. I like new enterprises, and I've been thinking about something." Here he paused and ate one more raisin, balancing it for a moment upon the palm of his hand before he swallowed it. "I've been thinking of picking up that railroad at Old Fort and pushing it right through to this place, and on to Tennessee; a branch, later, to tap South Carolina and Georgia. That isn't all, however." He paused again. Then with a glance which rested for a moment on each face, and finally stopped at Mrs. Franklin's, "What do you say," he added, with an hospitable smile, "to my making a big watering-place of your hilly little village?"

"*Asheville* watered? What next!" said Dolly.

"The next is that the stock won't be," replied Chase, laughing. "I mean, the stock of the company that undertakes the affair, if it does undertake it. You'd better apply for some right off; all of you. Shall I tell you how the thing strikes me, while you are finishing your nuts? Well, then, this is about it. The whole South is a hot place in summer, ladies; from Baltimore down to the end of Florida and Louisiana they simply swelter from June to October, and always must swelter. If you will look at a map, you can see for yourselves that the only region where the people of all this big section can get fresh air during the heated term, without a long journey for it, is this one line of mountains, called Alleghanies in the lump, but in reality including the Blue Ridge, the Cumberlands, your Smokies and Blacks, and others about here. For a trip to the southern sea-coast isn't much relief; a hot beach is about the hottest place I know! Now, then, what is the best point among these mountains? The Alleghanies lie *this* way." (He made the Alleghanies with a table-spoon.) "Then *there* is the Blue Ridge." (A nut-cracker.) "And here you get your Smokies and so forth." (Almonds taken hastily from a dish and arranged in a line.) "And I'll just indicate the Cumberlands with this orange. Very well. Now where are the highest peaks of these lines? Let us follow the range down. Do we find them in Pennsylvania? No, sir. Do we find them in Virginia? We do not. Are they over there among the Cumberlands? Not by a long shot. Where are they, then? Right here, ladies, at your own door; right here, where I make a dot this minute." And taking a pencil from his pocket, he made a small mark on the table-cloth between the spoon and the nut-cracker. "In this neighborhood," he went on, emphasizing his statement by pointing his pencil at Miss Billy, "there are thirteen nearly seven thousand feet high. It seems to me, therefore, that in spite of all the jokes about talking for buncombe, the talk for Buncombe has not been half tall enough yet. For this very Buncombe County is bound to be the favorite watering-place for over twelve millions of people, some day or other."

"Watering-place?" commented Dolly. "Well, we *have* the two rivers, the French Broad and the Swannanoa. But the Swannanoa is small; if the millions should all drink at once, it would soon go dry."

"I meant summer resort, Miss Franklin, not watering-place," said Chase, inwardly entertained by the quickness bordering on the sharp with which "the sickly one," as he called her, always.took him up. "Though there are sulphur springs near by too: I have been out to look at them. And it isn't only the Southerners who will come here," he went on. "Northerners will flock also, when they understand what these mountains are. For, in comparison with them, the Catskills are a suburb; the White Mountains, ornamental rock-work; and the Adirondacks, a wood-lot. *Here* everything is absolutely wild; you can shoot because there are all sorts of things *to* shoot, from bears down. And then there's another point—for I haven't got to the bottom of the sack yet. This mountain valley of yours, being 2400 feet above the sea, has a wonderfully pure dry air, and yet, as it is so far south, it is not cold; its winter climate, therefore, is as good as its summer, and even better. So here's the situation: people who live in hot places will come here from June to October, and people who live in cold places will come from October to June." He returned the orange and the almonds to their dishes, replaced the table-spoon and nut-cracker, and then, looking at Mrs. Franklin, he gave her a cheerful nod. "That's it, ma'am; that's the whole in a nutshell."

Ruth gravely offered him an empty almond shell.

"We'll have something better than that, Miss Ruth —a philopena." And taking a nut-cracker, he opened several almonds. Finding a double kernel, he gave her one of the halves. "Now, if I win, I should be much favored if you would make me something of worsted—a tidy is the name, I think?"

Ruth began to laugh.

"Well, then, a picture-frame of cones."

And now the other ladies joined in Ruth's merriment.

"We must decline such rare objects," said Mrs. Franklin. "But we have our own small resources, Mr. Chase." And, leading the way back to the parlor, she showed him the mantel-cover with Dolly's verse.

"Why, that's beautiful, Miss Franklin," said Chase, with sincere admiration, when he had read the lines. "I didn't know you could write poetry."

"Oh yes," answered Dolly. "I think in elegies as a general thing, and I make sonnets as I dress. Epics are nothing to me, and I turn off triolets in no time. But I don't publish, Mr. Chase, because I don't want to be called a *minor* poet."

Here Rinda came in like a projectile, carrying a large box clasped in her arms. "Jess lef'! 'Spress!" she exclaimed excitedly.

"Express?" repeated Mrs. Franklin, trying to make out the address without her glasses. "Read it, Ruth."

Ruth looked at the label, and then broke into another laugh. She had hardly recovered from the preceding one, and Chase, with amusement, watched her start off again. But he soon found himself surrounded by laughers a second time.

"Why, what's wrong with it?" he asked, seeing that it was the label which excited their mirth. And in his turn he examined it. "Miss Ruth Franklin, Lommy Dew, Asheville? That's right, isn't it? Isn't Lommy Dew the name of your place?"

Rinda meanwhile, wildly curious, had been opening the box by main force with the aid of the poker. She now uncovered a huge cluster of hot-house roses, packed in moss.

"Flowers? Who could have sent them?" said Mrs. Franklin, surprised. She had no suspicion of her present guest; her thoughts had turned towards some of their old friends at the North. But Ruth, happening to catch the look in Horace Chase's eyes as he glanced for an instant at the blossoms, not so much admiringly as critically, exclaimed:

"*You* sent them, Mr. Chase. How perfectly lovely!"

"I'm afraid they're not much," Chase answered. "I thought they'd send more." He had wished to show that he appreciated the invitations to L'Hommedieu, and as, according to his idea, it was the young lady of the family to whom it was proper to pay such attentions, he had ordered the box to be sent to Ruth rather than to Mrs. Franklin or Dolly.

Ruth's laugh had stopped. She was passionately fond of hot-house flowers, and now both her hands together could hardly encircle even the stems alone of these superb tea-roses, whose gorgeous masses filled her arms as she raised them. With a quick movement she buried her face in the soft petals.

"But, I say, what was wrong with this?" asked Chase a second time, as he again looked at the label.

"L'Hommedieu is a French name—" began Dolly.

But Ruth interrupted her: "It is an ugly old French name, Mr. Chase, and as it is pronounced, in America at least, exactly as you wrote it, I think it might as well be spelled so, too. At present, however, this is the way—the silly way." And holding her flowers with her left arm, she detached her right hand, and scribbled the name on the edge of the Raleigh paper.

"Ah!" said Chase, looking at it. "I don't speak French myself. I thought perhaps it had something to do with dew." And frowning a little, a frown of attention, he spelled the word over.

An old negro woman, her head covered with a red kerchief folded like a turban, now came stiffly in

with the coffee-tray, her stiffness being an angry dignity. It was Zoe, the cook, tired of waiting for
Rinda, who, still in the parlor, was occupied in gazing with friendly interest at the roses. "Lawdy—ef
I ain't clean ferget!" remarked the waitress, genially,
to the company in general.

"You clar out, good-fer-nutt'n' nigger!" muttered
the offended cook, in an undertone to her coadjutor.

With the tray, or rather behind it, a lady came in.

"Just in time for coffee, Genevieve," remarked
Dolly, cheerfully.

"Thanks; I do not take it at night," Geneveive
answered.

This was a dialogue often repeated in one form or
another, for Dolly kept it up. The younger Mrs.
Franklin did not like evening dinners, and Dolly even
maintained that her sister-in-law thought them wicked.
"She sees a close connection between a late dinner
with coffee after it, and the devil." The Franklins
had always dined at the close of the day, for the elder
Jared Franklin, having been the editor of a daily
paper, had found that hour the most convenient one.
The editor was gone; his family had moved from the
North to the South, and life for them was changed
in many ways; but his habit of the evening dinner
they had never altered.

The younger Mrs. Franklin greeted Chase cordially.
Dolly listened, hoping to hear her call him "Horrie."
But Genevieve contented herself with giving him her
hand, and some frank words of welcome. Genevieve

was always frank. And in all she said and did, also, she was absolutely sincere. She was a beautiful woman with golden hair, fair skin, regular features, and ideally lovely eyes; her tall figure was of Juno-like proportions. Chase admired her, that was evident. But Dolly (who was noting this) had long ago discovered that men always admired her sister-in-law. In addition to her beauty, Genevieve had a sweet voice, and an earnest, half-appealing way of speaking. She was appealing to Chase now. "There is to be an entertainment at the rink to-night, Horace, for the benefit of the Mission; won't you go? I hope so. And, mamma, that is what I have come over for; to tell you about it, and beg you to go also." She had seated herself beside Chase; but, as she said these last words, she put out her hand and laid it affectionately on Mrs. Franklin's shoulder.

"I believe I am to have the pleasure of spending the evening here?" Chase answered, making a little bow towards his hostess.

"But if mamma herself goes to the rink, as I am sure she will, then won't you accompany her? The Mission and the Colored Home, Horace, are—"

But here Chase, like a madman, made a sudden bound, and grasped the top of Miss Billy Breeze's head.

Quick as his spring had been, however, Ruth's was quicker. She pulled his hands away. "Don't hurt him! *Don't!*"

But the squirrel was not under Chase's fingers; he

had already escaped, and, running down the front of Miss Billy's dress (to her unspeakable terror), he now made another leap, and landed on Dolly's arm, where Ruth caught him.

"What in creation is it?" said Chase, who had followed. "A bird? Or a mouse?"

"Mouse!" said Ruth, indignantly. "It's Bob, my dear little flying-squirrel; I saw him on the cornice, but I thought he would fly to me. It's amazing that any one can possibly be afraid of the darling," she added, with a reproachful glance towards Miss Billy, who was still cowering. "I had him when he was nothing but a baby, Mr. Chase—he had fallen from his nest—and I have brought him up myself. Now that he is getting to be a big boy, he naturally likes to fly about a little. He cannot be always climbing his one little tree in the dining-room. He is so soft and downy. Look at his bright eyes." Here she opened her hand so that Chase could see her pet. "Would you like to hold him for a moment?"

"Oh, I'll look at *you* holding him," answered Chase. "Hollo! here's another." For Petie Trone, Esq., his jealousy roused by his mistress's interest in the squirrel, had come out from under the sofa, and was now seated on his hind-legs at the edge of her dress, begging. "Wouldn't you like an owl?" Chase suggested. "Or a 'possum? A 'coon might be tamed, if caught young."

Ruth walked away, offended.

This made him laugh still more as he returned to his place beside Genevieve.

"She is only eighteen," murmured the younger Mrs. Franklin, apologetically. Her words were covered by a rapturous "Gen'lem!" from Rinda at the door. For Rinda was always perfectly delighted to see anybody; when, therefore, there were already two or three guests, and still another appeared, her voice became ecstatic. The new-comer was Anthony Etheridge.

"How fortunate!" said Genevieve. "For it makes another for our little charity party. There is to be an impromptu entertainment at the rink to-night, commodore, for the benefit of the Mission, and mamma is going, I hope. Won't you accompany her? Let me introduce Mr. Chase—a very old friend of mine. Mr. Chase, Commodore Etheridge."

"Happy to meet you," said Chase, rising in order to shake hands.

"Gen'lem!" called Rinda again; this time fairly in a yell.

The last "gen'lem" was a slender man of thirty-five, who came in with his overcoat on. "Thanks; I did not take it off," he said, in answer to Mrs. Franklin, "because I knew that you were all going to the" —(here Ruth gave a deep cough)— "because I thought it possible that you might be going to the rink to-night," he went on, changing the form of his sentence, with a slight smile; "and in that case I hoped to accompany you."

"Yes," said Genevieve, "mamma is going, Mr. Larue. I only wish I could go, also.

The cheeks of Miss Billy Breeze had become flushed with rose-color as the new-comer entered. Noticing instantly the change he had made in his sentence when Ruth coughed, she at once divined that the girl had gone, bareheaded and in the darkness, to his residence during that long absence before dinner, in order to secure his co-operation in the frolic of the evening. Ruth had, in fact, done this very thing; for nothing amused her so much as to watch Billy herself when Larue was present. The girl was now wicked enough to carry on her joke a little longer. "I am *so* sorry, Miss Billy, that you do not care to go," she said, regretfully.

Miss Billy passed her handkerchief over her mouth and tried to smile. But she was, in fact, winking to keep back tears.

And then Mrs. Franklin, always kind-hearted, came to the rescue. "Did you tell Ruth that you could not go, Billy? Change your mind, my dear; change it to please *me*."

"Oh, if *you* care about it, dear Mrs. Franklin," murmured Billy, escaping, and hurrying happily up the stairs to put on her wraps.

The rink was a large, bare structure of wood, with a circular arena for roller-skating. This evening the place was lighted, and the gallery was occupied by the colored band. The members of this band, a new organization, had volunteered their services with the heartiest good-will. It was true that they could play (without mistakes) but one selection, namely, "The lone starry hours give me, love." But they arranged this difficulty by playing it first, softly; then as a solo on the cornet; then fortissimo, with drums; by means of these alterations it lasted bravely throughout the evening. Nearly the whole village was present; the promenade was crowded, and there were many skaters on the floor below. The Rev. Malachi Hill, the originator of the entertainment, was distributing programmes, his face beaming with pleasure as he surveyed the assemblage. Presently he came to the party from L'Hommedieu. "Programmes, Mrs. Franklin? Programmes, gentlemen?" He had written these programmes himself, in his best handwriting. "The performance will soon begin," he explained. "The procession will skate round the arena five times, and afterwards most of the characters will join in a reel—" Here some one called him, and he hastened off.

Chase, who had received a programme, looked at it in a business-like way. "Christopher Columbus," he read aloud; "Romeo and Juliet; the Muses, Calliope, and—and others," he added, glancing down the list.

His Calliope had rhymed with hope, and a gleam of inward entertainment showed itself for one instant in the eyes of Etheridge and Larue. Ruth saw this scintillation; instantly she crossed to Chase's side, as he still studied the programme, and bending to look at it, said, "Please, may I see too?"

"Oh! I thought you had one," said Chase, giving her the sheet of paper.

"The Muses," read Ruth again, aloud. "Cally-ope," she went on, giving the word Chase's pronunciation. "And Terp-si-core." She made this name rhyme with "more." Then, standing beside her new acquaintance, she glared at the remainder of the party, defiantly.

Mrs. Franklin was so much overcome by this performance of her daughter's that she was obliged to turn away to conceal her laughter.

"What possesses her—the witch!" asked Etheridge, following.

"It is only because she thinks I don't like him. He has given her those magnificent roses, and so she intends to stand up for him. I never know whom she will fancy next. Do look at her now!"

"I am afraid you have spoiled her," commented Etheridge, but joining in the mother's laugh himself, as he caught a glimpse of Ruth starting off, with high-held head and firm step, to walk with Chase round the entire promenade.

Owing to this sudden departure, Miss Billy Breeze found herself unexpectedly alone with Larue. She was so much excited by this state of things that at first she could hardly speak. How many times, during this very month, had she arranged with herself exactly what she should say if such an opportunity should be given her. Her most original ideas, her most beautiful thoughts (she kept them written out in her diary), should be summoned to entertain him. The moment had come. And this is what she actually did say: "Oh!" (giggle), "how pretty it is, isn't it?" (Giggle.) "Really a most beautiful sight. So interesting to see so many persons, and all so happy, is it not? I don't know when I've seen anything lovelier. Yes, indeed—*lovely*. But I hope you won't take cold, Mr. Laruc? Really, now, do be careful. One takes cold so easily; and then it is sometimes so hard to recover." With despair she heard herself bringing out these inanities. "I hope you are not in a draught?" she wandered on. "Colds are *so* tiresome."

And now, with a loud burst from the band, the procession issued from an improvised tent at the end of the building. First came Christopher Columbus at the head; then Romeo and Juliet; the Muses, three and three; George Washington and his wife, accompanied by Plato and a shepherdess; other personages followed, and all were mounted on roller-skates, and were keeping time to the music as well as they could. Then the rear was closed by a single American Indian in a complete costume of copper-colored tights, with tomahawk, war-paint, and feathers.

This Indian, as he was alone, was conspicuous; and when he skated into the brighter light, there came from that part of the audience which was nearest to him, a sound of glee. The sound, however, was instantly suppressed. But it rose again as he sailed majestically onward, in long sweeps to the right and the left, his head erect, his tomahawk brandished; it increased to mirth which could not be stifled. For nature having given to this brave slender legs, the costume-maker had supplied a herculean pair of calves, and these appendages had shifted their position, and were now adorning the front of each limb at the knee, the chieftain meanwhile remaining unconscious of the accident, and continuing to perform his part with stateliness at the end of the skating line. Ruth, with her hands dropping helplessly by her side, laughed until her mother came to her. Mrs. Franklin herself was laughing so that she could hardly speak. But Ruth's laughs sometimes were almost dangerous; they took such complete possession of her.

"Give her your arm and make her walk up and down," said Mrs. Franklin to Etheridge.

And Etheridge took the girl under his charge.

Chase, who had grinned silently each time the unsuspecting Moose came into view (for the procession had passed round the arena three times), now stepped down to the skating-floor as he approached on his fourth circuit, and stopped him. There was a short conference, and then, amid peals of mirth, the Moose looked down, and for the first time discovered the aspect of his knees. Chase signalled to the band to stop.

"Ladies and gentlemen," he said, "this Indian was not aware of his attractions." (Applause.)

"But now that he knows what they are, he will take part in the reel (which he had not intended to do), and he will take part *as he is!* For the benefit of the Mission, ladies and gentlemen. The hat will be passed immediately afterwards." Signing to the musicians to go on again, he conducted the chief to the space which had been left free for the reel, and then, when the other couples had skated to their places, he led off with his companion in a sort of quickstep (as he had no skates); and it is safe to say that North Carolina had never beheld so original a dance as that which followed (to the inexhaustible "Starry Hours" played as a jig). Chase and the Indian led and reeled. Finally Chase, with his hat tilted back on his head, and his face extremely solemn, balanced with his partner, taking so much pains with remarkable fancy steps, which were immediately imitated by the Indian's embossed legs, that the entire audience was weak from its continuous mirth. Then removing his hat, Chase made the rounds, proffering it with cordial invitation to all: "For the Mission, ladies and gentlemen. For *Big Moose's* Mission."

Big Moose, on his way home later (in his clergyman's attire this time), was so happy that he gave thanks. He would have liked, indeed, to chant a gloria. For the Mission was very near his heart, and from its beginning it had been so painfully fettered by poverty that, several times, he had almost despaired. But now that magic hat had brought to the struggling little fund more than it had ever dreamed of possessing; for underneath the dimes and the quarters of Asheville had laid a fat roll, a veritable Golconda roll of greenbacks. But one person could have given this roll, namely, the one stranger, Horace Chase.

CHAPTER III

Mrs. Franklin was a widow, her husband, Jared Franklin, having died in 1860. Franklin, a handsome, hearty man, who had enjoyed every day of his life, had owned and edited a well-known newspaper in one of the large towns on the Hudson River. This paper had brought him in a good income, which he had spent in his liberal way, year after year. The Franklins were not extravagant; but they lived generously, and they all had what they wanted. Their days went on happily, for they were fond of each other, they had the same sense of humor, and they took life easily, one and all. But when Jared Franklin died (after a sudden and short illness), it was found that he at least had taken it too easily; for he had laid aside nothing, and there were large debts to pay. As he had put his only son, the younger Jared, into the navy, the newspaper was sold. But it did not bring in so much as was expected, and the executors were forced in the end to sell the residence also; when the estate was finally cleared, the widow found herself left with no home, and, for income, only the small sum which had come to her from her father, Major Seymour, of the army. In this condition of things her thoughts turned towards the South.

For her mother, Mrs. Seymour, was a Southerner of Huguenot descent, one of the L'Hommedieu family. And Mrs. Seymour's eldest sister, Miss Dora L'Hommedieu, had bequeathed to the niece (now Mrs. Franklin), who had been named after her, all she had to leave. This was not much. But the queer, obstinate old woman did own two houses, one for the summer among the mountains of North Carolina, one for the winter in Florida. For she believed that she owed her remarkable health and longevity to a careful change of climate twice each year; and, accompanied by an old negress as crossgrained as herself, she had arrived in turn at each of these residences for so many seasons that it had seemed as if she would continue to arrive forever. In 1859, however, her migrations ceased.

At that date the Franklins were still enjoying their prosperity, and this legacy of the two ramshackle L'Hommedieu abodes, far away in the South, was a good deal laughed at by Jared Franklin, who laughed often. But when, soon afterwards, the blow came, and his widow found herself homeless and bereft, these houses seemed to beckon to her. They could not be sold while the war lasted, and even after that great struggle was over no purchasers appeared. In the meantime they were her own; they would be a roof, two roofs, over her head; and the milder climate would be excellent for her invalid daughter Dolly. In addition, their reduced income would go much further there than here. As soon after the war, therefore, as it could be arranged, she had made the change, and now for seven years she had been living in old Dora's abodes, very thankful to have them.

Mrs. Franklin herself would have said that they lived in North Carolina; that their visits to Florida were occasional only. It was true that she had made every effort to dispose of the Florida place. "For sale—a good coquina house on the bay," had been a standing advertisement in the St. Augustine *Press* year after year. But her hopes had been disappointed, and as the house still remained hers, she had only once been able to withstand the temptation of giving Dolly the benefit of the Florida climate in the winter, little as she could afford the additional expense; in reality, therefore, they had divided their year much as Miss L'Hommedieu had divided hers.

The adjective ramshackle, applied at random by Jared Franklin, had proved to be appropriate enough as regarded the North Carolina house, which old Dora had named L'Hommedieu, after herself. L'Hommedieu was a rambling wooden structure surrounded by verandas; it had been built originally by a low-country planter who came up to these mountains in the summer. But old Miss L'Hommedieu had let everything run down; she had, in truth, no money for repairs. When the place, therefore, came into the hands of her niece, it was much dilapidated. And in her turn Mrs. Franklin had done very little in the way of renovation, beyond stopping the leaks of the roof. Her daughter-in-law, Genevieve, was distressed by the aspect of everything, both without and within. "You really ought to have the whole house done over, mamma," she had said more than once. "If you will watch all the details yourself, it need not cost so very much : see what I have accomplished at the Cottage.

"In time, in time," Mrs. Franklin had answered. But in her heart she was not fond of Genevieve's abode; she preferred the low-ceilinged rooms of L'Hommedieu, shabby though they might be. These rooms had, in fact, an air of great cheerfulness. Anthony Etheridge was accustomed to say that he had never seen anywhere a better collection of easy-chairs. "There are at least eight with the long seat which holds a man's body comfortably as far as the knees, as it ought to held ; not ending skimpily half-way between the knee and the hip in the usual miserable fashion!" Mrs. Franklin had saved three of these chairs from the wreck of her northern home, and the others had been made, of less expensive materials, under her own eye. Both she and her husband had by nature a strong love of ease, and their children had inherited the same disposition; it could truthfully be said that as a family they made themselves comfortable, and kept themselves comfortable, all day long.

They did this at present in the face of obstacles which would have made some minds forget the very name of comfort. For they were far from their old

home; they were cramped as to money; there was
Dolly's suffering to reckon with; and there was a
load of debt. The children, however, were ignorant
in a great measure of this last difficulty; whatever
property there was, belonged to Mrs. Franklin personally, and she kept her cares to herself. These
fresh debts, made after the estate had finally been
cleared, were incurred by the mother's deliberate act
—an act of folly or of beauty, according to the point
from which one views it; after her husband's death
she had borrowed money in order to give to her
daughter Dora every possible aid and advantage in
her contest with fate—the long struggle which the
girl made to ignore illness, to conquer pain. These
sums had never been repaid, and when the mother
thought of them, she was troubled. But she did not
think of them often; when she had succeeded (with
difficulty) in paying the interest each year, she was
able to dismiss the subject from her mind, and return to her old habit of taking life easily; for neither her father, the army officer, nor her husband, the
liberal-handed editor, had ever taught her with any
strictness the importance of a well-balanced account.
Poor Dolly's health had always been uncertain. But
when her childhood was over, her mother's tender help
from minute to minute had kept her up in a determined attempt to follow the life led by other girls of
her age. A mother's love can do much. But heredity,
coming from the past, blind and deaf to all appeal,
does more, and the brave effort failed. The elder Miss

Franklin had now been for years an invalid, and an invalid for whom no improvement could be expected; sometimes she was able, with the aid of her cane, to take a walk of a mile's length, or more, and often several weeks would pass in tolerable comfort; but sooner or later the pain was sure to come on again, and it was a pain very hard to bear. But although Dolly was an invalid, she was neither sad nor dull. Both she and her mother were talkers by nature, and they never seemed to reach the end of their interest in each other's remarks. Ruth, too, was never tired of listening and laughing over Dolly's sallies. The whole family, in fact, had been born gay-hearted, and they were always sufficiently entertained with their own conversation and their own jokes; on the stormy days, when they could expect no visitors, they enjoyed life on the whole rather more than they did when they had guests—though they were fond of company also.

One evening, a week after the masquerade at the rink, Mrs. Franklin, leaning back in her easy-chair with her feet on a footstool, was peacefully reading a novel, when she was surprised by the entrance of Miss Breeze; she was surprised because Billy had paid her a visit in the afternoon. "Yes, I thought I would come in again," began Billy, vaguely. "I thought perhaps—or rather I thought it would be better—"

"Take off your bonnet and jacket, won't you?" interposed Ruth.

"Why, how smart you are, Billy!" remarked Mrs. Franklin, as she noted her guest's best dress, and the pink ribbon round her throat above the collar.

"Yes," began Billy again; "I thought—it seemed better—"

"Dolly," interrupted Ruth, "get out planchette, and make it write Billy a love letter!" And she gave her sister a glance which said: "Head her off! Or she will let it all out."

Dolly comprehended. She motioned Miss Breeze solemnly to a chair near her table, and taking the planchette from its box, she arranged the paper under it.

"I don't like it! I don't like it!" protested Mrs. Franklin.

"His Grand, if you don't like it, beat it," said Ruth, jumping up. "Give it a question too hard to answer. Go to the dining-room and do something —anything you like. Then planchette shall tell us what it is—aha!"

"A good idea," said Mrs. Franklin, significantly. And with her light step she left the room. The mother was as active as a girl; no one was ever deterred, therefore, from asking her to rise, or to move about, by any idea of age. She was tall, with aquiline features, bright dark eyes, and thick silvery hair. As she was thin, her face showed the lines and fine wrinkles which at middle age offset a slender waist. But, when she was animated, these lines disappeared, for at such moments her color rose, the same beautiful color which Ruth had inherited.

Dolly sat with her hands on the little heart-shaped board, pondering what she should say; for her familiar spirit was simply her own quick invention. But while it would have been easy to mystify Miss Billy, it was not easy to imagine what her mother, a distinctly hostile element, might do for the especial purpose of perplexing the medium; for although Mrs. Franklin knew perfectly well that her daughter invented all of planchette's replies, she remained nevertheless strongly opposed to even this pretended occultism. Dolly therefore pondered. But, as she did so, she was saying to herself that it was useless to ponder, and that she might as well select something at random, when suddenly there sprang into her mind a word, a word apropos of nothing at all, and, obeying an impulse, she wrote it; that is, planchette wrote it under the unseen propelling power of her long fingers. Then Ruth pushed the board aside, and they all read the word; it was "grinning."

"Grinning?" repeated Ruth. "How absurd! Imagine mother grinning!"

"She opened the door, and called, "What did you do, His Grand?"

"Wishing to expose that very skilful pretender, Miss Dora Franklin, I did the most unlikely thing I could think of," answered Mrs. Franklin's voice. "I went to the mirror, and standing in front of it, I grinned at my own image; grinned like a Cheshire cat."

Miss Billy looked at Dolly with frightened eyes. Dolly herself was startled; she crumpled the paper and threw it hastily into the waste-basket.

Mrs. Franklin, returning through the hall, was met by Anthony Etheridge, who had entered without ringing, merely giving a preliminary tap on the outer door with his walking-stick. Dolly began to talk as soon as they came in, selecting a subject which had nothing to do with planchette. For the unconscious knowledge which, of late years, she seemed to possess, regarding the thoughts in her mother's mind, troubled them both.

"Commodore, I have something to tell you. It is for you especially, for I have long known your secret attachment! From my window, I can see that field behind the Mackintosh house. Imagine my beholding Maud Muriel opening the gate this afternoon, crossing to the big bush in the centre, seating herself behind it, taking a long clay pipe from her pocket, filling it, lighting it, and smoking it!"

"No!" exclaimed Etheridge, breaking into a resounding laugh. "Could she make it go?"

"Not very well, I think; I took my opera-glass and watched her. Her face, as she puffed away, was exactly as solemn as it is when she models her deadly busts."

"Ho, ho, ho!" roared Etheridge again. "Ladies, excuse me. I have always thought that girl might be a genius if she could only get drunk! Perhaps the pipe is a beginning."

While he was saying this, Horace Chase was ushered in. A moment later there came another ring, and the Rev. Mr. Hill appeared, followed by Achilles Larue.

"Why, I have a party!" said Mrs. Franklin, smiling, as she welcomed the last comer.

"Yes, His Grand, it *is* a party," said Ruth. "Now you may know, since they are here, and you cannot stop it. I invited them all myself, late this afternoon; and it is a molasses-candy-pulling; Dolly and I have arranged it. We did not tell you beforehand, because we knew you would say it was sticky."

"Sticky it is," replied Mrs. Franklin.

"Vilely sticky!" added Etheridge, emphatically.

"And then we knew, also, that you would say that you could not get up a supper in so short a time," Ruth went on. "But Zoe has had her sister to help her, and ever so many nice things are all ready; chicken salad, for instance; and—listen, His Grand —a long row of macaroon custards, each cup with *three* macaroons dissolved in madeira!" And then she intoned the family chant, Dolly joining in from her easy-chair:

> " Mother Franklin thinks,
> That General Jackson,
> Jared the Sixth,
> Macaroon custards,
> And Bishop Carew,
> Are per-*fec*-tion!"

"What does she mean by that?" said Chase to Miss Billy.

"Oh, it is only one of their jokes; they have so many! Dear Mrs. Franklin was brought up by her father to admire General Jackson, and Dolly and Ruth pretend that she thinks he is still at the White House. And Jared the Sixth means her son, you know. And they say she is fond of macaroon custards; that is, *fondish*," added Miss Billy, getting in the "ish" with inward satisfaction. "And she is much attached to Bishop Carew. But, for that matter, so are we all."

"A Roman Catholic?" inquired Chase.

"He is our bishop — the Episcopal Bishop of North Carolina," answered Miss Breeze, surprised.

"Oh! I didn't know. I'm a Baptist myself. Or at least my parents were," explained Chase.

The kitchen of L'Hommedieu was large and low, with the beams showing overhead; it had a huge fireplace with an iron crane. This evening a pot dangled from the crane; it held the boiling molasses, and Zoe, brilliant in a new scarlet turban in honor of the occasion, was stirring the syrup with a long-handled spoon. One of the easy-chairs had been brought from the parlor for Dolly. Malachi Hill seated himself beside her; he seemed uneasy; he kept his hat in his hand. "I did not know that Mr. Chase was to be here, Miss Dolly, or I would not have come," he said to his companion, in an undertone. "I can't think what to make of myself—I'm becoming a regular cormorant! Strange to say, instead of being satisfied with all he has given to the Mission, I want more. I keep thinking of all the good he might do in these mountains if he only knew the facts, and I have fairly to hold myself in when he is present, to keep from flattering him and getting further help. Yes, it's as bad as that! Clergymen, you know, are always accused of paying court to rich men, or rather to liberal men. For the first time in my life I understand the danger! It's a dreadful temptation—it is indeed. I really think, Miss Dolly, that I had better go."

"No, you needn't; I'll see to you," answered Dolly. "If I notice you edging up too near him, I'll give a loud ahem. Stay and amuse yourself; you know you like it."

And Malachi Hill did like it. In his mission-work he was tirelessly energetic, self-sacrificing, devoted; on the other hand, he was as fond of merrymaking as a boy. He pulled the candy with glee, but also with eager industry, covering platter after platter with his braided sticks. His only rival in diligence was Chase, who also showed great energy. Dolly pulled; Mrs. Franklin pulled; even Etheridge helped. Ruth did not accomplish much, for she stopped too often; but when she did work she drew out the fragrant strands to a greater length than any one else attempted, and she made wheels of it, and silhouettes of all the company, including Mr. Tronc. Miss Billy had begun with much interest; then, seeing that Larue had done nothing beyond arranging the platters and plates in mathematical order on the table, she stopped, slipped out, and went up-stairs to wash her hands. When she returned, fortune favored her; the only vacant seat was one near him, and, after a short hesitation, she took it. Larue did not speak; he was looking at Ruth, who was now pulling candy with Horace Chase, drawing out the golden rope to a yard's length, and throwing the end back to him gayly.

Finally, when not even the painstaking young missionary could scrape another drop from the exhausted pot, Dolly, taking her violin, played a waltz. The uncarpeted floor was tempting, and after all the sticky hands had been washed, the dancing began— Ruth with Chase, Etheridge with Miss Billy; then Etheridge with Mrs. Franklin, while Miss Billy returned quickly to her precious chair.

"But these dances do not compare with the old ones," said Mrs. Franklin, when they had paused to let Dolly rest. "There was the mazurka; and the varsovienne — how pretty that was! La-la-la, la, *la!*" And humming the tune, she took a step or two lightly. Etheridge, who knew the varsovienne, joined her.

"Go on," said Ruth. "I'll whistle it for you." And sitting on the edge of a table she whistled the tune, while the two dancers circled round the kitchen, looking extremely well together.

"Whistling girls, you know," said Chase, warningly.

He had joined Ruth, and was watching her as she performed her part. She kept on, undisturbed by his jests, bending her head a little to the right and to the left in time with the music; her whistling was as clear as a flute.

"And then there was the heel-and-toe polka. Surely you remember that, commodore," pursued Mrs. Franklin, with inward malice.

For the heel-and-toe was a very ancient memory. It was considered old when she herself had seen it as a child.

"Never heard of it in my life," answered Etheridge. "Hum—ha."

"Oh, I know the heel-and-toe," cried Ruth. "I learned it from mother ages ago, just for fun. Are you rested, Dolly? Play it, please, and mother and I will show them.

Dolly began, and then Mrs. Franklin and Ruth, tall, slender mother, and tall, slender daughter, each with one arm round the other's waist, and the remaining arm held curved above the head, danced down the long room together, taking the steps of the queer Polish dance with charming grace and precision.

"Oh, *dear* Mrs. Franklin, so young and cheerful! So pleasant to see her, is it not? So lovely! Don't you think so? And dancing is so interesting in so many ways! Though, of course, there are other amusements equally to be desired," murmured Miss Billy, incoherently, to Larue.

" Now we will have a quadrille, and I will improvise the figures," said Ruth. " Mother and the commodore; Miss Billy and Mr. Larue; Mr. Chase with me; and we will take turns in making the fourth couple."

" Unfortunately, I don't dance," observed Larue.

" Spoil-sport ! " said Ruth, annihilatingly.

" You got it that time," remarked Chase, condolingly, to the other man.

" Miss Ruth, I can take the senator's place, if you like," said Malachi Hill, springing up, good-naturedly.

Since the termination of the candy-pulling, he had been sitting contentedly beside Dolly, watching her play, and regaling himself meanwhile with a stick of the fresh compound, its end carefully enveloped in a holder of paper.

" Excellent," said Ruth. " Please take Miss Billy, then."

Poor Miss Billy, obliged to dance with a misguided clergyman ! This time there was not the excuse of the Mission ; it was a real dance. He already smoked; the next step certainly would be cards and horse-racing ! While she was taking her place, Rinda ushered in a new guest.

" Maud Muriel—how lucky !" exclaimed Ruth. " You are the very person we need, for we are trying to get up a quadrille, and have not enough persons. I know you like to dance ?"

" Yes, I like it very much—for hygienic reasons principally," responded the new-comer.

"Please take my place, then," Ruth went on. "This is Mr. Chase, Miss Maud Mackintosh. Now we will see if our generic geologist and sensational senator will refuse to dance with *me*." And sinking suddenly on her knees before Larue, Ruth extended her hands in petition.

"What is all that she called him, Miss Maud?" inquired Chase, laughing.

"Miss Mackintosh," said his partner, correctively. "They are only alliterative adjectives, Mr. Chase, rather indiscriminately applied. Ruth is apt to be indiscriminate."

Larue had risen, and Ruth triumphantly led him to his place. He knew that she was laughing at him; in fact, as he went through the figures calmly, his partner mimicked him to his face. But he was indifferent alike to her laughter and her mimicry; what he was noticing was her beauty. If he had been speaking of her, he would have called her "prettyish"; but as he was only thinking, he allowed himself to note the charm of her eyes for the moment, the color in her cheeks and lips. For he was sure that it was only for the moment. "The coloring is evanescent," was his mental criticism. "Her beauty will not last. For she is handsome only when she is happy, and happiness for her means doing exactly as she pleases, and having her own way unchecked. No woman can do that forever. By the time she is thirty she may be absolutely plain."

Maud Muriel had laid aside her hat and jacket. She possessed a wealth of beautiful red hair, whose thick mass was combed so tightly back from her forehead that it made her wink; her much-exposed countenance was not at all handsome, though her hazel eyes were large, calm, and clear. She was a spinster of thirty-six—tall and thin, with large bones. And from her hair to her heels she was abnormally, extraordinarily straight. She danced with much vigor, scrutinizing Chase, and talking to him in the intervals between the figures. These intervals, however, were short, for Ruth improvised with rapidity. Finally she kept them all flying round in a circle so long that Mrs. Franklin, breathless, signalled that she must pause.

"Now we are all hungry," said Ruth. "Zoe, see to the coffee. And, Rinda, you may make ready here. · We won't go to the dining-room, His Grand; it's much more fun in the kitchen."

Various inviting dishes were soon arrayed upon a table. And then Ruth, to pass away the time until the coffee should be ready, began to sing. All the Franklins sang; Miss Billy had a sweet soprano, Maud Muriel a resonant contralto, and Malachi Hill a tenor of power; Etheridge, when he chose, could add bass notes.

> "Hark, the merry merry Christ-Church bells,
>   One, two, three, four, five, six;
>   They sound so strong, so wondrous sweet,
>   And they troll so merrily, merrily."

Horace Chase took no part in the catch song; he
sat looking at the others. It was the Franklin family who held his attention—the mother singing with
light-hearted animation; Dolly playing her part on
her violin, and singing it also; and Ruth, who, with
her hands clasped behind her head, was carolling like
a bird. To Chase's mind it seemed odd that a
woman so old as Mrs. Franklin, a woman with silver
hair and grown-up children, should like to dance and
sing. Dolly was certainly a very "live" invalid!
And Ruth—well, Ruth was enchanting. Horace
Chase's nature was always touched by beauty; he
was open to its influences, it had been so from boyhood. What he admired was not regularity of feat-
ure, but simply the seductive sweetness of womanhood. And, young as she was, Ruth Franklin's face
was full of this charm. He looked at her again as
she sat singing the chorus:

> "Hark, the first and second bell,
> Ring every day at four and ten"—

Then his gaze wandered round the kitchen. From
part of the wall the plastering was gone; it had fallen,
and had never been replaced. The housewives whom
he had hitherto known, so he said to himself, would
have preferred to have their walls repaired, and
spend less, if necessary, upon dinners. Suppers, too!
(Here he noted the rich array on the kitchen table.)
This array was completed presently by the arrival
of the coffee, which filled the room with its fragrant

aroma, and the supper was consumed amid much merriment. When the clock struck twelve, Maud Muriel rose. "I must be going," she said. "Wilhelmina, I came for you; that is what brought me. When I learned at the hotel that you were here, I followed for the purpose of seeing you home."

"Allow me the pleasure of accompanying you both," said Chase.

"That is not necessary; I always see to Wilhelmina," answered Miss Mackintosh, as she put on her hat.

"Yes; she is so kind," murmured Miss Billy. But Miss Billy in her heart believed that in some way or other Achilles Larue would yet be her escort (though he never had been that, or anything else, in all the years of their acquaintance). He was still in the house, and so was she; something might happen!

What happened was that Larue took leave of Mrs. Franklin, and went off alone.

Then Billy said to herself: "On the whole, I'm glad he didn't suggest it. For it is only five minutes' walk to the hotel, and if he had gone with me it would have counted as a call, and then he needn't have done anything more for a long time. So I'm glad he did not come. Very."

"Maud Muriel," demanded Dolly, " why select a *clay* pipe ?"

"Oh, did you see me ?" inquired Miss Mackintosh, composedly. " I use a clay pipe, Dolly, because it is cleaner; I can always have a new one. Smoking is said to insure the night's rest, and so I thought it best to learn it, as my brother's children are singularly active at night. I have been practising for three weeks, and I generally go to the woods, where no one can see me. But to-day I did not have time."

Chase broke into a laugh. Etheridge had emitted another ho, ho, ho! Then he gave Maud a jovial tap. "My dear young lady, don't go to the woods. Let *me* come, with another clay pipe, and be your protector."

"I have never needed a protector in my life," replied Miss Mackintosh; "I don't know what that feeling is, commodore. I secrete myself simply because people might not understand my motives; they might think that I was secretly given to dissolute courses. Are you ready, Wilhelmina?"

As the two ladies opened the outer door and stepped forth into the darkness, Chase, not deterred by the rebuff he had received from the stalwart virgin, passed her, and offered his arm to the gentler Miss Billy. And then Malachi Hill, feeling that he must, advanced to offer himself as escort for the remaining lady.

"Poor manikin! Do you think I need *you?*" inquired the sculptress sarcastically, under her breath.

The young clergyman disappeared. He did not actually run. But he was round the corner in an astonishingly short space of time.

Etheridge was the last to take leave. "Well, you

made a very merry party for your bubbling friend," he said to Mrs. Franklin.

"It wasn't for *him*," she answered.

"He is not mother's bubbling friend, and he is not Dolly's, either," said Ruth; "he is mine alone. Mother and Dolly do not in the least appreciate him."

"Is he worth much appreciation?" inquired Etheridge, noting her beauty as Larue had noted it. "How striking she grows!" he thought. And, forgetting for the moment what they were talking about, he looked at her as Chase had looked.

Meanwhile Ruth was answering, girlishly: "Much appreciation? *All*, commodore—all. Mr. Chase is *splendid!*"

CHAPTER IV

NOTHING could exceed the charm of the early summer, that year, in this high valley. The amphitheatre of mountains had taken on fresher robes of green, the air was like champagne; it would have been difficult to say which river danced more gayly along its course, the foam-flecked French Broad, its clear water open to the sunshine, or the little Swannanoa, frolicking through the forest in the shade.

One morning, a few days after the candy-pulling at L'Hommedieu, even Maud Muriel was stirred to admiration as she threw open the blinds of her bedroom at her usual early hour. "No humidity. And great rarefaction," she said to herself, as she tried the atmosphere with a tentative snort. Maud Muriel lived with her brother, Thomas Mackintosh; that is, she had a room under his roof and a seat at his table. But she did not spend much time at home, rather to the relief of Mrs. Thomas Mackintosh, an easy-going Southern woman, with several young children, including an obstreperous pair of twins. Maud Muriel, dismissing the landscape, took a conscientious sponge-bath, and went down to breakfast. After breakfast, on her way to her studio, she stopped for a moment to see Miss Billy. "At any rate, I *walk* well," she

5

had often thought with pride. And to-day, as she approached the hotel, she was so straight that her shoulders tipped backward.

Miss Billy was staying at the inn. This hotel bore the name "The Old North State," the loving title given by native North-Carolinians to their commonwealth — a commonwealth which, in its small long-settled towns, its old farms, and in the names of its people, shows less change in a hundred years than any other portion of the Union. The Old North, as it was called, was a wooden structure painted white, with outside blinds of green; in front of it extended a row of magnificent maple-trees. Miss Billy had a small sitting-room on the second floor; Maud Muriel, paying no attention to the negro servants, went up the uncarpeted stairway to her friend's apartment, and, as she opened the door, she caught sight of this friend carefully rolling a waste bit of string into a small ball.

"Too late—I saw you," she said. (For Miss Billy had nervously tried to hide the ball.) "I know you have at least fifty more little wads of the same sort somewhere, arranged in graded rows! A new ball of string of the largest size—enough to last a year—costs a dime, Wilhelmina. You must have a singularly defective sense of proportion to be willing to give many minutes (for I have even seen you taking out knots!) to a substance whose value really amounts to about the thousandth part of a cent! I have stopped on my way to the barn to tell you two things,

Wilhelmina. One is that I do *not* like your 'Mountain Walk.'" Here she took a roll of delicately written manuscript, tied with blue ribbons, from her pocket, and placed it on the table. "It is supposed to be about trees, isn't it? But you do not describe a single one with the least accuracy; all you do is to impute to them various allegorical sentiments, which no tree—a purely vegetable production—*ever* had."

"It was only a beginning — leading up to a study of the pre-Adamite trees, which I hope to make, later," Miss Billy answered. "Ruskin, you know—"

"You need not quote Ruskin to me — a man who criticises sculpture without any practical knowledge whatever of human anatomy; a man who subordinates correct drawing in a picture to the virtuous state of mind of the artist! If Ruskin's theory is true, very good persons who visit the poor and go to church, are, if they dabble in water-colors, or pen-and-ink sketches, the greatest of artists, because their piety is sincere. And *vice versa.* The history of art shows that, doesn't it?" commented Maud, ironically. "I am sorry to see that you sat up so late last night, Wilhelmina."

"Why, how do you know?" said Miss Billy, guiltily conscious of midnight reading.

"By the deep line between your eyebrows. You must see to that, or you will be misjudged by scientific minds. For marked, lined, or wrinkled foreheads indicate criminal tendencies; the statistics of prisons prove it. To-night put on two pieces of strong sticking-plaster at the temples, to draw the skin back. The other thing I had to tell you is that the result of my inquiries of a friend at the North who keeps in touch with the latest investigations of Liébeault and the Germans, is, that there may, after all, be something in the subject you mentioned to me, namely, the possibility of influencing a person, not present, by means of an effort of will. So we will try it now — for five minutes. Fix your eyes steadily upon that figure of the carpet, Wilhelmina " —she indicated a figure with her parasol — " and I will do the same. As subject we will take my sister-in-law. We will will her to whip the twins. Are you ready?" She took out her watch. "Begin, then."

Miss Billy, though secretly disappointed in the choice of subject, tried hard to fix her mind upon the proposed castigation. But in spite of her efforts her thoughts would stray to the carpet itself, to the pattern of the figure, and its reds and greens.

"Time's up," announced Maud, replacing her watch in the strong watch-pocket on the outside of her skirt; " I'll tell you whether the whipping comes off. Do you think it is decent, Wilhelmina, to be dressing and undressing yourself whenever you wish to know what time it is?" (For Miss Billy, who tried to follow the fashions to some extent, was putting her own watch back in her bodice, which she had unbuttoned for the purpose.) " Woman will never be the equal of man until she has grasped the conception that the position of her pockets should be unchangeable," Maud went on.

"I think I will go with you as far as L'Hommedieu," suggested Billy, ignoring the subject of the watch-pocket (an old one). "I have some books to take, so I may as well." She put on her hat, and piled eight dilapidated paper-covered volumes on her arm.

"Are you still collecting vapid literature for that feather-headed woman?" inquired Maud. For Billy went all over Asheville, to every house she knew, and probed in old closets and bookcases in search of novels for Mrs. Franklin. For years she had performed this office. When Mrs. Franklin had finished reading one set of volumes, Billy carried them back to their owners, and then roamed and foraged for more.

"If you do go as far as L'Hommedieu, you must stop there definitely; you must not go on to the barn," Maud Muriel announced, as they went down the stairs. "For if you do, you will stay. And then I shall be going back with you, to see to you. And then you will be coming part way back with me, to talk. And thus we shall be going home with each other all the rest of the day!" She passed out and crossed the street, doing it in the face of the leaders of a team of six horses attached to one of the huge mountain wagons, which are shaped like boats tilted up behind; for two files of these wagons, heavily loaded, were coming slowly up the road. Miss Billy started to cross also, but after three or four steps she turned and hurried back to the curb-stone. Then suddenly she started a second time, running first in one direction, then in another, and finally and unexpectedly in a third, so that the drivers of the wagons nearest to her, and even the very horses themselves, were filled with perplexity as to the course which she wished to pursue. Miss Billy, meanwhile, finding herself hemmed in, began to shriek wildly. The drivers in front stretched their necks round the corners of the canvas hoods erected, like gigantic Shaker bonnets, over their high-piled loads, in order to see what was the matter. And the drivers who were behind stood up and peered forward. But they could make out nothing, and, as Miss Billy continued her yells, the whole procession, and with it the entire traffic of the main street, came slowly to a pause. The pause was not long. The energetic Maud Muriel, jerking up the heads of two of the leaders, made a dive, caught hold of her frightened friend, and drew her out by main strength. The horses whom she had thus attacked, shook themselves. "Hep!" called their driver. "Hep!" called the other drivers, in various keys. And then, one by one, with a jerk and a creak, the great wains started on again.

When the friends reached L'Hommedieu, Billy was still trembling.

"I'd better take them in for you," said Maud Muriel, referring to the load of books which Billy was carrying for her companion. They found Dolly in the parlor, winding silk for her next pair of stockings. "Here are some volumes which Wilhelmina is bringing to Mrs. Franklin," said Maud Muriel, depositing the pile on a table.

"More novels?" said Dolly. "I'm so glad. Thank you, Miss Billy. For mother really has nothing for to-day. The one she had yesterday was very dull; she said she was 'worrying' through it. It was a story about female suffrage—as though any one could care for that!"

"Care for it or not, it is sure to come," declared Miss Mackintosh.

"Yes, in A.D. 5000."

"Sooner, much sooner. *We* may not see it," pursued Maud Muriel, putting up her finger impressively. "But, mark my words, our *children* will."

Miss Billy listened to this statement with the deepest interest.

"Well, Maud Muriel—Miss Billy, yourself, and myself as *parents*—that certainly is a new idea!" Dolly replied.

Ruth came in. At the same moment Maud Muriel turned to go; and, unconsciously, Billy made a motion as if about to follow.

"Wilhelmina, you are to *stay*," said Maud, sternly, as she departed, straighter than ever.

"Yes, Miss Billy, please stay," said Ruth. "I want you to go with me to see Genevieve."

"Genevieve?" repeated Dolly, surprised.

"Yes. She has bought another new dress for me, and this time she is going to fit it herself, she says, so that there may be no more bagging," answered Ruth, laughing. "I know she intends to *squeeze* me up. And so I want Miss Billy to come and say it's dangerous!"

Ruth was naturally what is called short-waisted; this gave her the long step which in a tall, slender woman is so enchantingly graceful. Genevieve did not appreciate grace of this sort. In her opinion Ruth's waist was too large. If she had been told that it was the waist of Greek sculpture, the statement would not have altered her criticism; she had no admiration for Greek sculpture; the few life-sized casts from antique statues which she had seen had appeared to her highly unpleasant objects. Her ideas of feminine shape were derived, in fact, from the season's fashion plates. Her own costumes were always of one unbroken tint, the same from head to foot. To men's eyes, therefore, her attire had an air of great simplicity. Women perceived at once that this unvarying effect was not obtained without much thought, and Genevieve herself would have been the last to disclaim such attention. For she believed that it was each woman's duty to dress as becomingly as was possible, because it increased her attraction; and the greater her attraction, the greater her influence. If she had been asked, "influence for what?" she would have replied unhesitatingly, "influence for good!" Her view of dress, therefore,

being a serious one, she was disturbed by the entire
indifference of her husband's family to the subject,
both generally and in detail. She had the most sincere desire to assist them, to improve them ; most of
all she longed to improve Ruth (she had given up
Dolly), and more than once she had denied herself
something, and taken the money it would have cost,
to buy a new costume for the heedless girl, who generally ruined the gifts (in her sister-in-law's opinion)
by careless directions, or no directions at all, to the
Asheville dressmaker.

Ruth bore Miss Billy away. But as they crossed
the garden towards the cottage she said : "I may as
well tell you—there will be no fitting. For Mr.
Chase is there ; I have just caught a glimpse of him
from the upper window."

"Then why go now ?" inquired Miss Billy, who at
heart was much afraid of Genevieve.

"To see Mr. Chase, of course. I wish to thank
him for my philopena, which came late last night.
Mother and Dolly are not pleased. But *I* am, ever
so much." She took a morocco case from her
pocket, and, opening it, disclosed a ring of very delicate workmanship, the gold circlet hardly more than
a thread, and enclosing a diamond, not large, but
very pure and bright.

"Oh-ooh !" said Miss Billy, with deep admiration.

" Yes ; isn't it lovely ? Mother and Dolly say that
it is too much. But I have never seen anything in
the world yet which I thought too much ! I should

like to have ever so many rings, each set with one
gem only, but that gem perfect. And I should like
to have twenty or thirty bracelets, all of odd pat-
terns, to wear on my arms above the elbow. And I
should like close rows of jewels to wear round my
throat. And clasps of jewels for the belt; and shoe-
buckles too. I have never had an ornament, except
one dreadful silver thing. Let me see; it's on now!"
And feeling under her sleeve, she drew off a thin
silver circlet, and threw it as far as she could across
the grass.

"Oh, your pretty bracelet!" exclaimed Miss Billy.

"Pretty? Horrid!"

Horace Chase had called at the Cottage in answer
to a note from Genevieve, offering to take him to
the Colored Home. "As you have shown so much
kindly interest in the Mission, I feel sure that this
second good work of ours will also please you," she
wrote.

"I think I won't go to-day, Gen, if it's all the
same to you," said Chase, when he entered. "For
my horses have come and I ought not to delay any
longer about making some arrangements for them."

"Any other time will do for the Home," answered
Genevieve, graciously. "But can't you stay for a
little while, Horace? Let me show you my house."

Chase had already seen her parlor, with its velvet
carpet, its set of furniture covered with green, its pictures arranged according to the size of the frames,
with the largest below on a line with the eye, and

the others above in pyramidical gradations, so that the smallest were near the cornice. At that distance the subjects of the smaller pictures were more or less indistinguishable; but at least the arrangement of the frames was full of symmetry. In the second story, at the end of the house, was " Jay's smoking-room." " Jay likes to smoke; it is a habit he acquired in the navy; I have therefore fitted up this room on purpose," said Jay's wife.

It was a small chamber, with a sloping ceiling, a single window overlooking the kitchen roof, oil-cloth on the floor, one table, and one chair.

" Do put in *two* chairs," suggested Chase, jocularly. For though he thought the husband of Genevieve a fortunate man, he could not say that his smoking-room was a cheerful place.

" Oh, *I* never sit here," answered Genevieve. " Now come down and take a peep at my kitchen, Horace. I have been kneading the bread; there it is on the table. I prefer to knead it myself, though I hope that in time Susannah will be able to do it according to my method " (with a glance towards the negro servant, who returned no answering smile). " And this is my garden. I can never tell you how glad I am that we have at last a fixed home of our own, Horrie. No more wandering about! Jay is able to spend a large part of his summers here, and, later, when he has made a little more money, he will come for the whole summer—four months. And I go to Raleigh to be with him in the winter; I am hoping that we can have a winter home there too, very soon. We are *so* much more comfortable in every way than we used to be. And looking at it from another point of view, it is inexpressibly better for Jay himself to be out of the navy. It always disturbed me—such a limited life!"

Jared Franklin, when an ensign, had met Genevieve Gray, fallen in love with her, and married her, in the short space of three months. He had remained in the navy throughout the war, and for two years longer; then, yielding at last to his wife's urgent entreaties, he had resigned. After his resignation he had been for a time a clerk in Atlanta. Now he was in business for himself in a small way at Raleigh; it was upon his establishment there that Genevieve had started this summer home in Asheville. "Our prospects are much brighter," she went on, cheerfully; "for at present we have a future. No one has a future in the navy; no one can make money there. But now there is no reason why Jay should not succeed, as other men have succeeded; that is what I always tell him. And I am not thinking only of ourselves, Horrie, as I say that; when Jay is a rich man, my principal pleasure in it will be the power which we shall have to give more in charity, to do more in all good works." And in saying this, Genevieve Franklin was entirely sincere.

"You must keep me posted about the railroad," she went on, as she led the way across the garden.

"Oh yes; if we decide to take hold of it, you

shall be admitted into the ring," answered Chase— "the inside track."

"I could buy land here beforehand—quietly, you know?"

"You've got a capital head for business, haven't you, Gen! Better than any one has at your mother-in-law's, I reckon?"

"They are not clever in that way; I have always regretted it. But they are very amiable."

"Not that Dolly!"

"Oh, Dolly? My principal feeling for poor Dolly, of course, is simply pity. This is my little dairy, Horrie; come in. I have been churning butter this morning."

Ruth and Miss Billy, finding no one in the house, had followed to the dairy; and they entered in time to hear this last phrase.

"She does churning and everything else, Mr. Chase, at three o'clock in the morning," said Ruth, with great seriousness.

"Not quite so early," Genevieve corrected.

The point was not taken up. The younger Mrs. Franklin, a fresh, strong, equable creature, who woke at dawn as a child wakes, liked an early breakfast as a child likes it. She found it difficult, therefore, to understand her mother-in-law's hour of nine, or half-past nine. "But you lose so much time, mamma," she had remarked during the first weeks of her own residence at Asheville.

"Yes," Dolly answered. (It was always Dolly

who answered Genevieve; Dolly delighted in it.)
" We *do* lose it at that end of the morning—the raw
end, Genevieve. But when we are once up, we remain up, available, fully awake, get-at-able, until midnight; we do not go off and seclude ourselves im-
pregnably for two hours or so in the middle of the
day." For Dolly was aware that it was her sister-in-
law's habit to retire to her room immediately after her
one o'clock dinner, and take a nap; often a long one.

" Do you wish to see something pretty, Genevieve?" said Ruth, giving her the morocco case.
" Thank you, Mr. Chase; I have wanted a ring so
long; you can't think how long!"

" Have you?" said Chase, smiling.

" Yes. And this is such a beauty."

" Well, to me it seemed rather small. I wrote to
a friend of mine to get it; it was my partner, in fact,
Mr. Willoughby. I told him that it was for a young
lady. That's his taste, I suppose."

" The taste is perfect," said Miss Billy. For poor
Miss Billy, browbeaten though she was by almost
everybody, possessed a very delicate and true per-
ception in all such matters.

" I have been *perfectly* happy ever since it came,"
Ruth declared, as she took the ring, slipped it on
her finger, and looked at the effect.

" You make me proud, Miss Ruth."

" Don't you want to be a little prouder?" and she
came up to him coaxingly. " I am sure Genevieve
has been asking you to go with her to the Colored

Home?" This quick guess made Chase laugh. "For it is the weekly reception day, and all her old women have on their clean turbans. The Colored Home is excellent, of course, but it won't fly away; there'll be more clean turbans next week. Meanwhile, *I* have something very pressing. I have long wanted Miss Mackintosh to make a bust of Petie Trone, Esq. And she won't, because she thinks it is frivolous. But if *you* will go with me, Mr. Chase, and speak of it as a fine thing to do, she will be impressed, I know; for she has a sort of concealed liking for you." Chase made a grimace. "I don't mean anything fiery," Ruth went on; "it's only a reasonable scientific interest. She is at the barn now: won't you come? For Petie Trone, Esq., is not a young dog any longer. He is more than eight years old," concluded the girl, mournfully.

Genevieve, who had been greatly struck by the ring, glanced at Chase with inward despair, as her sister-in-law made this ineffective conclusion. They had left the dairy, and were standing in the garden, and her despair renewed itself as, in the brighter light, she noted Ruth's faded dress, and the battered garden hat, whose half-detached feather had been temporarily secured with a large white pin.

But Chase was not looking at the hat. "Of course I'll go," he answered. "We'll have the little scamp in bronze, if you like. Don't worry about his age, Miss Ruth; he is so tremendously lively that he will see us all out yet."

"Come, then," said Ruth, exultingly. She linked her arm in Miss Billy's. "You must go, too, Miss Billy, so that you can tell mother that I did not tease Mr. Chase *too* hard."

Maud Muriel's studio was in an unused hay-barn. Here, ranged on rough shelves, were her "works," as Miss Billy called them — many studies of arms, and hands, and a dozen finished portrait-busts in clay. The subjects of the busts appeared to have been selected, one and all, for their strictly commonplace aspect; they had not even the distinction of ugliness. There were three old men with ordinary features, and no marked expression of any kind; there were six middle-aged women, each with the type of face which one forgets the moment after seeing it; and there were three uncompromisingly uninteresting little boys. The modelling was conscientious, and it was evident in each case that the likeness was faithful.

"But Petie Trone, Esq., is a *pretty* dog," objected the sculptress, when Ruth had made her request, backed up by Chase, who described the "dogs and animals of all sorts" which he had seen in bronze and marble in the galleries abroad. No one laughed, as the formal title came out from Maud's lips, Asheville had long ago accepted the name; Petie Trone, Esq., was as well known as Mount Pisgah.

"Don't you like pretty things?" Chase asked, gazing at the busts, and then at the studies of arms and hands—scraggy arms with sharp elbows and thin fingers, withered old arms with clawlike phalanges, lean arms of growing boys with hands like paws, hard-worked arms with distorted muscles — every and any human arm and hand save a beautiful one.

"Prettiness is the exception, not the rule," replied Maud, with decision. "I prefer to model the usual, the average; for in that direction, and in that only, lies truth."

"Yes; and I suppose that if I should make a usual cur of Petie Trone, Esq., cover him with average mud, and beat him so that he would cower and slink in his poor little tail, *then* you would do him?" said Ruth, indignantly.

"See here, Miss Mackintosh, your principles needn't be upset by one small dog. Come, do him; not his bust, but the whole of him. A life-sized statue," added Chase, laughing; "he must be about eleven inches long! Do him for me," he went on, boldly, looking at her with secret amusement; for he had never seen such an oaken bearing as that of this Asheville spinster.

Maud Muriel did not relax the tension of her muscles; in fact, she could not. The condition called "clinched," which with most persons is occasional only, had with her become chronic. Nevertheless, somehow, she consented.

"I'll get the darling this minute," cried Ruth, hurrying out. And Chase followed her.

"Well, here you are again! What did I tell

you?" said the sculptress to Miss Billy, when they were left alone.

"I did not mean to come, Maud Muriel. I really did not intend—" Billy began.

"What place, Wilhelmina, is *paved* with good intentions? Now, of course, we shall be going home with each other all the rest of the day!" declared the sculptress, good-humoredly.

Meanwhile, outside, Ruth was suggesting to Horace Chase, coaxingly, that he should wait until she could find her dog, and bring him to the barn. "Because if *you* are not with me, Maud Muriel will be sure to change her mind!"

"Not she. She is no more changeable than a telegraph pole. I am afraid I must leave you now, Miss Ruth; for the men are waiting to see me about the horses."

"Whose horses?"

"Mine."

"Did you send for them? Oh, *I* love horses too. Where are they?"

"At the Old North stables. So you like horses? I'll drive the pair round, then, in a day or two, to show them to you." And after shaking hands with her—Chase always shook hands—he went towards the village; for Maud Muriel's barn was on the outskirts. In figure he was tall, thin, and muscular. He never appeared to be in haste; all his movements were leisurely, even his words coming out with deliberation. His voice was pitched in a low key; his articulation was extremely distinct; sometimes, when amused, he had a slight humorous drawl.

Ruth looked after him for a moment. Then she went in search of her dog.

A little later Anthony Etheridge paid his usual morning visit to the post-office. On his return, when near his own abode, he met Horace Chase.

"A mail in?" inquired Chase, quickly, as he saw the letters.

"No; they came last night. *I* am never in a hurry about mails," answered Etheridge. "You younger fellows have not learned, as I have, that among every six letters, say, four at least are sure to be more or less disagreeable. Well, have you decided? Are you coming to my place?" For Etheridge had rooms in a private house, where he paid for a whole wing in order that his night's rest should not be disturbed by other tenants, who might perhaps bring in young children; with his usual thriftiness, he had offered his lower floor to Chase.

"Well, no, I guess not; I'm thinking of coming here," Chase answered, indicating the hotel near by with a backward turn of his thumb. "My horses are here; they came last night. I'm making some arrangements for them, now."

Anthony Etheridge cared more for a good horse than for anything else in the world. In spite of his title of Commodore, sailing had only a second place in his list of tastes. He had commanded a holiday squadron only, a fleet of yachts. Some years before, he had resigned his commandership in the Northern club. But he was still a commodore, almost in spite of himself, for he had again been elected, this time by the winter yacht club of St. Augustine. At the word " horses " his face had lighted up. " Can I have a look at them ?" he said, eagerly. " Did they stand the journey well ?"

" O. K. They're round in the stable, if you want to come."

The three horses were beautiful specimens of their kind. " The pair, I intend to drive ; I found that there was nothing in Asheville, and as I'm going to stay awhile longer (for the air is bringing me right up), I had to have something," Chase remarked. "The mare is for riding."

" She looks like a racer ?"

" Well, she *has* taken one prize. But I shall never race her again ; I don't care about it. I remember when I thought a race just heaven ! When I wasn't more than nineteen, I took a prize with a trotter ; 'twas a very small race, to be sure ; but a big thing to me. Not long after that, there was another prize offered for a well-matched pair, and by that time I had a pair—temporarily—bays. One of them, however, had a white spot on his nose. Well, sir, I painted his nose, and won the premium !" He broke into a laugh.

"Was that before you invented the Bubble Baking-powder ?" inquired Etheridge.

In this question, there was a tinge of superciliousness. Chase did not suspect it; in his estimation, a baking-powder was as good a means as anything else, the sole important point being its success. But even if he had perceived the tinge, it would only have amused him; with his far - stretching plans—plans which extended across a continent—his large interests and broad ambitions, criticism from this obscure old man would have seemed comical. Anthony Etheridge was not so obscure a personage as Chase fancied. But he was not known in the world of business or of speculation, and he had very little money. This last fact Chase had immediately divined. For he recognized in Etheridge a man who would never have denied himself luxury unless forced to do it, a man who would never have been at Asheville if he could have afforded Newport; the talk about "nature undraped" was simply an excuse. And he had discovered also another secret which no one (save Mrs. Franklin) suspected, namely, that the handsome commodore was in reality far older than his gallant bearing would seem to indicate.

"*I* didn't invent the Bubble," he had said, explanatorily. "I only bought it. Then the inventor and I ran it together, in a sort of partnership, as long as he lived. 'Twas as good as a silver mine for a while. Nothing could stand against it, sir—nothing."

But Etheridge was not interested in the Bubble. "I should like greatly to see your mare go," he said. "Here, boy, isn't that track in the field in pretty fair condition still?"

"Yes, boss," answered the negro, whom he had addressed.

"Why not let her go round it, Chase? It will do her good to stretch her legs this fine morning."

Here a shadow in the doorway caused them both to turn their heads. It was Ruth Franklin.

"Good heavens, Ruth, what are you doing here in the stables?" asked Etheridge, astonished.

"I have come to see the horses," replied Ruth, confidently. She addressed Chase. She had already learned that she could count upon indulgence from him, no matter what fancies might seize her.

"Here they are, then," Chase answered. "Come closer. This is Peter, and that is Piper. And here is the mare, Kentucky Belle. Your friend, the commodore, was urging me, as you came in, to send Kentucky round a race-course you have here somewhere."

"Yes, I know; the old ring," said Ruth. "Oh, please do! Please have a real race."

"But there's nothing to run against her, Miss Ruth. The pair are not racers."

"You go to Cyrus Jaycox," said Etheridge to the negro, "and ask him for—for" (he could not remember the name)—"for the colt," he concluded, in an enraged voice.

"Fer Tipkinoo, sah? Yassah."

"Tell him to come himself."

"Yassah." The negro started off on a run.

"It's the landlord of the Old North," Etheridge

explained. "He has a promising colt, Tippecanoe" (he brought it out this time sonorously). "No match, of course, for your mare, Chase. Still, it will make a little sport." His color had risen; his face was young with anticipation. "Now, Ruth, go home; you have seen the horses, and that is enough. Your mother would be much displeased if she knew you were here."

For answer, Ruth looked at Chase. "I won't be the least trouble," she said, winningly.

"Oh, do be! I like trouble — feel all the better for lots of it," he answered. "Come along with me. And make all the trouble you can!"

Three little negro boys, highly excited, had already started off to act as pilots to the field. Ruth put her hand in Chase's arm; for if the owner of Kentucky Belle wished to have her with him, or at least if he had the appearance of wishing it, there was less to be said against her presence. They led the way, therefore. Then came Chase's man with the mare, Etheridge keeping close to the beautiful beast, and watching her gait with critical eyes. All the hangers-on of the stable brought up the rear. The field, where an amateur race had been held during the preceding year, was not far distant; its course was a small one. Some minutes later their group was completed by the arrival of Cyrus Jaycox with his colt, Tippecanoe.

"But where is Groves?" said Chase to his men. "Groves is the only one of you who can ride her properly." It turned out, however, that Groves had gone to bed ill; he had taken a chill on the journey.

"I didn't observe that he wasn't here," said Chase. (This was because he had been talking to Ruth.) "We shall have to postpone it, commodore."

"Let her go round with one of the other men just once, to show her action," Etheridge urged.

"Yes, please, please," said Ruth.

The mare, therefore, went round the course with the groom Cartright, followed by the Asheville colt, ridden by a little negro boy, who clung on with grins and goggling eyes.

"There is Mr. Hill, watching us over the fence," said Ruth. "How astonished he looks!" And she beckoned to the distant figure.

Malachi Hill, who had been up the mountain to pay a visit to a family in bereavement, had recognized them, and stopped his horse in the road to see what was going on. In response to Ruth's invitation, he found a gate, opened it by leaning from his saddle, and came across to join them. As he rode up, Etheridge was urging another round. "If I were not such a heavy weight, I'd ride the mare myself!" he declared, with enthusiasm. Cyrus Jaycox offered a second little negro, as jockey. But Chase preferred to trust Cartright, unfitted though he was. In reality he consented not on account of the urgency of Etheridge, but solely to please the girl by his side.

There was trouble about this second start; the

colt, not having been trained, boggled and balked. Kentucky Belle, on her side, could not comprehend such awkwardness. "I'll go a few paces with them, just to get them well off," suggested Malachi Hill. And, touching Daniel with his whip, he rode forward, coming up behind the other two.

Mr. Hill's Daniel was the laughing‑stock of the irreverent; he was a very tall, ancient horse, lean and rawboned, with a rat tail. But he must have had a spark of youthful fire left in him somewhere, or else a long-thwarted ambition, for he made more than the start which his rider had intended; breaking into a pounding pace, he went round the entire course, in spite of the clergyman's efforts to pull him up. The mare, hearing the thundering sound of his advance behind her, began to go faster. Old Daniel passed the Asheville colt as though he were nothing at all; then, stretching out his gaunt head, he went in pursuit of the steed in front like a mad creature, the dust of the ring rising in clouds behind him. Nothing could now stop either horse. Cartright was powerless with Kentucky Belle, and Daniel paid no heed to his rider. But, the second time round, it was not quite clear whether the clergyman was trying to stop or not. The third time there was no question—he would not have stopped for the world; his flushed face showed the deepest delight.

Meanwhile people had collected as flies collect round honey; the negroes who lived in the shanties behind the Old North had come running to the

scene in a body, the big children "toting" the little
ones; and down the lane which led from the main
street had rushed all the whites within call, led by
the postmaster himself, a veteran of the Mexican
War. After the fourth round, Kentucky Belle decided to stop of her own accord. She was, of course,
ahead. But not very far behind her, still thundering along with his rat tail held stiffly out, came old
Daniel, in his turn ahead of Tippecanoe.

As Daniel drew near, exhausted but still ardent,
there rose loud laughter and cheers. "Good gracious!" murmured the missionary, as he quickly dismounted, pulled his hat straight, and involuntarily
tried to hide himself between Etheridge and Chase.
"What *have* I done!"

His perturbation was genuine. "Come along,"
said Chase, who had been laughing uproariously himself; "we'll protect you." He gave his arm to Mr.
Hill, and with Ruth (who still kept her hold tightly)
on his left, he made with his two companions a stately progress back to the hotel, followed by the mare
led by Cartright, with Etheridge as body-guard;
then by Cyrus Jaycox, with Tippecanoe; and finally
by all the spectators, who now numbered nearly a
hundred. But at the head of the whole file (Chase
insisted upon this) marched old Daniel, led by the
other groom.

"Go round to the front," called Chase. And round
they all went to the main street, amid the hurrahs of
the accompanying crowd, white and black. At the

door of the Old North, Ruth escaped and took refuge
within, accompanied by the troubled clergyman; and
a moment later Chase and Etheridge followed. Ruth
had led the way to Miss Billy's sitting-room. Miss
Billy received her guests with wonder; Maud Muriel was with her (for her prophecy had come true;
the two had already begun the "going home" with
each other).

"We have had the most exciting race, Miss Billy,"
explained Ruth. "A real horse-race round the old
track out in the field. And Mr. Hill came in second
on Daniel!"

The eyes of Miss Billy, turning to the clergyman
with horror, moved Chase to fresh laughter. "I say
—why not all stay and dine with me?" he suggested.
"To celebrate Daniel's triumph, you know? I am
coming here to stay, so I might as well begin. The
dinner hour is two o'clock, and it is almost that now.
We can have a table to ourselves, and perhaps they
can find us some champagne."

"That will be great fun; I'll stay," said Ruth.
"And the commodore will, I'm sure. Mr. Hill,
too."

"Thanks, no. I must go. Good-day," said the
missionary, hastening out.

Chase pursued him. "Why, you are the hero of
the whole thing," he said; "the man of the hour!
We can't bring old Daniel into the dining-room. So
we must have you, Hill."

"I am sorry to spoil it; but you will have to excuse me," answered the other man, hurriedly. Then, with an outburst of confidence: "It is impossible for me to remain where Miss Mackintosh is present. There is something perfectly awful to me, Mr. Chase, in that woman's eye!"

"Is that all? Come back; I'll see to her," responded Chase. And see to her he did. Aided by Etheridge, who liked nothing better than to assail the sculptress with lovelorn compliments, Chase paid Maud Muriel such devoted attention that for the moment she forgot poor Hill, or rather she left him to himself. He was able, therefore, to eat his dinner. But he still said, mutely, "Good gracious!" and, taking out his handkerchief, he furtively wiped his brow.

The Old North had provided for its patrons that day roast beef, spring chickens, new potatoes, and apple puddings. All the diners at the other tables asked for "a dish of gravy." A saucer containing gravy was then brought and placed by the side of each plate. Small hot biscuits were offered instead of bread, and eaten with the golden mountain butter. Mrs. Jaycox, stimulated by the liberal order for champagne, sent to Chase's table the additional splendors of three kinds of fresh cake, peach preserves, and a glass jug of cream.

CHAPTER V

THE spring deepened into summer, and July opened. On the 10th, the sojourners at the Warm Springs, the beautiful pools that well up in the valley of the French Broad River, were assembled on the veranda of the rambling wooden hotel, after their six o'clock supper, when they saw two carriages approaching.. "Phew! who can they be?" "What horses!"

The horses were indeed remarkably handsome—two bays and a lighter-limbed pair of sorrels; in addition there was a mounted groom. The house-keeper, who had come out on the veranda, mention-ed in a low tone that a second groom had arrived, three hours earlier, to engage rooms for the party, and make preparations. "They are to have supper by themselves, later; we're to do our best. Extras have been ordered, and they've sent all sorts of sup-plies. And champagne!"

"Chase, did you say the name was? That's a hoax. It's General Grant himself, I reckon, coming along yere like a conqueror in disguise," said a wag.

The bays were Horace Chase's Peter and Piper, attached to a two-seated carriage which was a model as regarded comfort; Anthony Etheridge was driv-

ing, and with him were Mrs. Franklin, Dolly, and
Ruth. Horace Chase himself, in a light vehicle for
two, which he called his cart, had the sorrels. His
companion was a gaunt, dark man, who looked as
though he had been ill. This man was Mrs. Franklin's son Jared.

Franklin had been stricken by that disheartening
malady which is formed by the union of fever and
ague. After bearing it for several weeks, and sending no tidings of his condition to his family (for he
considered it a rather unmasculine ailment), he had
journeyed to Asheville with the last remnants of his
strength, and arriving by stage, and finding no one
at the cottage (for it was his wife's day at the Colored Home), he had come with uncertain steps
across the field to L'Hommedieu, entering the parlor
like a yellow spectre, his eyes sunken, his mind
slightly wandering. "Ye—es, here I am," he said,
vaguely. "I was coming next week, you know.
But I — I didn't feel well. And so I've — come
now."

His mother had given a cry; then, with an instinctive movement, her tall figure looking taller than ever,
she had rushed forward and clasped her dazed, fever-
stricken son in her arms.

The mountain air, prompt remedies, and the vig-
ilant nursing of Genevieve, soon routed the insidious
foes. Routed them, that is, for the moment; for
their strength lies in stealthy returns; as Jared said
(he made jokes even at the worst stages), they never

know when they are beaten. But as soon as there
was even a truce, their victim, though still yellow
and weak, announced that he must return to his business immediately.

"But I thought you spent your summers here,
Mr. Franklin?" remarked Horace Chase, inquiringly.

"Yes, that is the plan, and I have been here a
good deal for the past three seasons. But this year
I can't stay," Jared answered.

This was said at L'Hommedieu. Ruth was sitting
beside her brother on the sofa, her arm in his. "But
you must stay," she protested. "You are not strong
yet; you are not strong at all." She put her other
arm across his breast, as if to keep him. "I shall
not let you go!"

Jared Franklin was tall and broad-shouldered, with
dark eyes whose expression was always sad. In spite
of this sadness, he had Dolly's habit of making jocular remarks. But he had not Dolly's sharpness;
where she was sarcastic, the brother was only ironical.
In looks Jared did not resemble his mother or Dolly.
But there was a strong likeness between his face and
Ruth's; they had the same contours, the same mouth.

While Ruth was protesting, Mrs. Franklin, making
no pretence of busying herself with anything, not
even with lamplighters, sat looking at her son with
eyes which seemed to have grown larger, owing to
the depth of love within them. Chase, who had happened to be at L'Hommedieu when Jared arrived, had
never forgotten that rush of the mother—the mother

whose easy indolence he had, up to that moment,
condemned. So now he said, with his slight drawl:
"Oh, you want to give the fever another round of
shot before you go back, Mr. Franklin. Why not
take a few days more, and drive with me over the
Great Smokies into Tennessee?" And the result was
the party already described.

The evening before the start, Ruth had come out
on the veranda of L'Hommedieu. Chase and her
brother had been smoking there (for Jared had not
shown any deep attachment to his smoking-room),
and Dolly, who loved the aroma of cigars, had seated herself near them. Jared had now strolled off
with his mother, and Genevieve, coming over from
the cottage, had taken her husband's place. As she
approached, Chase had extinguished his cigar and
tossed it into the grass; for tobacco smoke always
gave the younger Mrs. Franklin a headache.

Ruth had walked up to Chase's chair. "No, please
don't rise; I am only looking at you, Mr. Chase.
You are so wonderful!"

"Now don't be *too* hard on me!" interposed the
visitor, humorously.

"First, you are making my brother take this long
drive," Ruth went on; "the very thing of all others
that will do him good—and I could go down on my
knees to you just for that! Then you have sent for
that easy carriage, so that Dolly can go, too. Then
you are taking *me*. The commodore also, who would
rather drive Peter and Piper than go to heaven! I

have always wanted to see somebody who could do *everything.* It must be very nice to have money," she concluded, reflectively.

"And to do so much good with it," added Genevieve. Genevieve had insisted that her mother-in-law should take the fourth place in the carriage; for the drive would be excellent for Mrs. Franklin, who was far from strong; whereas, for herself, as she was in perfect health, no change was necessary. Genevieve might have mentioned, also, that she had had change enough for her whole life, and to spare, during the years which her husband had spent in the navy; for the younger Mrs. Franklin did not enjoy varying scenes. A house of her own and everything in it hers; prearranged occupations, all useful or beneficent, following each other regularly in an unbroken round; a leading place in the management of charitable institutions; the writing and despatching of letters, asking for contributions to these institutions; the general supervision of the clergy, with an eye to dangerous ritualistic tendencies; the conscientious endeavor to tell her friends on all occasions what they ought to do (Genevieve was never angry when they disagreed with her, she only pitied them. There was, in fact, no one she knew whom she had not felt herself competent, at one time or another, to pity) — all this gave her the sense of doing good. And to Genevieve that was more precious than all else—the feeling that she was doing good. "Ruth is right; it must be enchanting to have money," she went on. "I have often planned what I should do myself if I had a fortune. I think I may say that I can direct, administer; I have never seen or read of any charitable institution, refuge, hospital, home, asylum, or whatever it may be, which seemed too large or too complicated for me to undertake. On the contrary, I know I should like it; I feel that I have that sort of capacity." Her face kindled as she spoke; her genius (for she had a genius, that of directorship) was stirring within her.

"You certainly have one part of the capacity, and that is the despotism," remarked Dolly, laughing. "The other members of your Board of Managers for the Colored Home, for instance—Mrs. Baxter, Miss Wynne, Miss Kent—they haven't a voice in even the smallest matter, poor souls! You rule them with a rod of iron—all for their good, no doubt."

"As it is," continued the younger Mrs. Franklin, combating not Dolly's sarcasms (to which she had paid no attention), but her own sincere longings— "as it is, I cannot build a hospital at present, though I don't give up hope for the future. But I can at least give my prayers to all, and that I do; I never ring a door-bell without offering an inward petition that something I may say will help those whom I shall see when I go in."

"Now that's generous," commented Dolly. "But don't be too unselfish, Genevieve; think of yourself occasionally; why not pray that something *they* may say will be a help to *you?*"

After the arrival of his party at the Warm Springs, Chase devoted a half-hour to a brief but exhaustive examination of the site, the pool, and the buildings. "When we have made a Tyrol of Buncombe, we'll annex this place as a sort of Baden-Baden," he said. "Thirty-five miles from Asheville—that will just do. Ever tried the baths, commodore?"

"You must apply to somebody who has rheumatism, Mr. Chase," answered Etheridge, loftily.

"The pool has an abundant supply at a temperature of 104 Fahrenheit," Chase went on, with the gleam of a smile showing itself in his eyes for a moment (for the commodore's air of youth always amused him; it was so determined). "Baden-Baden was one of the prettiest little places I saw over there, on the other side of the big pond. They've taken lots of pains to lay out a promenade along a stream, and the stream is about as big as one from a garden-hose! But here there could be a walk worth something—along this French Broad."

They were strolling near the river in the red light of the sunset. "Their forest that they talk about, their Black Forest, is all guarded and patrolled," Chase continued; "every tree counted! I don't call that a forest at all. Now *these* woods are perfectly wild. Why—they're as wild as Noah!"

"Don't you mean old as Noah?" inquired Ruth, laughing.

"Certainly not," commented Jared. "Noah was

extremely wild. And not in his youth only; in his age as well."

"The first thing, however, would be the roads," Chase went on. "I never thought I should have to take a back seat about the United States of America! But I returned from Europe singing small, I can tell you, about our roads. Talk about the difficulty of making 'em? Go and look at Switzerland!"

"By all means," said Ruth, promptly. "Only tell us how, Mr. Chase. We'll go at once." She was walking with her brother, her hat dangling by its elastic cord from her arm.

Chase came out of his plans. "So you want to see Switzerland, do you?" he said, in an indulgent tone.

Ruth lifted her hat, and made with it a gesture which took in the entire horizon. "I wish to see everything in the world!" Jared took her hat away from her, put it on her head and secured it, or tried to secure it. "Will you take me, Jared? I mean some day?" she said, as he bungled with the cord, endeavoring to get it over her hair. "That's not the way." She unbuttoned the loop and adjusted it. It was a straw hat (thanks to Genevieve, a new one), which shaded her face, but left free, behind, the thick braids which covered her small head from crown to throat.

"Once, pussy, I might have answered yes. But now I'm not so sure," replied Jared, rather gloomily.

"I don't want to go, I wasn't in earnest; I only

want to stay where you are," exclaimed his young
sister, her mood changing. "But if only you had
never left the navy! If only you were not tied down
in that horrid, horrid Raleigh!"

"Is Raleigh so very horrid?" inquired Chase.

"Any place is horrid that keeps Jared shut up in a
warehouse all day," announced Ruth, indignantly.

Mrs. Franklin, who was behind with Etheridge,
came forward, took Ruth's arm, and led her back.

"She is sorry that you left the service?" Chase inquired of the brother.

Ruth overheard this question. "Jared was always
well when he was in the navy," she called out. "No,
His Grand, I *will* say it: he was always well, and he
was happy too; Dolly has told me so. Now he is
never well; he is growing so thin that I can't bear to
see it. And as for happiness — he is *miserable!*"
Her voice broke; she stood still, her breast heaving.

Jared strolled on, his hands in the pockets of his
flannel coat. "It's nothing," he said to Chase, who
was looking back; "she'll get over it in a moment.
She says whatever comes into her head; we have
spoiled her, I suppose. She was so much younger,
you see; the last of my mother's six children. And
the three who came before her had died in infancy,
so there was a great to-do when this one lived."

Chase glanced back a second time. Ruth, Mrs.
Franklin, and Etheridge had turned, and were going
towards the hotel. "She appears to wish that you
had remained in the navy; isn't that rather odd?"

he inquired, the idea in his mind being simply the facilities that existed for seeing this idolized brother, now that Raleigh was his home instead of the ocean.

"Odd?" repeated Jared. And his tone had such a strange vibration that his companion turned and looked at him.

They continued their walk for an hour longer. When they came back, they found the commodore seated on the veranda of the cottage which had been arranged for their use by Chase's courier. Ruth and Mrs. Franklin were his companions, and Dolly was also there, resting on a sofa which had been rolled out from the room behind. Chase and Jared lighted cigars; Etheridge took out a cigarette.

"Now if we only had Maud Muriel with her long clay pipe!" said Ruth. There was no trace of trouble left in her voice; she had drawn her chair close to her brother's, and seated herself contentedly.

"It's to the pipe you owe the very clever likeness she has made of your scamp of a dog," remarked Etheridge. "The smoking relaxed her a little, without her knowing it, and so she didn't confine herself, as she usually does, to the purely commonplace side."

"Petie! A *commonplace* side!" protested Ruth.

"She now wishes *me* to sit to her," said Mrs. Franklin; "for my wrinkles have grown so deep lately that she is sure she can make something satisfactorily hideous. Oh, I don't mind the wrinkles, Mr. Chase!" (for Chase had begun to say, "Not at all, ma'am "). "I received my quietus long ago. When I was not quite forty, there was some question about a particular dress-maker whom I wished to see at McCreery's. 'Was she an *old* woman?' inquired an assistant. 'We have only one *old* fitter.' It proved to be the person I meant. She was of my own age. The same year I asked a young friend about a party which he had attended the night before. 'Dreadfully dull,' he answered. 'Nobody there but old frumps.' And the old frumps (as I happened to know) were simply twenty or thirty of my contemporaries."

"Yes, it's hard; I have often thought so!" said Etheridge, with conviction. "Men, you see, have no age. But nothing saves a woman."

"Yes, one thing—namely, to look like a sheep," replied Mrs. Franklin. "If a woman wishes her face to remain young, she must cultivate calm, and even stolidity; she must banish changing expressions; she must give her facial muscles many hours, daily, of absolute repose. Most of my wrinkles have been caused by my wretched habit of contorting my poor thin slave of a face, partly of course to show my intelligence and appreciation, but really, also, in a large measure from sympathy. I have smiled unflinchingly at other people's jokes, looked sad for their griefs, angry for their injuries; I have raised my eyebrows to my hair over their surprises, and knitted my forehead into knots over their mysteries; in short, I have never ceased to grimace. However, even to the sheep-women there comes the fatal moment when their cheeks begin to look like those of an old baby," she concluded, laughing.

Dolly, for once untalkative, had not paid attention to this conversation; the moon had risen, and she had been watching its radiance descend slowly and make a silver path across the river. It was so beautiful! And (a rare occurrence with Dolly) it led her to think of herself. "How I should have enjoyed, enjoyed, *enjoyed* everything if I had only been well!" Even the tenderly loving mother could not have comprehended fully her daughter's heart at that moment. For Mrs. Franklin had had her part, such as it was, on the stage of human existence, and had played it. But Dolly's regret was for a life unlived. "How enchantingly lovely!" she murmured aloud, looking at the moonlit water.

"Yes," said Etheridge; "and its greatest beauty is that it's primeval. Larue, I suppose, would call it primevalish!"

"I had thought of asking the senator to come along with us," observed Chase.

"In a sedan-chair?" inquired Etheridge. "I don't think you know what a petrified squam-doodle he is!"

"No, I can't say I do. I only know he's a senator, and we want some senators. To boom our Tyrol, you know. Generals, too. Cottages might be put up at pleasant points near Asheville — on Beaucatcher, for instance—and presented to half a dozen of the best-known Southern generals? What do you say to that?"

"Generals as much as you like; but when you and the Willoughbys spread your nets for senators, do select better specimens than Achilles Larue! He is only in the place temporarily at best; he'll be kicked out soon. He succeeded the celebrated old senator who had represented this state for years, and was as well known here, he and his trunk, as the mountains themselves. When he resigned, there happened to be no one of the right sort ready in the political field. Larue was here, he was a college-bred man, and he had some reputation as an author (he has written a dreadfully dull book, *The Blue Ridge in the Glacial Period*). He had a little money, too, and that was in his favor. So they put him in; and now they wish they hadn't! He has no magnetism, no go; nothing but his tiresome drawing-copy profile and his good clothes. You say you don't know what sort of a person he is? He is a decrier, sir; nothing ever fully pleases him. His opinions on all subjects are so clipped to the bone, so closely shaved and denuded, that they are like the plucked chickens, blue and skinny, that one sees for sale at a stall. Achilles Larue never smokes. On the hottest day Achilles Larue remains clammily cold. He has no appreciation of a good dinner; he lives on salt mackerel and digestive crackers. Finally, to sum him up, he is a man, sir, who can neither ride nor drive—a man who knows nothing whatever about a horse! What do you suppose he asked me, when I was looking at a Blue-Grass pacer last year? ' Does he possess endurance ?' Yes—actually those words of a *horse!* ' Does he possess endurance ?' " repeated Etheridge, pursing up his lips and pronouncing the syllables in a mincing tone.

"You say he has nothing but his drawing-copy profile and his good clothes," remarked Dolly. " But he has something more, commodore: the devotion of Mrs. Kip and Miss Billy Breeze."

Etheridge looked discomfited.

"*Two* ladies ?" said Chase. " Why, he's in luck! Bachelor, I suppose ?"

" He is a widower," answered Mrs. Franklin. " His wife happened to have been a fool. He now believes that all women are idiots."

" He is a man who has never written, and who never will write, a book that stands on its own feet, whether good or bad; but only books *about* books," grumbled Etheridge. " He has merely the commentator's mind. His views on the Glacial Period are all borrowed. He can't be original even about an iceberg !"

" The ladies I have mentioned think that his originality is his strongest point," objected Dolly. " He produces great effects by describing some one in this way, for instance : ' He had small eyes and a grin. He was remarkably handsome.' This leaves them open-mouthed. But Miss Billy herself, as she stands, is his greatest effect; she was never outlined

in very vivid hues, and now she has so effaced herself, rubbed herself out, as it were (from fear lest he
should call her 'sensational'), that she is like a
skeleton leaf. She has the greatest desire to be
'delicate,' extremely delicate, in everything that she
does; and she tries to sing, therefore, with so much
expression that it's all expression and very little singing! 'Coarse!' — that is to her the most terrible
word in the whole vocabulary. I asked her once
whether her horned tryceratops, with his seventy-
five feet of length, might not have been a little
coarse in his manners."

"I declare I'll never go to see the woman again;
she *is* such a goose!" exclaimed Etheridge, angrily.

Jared laughed. And then his mother laughed also,
happy to see him amused. But at the same time she
was thinking: "You may not go to see Billy. But,
dear me! you will come to see *us* forever and forever!" And she had a weary vision of Etheridge,
entering with his "hum-ha," and his air of youth, five
or six times a week as long as she lived.

"Commodore," said Dolly, "you may not go to
see Miss Breeze. But I am sure you will come to see
us, with your cheerful hum-ha, and your youthful
face, as long as we live."

Mrs. Franklin passed her hand over her forehead.
"There it is again!" she thought. For, strangely
often, Dolly would give voice to the very ideas that
were passing through her mother's mind at the moment. At L'Hommedieu the two would fall into

silence sometimes, and remain silent for a half-hour, one with her embroidery, the other with her knitting. And then when Dolly spoke at last, it would be of the exact subject which was in her mother's mind. Mrs. Franklin no longer exclaimed: "How could you know I was thinking of that!" It happened too often. She herself never divined Dolly's thoughts. It was Dolly who divined hers, most of the time unconsciously.

Meanwhile Etheridge had replied, in a reassuring voice: " Well, Dolly, I'll do my best; you may count upon *that*." And then Ruth, leaning her head against her brother's arm so that her face was hidden, laughed silently.

From the Warm Springs they drove over the Great Smoky Mountains into Tennessee. Then returning, making no haste, they climbed slowly up again among the peaks. At the top of the pass they paused to gaze at the far-stretching view—Tennessee, Kentucky, Virginia, North Carolina, South Carolina, and Georgia; on the west, the Cumberland ranges sloping towards Chattanooga; in the east, the crowded summits of the Blue Ridge, their hue an unchanging azure; the Black Mountains with Mitchell, the Cat-tail Peak, the Balsams, the Hairy Bear, the Big Craggy, Great Pisgah, the Grandfather, and many more. The brilliant sunshine and the crystalline atmosphere revealed every detail— the golden and red tints of the gigantic bald cliffs near them, the foliage of every tree; the farm-houses like white dots thousands of feet below. Up here at the top of the pass there were no clearings visible; for long miles in every direction the forest held unbroken sway, filling the gorges like a leafy ocean, and sweeping up to the surrounding summits in the darker tints of the black balsams. The air was filled with delicate wild odors, a fragrance which is like no other—the breath of a virgin forest.

"And you want to put a railroad here?" broke out Dolly, suddenly. She addressed Horace Chase, who had drawn up his sorrels beside the carriage.

"Oh no, Miss Dolly; it can't get up so high, you know," he answered, not comprehending her dislike. "It will have to go through down below; tunnels."

"The principal objection I have to your railroad, Chase, is that it will bring railroad good-byes to this uncorrupted neighborhood," said Jared. "For there will be, of course, a station. And people will have to go there to see their friends off. The train will always be late in starting; then the heretofore sincere Ashevillians will be driven to all the usual exaggerations and falsities to fill the eternal time; they will have to repeat the same things over and over, stand first on one leg and then on the other, and smile until they are absolute clowns. Meanwhile their departing friends will be obliged to lean out of the car-windows in return, and repeat inanities and grin, until they too are perfectly haggard." Jared was now seated beside Etheridge; he had given up his place in the cart to Ruth for an hour or two. Sev-

eral times Mrs. Franklin herself had tried the cart.
She was very happy, for Jared had undoubtedly
gained strength; there was a faint color in his
cheeks, and his face looked less worn, his eyes a
little less dreary.

"How I should like to see *all* the mountains!"
exclaimed Ruth, suddenly, looking at the crowded
circle of peaks.

"Well—I suppose there are some sort of roads?"
Chase answered.

"Put the two pairs together and make a four-in-
hand," suggested Etheridge, eagerly. "Then we
might drive down Transylvania way. When I wasn't
more than eighteen I often drove a four-in-hand over
the—the—the range up there where I was born," he
concluded, with fresh inward disgust over the forgotten name.

"The Green Mountains," said Mrs. Franklin.

"Not at all. The Catskills," Etheridge answered,
curtly. His birthplace was Rutland, Vermont. But
on principle he never acknowledged a forgotten title.

"This is the country of the moonshiners, isn't it?"
asked Chase, his keen eyes glancing down a wild
gorge.

"The young lady beside you can tell about that,"
Etheridge answered.

Chase turned to Ruth, surprised. The color was
leaving her face. "Yes, I *did* see; I saw a man
shot!" she said, her dark-fringed blue eyes lifted
to his with an awe-struck expression. "It was at

Crumb's, the house where we stayed the first night,
you know. I was standing at the door. A man
came running along the road, trying to reach the
house. Behind him, not more than ten feet distant,
came another man, also running. He held a pistol
at arm's - length. He fired twice. After the first
shot, the man in front still ran. After the second, he
staggered along for a step or two, and then fell. And
the other man disappeared." These short sentences
came out in whispered tones; when she finished, her
face was blanched.

"You ought not to have seen it. You ought not
to have told me," said Chase, giving an indignant
glance towards the carriage; he thought they should
have prevented the narration.

"Oh, don't be disturbed, Mr. Chase," said Dolly,
looking at him from her cushions with an amused
smile. "The balls were extracted, and the man is
now in excellent health. Ruth has a way of turning
perfectly white and then enormously red on all occasions. She was much whiter last week when it was
supposed that Petie Trone, Esq., had inflammation of
the lungs."

And Ruth herself was already laughing again, and
the red had returned.

"It was a revenue detective," explained Mrs. Franklin; "I mean the man who was shot. The mountaineers have always made whiskey, and they think
that they have a right to make it; they look upon
the detectives as spies."

But Chase had no sympathy for moonshiners ; he was on the side of law and order. " The government should send up troops," he said. " What else are they for ?"

" It is not the business of the army to hunt out illicit stills," replied Jared Franklin, all the ex-officer in his haughty tone.

" Well, maybe not ; you see I'm only a civilian myself," remarked Chase, in a pacific voice. " Shall we go on ?"

They started down the eastern slope. When the cart was at some distance in front, Ruth said : " Oh, Mr. Chase, thank you for answering so good-naturedly. My brother has in reality a sweet temper. But lately he has been so out of sorts, so unhappy."

" Yes, I am beginning to understand about that, Miss Ruth ; I didn't at first. It's a great pity. Perhaps something can be done ?"

" No ; he can't get back into the navy now," said Ruth, sadly.

" But a change of some kind might be arranged," answered Chase, touching the off horse.

At the base of the mountains they followed the river road again, a rocky track, sometimes almost in the water, under towering cliffs that rose steeply, their summits leaning forward a little as though they would soon topple over. At many points it was a veritable cañon, and the swift current of the stream foamed so whitely over the scattered rocks of its bed that it was like the rapids of Niagara.

Here and there were bold islands; the forest on both sides was splendid with the rich tints of the *Rhododendron maximum* in full bloom; not patches or single bushes, but high thickets, a solid wall of blazing color.

Their stopping-place for the last evening was the farm-house called Crumb's, where they had also spent the first night of their journey on their way westward. Crumb's was one of the old farms; the grandfather of David Crumb had tilled the same acres. It was a pleasant place near the river, the house comparatively large and comfortable. The Crumbs were well-to-do in the limited mountain sense of the term, though they had probably never had a hundred dollars in cash in their lives. Mrs. Crumb, a lank woman with stooping shoulders and a soft, flat voice, received them without excitement. Nothing that life had to offer, for good or for ill, could ever bring excitement again to Portia Crumb. Her four sons had been killed in battle in Virginia, one after the other, and the mother lived on patiently. David Crumb was more rebellious against what he called their "bad luck." Once a week, and sometimes twice, he went to Asheville, making the journey a pretext for forgetting troubles according to the ancient way. He was at Asheville now, his wife explained, "with a load of wood." She did not add that he would probably return with a load of another sort — namely, a mixture of whiskey and repentance. The two never spoke of their lost boys;

when they talked together it was always about "the craps."

Porshy, as her friends called her, having been warned by Chase's courier that her former guests were returning, had set her supper-table with care. People stopped at Crumb's perforce; for, save at Warm Springs, there were no inns in the French Broad Valley. Ruth had been there often. For the girl, who was a fearless horsewoman, was extravagantly fond of riding; at one time or another she had ridden almost every horse in Asheville, including old Daniel himself. Of late years the Crumbs would have been glad to be relieved of all visitors. But the mountain farmers of the South are invariably hospitable—hospitable even with their last slice of corn-bread, their last cup of coffee. Porshy, therefore, had brought out her best table-cloth (homespun, like her sheets), her six thin silver teaspoons, her three china teacups and saucers. "Yes, rale chiny, you bet," she had said, in her gentle, lifeless voice, when Mrs. Franklin, who knew the tragedy of the house, was benevolently admiring the painstaking effort. The inevitable hot biscuits were waiting in a flat pan, together with fried bacon and potatoes and coffee. Chase's supplies of potted meats, hothouse fruit, and excellent champagne made the meal an extraordinary combination. The table was set in the kitchen, which was also the living-room. One end of the large, low-browed apartment was blocked by the loom, for Portia had been accustomed to spin, weave, dye, and fashion all the garments worn by herself and her family.

As they left the table, the sinking sun sent his horizontal beams through the open windows in a flood of golden light. "Let us go up to the terrace," said Ruth.

The terrace was a plateau on the mountain-side at some distance above; a winding path led thither through the thick forest. "It is too far," said Mrs. Franklin. "It is at least a mile from here, and a steep climb all the way; and, besides, it will soon be dark."

"Oh, but I want to go immensely, His Grand. Mr. Chase liked it so much when we were up there on our way out that he says it shall be named after me. And perhaps they will put up a cottage."

"Yes, Ruth's Terrace, ma'am. That is the name I propose," said Chase.

"There will be light enough to go up; and then we can wait there until the moon rises," continued Ruth. "The moon is full to-night, and the view will be lovely. You will go, Jared, won't you? Oh, please!"

She had her way, as usual. Chase and Jared, lighting cigars, prepared to accompany her.

"You'll stay here, I suppose, commodore?" said Chase.

"Stay here! By no means. There is nothing I like better than an evening stroll," answered Etheridge, heroically. And, lighting a cigarette, he walked on in advance, swinging his cane with an air of meditative enjoyment.

Dolly and Mrs. Franklin, meanwhile, sat beside the small fire which Portia had made on the broad hearth of her "best room." The fire, of aromatic "fat-pine" splinters only, without large sticks, had been kindled more on account of the light than from any need of its warmth; for the evening, though cool, was not cold. The best room, however, was large, and the great forest and cliffs outside, and the wild river, made the little blaze seem cheerful. Portia had been proud of this apartment in the old days before the war. In one corner there was a bed covered with a brilliant patch-work quilt; on the mantel-piece there was an old accordion, and a vase for flowers whose design was a hand holding a cornucopia; the floor was covered by a rag carpet; and tacked on the walls in a long row were colored fashion plates from *Godey's Lady's Book* for 1858. At ten o'clock Ruth and the commodore came in. But long after midnight, when the others were asleep, Chase and Jared Franklin still strolled to and fro along the river road in the moonlight, talking. The next day they all returned to Asheville.

At the end of the week, when Jared went back to his business, Chase accompanied him. "I thought I might as well take a look at that horrid Raleigh," he said to Ruth, with solemn humor. "You see, I have been laboring under the impression that it was a very pretty place—a mistake which evidently wants to be cleared up."

Ten days later the mud-bespattered Blue Ridge stage came slowly into Asheville at its accustomed hour. The mail-bags were thrown out, and then the postmaster, in his shirt-sleeves, with his spectacles on his nose and his straw hat tilted back on his head, began the distribution of their contents, assisted (through the open windows) by the usual group of loungers. This friendly audience had its elbows on the sill. It made accompanying comments as follows: "Hurry up, you veteran of the Mexican war!" "That letter ain't for Johnny Monroe. It's for Jem Morse; I can see the direction from here. Where's your eyes?" "*Six* for General Cyarter? Lucky reb, *he* is!"

Twenty minutes later Genevieve Franklin entered the parlor of L'Hommedieu, a flush of deep rose-color in each cheek, her eyes lustrous. "Mamma, a letter from Jay! It is too good— I cannot tell you—" Her words came out pantingly, for she had been running; she sat down with her hand over her breast as if to help herself breathe.

"From Jared? Oh, where are my glasses?" said Mrs. Franklin, searching vainly in her pocket and then on the table. "Here, Dolly. Quick! Read it!"

And then Dolly, also excited, read Jared's letter aloud.

Ruth came in in time to hear this sentence: "I

am to have charge of their Charleston office (the office of the Columbian Line), at a salary of three thousand dollars a year."

"Who? What? Not Jared? And at *Charleston?*" cried the girl, clapping her hands. "Oh, how splendid! For it's the water, you know; the salt-water at last. With the ships coming and going, and the ocean, it won't be so awfully inland to him, poor fellow, as Raleigh and Atlanta."

"And the large salary," said Genevieve, still breathless. "*That's* Horrie! I have felt sure, from the first, that he would do something for us. Such an old friend of mine. Dear, dear Horrie!"

A week later Chase returned. "Yes, he'll get off to Charleston, ma'am, in a few days," he said to Mrs. Franklin. "When he is settled there, you must pay him a visit. I guess you'll end by going there to live."

"Oh, we can't; we have this house, and no house there. If I could only sell that place in Florida! However, we can stop in Charleston when we go to Florida this winter. That is, if we go," added the mother, remembering her load of debts. But she soon forgot it again; she forgot everything save her joy in the brighter life for her son. "How can I thank you?" she said to Chase, gratefully.

"Oh, it's no favor, ma'am. We have always needed a first-class man at Charleston, and we've never had it; we think ourselves very lucky in being able to secure Mr. Franklin."

As he went back to the Old North with Etheridge,

whom he had met at L'Hommedieu (as Mrs. Franklin
would have said, "of course!"), Chase added some
further particulars. "You never saw such a mess as
he'd made of it, commodore. He told me—we had
a good deal of talk when we took that French Broad
drive—that his business wasn't what he had hoped
it would be when he went into it; that he was afraid
it was running down. Running down? It was at a
standstill; six months more, and he would have been
utterly swamped. The truth is, he didn't know how
to manage it. How should he? What does a navy
man know about leather? He saw that it was all
wrong, yet he didn't know how to help it; that took
the heart out of him, you see. There was no use in
going on with it a day longer; and so I told him, as
soon as I had looked into the thing a little. He has,
therefore, made an arrangement—sold out. And now
he is going to take a place at Charleston—our Columbian Line."

"To the tune of three thousand dollars a year, I
understand?"

"He'll be worth it to us. A navy officer as agent
will be a feather in our caps. It's a pity he couldn't
take command of one of our steamers—with his
hankering for the sea. Our steamer officers wear
uniforms, you know?"

"Take care that he doesn't knock you down," said
Etheridge, dryly.

"Oh, I haven't suggested it. I see he's cranky,"
Chase answered.

When Jared Franklin reached Charleston, he went to the office of the Columbian Company. It faced a wharf or dock, and from its windows he could see the broad harbor, the most beautiful port of the South Atlantic coast. He looked at Fort Sumter, then off towards the low white beaches of Morris Island; he knew the region well; his ship had lain outside during the war. Deliciously sweet to him was the salt tang of the sea; already, miles inland, he had perceived it, and had put his head out of the car window; the salt marshes had been to him like a tonic, as the train rushed past. The ocean out there in the east, too, that was rather better than a clattering street! Words could never express how he loathed the remembrance of the hides and the leather. A steamer of the Columbian Line came in. He went on board, contemptuous of everything, of course, but enjoying that especial species of contempt. Ascending to the upper deck, he glanced at the rigging and smoke-stacks. They were not what he approved of; but, oh! the solace of abusing any sort of rigging outlined against the sky! He went down and looked at the engines; he spoke to the engineer; he prowled all over the ship, from stem to stern, his feet enjoying the sensation of something underneath them that floated. That evening, seated on a bench at the Battery, with his arms on the railing, he looked out to sea. His beloved old life came back to him; all his cruises—the Mediterranean ports, Villefranche and the Bay of Naples; the

harbors of China, Rio Janeiro, Alexandria; tropical
islands; the color of the Pacific—while the wash of
the water below sounded in his ears. At last, long
after midnight, he rose; he came back to reality
again. "Well, even this is a great windfall. And I
must certainly do the best I can for that long-legged
fellow"—so he said to himself as he went up Meeting Street towards his hotel. He liked Chase after
a fashion; he appreciated his friendliness and his
genius for business. But this was the way he
thought of him—"that long-legged fellow." Chase's
fortune made no impression upon him. At heart he
had the sailor's chronic indifference to money-making. But at heart he had also something else—
Genevieve; Genevieve and her principles and plans,
Genevieve and her rules.

CHAPTER VI

ONE afternoon early in September, Miss Billy Breeze, her cheeks pink, her gentle eyes excited, entered the principal store of Asheville, the establishment of Messrs. Pinkham & Bebb. "Kid gloves, if you please, Mr. Bebb. Delicate shades. No. 6." The box of gloves having been produced, Miss Billy selected quickly twelve pairs. "I will take these. And please add twelve pairs of white."

Mr. Bebb was astounded, the order seemed to him reckless. Everybody in Asheville knew that Miss Billy's income was six hundred dollars a year. He made up the parcel slowly, in order to give her time to change her mind. But Miss Billy paid for the twenty-four pairs without a quiver, and, with the same excited look, took the package and went out. She walked down the main street to its last houses; she came back on the other side. Turning to the right, she traversed all the cross-roads in that direction. When this was done, she re-entered the main street again, and passed through its entire length a second time. It was Saturday, the day when the country people came to town. Ten mountaineers in a row were sitting on their heels in front of the post-office. Mountain women on horseback, wearing deep sun-bonnets, rode up and down the street, bartering. Wagons passed along, loaded with peaches heaped together as though they were potatoes. Miss Billy was now traversing all the cross-roads to the left. When this was accomplished she came back to the main street, and began over again. It took about an hour to make the entire circuit. At half-past five, on her fourth round, still walking quickly and always with an air of being bound to some especial point, she met Achilles Larue. "Oh — really — is this *you*, Mr. Larue? Such a *surprise* to see you! Lovely day, isn't it? I've been buying gloves." She opened the package and turned over the gloves hastily. "Light shades, you see. I — I thought I'd better."

Larue, slightly lifting his hat, was about to pass on.

But Miss Billy detained him. "Of course you are interested in the news, Mr. Larue? Weren't you surprised? I was. I am afraid she is a little too young for him. I think it is rather better when they are of *about* the same age — don't you?" She had no idea that she had been walking, and at twice her usual speed, for more than four hours. But her slender body knew; it trembled from fatigue.

Larue made another move, as if about to continue his course.

"But do tell me—weren't you surprised?" Billy repeated, hastily. (For, oh! he *must* not go so soon.)

"I don't think I am ever surprised, Miss Breeze."

Here Anthony Etheridge came by, and stopped. He looked sternly at Miss Billy. "But what do you *think* of it, Mr. Larue?" Billy was inquiring.

"I have not thought of it," Larue responded, coldly.

"Are you selling gloves?" inquired Etheridge. For the paper having fallen to the ground, the two dozen pairs were visible, lying in confusion over Billy's arm.

"To Mr. Larue?" (Giggle.) "Oh, I couldn't." (Giggle.) "They're only No. 6." For poor Billy had one humble little pride—her pretty hand.

There was a sound of horses' feet, and Ruth Franklin rode round the corner, on Kentucky Belle, giving them a gay nod as she passed. Horace Chase and Malachi Hill were with her, both mounted on beautiful horses — one black, one chestnut; and at some distance behind followed Chase's groom. "How *happy* she looks!" murmured Miss Billy, with an involuntary sigh.

"Yes. She has obtained what she likes," commented Larue. "Hers is a frivolous nature; she requires gayety, change, luxury, and now she will have them. Her family are very wise to consent. For they have, I suspect, but little money. Her good looks will soon disappear; at thirty she will be plain." And this time, decidedly, he walked away.

Miss Billy, her eyes dimmed by unshed tears,

looked after him. "Such a—such a *worldly* view of marriage!" she managed to articulate.

"What can you expect from a fish?" answered Ethridge, secretly glad of his opportunity. "Achilles Larue is as cold-blooded as a mackerel, and always was. I don't say he will never marry again; but if he does, the woman he selects will have to go down on her knees and stay there" (Miss Billy's eyes looked hopeful); "and bring him, also, a good big sum of money in her hand." Here, noticing that one of the pairs of gloves had slipped down so far that it was held by the tips of its fingers only, he turned away with a sudden "Good-afternoon." For he had had rheumatism all night in the small of his back; he could walk, but he could not stoop.

Miss Billy went home much depressed. The night before, after her usual devotions and an hour's perusal of *The Blue Ridge in the Glacial Period* (she read the volume through regularly once a month), she had attempted a thought-transference. She had, indeed, made many such experiments since Maud Muriel's explanation of the process. But last night she had for the first time succeeded in keeping her mind strictly to the subject; for nearly ten minutes, with her face screwed up by the intensity of the effort, she had willed continuously, "Like me, Achilles, like me!" (She was too modest even to *think* "love" instead of "like.") "You must! You *shall!*" And now, when at last she had succeeded in meeting him, this was the result! She put away the gloves mechanically : she had bought them not from any need, but simply because she had felt the wish to go out and *do* something when the exciting news of Ruth Franklin's engagement had reached her at noon. Stirred as she already was by her own private experiment of the previous night, the thought in her heart was : " Well, it isn't extravagance, for light gloves are always useful. And then in case of—of anything happening to *me*, they'd be all ready."

When Anthony Etheridge left her, he went to L'Hommedieu, where he found Dolly in the parlor with Petie Tronc, Esq. Tronc's basket had been established by Ruth under the pedestal which now held his own likeness. For Chase had kept his word ; Maud Muriel's clever work had been reproduced in bronze. The squirrel also was present ; he was climbing up the window - curtain. " So *you* have to see to the pets, do you ?" remarked the visitor as he seated himself. He had known of the engagement for several days ; he had already made what he called " the proper speeches " to Mrs. Franklin and Ruth, and to Chase himself. " I have just seen her—on Kentucky Belle," he went on. " Well, he will give her everything, that's one certainty. On the whole, she's a lucky girl."

" It is Mr. Chase who is lucky," answered Dolly, stiffly. She was finishing off the toe of a stocking, and did not look up. " I consider Mr. Chase a miraculously fortunate man."

"Miraculously? How do you mean? Because she is young? The good-fortune, as regards that, is for the wife, not the husband; for she will always be so much his junior that he will have to consider her—he will never dare to neglect her. Well, Dolly, all Asheville has heard the news this morning; the town is ringing with it. And it is such an amiable community that it has immediately given its benediction in the most optimistic way. Of course, though, there are some who maintain that she is marrying him for his money."

Dolly knitted more rapidly.

"And so she is," Etheridge added. "Though not in their sense, for she has never reflected, never thought about it, never made a plan. All the same, it is his wealth, you know, which has fascinated her—his wealth and his liberality. She has never seen anything like it. No one she knows has ever done such things—flowers, jewels, journeys, her brother lifted out of his troubles as if by magic, a future sparkling and splendid opening before her; no wonder she is dazzled. In addition, she herself has an ingrained love of ease—"

Dolly dropped her stocking. "Do you think I intend to sit here and listen to you?" she demanded, with flashing eyes.

"Wait, wait," answered Etheridge, putting out his hand as if to explain; "you don't see what I am driving at, Dolly. As Mrs. Chase, your sister will have everything she wishes for; all her tastes and fancies gratified to the full; and that is no small affair! Chase will be fond of her; in addition, he will be excessively indulgent to her in every way. With her nature and disposition, her training, too (for you have spoiled her, all of you), it is really an ideal marriage for the girl, and that is what I am trying to tell you. You might search the world over, and you could not find a better one."

"I don't like it; I never shall like it," answered Dolly, implacably. "And mother in her heart agrees with me, though she has, somehow, a higher idea of the man than I have. As for Ruth—Ruth is simply swept away—"

"Exactly; swept into her proper sphere," interrupted Etheridge. "Don't interfere with the process."

"She doesn't understand—" Dolly began.

"She understands immensely well what she likes! Give Ruth indulgence, amusement, pleasure, and she will be kind-hearted, amiable, generous; in short, good and happy. On the other hand, there might be another story. Come, I am going to be brutal; I don't know how much money your mother has; but I suspect very little, with the possibility, perhaps, of less. And I can't imagine, Dolly, any one more unhappy than your sister would be, ten years hence, say, if shut up here in Asheville, poor, her good looks gone, to face a life of dull sameness forever. I think it would kill her! She is not at all the girl to accept monotony with resignation or heroism; to settle down to mending and reading, book-clubs and whist-clubs, puddings and embroidery, gossip and good works."

Here the house-door opened; Mrs. Franklin and Genevieve came in together, and entered the parlor. When Dolly heard Genevieve's step, she rose. Obliged to walk slowly, she could not slip out; but she made a progress which was almost stately, as, without speaking to her sister-in-law, or looking at her, she left the room.

Genevieve, however, required no notice from Dolly. Her face was radiant with satisfaction. She shook hands with Etheridge warmly. "I have not seen you since it happened, commodore. I know you are with us in our pleasure? I know you congratulate us?"

Etheridge had always thought the younger Mrs. Franklin a beautiful woman; she reminded him of the Madonna del Granduca at Florence. Now she held his hand so long, and looked at him with such cordial friendliness, that he came out with the gallant exclamation, "Chase is the one I congratulate, by Jove!—on getting such a sister-in-law!"

"Think of all Ruth will now be able to do—all the good! I seem to see even my hospital," added Genevieve, gayly.

"Hum—yes," added Etheridge. Walking away a step or two, he put his hands in the pockets of his trousers and looked towards his legs reflectively for a moment, as though surveying the pattern of the gar-

9

ments—a convenient gesture to which a (slender) man
can resort when he wishes to cover a silence.

"For dear mamma, too, it is so delightful," continued Genevieve. She had seated herself, and she
now drew her mother-in-law down beside her. "Ruth
will never permit mamma to have another care."

"Yes—I think I'll just run up and take off my
bonnet," said Mrs. Franklin, disengaging herself.
And she left the room.

Genevieve was not disturbed by this second departure; she was never disturbed by any of the actions or the speeches of her husband's family. She
did her own duty regarding them regularly and
steadily, month after month; it was part of her rule
of conduct. But what they did or said to her in return was less important. "Ruth is a fortunate girl,"
she went on, as she drew off her gloves with careful
touches. "And she appreciates it, commodore—I
am glad to tell you that; I have been talking to her.
She is very happy. Horace is such an able and
splendidly successful man—a man whom every one
must respect and admire most warmly."

"Yes, a clever speculator indeed!" commented
Etheridge, ungratefully, throwing over his drive with
the bays.

"Speculator? Oh no; it is all genuine business;
I can assure you of that," answered Genevieve, seriously. "And now perhaps you can help us a little.
Horace is anxious to have the marriage take place
this fall. And I am on his side. For why, indeed,

should they wait? The usual delays are prudential, or for the purpose of making preparations. But in this case there are no such conditions; he already has a house in New York, for he has always preferred home life. Ruth is willing to have it so. But mamma decidedly, almost obstinately, opposes it."

"Dolly too, I suppose?"

"Oh, I never count Dolly; her temper is so uncertain. But it is very natural that it should be so, and one always excuses her, poor dear! Couldn't *you* say a word or two to mamma, commodore? You have known her so long; I am sure you have influence. But my chief dependence, of course, is upon Jay. Mamma always yields to Jay."

"Franklin, then, is pleased with the engagement?" said Etheridge, walking about the room, taking up books, looking at them vaguely, and laying them down again.

"How could he *not* be! As it happens, however, we have not yet heard from him, for when our letters reached Charleston he had just started for New York on one of their steamers; some business errand. But he was to return by train, and I am expecting to hear from him to-morrow."

There was a sound outside. "Here they come," said Etheridge, looking out.

Genevieve rose quickly to join him at the window. Chase and Malachi Hill were dismounting. Then Chase lifted Ruth from Kentucky Belle. "Those are two new horses, you know," explained Genevieve, in

a low tone; "Horrie sent for them. And he lets Mr.
Hill ride one of them every day."

"Yes; *horses* enough!" grumbled Etheridge, dis-
contentedly.

Ruth, holding up the skirt of her habit, was coming towards the house, talking to her two escorts.
When she entered the parlor, Genevieve went forward and put her arm round her. "I know you
have enjoyed your ride, dear?"

"Of course I have. How do you do, commodore?
I have just been planning another excursion with
Horace." (The name came out happily and securely.)
"To Cæsar's Head this time; you to drive the four-
in-hand, and I to ride Kentucky Belle."

"Yes, that's right; arrange it with him," said
Chase. "For I must go; I have letters to write
which can be postponed no longer. You have had
enough of me for to-day, I guess? May I come in
to-morrow afternoon—early?"

"Come to lunch," said Ruth, giving him her hand.
He held it out for a moment, looking at her with
kindly eyes. "You don't know how much I enjoyed
my ride," said the girl, heartily. "It is such a joy
to be on Kentucky Belle; she is so beautiful, and
she moves so lightly! It was the nicest ride I have
ever had in my life!"

This seemed to please Chase. He took leave of
the others and went away.

"I will wait here, if you will allow it, Miss Ruth,
until he is out of sight," said Malachi Hill. "For I

may as well confess to you—I have already told Miss
Dolly—that I seem fairly to lose my head when I
find myself with Mr. Chase alone! I am so haunted
by the idea of all he could do for the Church in these
mountains that in spite of the generous gifts he has
already made, I keep hankering after more—like a
regular *gorilla* of covetousness!"

"I shall have to see that he is never left alone with
you," said Ruth, laughing.

"There! he has turned the corner. Now *I'll* go
the other way," continued the missionary, his seriousness unbroken.

"Mr. Hill is such a *good* man," remarked Genevieve as she closed the window.

"Miss Billy thinks him full of the darkest evil,"
commented Ruth. "Why do you shut the window?"

"You were in a draught. After your ride you
must be warm."

"I'm a precious object, am I?"

"Yes, dear, you certainly are," replied Genevieve,
with all the seriousness of Malachi Hill.

"If that simpleton of a Billy could see the parson
eat apples, she would change her opinion about him,"
remarked Etheridge. "A man who can devour with
relish four, five, and even six, cold raw apples (and
the Asheville apples are sixteen inches round) late
in the evening, cores, seeds, and all, *must* be virtuous—as virtuous as mutton!" He was looking at
Ruth as he spoke. The girl was leaning back in an
easy-chair; Petie Trone, Esq., had lost no time, he

was already established in her lap, and the squirrel had flown to her shoulder. She had taken off her gauntlets, and as she lifted her hands to remove her hat, he saw a flash. "Trinkets?" he said.

"Oh—you haven't seen it?" She drew off a ring and tossed it across to him.

"Take care!" said Genevieve.

But Etheridge had already caught it. It was a solitaire diamond ring, the stone of splendid beauty, large, pure, brilliant.

"It came yesterday," Genevieve explained. Then she folded her hands—this with Genevieve was always a deliberate motion. "There will be diamonds—yes. But there will be other things also; surely our dear Ruth will remember the duties of wealth as well as its pleasures."

Ruth paid no heed to this; put on her ring again, using the philopena circlet as a guard; then she said, "Petie Trone, Esq., there will be just time before dinner for your Saturday scrubbing."

Half an hour later when she returned, the little dog trotting behind her, his small body pinned up in a hot towel, Genevieve cried in alarm, "Where are your rings?"

"Oh," said Ruth, looking at her hands, "I didn't miss them; they must have come off in the tub. Since then I have been in my room, dressing."

"And Rinda may have thrown away the water!" exclaimed her sister-in-law, rushing up the stairs in breathless haste.

But Rinda was never in a hurry to perform any of her duties, and the wooden tub devoted to Mr. Trone still stood in its place. Genevieve, baring her white arms, plunged both her hands into the water, her heart beating with anxiety. But the rings, very soapy, were there.

That evening, at nine o'clock, Mrs. Franklin was galloping through the latest tale of Anthony Trollope. For she always read a novel with racing speed to get at the story, skipping every description; then, if she had been interested, she went back and reperused it in more leisurely fashion. It was unusual to have a book fresh from the press; the well-fingered volumes which Miss Billy borrowed for her so industriously were generally two or three years old. Horace Chase, learning from Ruth the mother's liking for novels, had sent a note to New York, ordering in his large way "all the latest articles in fiction;" a package to be sent to L'Hommedieu once a month. The first parcel had just arrived, and Mrs. Franklin, opening it, much surprised, had surveyed the gift with mixed feelings. She was alone; Dolly was upstairs. Ruth, seized with a sudden fancy for a glass of cream, had gone, with Rinda as protector, to a house at some distance, where cream was sold; for with Ruth fancies were so vivid that it always seemed to her absolutely necessary to follow them instantly. The mother turned over the volumes. "It doesn't make me like him a bit better!" she said to herself. But her easy-chair was comfortable; the reading-lamp was burning brightly at her elbow. For fourteen years novels had been her opiates; she put on her glasses, took up the Trollope, and began. She had not been reading long, when her attention suddenly jumped back to the present, owing to a sound outside. For the window was open, somebody was coming up the path from the gate, and she recognized—yes, she recognized the step. Letting the book drop, she ran to the house-door. "Jared! Why—how did you get here? The stage came in long ago."

"I drove over from Old Fort," answered her son as he entered.

"And you did not find Genevieve? She has gone with Mr. Hill to—"

"I haven't been to the Cottage yet; I came directly here. Where is Ruth?"

"Out. But she will be in soon. Dolly isn't well to-night; she has gone to bed."

"The coast is clear, then, and we can talk," said Jared. "So much the better." They were now in the parlor; before seating himself he closed the door. "I have come up, mother, about this affair of Ruth's. As soon as I got back to Charleston and read your letters, I started at once. You have been careless, I fear; but at least I hope that nothing has been said, that no one knows?"

"Everybody knows, Jared. At least, everybody in Asheville."

"Who has told? Chase?" asked Jared, angrily.

"Oh no; he left that to us. I have said nothing, and Dolly has said nothing. But—but—"

"But what?"

"Genevieve has announced it everywhere," answered Mrs. Franklin, her inward feeling against her daughter-in-law for once getting the better of her.

"I will speak to Genevieve. But she is not the one most in fault, mother; she could not have announced it unless *you* had given your consent. And how came you to do that?"

"I don't think I have consented. I have been waiting for you."

"Very well, then; we can act together. Now that *I* have come, Horace Chase will find that there's some one on hand to look after you; he will no longer be able to do as he pleases!"

"Our difficulty is, Jared, that it is not so much a question of his doing as he pleases as it is of Ruth's doing as *she* pleases; she thinks it is all enchanting; and she is headstrong, you know."

"Yes. That is the very reason why I think you have been careless, mother. You were here and I was not; you, therefore, were the one to act. You should have taken Ruth out of town at once; you should have taken her north, if necessary, and kept her there; you should have done this at any sacrifice."

"It is not so easy—" began his mother. Then she stopped. For she was living on credit; she owed money everywhere, and there were still ten days to elapse before any remittances could reach her. But she would have borne anything, and resorted to everything, rather than let Jared know this. "It took me so completely by surprise," she said, beginning again. "I am sure that you yourself had no suspicion of any such possibility when we took that French Broad drive?"

"No, I had not. And it enrages me to think how blind I was! He was laying his plans even then; the whole trip, and all those costly things he did—that was simply part of it." And leaving his chair, the brother walked up and down the room, his face darkly flushed with anger. "Ruth—a child! And he—thirty years older!"

"Not that, dear. He is thirty-eight; and she was nineteen last week."

"He looks much more than thirty-eight. But that isn't the point. You don't seem to see, mother, what makes it so insufferable; he has bribed her about *me*, bribed her with that place in Charleston; that's the whole story! She is so happy about that, that she forgets all else."

"I don't like the idea of an engagement between them any better than you do, Jared. But I ought to say two things. One is, that I don't believe he made any plot as to the Charleston place; I think he likes to help people—"

"Yes, our family!" interrupted the son, hotly. "No, mother, you don't understand him in the least. Horace Chase is purely a business man, a long-headed, driving, money-making fellow; all his ambition (and he has plenty of it) is along that one line. It's the only line, in fact, which he thinks important. But the idea of his being a philanthropist would make any one who has ever had business dealings with him laugh for a week!"

"Well, have that as you like. But even if he first gave you the place on Ruth's account (for he has fallen very much in love with her, there is no doubt of that), I don't see that he has any need to be a benefactor in keeping you there. They are no doubt delighted to have you; he says so himself, in fact. A navy officer, a gentleman—they may well be!" added Mrs. Franklin, looking for the moment very much like her father, old Major Seymour, with his aristocratic notions.

"Why, mother, don't you know that people with that brutal amount of money—Chaise and the Willoughbys, for instance—don't you know that they look upon the salaries of army and navy officers simply as genteel poverty?" said Jared, forgetting for the moment his anger in amusement over her old-fashioned mistake.

But he could not have made Mrs. Franklin believe this in ten years of repetition, much less in ten minutes. "And the other thing I had to say," she went on, "is that I don't think Ruth is marrying him on *your* account solely."

"Oh yes, she is, though she may not be conscious of it. But when I have given up the Charleston place, which I shall do to-morrow, then she will be free again. The moment she sees that she can do *me* no good, all will look different to her. I'd rather do anything—sell the Cottage, and live on a crust all the rest of my days—than have a sister of mine help me along in that way!"

His mother watched him as he paced to and fro. He looked ill; there were hollows at his temples and dark circles under his eyes; his tall figure had begun to stoop. He was the dearest of all her children; his incurable, unspoken regrets, his broken life, were like a dagger in her heart at all times. He would give up his place, and then he would have nothing; and she, his mother, could not help him with a penny. He would give up his place and sell the Cottage, and then—Genevieve! It all came back to that; it would always come back to that—Genevieve! She swallowed hard to keep down the sob in her throat. "He is very much in love with her," she repeated, vaguely, in order to say something.

"Who cares if he is! I almost begin to think you like it, after all?"

"No, dear, no; neither Dolly nor I like it in the least. But Ruth is not easy to manage. And Genevieve was sure that you—"

"This is not Genevieve's affair. It is mine!" thundered Jared.

His mother jumped up, ran to him, and gave him a kiss. For the moment she forgot his illness, his uncertain future, her own debts, all her troubles, in the joy of hearing him at last assert his will against that

of his wife. But it was only for a moment; she knew
—knew far better than he did—that the even-tem-
pered feminine pertinacity would always in the end
have its way. Jared, impulsive, generous, affectionate, was no match for Genevieve. In a contest of
this sort it is the nobler nature, always, that yields;
the self-satisfied, limited mind has an obstinacy that
never gives way. She leaned her head against her
son's breast, and all the bitterness of his marriage
came over her afresh like a flood.

"Why, mother, what is it?" asked Jared, feeling
her tremble. He put his arm round her, and
smoothed her hair tenderly. "Tell me what it is
that troubles you so?"

The gate swung to. Mrs. Franklin lifted her
head. "Ruth is coming," she whispered. "Say
what you like to her. But, under all circumstances,
remember to be kind. I will come back presently."
She hurried out.

Rinda and Ruth entered. Rinda went to the
kitchen, and Ruth, after taking off her hat, came into
the parlor, carrying her glass of cream. "Jared!"
She put down the glass on the table, and threw her
arms round her brother's neck. "Oh, I am *so* glad
you have come!"

"Sit down. Here, by me. I wish to speak to
you, Ruth."

"Yes—about my engagement. It's very good of
you to come so soon;" and she put her hand through
his arm in her old affectionate way.

"I do not call it an engagement when you have neither your mother's consent nor mine," answered her brother. "Whatever it is, however, you must make an end of it."

"An end of it? Why?"

"Because we all dislike the idea. You are too young to comprehend what you are doing."

"I am nineteen; that is not so very young. I comprehend that I am going to be happy. And I *love* to be happy! I have never seen any one half so kind as Mr. Chase. If there is anything I want to do, he arranges it. He doesn't wait, and hesitate, and consider; he *does* it. He thinks of everything; it is perfectly beautiful! Why, Jared—what he did for you, wasn't that kind?"

"Exactly. That is what he has bribed you with!"

"Bribed?" repeated Ruth, surprised, as she saw the indignation in his eyes. Then comprehending what he meant, she laughed, coloring a little also. "But I am not marrying him on your account; I am marrying him on my own. I am marrying because I like it, because I want to. You don't believe it? Why—look at me." She rose and stood before him. "I am the happiest girl in the world as I stand here! I should think you could see it for yourself?" And in truth her face was radiant. "If I have ever had any dreams of what I should like my life to be (and I have had plenty), they have all come true," she went on, with her hands behind her, looking at him reflectively. "Think of all I shall have!

And of where I can go! And of what I can do! Why—there's no end of it!"

"That is not the way to talk of marriage."

"How one talks of it is not important. The important point is to be happy *in* it, and that I shall be to the full—yes, to the full. His Grand shall have whatever she likes; and Dolly too. First of all, Dolly shall have a phaeton, so that she can drive to the woods every day. The house shall be put in order from top to bottom. And—oh, everything!"

"Is that the way you talk to *him?*"

But the sarcasm fell to the ground. "Precisely. Word for word," answered Ruth, lightly. And he saw that she spoke the truth.

"He is much too old for you. If there were no other—"

But Ruth interrupted him with a sort of sweet obstinacy. "That is for me to judge, isn't it?"

"He is not at all the person you fancy he is."

"I don't care what he is generally, what he is to other people; all I care for is what he is to me. And about that you know nothing; I am the one to know. He is nicer to me, and he always will be nicer, than Genevieve has ever been to *you!*" And turning, the girl walked across the room.

"If I have been unhappy, that is the very reason I don't want you to be," answered her brother, after a moment's pause.

His tone touched her. She ran back to him, and seated herself on his knee, with her cheek against his.

"I didn't mean it, dear; forgive me," she whispered, softly. "But please don't be cross. You are angry because you believe I am marrying to help *you*. But you are mistaken; I am marrying for myself. You might be back in the navy, and mother and Dolly might have more money, and I should still marry him. It would be because I want to, because I like him. If you had anything to say against him personally, it would be different, but you haven't. He is waiting to tell you about himself, to introduce you to his family (he has only sisters), and to his partners, the Willoughbys. Your only objections appear to be that I am marrying him on your account, and I have told you that I am not; and that he is older than I am, and *that* I like; and that he has money, while we are poor. But he gets something in getting me," she added, in a lighter tone, as she raised her head and looked at him gayly. "Wait till you see how pretty I shall be in fine clothes."

The door opened, and Mrs. Franklin came in.

Ruth rose. "Here is mother. Now I must say the whole. Listen, mother; and you too, Jared. I intend to marry Horace Chase. If not with your consent, then without it. If you will not let me be married at home, then I shall walk out of the house, go to Horace, and the first clergyman or minister he can find shall marry us. There! I have said it. But *why* should you treat me so? Don't make me so dreadfully unhappy."

She had spoken wilfully, determinedly. But now she was pleading — though it was pleading to have her own way. Into her beautiful eyes came two big tears as she gazed at them. Neither Mrs. Franklin nor Jared could withstand those drops.

10

THE wedding was over. Pretty little Trinity Church was left alone with its decorations of flowers and vines, the work of Miss Billy Breeze. Miss Billy, much excited, was now standing beside Ruth in the parlor at L'Hommedieu; for Miss Billy and Maud Muriel were the bridesmaids. Maud Muriel had consented with solemnity. "It is strange that such a man as Horace Chase, a man of sense and importance, should be taken with a child like Ruth Franklin," she confided to Miss Billy. "However, I won't desert him at such a moment. I'll stand by him." She was in reality not so much bridesmaid as groomsman.

L'Hommedieu was decked with flowers. It was a warm autumn day, the windows and doors were open. All Asheville was in attendance, if not in the house and on the verandas, then gazing over the fence, and waiting outside the gate. For there were many things to engage its attention. First, there was Mrs. Franklin, looking very distinguished; then Genevieve, the most beautiful woman present. Then there was Bishop Carew, who had come from Wilmington to officiate. All Asheville admired the bishop — the handsome, kindly, noble old man, full of dignity, full of sweetness as well; they were proud that he had come to "their" wedding. For that was the way they thought of it. Even the negroes—those who had flocked to old Daniel's race —had a sense of ownership in the affair.

A third point of interest was the general surprise over Maud. As Ruth had selected the costumes of her bridesmaids, Miss Mackintosh was attired for the first time in her life in ample soft draperies. Her hair, too, arranged by Miss Billy, had no longer the look of the penitentiary, and the result was that (to the amazement of the town) the sculptress was almost handsome.

Anthony Etheridge, much struck by this (and haunted by his old idea), pressed upon her a glass of punch.

"Take it," he urged, in a low tone, "take two or three. Then, as soon as this is over, hurry to your studio and *let yourself go.* You'll do wonders!"

Two of Chase's partners were present, Nicholas Willoughby, a quiet-looking man of fifty-eight, and his nephew Walter of the same name; Walter was acting as "best man." The elder Willoughby had made use of the occasion to take a general look at this mountain country, with reference to Chase's ideas concerning it, in order to make a report to his brother Richard. For Nicholas and Richard were millionaires many times over; their business in life was investment. Asheville itself, meanwhile, hardly comprehended the importance of such an event as the presence within its borders of a New York capitalist; it knew very little about New York, still less about capitalists. Mrs. Franklin, however, possessed a wider knowledge; she understood what was represented by the name of Willoughby. And it had solaced her unspeakably also to note that the uncle had a genuine liking for her future son-in-law. "They have a real regard for him," she said to her son, in private. "And I myself like him rather better than I once thought I should."

Jared had come from Charleston on the preceding day. "Oh, that's far too guarded, mother," he answered. "The only way for us now is to like Horace Chase with enthusiasm, to cling to him with the deepest affection. We must admire unflinchingly everything he says and everything he does—swallow him whole, as it were; it isn't difficult to swallow things *whole!* Just watch me." And, in truth, it was Jared's jocularity that enlivened the reception, and made it so gay; it reached even Dolly, who (to aid him) became herself a veritable Catherine-wheel of jokes, so that every one noticed how happy all the Franklins were—how delighted with the marriage.

Chase himself appeared well. His rather ordinary face was lighted by an expression of deep inward happiness which was touching; its set lines were relaxed; his eyes, which were usually too keen, had a softness that was new to them. He was very silent; he let his best man talk for him. Walter Willoughby performed this part admirably; standing beside the bridegroom, he "supported" him gayly through the two hours which were given up to the outside friends.

Ruth looked happy, but not particularly pretty. The excitement had given her a deep flush; even her throat was red.

At three o'clock Peter and Piper were brought round to the door; Chase was to drive his wife over the mountains, through the magnificent forest, now gorgeous with the tints of autumn, and at Old Fort a special train was waiting to take them eastward.

A few more minutes and then they were gone. There was nothing left but the scattered rice on the ground, and Petie Trone, Esq., barking his little heart out at the gate.

CHAPTER VIII

EARLY on a moonlit evening in January, 1875, Mr. and Mrs. Horace Chase were approaching St. Augustine. They had come by steamer up the broad St. Johns, the beautiful river of Florida, to the lonely little landing called Tocoi; here they had intrusted themselves to the Atlantic Ocean Railroad. This railroad undertook to convey travellers across the peninsula to the sea-coast, fifteen miles distant; and the promise was kept. But it was kept in a manner so leisurely that more than once Horace Chase had risen and walked to and fro, as though, somehow, that would serve to increase the speed. The rolling-stock possessed by the Atlantic Ocean Railroad at that date consisted of two small street-cars, one for passengers, one for luggage; Chase's promenade, therefore, confined as it was to the first car, had a range of about four steps. "I'm ridiculously fidgety, and that's a fact," he said to his wife, laughing at himself. "I can be lazy enough in a Pullman, for then I can either read the papers or go to sleep. But down here there are no papers to read. And who can sleep in this jolting? I believe I'll ask that darky to let me drive the mules!"

"Do," said Ruth. "Then I can be out there with you on the front platform."

As there were no other passengers (save Petie Trone, Esq., asleep in his travelling basket), Abram, the negro driver, gave up the reins with a grin. Taking his station on the step, he then admonished the volunteer from time to time as follows: "Dish yere's a bad bit; take keer, boss." "Jess ahead de rail am splayed out on de lef'. Yank 'em hard to de right, or we'll sut'ny run off de track. We ginerally *do* run off de track 'bout yere." On each side was a dense forest veiled in the gray long moss. Could that be snow between the two black lines of track ahead? No snow, however, was possible in this warm atmosphere; it was but the spectral effect of the moonlight, blanching to an even paler whiteness the silvery sand which formed the road-bed between the rails. This sand covered the sleepers to such a depth that the mules could not step quickly; there was always a pailful of it on each foot to lift and throw off. They moved on, therefore, in a sluggish trot, the cow-bells attached to their collars keeping up a regular tink-tank, tink-tank.

The tableau of her husband driving these spirited steeds struck Ruth as comical. She was seated on a camp-stool by his side, and presently she broke into a laugh. "Oh, you do look *so* funny, Horace! If you could only see yourself! You, so particular about horses that you won't drive anything that is not absolutely perfect, there you stand taking the greatest pains, and watching solemnly every quiver of the ear of those old mules!"

They were alone, Abram having gone to the baggage-car to get his tin horn. "Come, now, are you never going to stop making fun of me?" inquired Chase. "How do you expect to hit St. Augustine to-night if this fast express runs off the track?" But in spite of his protest, it was easy to see that he liked to hear her laugh.

Abram, coming back, put the horn to his lips and blew a resounding blast; and presently, round a curve, the half-way station came into view—namely, a hut of palmetto boughs on the barren, with a bonfire before it. The negro station-men, beguiling their evening leisure by dancing on the track to their own singing and the music of a banjo, did not think it necessary to stop their gyrations until the heads of the mules actually touched their shoulders. Even then they made no haste in bringing out the fresh team which was to serve as motive power to St. Augustine, and Mr. and Mrs. Chase, leaving the car, strolled up and down near by. The veiled forest had been left behind; the rest of the way lay over the open pine-barrens. The leaping bonfire, the singing negroes, and the little train on its elevated snow-like track contrasted with the wild, lonely, silent, tree-dotted plain, stretching away limitlessly in the moonlight on all sides.

"Perhaps Petie Trone, Esq., would like to take a run," said Ruth. Hastening into the car with her usual heedlessness, she tripped and nearly fell, Chase, who had followed, catching her arm just in time to save her.

"Some of these days, Ruthie, you will break your neck. Why are you always in such a desperate hurry?"

"Talk about hurry!" answered Ruth, as she unstrapped the basket and woke the lazy Mr. Trone. "Who saw the whole of Switzerland in five days? and found it slow at that?" And then they both laughed.

After a stretch, Petie Trone decided to make a foray over the barren; his little black figure was soon out of sight. "Horace, now that we are here, I wish you would promise to stay. Can't we stay at least until the middle of March? It's lovely in Florida in the winter," Ruth declared, as they resumed their walk.

"Well, I'll stay as long as I can. But I must go to California on business between this and spring," Chase answered.

"Why don't you make one of the Willoughbys do that? They never do anything!"

"That's all right; I'm the working partner of the firm; it was so understood from the beginning. The Willoughbys only put in capital; all but Walter, of course, who hasn't got much. But Walter's a knowing young chap, who will put in brains. My California business, however, has nothing to do with the Willoughbys, Ruthie; it's my own private affair, *that* is. If I succeed, and I think I shall, it 'll about double my pile. Come, you know you like money." He drew her hand through his arm and held it.

"How many more rings do you want? How many more houses? How many more French maids and flounces? How many more carriages?"

"Oh, leave out the carriages, do," interrupted Ruth. "When it comes to anything connected with a horse, who spends money—you or I?"

"My one small spree compared to your fifty!"

"Small!" she repeated. "Wherever we go, whole troops of horses appear by magic!" Then, after a moment, she let her head rest against his shoulder as they strolled slowly on. "You are only too good to me," she added, in another tone.

"Well, I guess that's about what I want to be," Chase answered, covering, as he often did, the deep tenderness in his heart with a vein of jocularity.

The Atlantic Ocean Railroad's terminal station at St. Augustine consisted of a platform in the sand and another flaring bonfire. At half-past six Mrs. Franklin, Dolly, and Anthony Etheridge were waiting on this platform for the evening train. With them was a fourth person—Mrs. Lilian Kip. "Oh, I can scarcely wait to see her!" exclaimed this lady, excitedly. "Will she be the same? But no. Impossible!"

"She is exactly the same," answered Dolly, who, seated on an empty dry-goods box, was watching the bonfire.

"But you must remember that Ruth did not come to Florida last winter after her marriage. And this summer, when I was in Asheville, she was abroad.

And as none of you came south winter before last—
don't you see that it makes nearly *two* years since I
have seen her?" Mrs. Kip went on. "In addition,
marriage changes a woman's face so—deepens its
expression and makes it so *much* more beautiful.
I am sure, commodore, that *you* agree with me
there?" And she turned to the only man present.

"Yes, yes," answered Etheridge, gallantly. In his
heart he added: "And therefore the more marriage
the better? Is that what you are thinking of, you
idiot?"

The presence of Mrs. Kip always tore Etheridge
to pieces. He had never had any intention of marrying, and he certainly had no such intention now.
Yet he could not help admiring this doubly widowed
Lilian very deeply, after a fashion. And he knew,
too—jealously and angrily he knew it—that before
long she would inevitably be led to the altar a third
time; so extremely marriageable a woman would
never lack for leaders.

"Ruth is handsomer," remarked Mrs. Franklin;
"otherwise she is unchanged. You will see it for
yourself, Lilian, when she comes."

The mother's tone was placid. All her forebodings had faded away, and she had watched them disappear with thankful eyes. For Ruth was happy;
there could be no doubt about that. In the year that
had passed since her marriage, she had returned twice
to Asheville, and Mrs. Franklin also had spent a
month at her son-in-law's home in New York. On

all these occasions it had been evident that the girl
was enjoying greatly her new life; that she was delightedly, exultantly, and gleefully contented, and all
in a natural way, without analyzing it. She delighted
in the boundless gratification of her taste for personal ease and luxury; she exulted in all that she
was able to do for her own family; she was full of
glee over the amusements, the entertainments, and
especially the change, that surrounded her like a
boundless horizon. For her husband denied her
nothing; she had only to choose. He was not what
is known as set in his ways; he had no fixed habits
(save the habit of making money); in everything,
therefore, except his business affairs, he allowed his
young wife to arrange their life according to her
fancy. This freedom, this power, and the wealth,
had not yet become an old story to Ruth, and, with
the enjoyment which she found in all three, it seemed
as if they never would become that. It had been an
immense delight to her, for instance, to put L'Hommedieu in order for her mother. A month after her
marriage, on returning to Asheville for a short visit,
she had described her plan to Dolly. "And think
what fun it will be, Dolly, to have the whole house
done over, not counting each cent in Genevieve's
deadly way, but just *recklessly!* And then to see
her squirm, and say 'surely!' And you and mother
must pretend not to care much about it; you must
hardly know what is going on, while they are actually putting in steam-heaters, and hard-wood floors,

and bath-rooms with porcelain tubs—hurrah!" And, with Petie Trone barking in her arms, she whirled round in a dance of glee.

Chase happening to come in at this moment, she immediately repeated to him all that she had been saying.

He agreed; then added, with his humorous deliberation, "But you don't seem to think quite so much of my old school-mate as I supposed you did?"

"Sisters-in-law, Mr. Chase, are seldom *very* devoted friends," explained Dolly, going on with her embroidery. Dolly always did something that required her close attention whenever Horace Chase was present. "How, indeed, can they be? A sister sees one side of her brother's nature, and sees it correctly; a wife sees another side, and with equal accuracy. Each honestly believes that the other is entirely wrong. Their point of view, you see, is so different!"

The waiting group at the St. Augustine station on this January evening heard at last the blast of Abram's horn, and presently the train came in, the mules for the last few yards galloping madly, their tin bells giving out a clattering peal, and Chase still acting as driver, with Ruth beside him. Affectionate greetings followed, for all the Franklins were warmly attached to each other. Mrs. Kip was not a Franklin, but she was by nature largely affectionate; she was probably the most affectionate person in Florida. To the present occasion she contributed several tears of joy. Then she signalled to Juniper, her colored waiter; for, being not only affectionate, but romantic as well, she had brought in her phaeton a bridal ornament, a heart three feet high, made of roses reposing upon myrtle, and this symbol, amid the admiration of all the bystanders, black and white, was now borne forward in the arms of Juniper (who, being a slender lad, staggered under its weight). Ruth laughed and laughed as this edifice was presented to her. But as, amid her mirth, she had kissed the donor and thanked her very prettily, Mrs. Kip was satisfied. For Ruth might laugh—Ruth, in fact, always laughed—but marriage was marriage none the less; the most beautiful human relation; and it was certainly fit that the first visit of a happily wedded pair to the land of flowers should be commemorated florally. Mrs. Kip volunteered to carry her heart to Mrs. Franklin's residence; she drove away, therefore, Etheridge accompanying her, and Juniper behind, balancing the structure as well as he could on his knees, with his arms stretched upward to their fullest extent in order to grasp its top.

In a rickety barouche drawn by two lean horses the others followed, laughing and talking gayly. Chase got on very well with his mother-in-law; and he supposed, also, that he got on fairly well with Dolly: he had not divined Dolly's mental attitude towards him, which was that simply of an armed neutrality. Dolly would have been wildly happy if, for herself and her mother at least, she could have refused every cent of his money. This had not been

possible. Chase had settled upon his wife a sum
which gave her a large income for her personal use,
independent of all their common expenses; it was
upon this income that Ruth had drawn for the restoration of L'Hommedieu, and also for the refurnish-
ing of her mother's house at St. Augustine. "I can't
be happy, His Grand, I can't enjoy New York, or our
trip to Europe, or anything, unless I feel certain that
you are perfectly comfortable in every way," she had
said during that first visit at home. "All this money
is mine; I am not asked what I do with it, and I
never shall be asked; you don't know Horace if you
think he will ever even allude to the subject. He intends it for my ownest own, and of course he knows
what I care the most for, and that is you and Jared
and Dolly. I have always suspected that something
troubled you every now and then, though I didn't
know what. And if it was money, His Grand, you
must take some from me, now that I have it; you
must take it, and make your little girl really happy.
For she can't be happy until you do."

This youngest child really was still, in the mother's
eyes, her "baby." And when the baby, sitting down
in her lap, put her arms round her neck and pleaded
so lovingly, the mother yielded. Her debts were now
all paid; it was a secret between herself and Ruth.
The disappearance of the burden was a great relief
to the mother, though not so much so as it would
have been to some women; for it was characteristic
of Mrs. Franklin that she had never thought there

was anything wrong in being in debt; she had only thought that it was unfortunate. It would not have occurred to her, even in her worst anxieties, to reduce sternly her expenses until they accorded with her means, no matter how low that might lead her; there was a point, so she believed, beyond which a Mrs. Franklin could not descend with justice to her children. And justice to her children was certainly a mother's first duty; justice to creditors must take a second place.

To Dolly, unaware of the payment of the debts, the acceptance even of the restoration of the two houses had been bitter enough; for though the money came through Ruth's hands, it was nevertheless provided by this stranger. "If I had only been well, I could have worked and saved mother from this," she thought. "But I am helpless. Not only that, but a care! Nobody stops to think how dreary a lot it is to be always a care. And how hard, hard, never to be able to give, but always to have to accept, accept, and be thankful!" But Dolly, at heart, had a generous nature; she would not cloud even by a look her mother's contentment or the happiness of Ruth. So when Chase said, as the barouche swayed crazily through the deep mud-hole which for years formed the junction between the station lane and the main road, "This old rattletrap isn't safe, ma'am. Is it the best St. Augustine can do? You ought to have something better!" — when Chase said this to her mother, Dolly even brought forward a smile.

The rattletrap followed the long causeway which crossed the salt-marsh and the San Sebastian River. Entering the town beneath an archway of foliage, this causeway broadened into a sandy street under huge pride-of-India trees, whose branches met overhead. Old Miss L'Hommedieu's winter residence was not far from St. Francis Barracks, at the south end of the town. It was an old coquina house which rose directly from a little-travelled roadway. An open space on the other side of this roadway, and the absence of houses, gave it the air of being "on the bay," as it was called. Chase had taken, for a term of years, another house not far distant, which really was on the bay. He had done this to please Ruth. It was not probable that they should spend many winters in Florida; but in case they should wish to come occasionally, it would be convenient to have a house ready. "And when we don't want it, Jared could stay here now and then," Ruth had suggested.

"Your brother? I guess he isn't going to be a very easy chap to arrange for, here or anywhere," Chase had answered, laughing. "We've already slipped up once pretty well—Charleston, you know." Then, seeing her face grow troubled, "But he'll take another view of something else I have in mind," he went on. "If my California project turns out as I hope, it will be absolutely necessary for me to have a confidential man to see to the New York part of it—some one whom I can trust. And I shall be able to convince Franklin that this time, at any rate, instead of its being a favor to him, it 'll be a favor to me.   He won't kick at *that*, I reckon."

For Jared was now again at Raleigh, working as a clerk for the man who had bought his former business; he had resigned his Charleston place in spite of Ruth, in spite even of Genevieve.   He had waited until the wedding was over, in order that Ruth might not be made unhappy at the moment; and then he had done it.

Notwithstanding this, his wife had never had so much money in her life as she had now.   For she and Ruth, with the perfectly good conscience which women have in such matters, had combined together, as it were, to circumvent secretly the obstinate naval officer.   Ruth was warmly attached to her brother; he was the one person who had been able to control her when she was a child; his good opinion had been a hundred times more important to her than that of her mother and Dolly.   Now that she was rich, she was bent upon helping him; and having found that she could not do it directly, she had turned all her intelligence towards doing it indirectly, through the capable, the willing Genevieve.   Mrs. Jared Franklin, Junior, had quietly and skilfully bought land in Asheville (in readiness for the coming railroad); she had an account at the bank; she had come into the possession of bonds and stock; she had enlarged her house, and she had also given herself the pleasure (she called it the benediction) of laying the foundations of an addition to the Colored Home.   As she kept up a private correspondence with Ruth, she had heard of the proposed place in New York for Jared, the place where his services would be of value. She was not surprised; it was what she had been counting upon. Jared's obstinacy would give way, *must* give way, before this new opportunity; and in the meanwhile, here at Asheville, all was going splendidly well.

Amid these various transactions Jared Franklin's mother had been obliged to make up her mind as to what her own attitude should be. It had been to her a relief unspeakable, an overmastering joy, to know that her son would not, after all, sink to harassing poverty. Soothed by this, lulled also by the hope that before very long he would of his own accord consent to give up what was so distasteful to him, she had virtually condoned the underhand partnership between Ruth and Genevieve, arranging the matter with her conscience after her own fashion, by simply turning her head away from the subject entirely. As she had plenty of imagination, she had ended by really convincing herself that she was not aware of what was going on, because she had not heard any of the details. (She had, in fact, refused to hear them.) This left her free to say to Jared (if necessary) that she had known nothing. But she hoped that no actual words of this sort would be required. Her temperament, indeed, had always been largely made up of hope.

It was true that Jared for the present was still at

Raleigh, drudging away at a very small salary. That, however, would not last forever. And in the meantime (and this was also extraordinarily agreeable to the mother) Madame Genevieve was learning that she could not lead her husband quite so easily as she had supposed she could. In her enjoyment of this fact, Mrs. Franklin, in certain moods, almost hoped that (as his affairs were in reality going on so well) her son would continue to hold out for some time longer.

The house which Horace Chase had taken at St. Augustine was much larger than old Miss L'Hommedieu's abode; it was built of coquina, like hers, but it faced the sea-wall directly, commanding the inlet; from its upper windows one could see over Anastasia Island opposite, and follow miles of the blue southern sea. Ruth's French maid, Félicité, had arrived at this brown mansion the day before, with the heavy luggage; to-night, however, new-comers were to remain with the mother in the smaller house.

When the barouche reached Mrs. Franklin's door, Etheridge, Mrs. Kip, and the heart were already there. "I won't stay now," said Mrs. Kip. "But may I look in later? Evangeline Taylor is perfectly *wild* to come."

When she returned, a little after eight, Chase was still in the dining-room with Anthony Etheridge, who had dined there. The heart had been suspended from a stout hook on the parlor wall, and Ruth happened a moment before to have placed herself under it, when, having discovered her old guitar in a closet, she had seated herself to tune it. "It's *so* sweet, Ruth, your sitting there under my flowers," said the visitor, tearfully. "And yet, for *me*, such an—such an *association!*"

"I thought your daughter was coming?" said Mrs. Franklin, peering towards the door over her glasses.

"Evangeline Taylor will be here in a moment," answered her mother; "her governess is bringing her." And presently there entered a tall, a gigantically tall girl, with a long, solemn, pale face. As she was barely twelve, she was dressed youthfully in a short school-girl frock with a blue sash. Advancing, she kissed Ruth; then, retiring to a corner, she seated herself, arranged her feet in an appropriate pose, and crossed her hands in her lap. A little later, when no one was looking, she furtively altered the position of her feet. Then she changed once or twice the arrangement of her hands. This being settled at last to her satisfaction, she turned her attention to her features, trying several different contortions, and finally settling upon a drawing in of the lips and a slight dilatation of the nostrils. And all this not in the least from vanity, but simply from an intense personal conscientiousness.

"The dear child longed to see you, Ruth. She danced for joy when she heard you had come," explained the mother.

"Yes, Evangeline and I have always been great chums," answered Ruth, good-naturedly.

The room was brightly lighted, and the light showed

that the young wife's face was more beautiful than
ever; the grace of her figure also was now height-
ened by all the aids that dress can bestow. Ruth
had said to Jared, jokingly, "Wait till you see how
pretty I shall be in fine clothes!" The fine clothes
had been purchased in profusion, and, what was better, Félicité knew how to adapt them perfectly to her
slender young mistress.

Mrs. Kip, having paid her tribute to "the association" (she did not say whether the feeling was connected with Andrew Taylor, her first husband, or
with the equally departed John Kip, her second),
now seated herself beside Ruth, and, with the freedom of old friendship, examined her costume. "I
know you had that made in Paris!" she said. "Simple as it is, it has a sort of something or other! And,
oh, what a beautiful bracelet! What splendid rings!"

Ruth wore no ornaments save that on her right
wrist was a band of sapphires, and on her right
hand three of the same gems, all the stones being of
great beauty. On her left hand she wore the wedding circlet, with her engagement-ring and the philopena guard over it. In answer to the exclamation,
she had taken off the jewels and tossed them all into
Mrs. Kip's lap. Mrs. Kip looked at them, her red
lips open.

To some persons, Lilian Kip seemed beautiful, in
spite of the fact that the outline of her features,
from certain points of view, was almost grotesque;
she had a short nose, a wide mouth, a broad face,

and a receding chin. Her dark-brown eyes were
neither large nor bright, but they had a soft, dove-
like expression; her curling hair was of a mahogany-
red tint, and she had the exquisitely beautiful skin
which sometimes accompanies hair of this hue;
her cheeks really had the coloring of peaches and
cream; her lips were like strawberries; her neck,
arms, and hands were as fair as the inner petals of a
tea-rose. With the exception of her imperfect facial
outlines, she was as faultlessly modelled as a Venus.
A short Venus, it is true, and a well-fed one; still a
Venus. No one would ever have imagined her to be
the mother of that light-house of a daughter; it was
necessary to recall the fact that the height of the late
Andrew Taylor had been six feet four inches. Andrew Taylor having married Lilian Howard when
she was but seventeen, Lilian Kip, in spite of two
husbands and her embarrassingly overtopping child,
found herself even now but thirty.

She had put Ruth's rings on her hands and the
bracelet on her wrist; now she surveyed the effect
with her head on one side, consideringly. While
she was thus engaged, Mrs. Franklin's little negro
boy, Samp, ushered in another visitor—Walter Willoughby.

"Welcome to Florida, Mrs. Chase," he said, as he
shook hands with Ruth. "As you are an old resi-
dent, however, it's really your husband whom I have
come to greet; he is here, isn't he?"

"Yes; he is in the dining-room with Commodore

Etheridge," Ruth answered. "Will you go out?" For it was literally out; the old house was built in the Spanish fashion round an interior court, and to reach the dining-room one traversed a long veranda.

"Thanks; I'll wait here," Walter answered. In reality he would have preferred to go and have a cigar with Chase. But as he had not seen his partner's wife since she returned from Europe, it was only courtesy as well as good policy to remain where he was. For Mrs. Chase was a power. She was a power because her husband would always wish to please her; this desire would come next to his money-making, and would even, in Walter's opinion (in case there should ever be a contest between the two influences), "run in close!"

Mrs. Kip had hastily divested herself of the jewels, and replaced them on Ruth's wrist and hands, with many caressing touches. "Aren't they *lovely?*" she said to Walter.

"That little one, the guard, was *my* selection," he replied, indicating the philopena circlet.

"And not this also?" said Ruth, touching her engagement ring.

"No; that was my uncle Richard's choice; Chase wrote to *him* the second time, not to me," Walter answered. "I'm afraid he didn't like my taste." He laughed; then turned to another subject. "You were playing the guitar when I came in, Mrs. Chase; won't you sing something?"

"I neither play nor sing in a civilized way," Ruth

answered. "None of us do. In music we are all awful barbarians."

"How can you say so," protested Mrs. Kip, "when, as a family, you are *so* musical?" Then, summoning to her eyes an expression of great intelligence, she added : "And I should know that you were, all of you, from your thick eyebrows and very thick hair. You have heard of that theory, haven't you, Mr. Willoughby? That all true musicians have very thick hair?"

"Also murderers ; I mean the women — the murderesses," remarked Dolly.

"Oh, Dolly, what ideas you do have! Who would ever think of associating murderesses with music? Music is *so* uplifting," protested the rosy widow.

"We should take care that it is not too much so," Dolly answered. "Lots of us are ridiculously uplifted. We know one thing perhaps, and like it. But we remain flatly ignorant about almost everything else. In a busy world this would do no harm, if we could only be conscious of it. But no; on we go, deeply conceited about the one thing we know and like, and loftily severe as to the ignorance of other persons concerning it. It doesn't occur to us that upon other subjects save our own, we ourselves are presenting precisely the same spectacle. A Beethoven, when it comes to pictures, may find something very taking in a daub representing a plump child with a skipping - rope, and the legend : 'See me jump!' A painter of the highest power may think 'The Sweet By-and-By' on the cornet the acme of musical expression. A distinguished sculptor may appreciate on the stage only negro minstrels or a tenth-rate farce. A great historian may see nothing to choose, in the way of beauty, between a fine etching and a chromo. It is well known that the most celebrated, and deservedly celebrated, scientific man of our day devours regularly the weakest fiction that we have. And people who love the best classical music and can endure nothing else, have no idea, very often, whether they belong to the mammalia or the crustacea, or whether the Cologne cathedral is Doric or late Tudor."

"Carry it a little further, Miss Franklin," said Walter Willoughby; "it has often been noted that criminals delight in the most sentimental tales."

"That isn't the same thing," Dolly answered. "However, to take up your idea, Mr. Willoughby, it is certainly true that it is often the good women who read with the most breathless interest the newspaper reports of crimes."

"Oh no!" exclaimed Mrs. Kip.

"Yes, they do, Lilian," Dolly responded. "And when it comes to tales, they like dreadful events, with plenty of moral reflections thrown in; the moral reflections make it all right. A plain narrative of an even much less degree of evil, given impartially, and without a word of comment by the author — *that* seems to them the unpardonable thing."

" Well, and isn't it?" said Mrs. Kip. " Shouldn't people be *taught—counselled ?*"

" And it's for the sake of the counsel that they read such stories?" inquired Dolly.

During this conversation, Chase, in the dining-room, had risen and given a stretch, with his long arms out horizontally. He was beginning to feel bored by the talk of Anthony Etheridge, " the ancient swell," as he called him. In addition, he had a vision of finishing this second cigar in a comfortable chair in the parlor (for Mrs. Franklin had no objection to cigar smoke), with Ruth near by; for it always amused him to hear his wife laugh and talk. The commodore, meanwhile, having assigned to himself from the day of the wedding the task of " helping to civilize the Bubble," never lost an opportunity to tell him stories from his own more cultivated experience —" stories that will give him ideas, and, by Jove ! phrases, too. He needs 'em !" He had risen also. But he now detained his companion until he had finished what he was saying. " So there you have the reason, Mr. Chase, why *I* didn't marry. I simply couldn't endure the idea of an old woman's face opposite mine at table year after year; for our women grow old so soon ! Now you, sir, have shown the highest wisdom in this respect. I congratulate you."

" I don't know about that," answered Chase, as he turned towards the door. " Ruth will have an old man's face opposite *her* before very long, won't she ?"

" Not at all, my good friend; not at all. Men

have no age. At least, they *need* not have it," answered Etheridge, bringing forward with joviality his favorite axiom.

Cordial greetings took place between Chase and Walter Willoughby. "Your uncles weren't sure you would still be here," Chase remarked. "They thought perhaps you wouldn't stay."

"I shall stay awhile—outstay you, probably," answered Walter, smiling. "I can't imagine that you'll stand it long."

"Doing nothing, you mean? Well, it's true I have never loafed *much*," Chase admitted.

"You loafed all summer in Europe," the younger man replied, and his voice had almost an intonation of complaint. He perceived this himself, and smiled a little over it.

"So that was loafing, was it," commented Ruth, in a musing tone—"catching trains and coaches on a full run, seeing three or four cantons, half a dozen towns, two passes, and several ranges of mountains every day?"

All laughed, and Mrs. Kip said: "Did you rush along at that rate? That was baddish. There's no hurry *here;* that's one good thing. The laziest place! We must get up a boat-ride soon, Ruth. Boat-drive, I mean."

Mrs. Franklin meanwhile, rising to get something, knocked over accidentally the lamplighters which she had just completed, and Chase, who saw it, jumped up to help her collect them.

"Why, how many you have made!" he said, gallantly.

She was not pleased by this innocent speech; she had no desire to be patted on the back, as it were, about her curled strips of paper; she curled them to please herself. She made no reply, save that her nose looked unusually aquiline.

"Yes, mother is tremendously industrious in lamplighters," remarked Dolly. "Her only grief is that she cannot send them to the Indian missions. You can send *almost* everything to the Indian missions; but somehow lamplighters fill no void."

"Do you mean the new mission we are to have here—the Indians at the fort?" asked Walter Willoughby. "They are having a big dance to-night."

Ruth looked up.

"Should you like to see it?" he went on, instantly taking advantage of an opportunity to please her. "Nothing easier. We could watch it quite comfortably, you know, from the ramparts."

"I should like it ever so much! Let us go at once, before it is over!" exclaimed Ruth, eagerly.

"Ruth! Ruth!" said her mother. "After travelling all day, Mr. Chase may be tired."

"Not at all, ma'am," said Chase. "I don't take much stock in Indians myself," he went on, to his wife. "Do you really want to go?"

"Oh yes, Horace. Please."

"And the commodore will go with *me*," said Mrs.

Kip, turning her soft eyes towards Etheridge, who went down before the glance like a house of cards.

"But we must take Evangeline Taylor home first," said Mrs. Kip. "We'll go round by way of Andalusia, commodore. It would never do to let her see an Indian dance at *her* age," she added, affectionately, lifting her hand high to pat her daughter's aerial cheek. "It would make her tremble like a babe."

"Oh, *did* you hear her 'baddish'!" said Dolly, as, a few minutes later, they went up the steps that led to the sea-wall, Chase and Walter Willoughby, Ruth and herself. "And did you hear her 'boat-drive'? She has become so densely confused by hearing Achilles Larue inveigh against the use of 'ride' for 'drive' that now she thinks everything must be drive."

Chase and Walter Willoughby smiled; but not unkindly. There are some things which the Dolly Franklins of the world are incapable, with all their cleverness, of comprehending; one of them is the attraction of a sweet fool.

The sea-wall of St. Augustine stretches, with its smooth granite coping, along the entire front of the old town, nearly a mile in length. On the land side its top is but four or five feet above the roadway; towards the water it presents a high, dark, wet surface, against which comes the wash of the ocean, or rather of the inlet; for the harbor is protected by a long, low island lying outside. It is this island, called Anastasia, that has the ocean beach. The

walk on top of the wall is just wide enough for two.
Walter Willoughby led the way with Dolly, and
Chase and his wife followed, a short distance be-
hind.

Walter thought Miss Franklin tiresome. With the
impatience of a young fellow, he did not care for her
clever talk. He was interested in clever men; in
woman he admired other qualities. He had spent
ten days in Asheville during the preceding summer
in connection with Chase's plans for investment
there, and he had been often at L'Hommedieu during
his stay; but he had found Genevieve more attractive than Dolly—Genevieve and Mrs. Kip. For Mrs.
Kip, since her second widowhood, had spent her
summers at Asheville, for the sake of "the mountain
atmosphere;" ("which means Achilles atmosphere,"
Mrs. Franklin declared). This evening Walter had
felt a distinct sense of annoyance when Dolly had
announced her intention of going with them to see
the Indian dance, for this would arrange their party
in twos. He had no desire for a tête-à-tête with
Dolly, and neither did he care for a tête-à-tête with
Ruth; his idea had been to accompany Mr. and Mrs.
Chase as a third. However, he made the best of it;
Walter always did that. He had the happy faculty
of getting all the enjoyment possible out of the present, whatever it might be. Postponing, therefore,
to the next day his plan for making himself agreeable to the Chases, he led the way gayly enough to
the fort.

Fort San Marco is the most imposing ancient structure which the United States can show. Begun in the seventeenth century, when Florida was a province of Spain, it has turrets, ramparts, and bastions, a portcullis and barbacan, a moat and drawbridge. Its water-battery, where once stood the Spanish cannon, looks out to sea. Having outlived its use as a fortification, it was now sheltering temporarily a band of Indians from the far West, most of whom had been sentenced to imprisonment for crime. With the captives had come their families, for this imprisonment was to serve also as an experiment; the red men were to be instructed, influenced, helped. At present the education had not had time to progress far.

The large square interior court, open to the sky, was to-night lighted by torches of pine, which were thrust into the iron rings that had served the Spaniards for the same purpose long before. The Indians, adorned with paint and feathers, were going through their wild evolutions, now moving round a large circle in a strange squatting attitude, now bounding aloft. Their dark faces, either from their actual feelings or from the simulated ferocity appropriate to a war-dance, were very savage, and with their half-naked bodies, their whoops and yells, they made a picture that was terribly realistic to the whites who looked on from the ramparts above, for it needed but little imagination to fancy a *bona fide* attack — the surprise of the lonely frontier farm-house, with the following massacre and dreadful shrieks.

Ruth, half frightened, clung to her husband's arm. Mrs. Kip, after a while, began to sob a little.

" I'm *thinking*—of the *wo-women* they have probably *scalped* on the *pla-ains*," she said to Etheridge.

" What ?" he asked, unable to hear.

" Never mind; we'll *convert* them," she went on, drying her eyes hopefully. For a Sunday-school was to be established at the fort, and she had already promised to take a class.

But Dolly was on the side of the Indians. "The crimes for which these poor creatures are imprisoned here are nothing but virtues upside down," she shouted. "They killed white men? Of course they did. Haven't the white men stolen all their land ?"

" But we're going to *Christianize* them," yelled Mrs. Kip, in reply. They were obliged to yell, amid the deafening noise of the dance and the whoopings below.

Ruth had a humorous remark ready, when suddenly her husband, to Walter's amusement, put his hand over her lips. She looked up at him, laughing. She understood.

" Funniest thing in the world," he had once said to her, " but the more noise there is, the more incessantly women *will* talk. Ever noticed? They are capable of carrying on a shrieking conversation in the cars all day long."

The atmosphere grew dense with the smoke from

the pitch-pine torches, and suddenly, ten minutes later, Dolly fainted. This in itself was not alarming; with Dolly it happened not infrequently. But under the present circumstances it was awkward.

"Why did you let her come? I was amazed when I saw her here," said Etheridge, testily.

For Etheridge was dead tired. He hated the Indians; he detested the choking smoke; he loathed open ramparts at this time of night. Ruth and Mrs. Franklin had themselves been surprised by Dolly's desire to see the dance. But they always encouraged any wish of hers to go anywhere; such inclinations were so few.

Walter Willoughby, meanwhile, prompt as ever, had already found a vehicle — namely, the phaeton of Captain March, the army officer in charge of the Indians; it was waiting outside to take Mrs. March back to the Magnolia Hotel. "The captain lends it with pleasure; as soon, therefore, as Miss Franklin is able, I can drive her home," suggested Walter.

But Chase, who knew through his wife some of the secrets of Dolly's suffering, feared lest she might now be attacked by pain; he would not trust her to a careless young fellow like Walter. "I'll take her myself," he said. "And Ruth, you can come back with the others, along the sea-wall."

Dolly, who had recovered consciousness, protested against this arrangement. But her voice was only a whisper; Chase, paying no attention to it, lifted her and helped her down to the phaeton. He was certainly the one to do it, so he thought; his wife's sister was his sister as well. It was a pity that she was not rather more amiable. But that made no difference regarding one's duty towards her.

The others also left the ramparts, and started homeward, following the sea-wall.

This granite pathway is not straight; it curves a little here and there, adapting itself to the line of the shore. To-night it glittered in the moonlight. It was high tide, and the water also glittered as it came lapping against the stones waveringly, so that the granite somehow seemed to waver, too. Etheridge was last, behind Mrs. Kip. He did not wish to make her dizzy by walking beside her, he said. Suddenly he descended. On the land side.

Mrs. Kip, hearing the thud of his jump, turned her head, surprised. And then the commodore (though he was still staggering) held out his hand, saying, "We get off here, of course; it is much our nearest way. That's the reason I stepped down," he carelessly added.

Mrs. Kip had intended to follow the wall as far as the Basin. But she always instinctively obeyed directions given in a masculine voice. If there were two masculine voices, she obeyed the younger. In this case the younger man did not speak. She acquiesced, therefore, in the elder's sharp "Come!" For poor Etheridge had been so jarred by his fall that his voice had become for the moment falsetto.

Mrs. Chase and Walter Willoughby, thus deserted, continued on their way alone.

It was a beautiful night. The moon lighted the water so brilliantly that the flash of the light-house on Anastasia seemed superfluous; the dark fort loomed up in massive outlines; a narrow black boat was coming across from the island, and, as there was a breeze, the two Minorcans it carried had put up a rag of a sail, which shone like silver. "How fast they go!" said Ruth.

"Would you like to sail home?" asked Walter. He did not wait for her answer, for, quick at divination, he had caught the wish in her voice. He hailed the Minorcans; they brought their boat up to the next flight of water-steps; in two minutes from the time she had first spoken, Ruth, much amused by this unexpected adventure, was sailing down the inlet. "Oh, how wet! I didn't think of that," Walter had exclaimed as he saw the water in the bottom of the boat; and with a quick movement he had divested himself of his coat, and made a seat of it for her in the driest place. She had had no time to object, they were already off; she must sit down, and sit still, for their tottlish craft was only a dugout. Walter, squatting opposite, made jocular remarks about his appearance as he sat there in his shirt-sleeves.

It was never difficult for Ruth to laugh, and presently, as the water gained on her companion in spite of all his efforts, she gave way to mirth. She laughed so long that Walter began to feel that he knew her better, that he even knew her well. He laughed himself. But he also took the greatest pains at the same time to guard her pretty dress from injury.

The breeze and the tide were both in their favor; they glided rapidly past the bathing-house, the Plaza, the Basin, and the old mansion which Chase had taken. Then Walter directed the Minorcans towards another flight of water-steps. " Here we are," he said. " And in half the time it would have taken us if we had walked. We have come like a shot."

He took her to her mother's door. Then, pretty wet, with his ruined coat over his arm, he walked back along the sea-wall to the St. Augustine Hotel.

CHAPTER IX

Two weeks later Mrs. Kip gave an afternoon party
for the Indians. Captain March had not been struck
by her idea that the sight of "a lady's quiet home"
would have a soothing effect upon these children of
the plains. Mrs. Kip had invited the whole band,
but the captain had sent only a carefully selected
half-dozen in charge of the interpreter. And he had
also added, uninvited, several soldiers from the small
force at his disposal. Mrs. Kip was sure that these
soldiers were present "merely for form." There are
various kinds of form. Captain March, having confided to the colonel who commanded at the other
end of the sea-wall, that he could answer for the de-
corum of his six "unless the young ladies get hold
of them," a further detachment of men had arrived
from St. Francis Barracks; for the colonel was aware
that the party was to be largely feminine. The fes-
tivities, therefore, went on with double brilliancy,
owing to the many uniforms visible under the trees.

These trees were magnificent. Mrs. Kip occupied,
as tenant, the old Buckingham Smith place, which
she had named Andalusia. Here, in addition to the
majestic live-oaks, were date-palms, palmettoes, mag-
nolias, crape-myrtles, figs, and bananas, hedges of

Spanish-bayonet, and a half-mile of orange walks, which resembled tunnels through a glossy-green foliage, the daylight at each end looking like a far-away yellow spot. All this superb vegetation rose, strangely enough to Northern eyes, from a silver-white soil. It was a beautiful day, warm and bright. Above, the sky seemed very near; it closed down over the flat land like a soft blue cover. The air was full of fragrance, for both here and in the neighboring grove of Dr. Carrington the orange-trees were in bloom. Andalusia was near the San Sebastian border of the town, and to reach it on foot one was obliged to toil through a lane so deep in sand that it was practically bottomless.

There was no toil, however, for Mrs. Horace Chase; on the day of the party she arrived at Andalusia in a phaeton drawn by two pretty ponies. She was driving, for the ponies were hers. Her husband was beside her, and, in the little seat behind, Walter Willoughby had perched himself. It was a very early party, having begun with a dinner for the Indians at one o'clock; Mr. and Mrs. Chase arrived at half-past two. Dressed in white, Mrs. Kip was hovering round her dark-skinned guests. When she could not think of anything else to do, she shook hands with them; she had already been through this ceremony eight times. "If I could only speak to them in their own tongue!" she said, yearningly. And the long sentences, expressive of friendship, which she begged the interpreter to translate to them, would have filled a volume. The interpreter, a very intelligent young man, obeyed all her requests with much politeness. "Tell them that we *love* them," said Mrs. Kip. "Tell them that we think of their *souls*."

The interpreter bowed; then he translated as follows: "The white squaw says that you have had enough to eat, and more than enough; and she hopes that you won't make pigs of yourselves if anything else is offered — especially Drowning Raven!"

The Chases and Walter Willoughby had come to the Indian party for a particular purpose, or rather Walter had asked the assistance of the other two in carrying out a purpose of his own, which was to make Mrs. Kip give them a ball. For Andalusia possessed a capital room for dancing. The room was, in fact, an old gymnasium—a one-story building near the house. Mrs. Kip was in the habit of lending this gymnasium for tableaux and Sunday-school festivals; to-day it had served as a dining-room for the Indians. Walter declared that with the aid of flags and flowers the gymnasium would make an excellent ball-room; and as the regimental band had arrived at St. Francis Barracks that morning for a short stay, the mistress of Andalusia must be attacked at once.

"We'll go to her Indian party, and compliment her out of her shoes," he suggested. "You, Mrs. Chase, must be struck with her dress. I shall simply make love to her. And let me see — what can you do?"

he went on, addressing Chase. "I have it; you can admire her chiefs."

"Dirty lot!" Chase answered. "I'd rather admire the hostess."

But the six Indians were not at all dirty; they had never been half so clean since they were born; they fairly shone with soap and ablutions. Dressed in trousers and calico shirts, with moccasins on their feet, and their black hair carefully anointed, they walked, stood, or sat in a straight row all together, according to the strongly emphasized instructions which they had received before setting out. Two old warriors, one of them the gluttonous Drowning Raven reproved by the interpreter, grinned affably at everything. The others preserved the dignified Indian impassiveness.

Soon after his arrival, Walter, who had paid his greetings upon entering, returned to his fair hostess. "I hear you have a rose-tree that is a wonder, Mrs. Kip; where is it?"

Mrs. Kip began to explain. "Go through the first orange-walk. Then turn to the right. Then—"

"I am afraid I can't remember. Take me there yourself," said Walter, calmly.

"Oh, I ought to be here, I think. People are still coming, you know," answered the lady. Then, as he did not withdraw his order, "Well," she said, assentingly.

They were absent twenty minutes.

When they returned, the soft brown eyes of the

widow had a partly pleased, partly deprecatory expression. Another young man in love with her!
What could she do to prevent these occurrences?

Walter, meanwhile, had returned to Mr. and Mrs.
Chase. "It's all right," he said to Ruth. "The ball
will come off to-morrow night. Impromptu."

"Well, you *have* got cheek!" commented Chase.

Mrs. Kip herself soon came up. "Ruth, dear, do
you know that the artillery band is only to stay a
short time? My gymnasium has a capital floor;
what do you say to an impromptu dance there to-
morrow night? I've just thought of it; it's my own
idea entirely."

"Now what made her lug in that unnecessary lie
at the end?" inquired Chase, in a reasoning tone,
when their hostess, after a few minutes more of conversation, had returned to her duties. "It's of no
importance to anybody whose idea it was. That's
what I call taking trouble for nothing!"

"If you believe your lie, it's no longer a lie," answered Walter; "and she believes hers. A quarter of
a minute after a thing has happened, a woman can
often succeed in convincing herself that it happened
not *quite* in that way, but in another. Then she tells
it in *her* way forever after."

Chase gave a yawn. "Well, haven't you had
about enough of this fool business?" he said to his
wife, using the words humorously.

"I am ready to go whenever you like," she answered. For if he allowed her to arrange their days

as she pleased, she, on her side, always yielded to his wishes whenever he expressed them.

"I'll go and see if the ponies have come," he suggested, and he made his way towards the gate.

"You don't give us a very nice character," Ruth went on to Walter.

"About fibs, do you mean? I only said that you ladies have very powerful beliefs. Proof is nothing to you; faith is all. There is another odd fact connected with the subject, Mrs. Chase, and that is that an absolutely veracious woman, one who tells the exact, bare, cold truth on all occasions and nothing more; who never exaggerates or is tempted to exaggerate, by even a hair's-breadth—who is never conscious that she is coloring things too rosily—such a woman is somehow a very uninteresting person to men! I can't explain it, and it doesn't seem just. But it's so. Women of that sort (for they exist—a few of them) move through life very admirably; but quite without masculine adorers." Then he stopped himself. "I'm not here, however, to discuss problems with her," he thought. "Several hours more of daylight; let me see, what can I suggest next to amuse her?"

This young man—he was twenty-seven—had had an intention in seeking St. Augustine at this time; he wished to become well acquainted, if possible intimate, with the enterprising member of his uncle's firm. He had some money, but not much. His father, the elder Walter, had been the one black sheep of the Willoughby flock, the one spendthrift

of that prudent family circle. After the death of the
prodigal, Richard and Nicholas had befriended the
son; the younger Walter was a graduate of Columbia; he had spent eighteen months in Europe; and
when not at college or abroad, he had lived with his
rich uncles. But this did not satisfy him, he was intensely ambitious; the other Willoughbys had no
suspicion of the reach of this nephew's plans. For
his ambitions extended in half a dozen different directions, whereas what might have been called the
family idea had moved always along one line. Walter had more taste than his uncles; he knew a good
picture when he saw it; he liked good architecture;
he admired a well-bound book. But these things
were subordinate; his first wish was to be rich; that
was the stepping-stone to all the rest. As his uncles
had children, he could not expect to be their heir;
but he had the advantage of the name and the rela-
tionship, and they had already done much by making
him, nominally at least, a junior partner in this new
(comparatively new) firm—a firm which was, however, but one of their interests. The very first time
that Walter had met the Chase of Willoughby &
Chase he had made up his mind that this was the
person he needed, the person to give him a lift.
Richard and Nicholas were too cautious, too conserv-
ative, for daring enterprises, for outside speculations; in addition, they had no need to turn to things
of that sort. Their nephew, however, was in a hurry,
and here, ready to his hand, appeared a man of re-

sources; a man who had made one fortune in a baking-powder, another by the bold purchase of three-
quarters of an uncertain silver mine, a third by speculation on a large scale in lumber, while a fourth was
now in progress, founded (more regularly) in steamers. At present also there was a rumor that he had
something new on foot, something in California;
Walter had an ardent desire to be admitted to a part
in this Californian enterprise, whatever it might be.
But Chase's trip to Europe had delayed any progress
he might have hoped for in this direction, just as it
had delayed the carrying out of the Asheville speculation. The Chases had returned to New York in
November. But immediately (for it had seemed immediately to the impatient junior partner) Chase had
been hurried off again, this time to Florida, by his
silly wife. Walter did not really mean that Ruth
was silly; he thought her pretty and amiable. But
as she was gay, restless, fond of change, she had interfered (unconsciously of course) with his plans and
his hopes for nearly a year; to call her silly, therefore, was, in comparison, a mild revenge. "What
under heaven is the use of her dragging poor Chase
'away down South to the land of the cotton,' when
she has already kept him a whole summer wandering
about Europe," he had said to himself, discomfited,
when he first heard of the proposed Florida journey.
The next day an idea came to him: "Why shouldn't
I go also? Chase will be sure to bore himself to
death down there, with nothing in the world to do.

And then I shall be on hand to help him through the eternal sunshiny days! In addition, I may as well try to make myself agreeable to his gadding wife; for, whether she knows it as yet or not, it is evident that *she* rules the roost." He followed, therefore. But as he came straight to Florida, and as Mr. and Mrs. Chase had stopped *en route* at Baltimore, Washington, Richmond, Charleston, and Savannah, Walter had been in St. Augustine nearly two weeks before they arrived.

So far, all had turned out as he had hoped it would. This was not surprising; for young Willoughby was, not merely in manner, but also in reality, a good-natured, agreeable fellow, full of life, fond of amusement. He was ambitious, it is true. But he was as far as possible from being a drudging moneymaker. He meant to carry out his plans, but he also meant to enjoy life as he went along. He had noticed, even as far back as the time of the wedding, that the girl whom Horace Chase was to marry had in her temperament both indolence and activity; now one of these moods predominated, now the other. As soon, therefore, as Mr. and Mrs. Chase were established in their St. Augustine house, he let himself go. Whenever the young wife's mood for activity appeared to be uppermost, he opened a door for it; he proposed an excursion, an entertainment of some sort. Already, under his leadership, they had sailed down the Matanzas River (as the inlet is called) to see the old Spanish lookout; they had rowed up

Moultrie Creek; they had sent horses across to Anastasia Island and had galloped for miles southward down the hard ocean beach. They had explored the barrens; they had had a bear-hunt; they had camped out; they had caught sharks. On these occasions they had always been a party of at least four, and often of seven, when Mrs. Franklin and Dolly, Mrs. Kip and Commodore Etheridge joined in the excursion. Dolly in particular had surprised everybody by her unexpected strength; she had accompanied them whenever it had been possible. When it was not, she had urged her mother to take the vacant place. "Do go, His Grand, so that you can tell me about it. For it does amuse me so!"

Walter's latest inspiration, the ball at Andalusia, having been arranged, he now suggested that they should slip out unobserved and finish the afternoon with a sail. "I noticed the *Owl and the Pussycat* moored at the pier as we came by," he said. "If she is still there, Paul Archer is at the club, probably, and I can easily borrow her."

"Anything to get away from these Apaches," Chase answered. "And I'm a good deal afraid, too, of that Evangeline Taylor! She has asked me three times, with such a voice from the tombs, if I feel well to-day, that she has turned me stiff."

"Why on earth does that girl make such *awful* faces?" inquired Walter.

Ruth gave way to laughter. "I can never make you two believe it, but it is really her deep sense of duty. She thinks that she ought to look earnest, or intelligent, or grateful, or whatever it may be, and so she constantly tries new ways to do it."

"What way is it when she glares at a fellow's collar for fifteen minutes steadily," said Walter; "at close range?"

"She *never* did!" protested Ruth.

"Yes—in the tea-room; *my* collar. And every now and then she gave a ghastly smile."

"She didn't know it was your collar; she was simply fixing her eyes upon a point in space, as less embarrassing than looking about. And she smiled because she thought she ought to, as it is a party."

"A point in space! My collar!" grumbled Walter.

At the gate they looked back for a moment. The guests, nearly a hundred in number, had gathered in a semicircle under a live-oak; they were gazing with fresh interest at the Indians, who had been drawn up before them. The six redskins were still in as close a row as though they had been handcuffed together; the serious spinsters had failed entirely in their attempts to break the rank, and have a gentle word with one or two of them, apart. The Rev. Mr. Harrison, who was to make an address, now advanced and began to speak; the listeners at the gate could hear his voice, though they were too far off to catch the words. The voice would go on for a minute or two, and pause. Then would follow the more staccato accents of the interpreter.

"The horse-joke comes in, Walter, when that interpreter begins," said Chase. "Who knows what he is saying?"

The interpreter, however, made a very good speech. It was, perhaps, less spiritual than Mr. Harrison's.

It turned out afterwards that the thing which had made the deepest impression upon the Apaches was not the "lady's quiet home," nor the Sunday-school teachers, nor the cabinet-organ, nor even the dinner; it was the extraordinary length of "the young-squaw-with-her-head-in-the-sky," as they designated Evangeline Taylor.

Ruth drove her ponies down to the Basin. The little yacht called the *Owl and the Pussycat* was still moored at the pier; but Paul Archer, her owner, was not at the club, as Walter had supposed; he had gone to the Florida House to call upon some friends. Commodore Etheridge was in the club-room; he was forcing himself to stay away from Andalusia, for he had an alarming vision of its mistress, dressed in white, with the sunshine lighting up her sea-shell complexion and bringing out, amorously, the rich tints of her hair. Delighted to have something to do, he immediately took charge of Walter.

"Write a line, Mr. Willoughby; write a line on your card, and our porter shall take it to the Florida House at once. In the meanwhile Mr. and Mrs. Chase can wait here. Not a bad place to wait in, Mrs. Chase? Simple, you see. Close to nature. And nature's great restorer" (for two of the club-men were asleep).

The room was close to restorers of all sorts, for
the land front was let to a druggist. The house
stood on the wooden pier facing the little Plaza,
across whose grassy space the old Spanish cathedral
and the more modern Episcopal church eyed each
other without rancour. The Plaza's third side was
occupied by the post-office, which had once been the
residence of the Spanish governor.

The club-room was a large, pleasant apartment,
with windows and verandas overlooking the water.
There was a general straightening up of lounging at-
titudes when Mrs. Chase came in. Etheridge had
already introduced Horace Chase to everybody at
the club, and Chase, in his turn, had introduced almost everybody to his wife. The club, to a man,
admired Mrs. Chase; while she waited, therefore,
she held a little court. The commodore, meanwhile,
kindly took upon himself, as usual, the duty of en-
tertaining the Bubble.

"Mr. Willoughby need not have gone to the Florida House in person; our porter could perfectly
well have taken a note, as I suggested. Capital
fellow, our porter; I never come South, Mr. Chase,
without being struck afresh with the excellence of
the negroes as servants; they are the best in the
world; they're born for it!"

"That's all right, if they're willing," Chase answered. "But not to force 'em, you know. That
slave-market in the Plaza, now—"

"Oh Lord! Slave-market! Have *you* got hold

of that story too?" interposed Etheridge, irritably.
"It was never anything but a fish-market in its life!
But I'm tired of explaining it; that, and the full-
length skeleton hanging by its neck in an iron cage
in the underground dungeon at the fort — if they're
not true, they ought to be; that's what people appear to think! '*Si non ee veero, ee ben trovatoro,*'
as the Italians say. And speaking of the fort, I
suppose you have been to that ridiculous Indian
party at Andalusia to-day? Mrs. Kip must have
looked grotesque, out-of-doors? In white too, I
dare say?"

"Grotesque? Why, she's pretty," answered Chase.

"Not to my eye," responded Etheridge, deter-
minedly. "She has the facial outlines of a frog.
Do you know the real reason why I didn't marry?
I couldn't endure, sir, the prospect of an old wom-
an's face opposite mine at table year after year.
For our women grow old so soon —"

As he brought this out, a dim remembrance of
having said it to Horace Chase before came into his
mind. Had he, or had he not? Chase's face be-
trayed nothing. If he had, what the devil did the
fellow mean by not answering naturally, "Yes, you
told me?" Could it be possible that he, Anthony
Etheridge, had fallen into a habit of repeating? —
So that people were accustomed— ? He went off
and pretended to look at a file of porpoises, who
were going out to sea in a long line, like so many
fat dark wheels rolling through the water.

Chase, left alone, took up a newspaper. But almost immediately he threw it down, saying, "Well, I didn't expect to see *you* here!"

The person whom he addressed was a stranger, who came in at this moment, brought by a member of the club. He shook hands with Chase, and they talked together for a while. Then Chase crossed the room, and, smiling a little as he noted the semicircle round his wife, he asked her to come out and walk up and down the pier while they waited for Willoughby. Once outside, he said:

"Ruthie, I want to have a talk with Patterson, that man you saw come in just now. I'm not very keen about sailing, anyhow. Will you let me off this time?"

"Oh yes; I don't care about going," Ruth answered.

"You needn't give it up because I do," said her husband, kindly; "you like to sail. Take the ancient swell in my place. He will be delighted to go, for it will make him appear so young. Just Ruth, Anthony, and Walter—three gay little chums together!"

As Chase had predicted, the commodore professed himself "enchanted." He went off smilingly in Paul Archer's yacht, whose device of an owl and pussycat confounded the practically minded, while to the initiated — the admirers of those immortal honey-mooners who "ate with a runcible spoon"— it gave delight; a glee which was increased by the delicate pea-green hue of the pretty little craft.

But in spite of his enchantment, the commodore soon brought the boat back. He had taken the helm, and, when he had shown himself and his young companions to everybody on the sea-wall; when he had dashed past the old fort ; and then, putting about, had gone beating across the inlet to the barracks, he turned the prow towards the yacht club again. It was the hour for his afternoon whist, and he never let anything interfere with that.

The excursion, therefore, had been a short one, and, as Walter walked home with Mrs. Chase, she lingered a little. " It's too early to go in," she declared. As they passed the second pier, a dilapidated construction with its flooring gone, she espied a boat she knew. " There is the *Shearwater* just coming in. I am sure Mr. Kean would lend it to us. Don't you want to go out again ?"

The *Shearwater* was an odd little craft, flat on the water, with a long, pointed, covered prow and one large sail. Ruth knew it well, for Mr. Kean was an old friend of the Franklin's, and, in former winters, he had often taken her out.

" My object certainly is to please her," Walter said to himself. " But she *does* keep one busy. Well, here goes !"

Mr. Kean lent his boat, and presently they were off again.

" Take me as far as the old light-house," Ruth suggested.

" Easy enough going; but the getting back will

be another matter," Walter answered. "We should have to tack."

"I like tacking. I insist upon the light-house," Mrs. Chase replied, gayly.

The little boat glided rapidly past the town and San Marco; then turned towards the sea. For the old light-house, an ancient Spanish beacon, was on the ocean side of Anastasia.

"We can see it now. Isn't this far enough?" Walter asked, after a while.

"No; take me to the very door; I've made a vow to go," Ruth declared.

"But at this rate we shall never get back. And when we do, your husband, powerfully hungry for his delayed dinner, will be sharpening the carving-knife on the sea-wall!"

"He is more likely to be sharpening pencils at the Magnolia. He is sure to be late himself; in fact, he told me so; for he has business matters to talk over with that Mr. Patterson."

Walter had not known, until now, the name of the person who had carried off Chase; he had supposed that it was some ordinary acquaintance; he had no idea that it was the Chicago man whose name he had heard mentioned in connection with Chase's California interests. "David Patterson, of Chicago?" he asked. "Is he going to stay?"

"No; he leaves to-morrow morning, I believe," replied Ruth, in an uninterested tone.

"And here I am, sailing all over creation with

this insatiable girl, when, if I had remained at the club, perhaps Chase would have introduced me; perhaps I might even have been with them now at the Magnolia," Walter reflected, with intense annoyance.

At last she allowed him to put about. The sun was sinking out of sight. Presently the after-glow gave a second daylight of deep gold. Down in the south the dark line of the dense forest rose like a range of hills. The perfume from the orange groves floated seaward and filled the air.

" I used to believe that I liked riding better than anything," remarked Ruth. " But ever since that little rush we had together in the dugout — do you remember? the night we arrived? — ever since then, somehow, sailing has seemed more delicious! For one thing, it's lazier."

They were seated opposite each other in the small open space, Walter holding the helm with one hand, while with the other he managed the sail, and Ruth leaning back against the miniature deck. Presently she began to sing, softly, Schubert's music set to Shakespeare's words:

> " ' Hark! hark! the lark at heaven's gate sings,
>   And Phœbus 'gins arise— ' "

" Not the lark already?" asked Walter.

He was exerting all his skill, but their progress was slow; the *Shearwater* crossed and recrossed, crossed and recrossed, gaining but a few feet in each transit.

> " ' Arise! arise!
> My lady sweet, arise!' "

sang Ruth.

"Do you think I could get a rise out of those Minorcans?" suggested her companion, indicating a fishing-boat at a little distance. "Perhaps they could lend me some oars. I was a great fool to come out without them!"

"Oh, don't get oars; that would spoil it. The tide has turned, and the wind is dying down; we can float slowly in. Everything is exactly right, and I am perfectly happy!"

Walter, his mind haunted by that vision of Chase and Patterson at the Magnolia, did not at first take in what she had said. Then, a minute or two afterwards, her phrase returned to him, and he smiled; it seemed so naïve. "It's delightful, in a discontented world, to hear you say that, Mrs. Chase. Is it generally, or in particular, that you are so blissful? St. Augustine? or life as a whole?"

"Both," replied Ruth, promptly. "For I have everything I like—and I like so many things! And everybody does whatever I want them to do. Why, you yourself, Mr. Willoughby! Because I love to dance, you have arranged that ball for to-morrow night. And when I asked you to take me out this second time in the *Shearwater*, you did it at once."

"Ah, my lady, with your blue eyes and dark lashes, you little know why!" thought Walter, with an inward laugh.

At last he got the boat up to the dilapidated pier again. It was long after dark. He took her to her door, and left her; she must explain her late arrival in her own way. Women, fortunately, are excellent at explanations.

But Chase was not there.

Twenty minutes afterwards he came in, late in his turn. "You didn't have dinner, Ruthie? I'm sorry you waited; I was detained."

"I was very late myself," Ruth answered.

"Even now I can't stay," Chase went on, hurriedly; "I came back to tell you, and to get a few things. I am going up to Savannah with Patterson for three or four days, on business. We are to have a special—a mule special—this evening, and hit a steamer. You'd better have your mother to stay with you while I'm away."

"Yes. To-morrow."

"She could come to-night, couldn't she?"

"Yes; but it's late; I won't make her turn out to-night. With seven servants in the house, I am not afraid," Ruth answered.

"I only thought you might be lonely?"

"I'll sing all my songs to Petie Trone, Esq."

He laughed and kissed her.

"You must come back soon," she said.

When he had gone she went up-stairs and changed her dress for a long, loose costume of pale pink tint, covered with lace; then, returning, she rang for dinner. Here, as in New York, there was a housekeeper, who relieved the young wife of all care. The dinner, in spite of the long postponement, was excellent; it was also dainty, for the housekeeper had learned Mrs. Chase's tastes. Mrs. Chase enjoyed it. She drank a glass of wine, and dallied over the sweets and the fruit. Afterwards, in the softly lighted drawing-room, she amused herself by singing half a dozen songs. Petie Trone, Esq., the supposed audience, was not fond of music, though the songs were sweet; he slinked out, and going softly up the stairs, deposited himself of his own accord in his basket behind the cheval-glass in the dressing-room. At eleven his mistress came up; she let Félicité undress her, and brush with skilful touch the long, thick mass of her hair. When the maid had gone, she read a little, leaning back in an easy-chair, with a shaded lamp beside her; then, letting the novel slip down on her lap, she sat there, looking about the room. Miss Billy Breeze had marvelled over the luxurious toilet table at L'Hommedieu; here the whole room was like that table. Presently its occupant put out her hand, and drew towards her a small stand which held her jewel-box. For she already had jewels, as Chase liked to buy them for her. He would have covered his wife with diamonds if Mrs. Franklin had not said (during that first visit at Asheville after the marriage), " Ruth is too young to wear diamonds, Mr. Chase; don't you think so?" Chase did not think so; but he had deferred to her opinion—at least, he supposed himself to be defer-

ring to it when he bought only rubies and sapphires
and pearls. His wife now turned over these ornaments. She put on the pearl necklace; then she
took it off, and held it against her cheek. But she
did not spend as much time as usual over the jewels.
Often she entertained herself with them for an hour;
it had been one of her husband's amusements to
watch her. To-night, putting the case aside, she
strolled to the window, opened it and looked out.
The stars were shining brilliantly overhead; she
could hear the soft lapping of the water against the
sea-wall. From Anastasia came at intervals the flash
of the light-house. "I was over there at sunset,"
she said to herself as she watched the gleam. Then
closing the window, she walked idly to and fro, with
her hands clasped behind her. "How happy I am!"
she thought; or rather she did not think it, she felt
it. She had no desire to sleep; the door of the
bedroom stood open behind her, but she did not go
in. She sat down on the divan, and let her head fall
back among the cushions: "Everything is perfect—
perfect. How delightful it is to live!"

CHAPTER X

Two days after the Indian party at Andalusia, the excursion which Mrs. Kip had called a "boat-drive" came off. Horace Chase was still absent; he had telegraphed to his wife that he could not return before the last of the week. As all the preparations had been made, the excursion was not postponed on his account. Nor was there any reason why it should be. It was not given in honor of his wife, especially; Ruth, after sixteen months of marriage, could hardly be called a bride. In addition, the little winter colony had learned that an hour or two of their leisurely pleasure-making was about as much as this man of affairs could enjoy (some persons said "could endure"); after that his face was apt to betray a vague boredom, although it was evident that (with his usual careful politeness) he was trying to conceal it.

Walter Willoughby, meanwhile, was making the best of an annoying situation. He had lost the chance of being introduced to David Patterson, and with it the opportunity of learning something definite, at last, about Chase's Californian interests, and this seemed to him a great misfortune. But there was no use in moaning over it; the course to follow was not still further to lose the five days of Chase's absence in sulking, but to employ them in the only profitable way that was left open (small profit, but better than nothing)—namely, in cementing still further a friendly feeling between himself and Chase's wife, that butterfly young wife who had been the cause of so many of his disappointments. "Every little helps, I suppose," he said to himself, philosophically. "And as the thing she likes best, apparently, is to go and keep going, why, I'll take her own pace and outrace her — the little gad-about!" For, to Walter's eyes, Ruth appeared very young; mentally unformed as yet, child-like. His adjective "little" could, in truth, only be applied to her in this sense, for in actual inches Mrs. Chase was almost as tall as he was. Walter was of medium height, robust and compact. He had a well-shaped, well-poised head, which joined his strong neck behind with no hollow and scarcely a curve. His thick, dark hair was kept very short; but, with his full temples and facial outlines, this curt fashion became him well. He was not called handsome, though his features were clearly cut and firm. His gray eyes were ordinarily rather cold. But when he was animated—and he was usually very animated—young Willoughby looked full of life. He was fond of pleasure, fond of amusement. But this did not prevent his possessing, underneath the surface, a resolute will, which he could enforce against himself as well as against others. He intended to enjoy life.

And as, according to his idea, there could be no lasting enjoyment without freedom from the pinch of anxiety about material things, he also intended to get money—first of all to get money. "For a few years, while one is young, to have small means doesn't so much matter," he had told himself. "But when one reaches middle age, or passes it, then, if one has children, care inevitably steps in. There are anxieties, of course, which cannot be prevented. But this particular one can be—with a certain amount of energy, and also of resolute self-control in the beginning. The 'have-a-good-time-while-you-are-young' policy doesn't compensate for having a bad time when you are old, in my opinion. And it's care that makes one old!"

Horace Chase had left St. Augustine on Monday. The next evening, at Mrs. Kip's impromptu ball in the gymnasium, the junior partner of Willoughby, Chase, & Company devoted his time to Mrs. Chase with much skill. His attentions remained unobtrusive; he did not dance with her often. The latter, indeed, would not have been possible in any case; for Mrs. Chase was surrounded, from first to last, by all that St. Augustine could offer. Graceful as she was in all her movements, Ruth's dancing was particularly charming. And it was also striking; for, sinuous, lithe, soon excited, she danced because she loved it, danced with unconscious abandon. That night, her slender figure in the white ball dress, that floated backward in the rapid motion, her happy face

with the starry eyes and beautiful color coming and
going—this made a picture which those who were
present remembered long. At ten o'clock she had
begun to dance; at two, when many persons were
taking leave, she was still on the floor; with her circle of admirers, it was now Mrs. Chase who was
keeping up the ball. Her mother, who was staying
with her during her husband's absence, had accompanied her to Andalusia. But there was no need to
ask whether Mrs. Franklin was tired; Mrs. Franklin
was never tired in scenes of gayety; she was as well
entertained as her daughter. Walter had danced but
twice with Mrs. Chase during the four hours. But
always between her dances he had been on hand. If
she had a fancy for spending a few moments on the
veranda, he had her white cloak ready; if she wished
for an ice, it appeared by magic; if there was any
one she did not care to dance with, she could always
say that she was engaged to Mr. Willoughby. It was
in this way, in fact, that Mr. Willoughby had obtained his two dances. The last dance, however, was
all his own. It was three o'clock; even the most
good-natured chaperons had collected their charges,
and the music had ceased. "How sorry I am! I do
so long for just one waltz more," said Ruth.

She spoke to her mother, but Walter overheard the
words. He went across to the musicians (in reality
he bribed them); then returning, he said: "I've arranged it, Mrs. Chase. You are to have that one
waltz more." A few of the young people, tempted

by the revived strains, threw aside their wraps and
joined them, but practically they had the floor to
themselves. Walter was an expert dancer, skilful
and strong; he bore his partner down the long room,
guiding her so securely that she was not obliged to
think of their course; she could leave that entirely
to him, and give herself up to the enjoyment of the
motion. As they returned towards the music for
the third time, she supposed that he would stop.
But he did not; he swept her down again, and in
shorter circles that made her, light as she was on her
feet, a little giddy. "Isn't this enough?" she asked.
But apparently he did not hear her. The floor began to spin. "Please stop," she murmured, her eyes
half closing from the increasing dizziness. But her
partner kept on until he felt that she was faltering;
then, with a final bewildering whirl, he deposited her
safely on a bench, and stood beside her, laughing a
little.

There was no one near them; Mrs. Franklin, Mrs.
Kip, and the few who still remained, were at the
other end of the room. Ruth, after a moment, began to laugh also, while she pressed her hands over
her eyes to help herself see more clearly. "What
possessed you?" she said. "Another instant and
I should certainly have fallen; I couldn't see a
thing!"

"No, you wouldn't have fallen, Mrs. Chase; I
could have held you up under any circumstances.
But I wanted to make you for once acknowledge

that we are not all so lethargic as you constantly accuse us of being."

"Accuse?" said Ruth, surprised. She was still panting.

"Yes, you accuse the whole world; you do nothing *but* accuse. You are never preoccupied yourself, and so preoccupation in others seems to you stupidity. You are never tired; so the rest of us strike you as owlish and lazy."

"Oh, but I'm often lazy myself," protested Ruth.

"Precisely. No doubt when you go in for being lazy at all, you carry it further than any poor, dull, reasonable man would ever dream of doing," Walter went on. "I dare say you are capable of lying motionless on a sofa, with a novel, for ten hours at a stretch!"

"Ten hours? That's nothing. Ten days," answered Ruth. "I have spent ten days at L'Hommedieu in that way many a time; Maud Muriel used to call it 'lucid stupor.'"

"Lucid?" said Walter, doubtfully. "Do you think you can walk?" he went on, as her mirth still continued. "Because the music really has stopped this time, and I see your mother's eyes turning this way. Your laughs are perfectly beautiful, of course. But do they leave you your walking powers?"

The musicians, seeing them rise, began suddenly to play again (for his bribe had been a generous one), and he took her back to her mother in a rapid *deux temps.*

14

"Splendid! I like dancing better than anything else in the world," Ruth declared.

"I thought it was sailing? However, whatever it is, please make use of me often, Mrs. Chase. When I've nothing to do I become terribly low-spirited: for my uncles are bent upon marrying me!"

"Have they selected any special person?" inquired Mrs. Franklin, laughing, as he helped her to put on her cloak.

"I think they have their eye on a widow, a widow of thirty-seven with a fortune," answered Walter, with exaggerated gloom.

"Will she have you?"

"Never in the world!" Walter declared; "that's just it! Why, therefore, should my uncles force me forward — such a tender flower as I am — to certain defeat? It is on that account that I have run away. I have come to hide in Florida — under your protection, Mrs. Chase."

The meeting-place for the water-party the next day was St. Francis Barracks—the long, brown structure with pointed gables and deep shady verandas, which stood on the site of an old Spanish monastery, at the south end of the sea-wall. The troops stationed at St. Francis that winter belonged to the First Artillery; to-day the colonel and his family, the captain and his wife, and the two handsome lieutenants took part in the excursion; there were fifty people in all, and many yachts, from the big *Seminole* down to the little *Shearwater*. Walter had *The Owl and the Pussycat,* and with him embarked Mrs. Franklin with her two daughters, Miss Franklin and Mrs. Chase ; Mrs. Lilian Kip ; and Commodore Etheridge. At two o'clock the little fleet sped gayly down the Matanzas.

"Matanzas, Sebastian, St. Augustine," said Walter ; "these names are all in character. It's an awful misfortune for your husband's budding summer resort in the North Carolina mountains, Mrs. Chase, that its name happens to be Asheville, after that stupid custom of tacking the French 'ville' to some man's name ; (for I take it that Ashe is a name, and not cinders). In this case, the first settlers were more than usually asinine ; for they had the beautiful Indian 'Swannanoa' ready to their hands."

"Oh, but first settlers have no love for Indian names,"·commented Dolly. "How can they have ? The Indians and the great forest — these are their enemies. To me there is something touching in our Higgsvilles and Slatervilles. I see the first log cabins in the little clearing ; then a short, stump-bedecked street ; then two or three streets and a court - house. The Higgs or the Slater was their best man, their leader, the one they looked up to. In North Carolina alone there are one hundred and ten towns or villages with names ending in 'ville.'"

"North Carolina ? Oh yes, I dare say !" remarked Etheridge.

"And two hundred and forty-one in New York," added Dolly.

"Well, we make up for it in other ways," said Mrs. Franklin. "If the men name the towns, the women name the children; I have known mothers to produce simply from their own imaginations such titles as Merilla, and Idelusia, for their daughters. I once knew a girl who had even been baptized Damask Rose."

"What did they call her for short?" inquired Walter.

"Oh, Mr. *Willoughby!*" said Lilian Kip, shocked.

"Damask's mother was trying to solace herself with names, I fancy," Mrs. Franklin went on, " because by the terms of her husband's will (she was a widow), she forfeited all she had if she married again."

"How outrageous?" exclaimed Mrs. Kip, bristling into vehemence. "If a woman has been a good wife to one man, is that any reason why she should be denied the *privilege* of being a good wife to another?"

"Privilege?" repeated Dolly.

"Surely there is no greater one," said Mrs. Kip, with a sigh. "Love is so beautiful! And it is such a benefit! The more one loves, the better, I think. And the more *persons* one loves, the more sweet and generous one's nature becomes. If any one has been bereaved, I am always *so* glad to hear that they are in love again. Even if the love is unreturned" (here she gave a little swallow), "I still think it in itself the greatest blessing we have ; and the most improving."

After a friendly race towards the south, the fleet turned and came back; the company disembarked and walked across the narrow breadth of Anastasia Island to the ocean beach, where, at the Spanish light-house, the collation was to be served later in the day. The old beacon stood, at high tide, almost in the water; for, in two hundred years, the ocean had encroached largely upon the shore. Its square stone tower, which had been topped in the Spanish days with an iron grating and a bonfire, now displayed a revolving light, which flashed and then faded, flashed and faded, signalling out to sea the harbor of St. Augustine. Under the tower stood a coquina house for the keeper, and the whole was fortified, having a defensive wall, with angles and loop-holes. Nothing could have been more beautiful than the soft sapphire tint of the ocean, whose long rollers, coming smoothly in, broke with a musical wash upon the broad white beach which, firm as a pavement, stretched towards the south in long curves. Not a ship was in sight. Overhead sailed an eagle. "Oh, why did we land so soon?" said Ruth, regretfully. "We might have stayed out two hours longer. For we are not to have the supper—or is it the dinner?—at any rate, it's chowder—until sunset."

"We can go out again, if you like," said Walter.

Here Etheridge came up. The implacably clear light which comes from a broad expanse of sea was revealing every minute line in Mrs. Franklin's delicate face. "How wrinkled she looks!" was his self-congratulatory thought. "Even fifteen years ago she was finished—done!" Then he added, aloud: "I think I'll accompany you, if you *are* going out again. The afternoon promises to be endlessly long here, with nothing to do but gawp for sea-beans, or squawk poetry!" This strenuous description of some of the amusements already in progress on the beach showed that, in the commodore's plans, something had gone wrong.

"Are you really going, commodore?" asked Mrs. Franklin. "Then I'll put Ruth in your charge."

"Put me in it, too," said Dolly. "I should much rather sail than sit here."

"Oh no, Dolly. You never can take that walk to the landing a second time so soon," said the mother.

And so it proved. Dolly started. But, after a few steps, she had to give it up. "I should think *you* would like to go, His Grand?" she suggested.

"I can't. I have promised to see to the chowder," answered Mrs. Franklin. "Sailing and sea-beans and poetry are all very well. But I have noticed that every one grows gloomy when the chowder is bad!"

Etheridge, Ruth, and Walter Willoughby, therefore, recrossed the island and embarked. The commodore took the helm.

"What boat is that ahead of us?" asked Walter. "Some of our people? Has any one else deserted the sea-beans?"

"I dare say," replied Etheridge, carelessly.

The commodore could manage a boat extremely

well; the *Owl and the Pussycat* flew after that sail
ahead, in a line as straight as a plummet.

"Why, it's Mrs. Kip," said Ruth, as they drew nearer. She had recognized the gypsy hat in the other boat.

"Yes, with Albert Tillotson," added Walter.

"What, that donkey?" inquired Etheridge, with
well-feigned surprise (and an anger that required no
feigning). "He can no more manage a boat than I
can manage a comet! Poor Mrs. Kip is in actual
danger of her life. The idea of that Tom Noddy of
a Tillotson daring to take her out! I must run this
boat up alongside, Mr. Willoughby, and get on board
immediately. Common humanity requires it."

"The commodore's common humanity is uncommonly like jealousy," said Walter to Ruth when the
Owl had dropped behind again after this manœuvre
had been successfully executed. "He is a clever old
fellow! Of course he knew she was out, and he came
with us on purpose. We'll keep near them, Mrs.
Chase, and watch their faces; it will be as good as a
play."

To his surprise, Ruth, who was generally so ready
to laugh, did not pay heed to this. "I am glad he
has gone," she said; "for now we need not talk—
just sail and sail! Let us go over so far—straight
down towards the south." Her eyes had a dreamy
expression which was new to him.

"What next!" thought her companion. He glanced
furtively at his watch. "I can keep on for half an
hour more, I suppose."

But when, at the end of that time, he put about, Ruth, who had scarcely spoken, straightened herself (she had been lying back indolently, with one hand behind her head), and watched the turning prow with regret. "*Must* we go back so soon? Why?"

"To look for sea-beans," answered Walter. "Are you aware, Mrs. Chase, of the awful significance of that New England phrase of condemnation, 'You don't know beans'? It will be said that *I* don't know if I take you any farther. For the tide will soon turn, and the wind is already against us."

But his tasks were not yet at an end; another idea soon took possession of his companion's imagination.

"How wild Anastasia looks from here! I have never landed at this point. Can't we land now, just for a few moments? It would be such fun."

"Won't it be more than fun, Mrs. Horace? A wild-goose—? Forgive the pun."

On Anastasia there are ancient trails running north and south. Ruth, discovering one of these paths, followed it inland. "I wish we could meet something, I wish we could have an adventure!" she said. "There are bears over here; and there are alligators too at the pools. Perhaps this trail leads to a pool?" The surmise was correct; the path soon brought them within sight of a dark-looking pond, partly covered with lily leaves. Ruth, who was first (for the old Indian trail was so narrow that they could not walk side by side), turned back suddenly. "There really *is* an alligator," she whispered. "He is half in and half out of the water. I am going to run round through the thicket, so as to have a nearer view of him." And hurrying with noiseless steps along the trail, she turned into the forest.

He followed. "Don't be foolhardy," he urged. For she seemed to him so fearless that there was no telling what she might do.

But when they reached the opposite side of the pool no alligator was visible, and Ruth, seating herself in the loop of a vine, which formed a natural swing, laughed her merriest.

"You are an excellent actress," he said. "I really believed that you had seen the creature."

"And if I had? They don't attack people; they are great cowards."

"I have an admirable air of being more timid than she is!" he thought, annoyed.

They returned towards the shore along a low ridge. On their way he saw something cross this ridge about thirty feet ahead of them—a slender dark line. He ran forward and looked down (for the ridge was four feet high).

"Come quickly!" he called back to Ruth. "Your alligator was a base invention. But here is something real. He is hardly more than an infant," he continued, his eyes still fixed on the lower slope. "But he is of the blood royal, I can tell by the shape of his neck. I'll get a long branch, Mrs. Chase, and then, as you like adventures, you can see him strike." Where they stood, they were safe, for the snake (it was a young rattlesnake) would not come up the ascent; when he moved, he would glide the other way into the thicket. Hastily cutting a long wand from a bush, he gave it to her. "Touch him," he directed; "on the body, not on the head. Then you will see him coil!" He himself kept his eyes meanwhile on the snake; he did not look at her. But the wand did not descend. "Make haste," he urged, "or he will be off!"

The wand came down slowly, paused, and then touched the reptile, who instantly coiled himself, reared his flat head, and struck at it with his fangs exposed. Walter, excited and interested, waited to see him strike again. But there was no opportunity, for the wand itself was dropping. He turned. Ruth, her face covered with her hands, was shuddering convulsively.

"The snake has gone," he said, reassuringly; "he went off like a shot into the thicket, he is a quarter of a mile away by this time." For he was alarmed by the violence of the tremor that had taken possession of her.

In spite of her tremor, she began to run; she hurried like a wild creature along the ridge until she came to a broad open space of white sand, over which no dark object could approach unseen; here she sank down, sobbing aloud.

He was at his wits' end. Why should a girl, who apparently had no fear of bears or alligators, be frightened out of her senses by one small snake?

"Supposing she should faint—that Dolly is always fainting! What on earth could I do?" he thought.

Ruth, however, did not faint. But she sobbed and sobbed as if she could not stop.

"It's just like her laughing," thought Walter, in despair. "Dear Mrs. Chase," he said aloud, "I am distracted to see how I have made you suffer. These Florida snakes do very little harm, unless one happens to step on them unawares. I did not imagine, I did not dream, that the mere sight— But that makes no difference; I shall never forgive myself; never!"

Ruth looked up, catching her breath. "It was so dreadful!" she murmured, brokenly. "Did you see its—its mouth?" She was so white that even her lips were colorless; her blue eyes were dilated strangely.

He grew more and more alarmed. Apparently she saw it, for she tried to control herself; and, after two or three minutes, she succeeded. "You must not mind if I happen to look rather pale," she said, timidly. "I am sometimes very pale for a moment or two. And then I get dreadfully red in the same way. Dolly often speaks of it. But it doesn't mean anything. I can go now," she added, still timidly.

"She thinks I am vexed," he said to himself, surprised. He was not vexed; on the contrary, in her pallor and this new shyness she was more interesting to him than she had ever been before. As he knew that they ought to be on their way back, he accepted her offer to start, in spite of her white cheeks. But her steps were so weak, and she still trembled so convulsively, that he drew her hand through his arm and held it. Giving her in this way all the help he could, he took her towards the shore, choosing a route through open spaces, so that there should be no vision of any gliding thing in the underbrush near by. When they were off again, crossing the Matanzas on a long tack, she was still very pallid. "I haven't been clever," he thought. "At present she is unnerved by fright. But by to-morrow it will be anger, and she will say that it was my fault." While thinking of this, he talked on various subjects. But it was a monologue; for a long time Ruth made no answer. Then suddenly the color came rushing back to her cheeks. "*Please* don't tell —don't tell any one how dreadfully frightened I was," she pleaded.

"I never tell anything; I have no talent for narrative," he answered, much relieved to see the returning red. "But I am dreadfully cut up and wretched about that fright I was stupid enough to give you. I wish I could make you forget it, Mrs. Chase; forget it forever."

"On the contrary, I am afraid I shall remember it forever," Ruth answered. Then she added, still timidly, "But you were so kind— It won't be *all* unpleasant."

"What a school-girl it is!" thought Walter. "And above all things, what a creature of extremes! She must lead Horace Chase a life! However, she is certainly seductively lovely."

CHAPTER XI

AT the end of this week Horace Chase returned. And the next morning he paid a visit to his mother-in-law. He still used his "ma'am" when talking to her; she still called him "Mr. Chase." In mentioning him to others, she sometimes succeeded in bringing out a "Horace." But when the tall, grave-looking business man was before her in person, she never got beyond the more formal title.

"My trip to Savannah, ma'am, was connected with business," Chase began, after he had gone through his usual elaborate inquiries about her health and "the health of Miss Dolly." "One of my friends, David Patterson by name, and myself, have been engaged for some time in arranging a new enterprise in which we are about to embark in California. Matters are now sufficiently advanced for me to mention that about May next we shall need a confidential man in New York to attend to the Eastern part of it. It is highly important to me, ma'am, to have for that position some one I know, some one I can trust. Mr. Patterson will go himself to California, and remain there, probably, a year or more. Meanwhile I, at the East, shall need just the right man under me; for *I* have other things to see to; I cannot give all my time to this new concern. Do you think, ma'am, that Mr. Franklin could be induced to take this place? Under the circumstances, I should esteem it a favor." And here he made Jared's mother a little bow.

"You are very kind," answered Mrs. Franklin. Having refused to know anything of the correspondence between Ruth and Genevieve, she had had until now no knowledge of the proposed New York place. "Jared's present position is certainly most wretched drudgery," she went on; "far beneath his abilities—which are really great."

"Just so. And what should you recommend, ma'am, as the best way to open the subject? Shall I take a run up to Raleigh? Or shall I drop him a line? Perhaps you yourself would like to write?"

The mother reflected. "If I do," she thought, "Jared will fancy that I have begged the place for him. If Ruth writes, he will be sure of it. If Mr. Chase writes, Jared will answer within the hour—a letter full of jokes and friendliness, but—declining. If Chase goes to Raleigh in person, Jared will decline verbally, and with even more unassailable good-humor. No, there is only one person in the world who could perhaps make him yield, and that person is Genevieve!" At this thought, her face, which always showed like a barometer her inward feelings, changed so markedly that her son-in-law hastened to interpose. "Don't bother about the ways and means, ma'am; I guess I can fix it all right." He spoke in a confident tone, in order to reassure her; for he had a liking for the "limber old lady," as he mentally called her. His confidence, however, was in a large measure assumed; where business matters were in question, the "offishness," as he termed it, of this ex-naval officer had seemed to him such a queer trait that he hardly knew how to grapple with it.

"I was only thinking that my daughter-in-law would perhaps be the best person to speak to Jared," replied Mrs. Franklin at last. (The words came out with an effort.)

"Gen? So she would; she is very clear-headed. But if she is to be the one, I must first let her know just what the place is, and all about it, and how can that be done, ma'am? Wouldn't Mr. Franklin see my letter?"

"No. For she isn't in Raleigh with her husband; she is at Asheville."

"Why, how's that?" inquired Chase, who had seen, from the first, Jared's deep attachment to his wife.

"How indeed!" thought the mother. Her lips quivered. She compressed them in order to conceal it. The satisfaction which she had, for a time, felt in the idea that Genevieve was learning, at last, that she could not always control her husband—this had now vanished in the sense of her son's long and dreary solitude. For the wife had not been in Raleigh during the entire winter; Jared had been left

to endure existence as best he could in his comfortless boarding-house. "My daughter-in-law has been
very closely occupied at Asheville," she explained,
after a moment. "They are improving their house
there, you know, and she can superintend work of
that sort remarkably well."

"That's so," said Chase, agreeingly.

"She is also much interested in a new wing for
the Colored Home," pursued Mrs. Franklin; and this
time a little of her deep inward bitterness showed
itself in her tone.

"Gen's pretty cute!" thought Chase. "She's not
only feathering her own nest up there in Asheville,
but at the same time she is starving out that wrong-
headed husband of hers." Then he went on aloud:
"Well, ma'am, if it's to be Mrs. Jared who is to attend to the matter for me, I guess I'll wait until I
can put the whole thing before her in a nutshell,
with the details arranged. That will be pretty soon
now—as soon as I come back from California. For
I must go to California myself before long."

"Are you going to take Ruth? How I shall miss
her!" said the mother, dispiritedly.

"We shall not be gone a great while—only five or
six weeks. On second thoughts, why shouldn't you
come along, ma'am?—come along with us? I guess
I could fix it so as you'd be pretty comfortable."

"You are very kind. But I could not leave Dolly."

"Of course not. I didn't mean that, ma'am; I
meant that Miss Dolly should come along too. That

French woman of Ruth's — Felicity — she's capital when travelling. Or we could have a trained nurse? They have very attractive nurses now, ma'am; real ladies; and good-looking too, and sprightly."

"You are always thoughtful," answered Mrs. Franklin, amused by this description. "But it is impossible. Dolly can travel for two or three days, if we take great precautions; but a longer time makes her ill. Ruth is coming to lunch, isn't she? With Malachi? I am so glad you brought him; he doesn't have many holidays."

"Well, ma'am, he was there in Savannah, buying a bell, or, rather, getting prices. A church bell, as I understood. He'd about got through, and was going back to Asheville, when I suggested to him to come along down to St. Augustine for three or four days. 'Come and look up your wandering flock'—that is what I remarked to him. For you know, ma'am, that with yourself and Miss Dolly, the commodore and Mrs. Kip, you make four—four of his sheep in Florida; including Miss Evangeline Taylor, four sheep and a first-prize lamb."

Mrs. Franklin smiled. But she felt herself called upon to explain a little. "We are not of his flock, exactly; Mr. Hill has a mission charge. But though he is not our rector, we are all much attached to him."

"He's a capital little fellow, and works hard; I've great respect for him. But somehow, ma'am, he's taken a queer way lately of stopping short when he is talking. Almost as though he had choked!"

15

"So he has—choked himself off," answered Mrs. Franklin, breaking into a laugh. "When with you, he is constantly tempted to ask for money for the Mission, he says. He knows, however, that the clergy are always accused of paying court to rich men for begging purposes, and he is determined to be an exception. But he finds it uncommonly difficult."

"How much does he want?" inquired Chase. Then he paused. "Perhaps his notions take the form of a church?" he went on. "I've been thinking a little of building a church, ma'am. You see, my mother was a great church-goer; she found her principal comfort in it. I've been very far from steady myself, I'm sorry to say; I haven't done much credit to her bringing-up. And so I've thought that I'd put up a church some day, as a sort of memory of her. Because, if she'd lived, she would have liked that better than anything else."

"Do you mean an Episcopal church?" inquired Mrs. Franklin, touched by these words.

"Well, she was a Baptist herself," Chase replied. "So perhaps I have rather a prejudice in favor of that denomination. But I'm not set upon it; I should think it might be built so as to be suitable for all persuasions. At any rate, I guess Hill and I could hit it off together somehow."

Here Dolly came in, and a moment afterwards Ruth appeared with the Rev. Malachi Hill. Dolly greeted the young missionary with cordiality. "How is Asheville?" she inquired. "How is Maud Muriel?"

Malachi's radiant face changed. "She is the same. When I see her coming, I do everything I can to keep out of the way. But sometimes there is no corner to turn, or no house to go into, and I *have* to pass her. And then I know just how she will say it!" And, tightening his lips, he brought out a low "Manikin!"

"Brace up," said Dolly. "You must look back at her and look her down; make her falter."

"Oh, falter!" repeated poor Malachi, hopelessly.

Another guest now appeared—Mrs. Kip. For Mrs. Franklin had invited them all to lunch before the jessamine hunt, which had been appointed for that afternoon. As it happened, Mrs. Kip's first question also was, "How is Miss Mackintosh?"

"Unchanged. At least, she treats *me* with the same contumely," answered the clergyman.

"If you indulge yourself with such words as 'contumely,' Mr. Hill, people will call you affected," said Dolly, in humorous warning.

"Now, Dolly, don't say that," interposed Mrs. Kip. "For unusual words are full of dignity. I don't know what I wouldn't give if *I* could bring in, just naturally and easily, when I am talking, such a word, for instance, as jejune! And for clergymen it is especially distinguished. Though there is *one* clerical word, Mr. Hill, that I do think might be altered, and that is closet. Why should we always be told to meditate in our closets? Generally there is no room for a chair; so all one can think of is people sitting on the floor among the shoes."

Every one laughed. Mrs. Kip, however, had made her remark in perfect good faith.

The entrance of Walter Willoughby completed the party, and lunch was announced. When the meal was over, and they came back to the parlor, they found Félicité in waiting with Petie Trone, Esq. Félicité, a French woman with a trim waist and large eyes, always looked as though she would like to be wicked. In reality, however, she was harmless, for one insatiable ambition within her swallowed up all else, namely, the ambition not to be middle-aged. As she was forty-eight, the struggle took all her time. "I bring to madame le petit trône for his promenade," she said, as, after a respectful salutation to the company, she detached the leader from the dog's collar.

"Must that **fat** little wretch go with us?" Chase inquired, after the maid had departed.

For answer, Ruth took up Mr. Trone and deposited him on her husband's knee. "Yes; and you are to see to him."

"Is the squirrel down here too?" inquired Walter. "I haven't seen him."

"Robert the Squirrel—" began Chase, with his hands in his trousers pockets; then he paused. "That's just like Robert the Devil, isn't it? I mean an opera, ma'am, of that name that they were giving in New York last winter," he explained to Mrs. Franklin, so that she should not think he was swearing.

"Robert the Devil will do excellently well as a

nickname for Bob," said Dolly. "It's the best he has had."

"Well, at any rate, Robert the Squirrel isn't here," Chase went on. "He boards with Mr. Hill for the winter, Walter; special terms made for nuts. And, by-the-way, Hill, you haven't mentioned Larue; how is the senator? I'm keeping my eye on him for future use in booming our resort, you know. The Governor of North Carolina remarking to the Governor of South Carolina—you've heard that story? Well, sir, what we propose now is to have the *senator* from North Carolina remark to the senator from South Carolina (and to all the other senators thrown in) that Asheville is bound to be the Lone Star of mountain resorts south of the Catskills."

Lilian Kip's heart had given a jump at Larue's name; to carry it off, she took up a new novel which was lying on the table. (For Chase's order had been a perennial one: "all the latest articles in fiction," pursued Mrs. Franklin hotly, month after month.) "Oh, I am sure you don't like *this*," said Lilian, when she had read the title.

"I have only just begun it," answered Mrs. Franklin. "But why shouldn't I like it? It is said to be original and amusing."

"It is not *at all* the book I should wish to put into the hands of Evangeline Taylor," replied Mrs. Kip, with decision.

"The one unfailing test of the American mother for the entire literature of the world!" commented Dolly.

The search for the first jessamine was in those days one of the regular amusements of a St. Augustine winter. Where St. George Street ends, beyond the two pomegranate-topped pillars of the old city gate, Mrs. Franklin's party came upon the other members of the searching expedition, and they all walked on together along the shell road. On the right, Fort San Marco loomed up, with the figures of several Indians on its top outlined against the sky. Beyond shone the white sand-hills of the North Beach. At the end of the road the searchers entered a long range of park-like glades; here the yellow jessamine, the loveliest wild flower of the Florida spring, unfolds its tendrils as it clambers over the trees and thickets, lighting up their evergreen foliage with its bell-shaped flowers. Dolly and Mrs. Frankl'n had accompanied the party in a phaeton. "I think I can drive everywhere, even without a road, as the ground is so level and open," Dolly suggested. "But you must serve as guide, Ruth. Please keep us in sight."

But after a while Ruth forgot this injunction. Mrs. Franklin, always interested in whatever was going on, had already disappeared, searching for the jessamine with the eagerness of a girl. Dolly, finding herself thus deserted, stopped. But her brother-in-law, who had had his eye on her pony from the beginning, soon appeared. "What, alone?" he said, coming up.

Upon seeing him, Dolly cleared her brow. "I don't mind it; the glades are so pretty."

Chase examined the glades ; but without any marked admiration in his glance.

"Where is Ruth?" Dolly went on.

"Just round the corner—I mean on the other side of that thicket. Walter has found some of the vine they are all hunting for, and she's in a great jubilation over it; she wanted to find it ahead of that Mr. Kean, who always gets it first."

"Please tell her to bring me a spray of it. As soon as she can."

Assuring himself that the pony felt no curiosity about the absence of a road under his feet, Chase, with his leisurely step, went in search of his wife. He found her catching jessamine, which Walter, who had climbed into a wild-plum tree, was throwing down. She had already adorned herself with the blossoms, and when she saw her husband approaching she went to meet him, and wound a spray round his hat.

"Your sister wants some ; she told me to tell you. She's back there a little way—on the left," said Chase. "Hullo ! here comes a wounded hero ;" for Petie Trone, Esq., had appeared, limping dolefully. "Never mind ; I'll see to the little porpoise if you want to go to Dolly." He stooped and took up the dog with gentle touch. "He has probably been interviewing some prickly-pears."

When Ruth had gone, Walter's interest in the jessamine vanished. He swung himself down to the ground. "Mrs. Chase has been telling me that you are thinking of going to California very soon?" he said, inquiringly.

"Yes; I guess we shall get off next week," Chase answered, examining Trone's little paws.

"I am going to be very bold," Walter went on. "I am going to ask you to take me with you."

Chase's features did not move, but his whole expression altered; the half-humorous look which his face always wore when, in the company of his young wife, he was "taking things easy," as he called it, gave place in a flash to the cool reticence of the man of business. "Take you?" he inquired, briefly. "Why?"

And then Willoughby, in the plainest and most direct words (a directness which was not, however, without the eloquence that comes from an intense desire), explained his wish to be admitted to a part, however small, in the California scheme. He allowed himself no reserves; he told the whole story of his father's spendthrift propensities, and his own small means in consequence. "I have a fixed determination to make money, Mr. Chase. I dare say you have thought me idle; but I should not have idled if I had had at any time the right thing to go into. Work? There is literally no amount of work that I should shrink from, if it led towards the fortune upon which I am bent. I can, and I will, work as hard as ever you yourself have worked."

"I'm afraid you're looking for a soft snap," said Chase, shifting Mr. Trone to his left arm, and putting his right hand into his trousers pocket, where he jingled a bunch of keys vaguely.

"If you will let me come in, even by a little edge. only, I am sure you won't regret it," Walter went on. "Can't you recall, by looking back, your own determination to succeed, and how far it carried you, how strong it made you? Well, that is the way I feel to-day! You ought to be able to comprehend me. You've been over the same road."

"The same road!" repeated Chase, ironically. "Let's size it up a little. I was taken out of school before I was fourteen—when my father died. From that day I had not only to earn every crumb of bread I ate, but help to earn the bread of my sisters too. Before I was eighteen I had worked at half a dozen different things, and always at the rate of thirteen or fourteen hours a day. By the time I was twenty I was old; I had already lived a long and hard life. Now your side: A good home; every luxury; school; college; Europe!"

"You think that because I have been through Columbia, and because I once had a yacht (the yacht was in reality my uncle's), I shall never make a good business man," replied Walter. "Unfortunately, I have no means of proving to you the contrary, unless you will give me the chance I ask for. I don't pretend, of course, to have anything like your talents; they are your own, and unapproached. But I do say that I have ability; I *feel* that I have."

"It's sizzling, is it?" commented Chase. "Why

don't you put it into the business you're in already, then; the steamship firm of Willoughby, Chase, & Co.? Boom that; put on steam, and boom it for all you're worth; your uncles and I will see you through. You say you only want a chance; why on earth don't you take the one that lies before you? If you wish to convince me you know something, *that's* the way."

"The steamship concern is too slow for me; I have looked into it, and I know. I might work at it for ten years, and with the small share I have in it I should not be very rich," Walter answered. "I'm in a hurry! I am willing to give everything on my side—all my time and my strength and my brains; but I want something good on the other."

"Now you're shouting!"

"The steamship firm is routine — regular; that isn't the way you made *your* money," Walter went on.

"My way is open to everybody. It isn't covered by any patent that I know of," remarked Chase, in his dry tones.

"Yes, it is," answered Walter, immediately taking him up. "Or rather it was; the Bubble Baking-Powder was very tightly patented."

Chase grinned a little over this sally. But he was not moved towards the least concession, and Walter saw that he was not; he therefore played his last card. "I have a great deal of influence with my uncles, I think; especially with my uncle Nicholas."

" Put your money on Nicholas Willoughby, and you're safe, every time," remarked Chase, in a general way.

"I don't know whether you and Patterson care for more capital in developing your California scheme?" Walter went on. " But if you do, I could probably help you to some."

Chase looked at him. The younger man's eyes met his, bright as steel.

The millionaire walked over to a block of coquina, which had once formed part of a Spanish house; here he seated himself, established Petie Trone comfortably on his knee, and lifting his hand, tilted back still farther on his head his jessamine-decked hat. "You've been blowing about being able to work, Walter. But we can get plenty of hard workers without letting 'em into the ring. And you've been talking about being sharp. Sharp you may be. But I rather guess that when it comes to *that*, Dave Patterson and I don't need any help. Capital, however, is another matter ; it's always another matter. By enlarging our scheme at its present stage by a third (which we could do easily if your uncle Nicholas came in), we should make a much bigger pile."

There was no second block of coquina ; Walter remained standing. But his compact figure looked sturdy and firm as he stood there beside the other man. " I could not go to my uncle without knowing what I am to tell him," he remarked, after a moment.

"Certainly not!" Chase answered. Then, after further reflection (this time Walter did not break the silence), he said: "Well, see here; I may as well state at the outset that unless your uncle will come in to a pretty big tune, we don't want him at all; 'twouldn't pay us; we'd prefer to play it alone. Now your uncles don't strike me as men who would be willing to take risks. You say you have influence with 'em, or rather with Nick. But I've got no proof of that. Of course it's possible; Nick has brought you up; he's got no son—only girls; perhaps he'd be willing to do for you what he'd do for a son of his own; perhaps he really would take a risk, to give you a first-class start. But I repeat that I've no proof of your having the least influence with him. What's more, I've a healthy amount of doubt about it! Oh, I dare say *you* believe you've got a pull; you're straight as far as that goes. My notion is simply that you're mistaken, that you're barking up the wrong tree; Nicholas ain't that sort! However, as it happens to be the moment when we *could* enlarge (and double the profits), I'll give you my terms. You have convinced me at least of one thing, and that is that you're very sharp set yourself as to money-making; you want tremendously to catch on. And it's *that* I'm going to take as my security. In this way. In order to learn whether your uncle Nicholas, to oblige *you*, is willing to come in with Patterson and myself in this affair, you must first know what the affair is (as you very justly remarked);

I must therefore tell you the whole scheme — show all my hand. Now, then, if I do this, and your uncle *doesn't* take it up, then not only you don't get in yourself, but if I see the slightest indication that my confidence has been abused, I sell out of that steamship firm instanter, and, as I'm virtually the firm, you know what that will mean! And the one other property you have—that stock—you'll be surprised to see how it 'll go down to next to nothing on the street. 'Twon't hurt *me*, you know. As for you, you'll deserve it all, and more, too, for having been a dunderhead!"

"I accept the terms," answered Willoughby. "Under the circumstances, they're not even hard. If I fail, I *am* a dunderhead!—I shall be the first to say it. But I sha'n't fail." (Even at this moment, though he was intensely absorbed, his eye was struck by the contrast between the keen, hard expression of Horace Chase's face and his flower-decked hat; between the dry tones of his voice and the care with which he still held his wife's little dog, who at this instant, after a long yawn, affectionately licked the hand that held him, ringing by the motion the three small silver bells with which his young mistress had adorned his collar.) "If I am to go to California with you next week, I have no time to lose," he went on, promptly. "For I must first go to New York, of course, to see my uncle."

"Well, rather!" interpolated Chase.

"Couldn't you tell me now whatever I have to

know?" Walter continued. "This is as good a place as any. We might walk off towards that house on the right, near the shore; there is no danger of there being any jessamine *there*."

Here Ruth appeared. "Haven't you found any more?" she asked, surprised. "Mr. Willoughby, you pretended to be so much interested! As for you, Horace, where is your spirit? I thought you liked to be first in everything?"

"First in war, first in peace, first in the hearts of his countrymen," quoted Chase. "Here—you'd better put your monkey in the phaeton," he went on, passing over Mr. Trone. "He has a little rheumatism in his paw. But you must try to bear it." His voice had again its humorous tones; the penetrating look in his eyes had vanished. His wife standing there, adorned with jessamine, her face looking child-like as she stroked her dog, seemed to change the man of a moment before into an entirely different being. In reality it did not do this; but it brought out another part of his nature, and a part equally strong. Ruth had taken off her gloves; the gems which her husband had given her flashed on her hands as she lifted Mr. Trone to her shoulder and laid her cheek against his little black head. "We are going for a short walk, Willoughby and I," Chase said—"over towards that house on the shore. We'll be back soon."

"That house is Dalton's," answered Ruth, looking in that direction. "Mrs. Dalton makes the loveliest baskets, Horace; won't you get me one? They are always a little one-sided, and that makes them much more original, you know, than those that are for sale in town."

"Oh, it makes them more original, does it?" repeated Chase.

When he returned, an hour later, he brought the ·basket.

Walter Willoughby started that night for New York.

CHAPTER XII

SEVEN weeks after she had searched for the first jessamine, Ruth Chase was again at St. Augustine. But in the meanwhile she had made a long journey, having accompanied her husband to California. Chase had unexpectedly come back to Florida, to see David Patterson. When he reached New York on his return from the West, and learned that Patterson had been stricken down by illness at Palatka, he decided that the best thing he could do would be to go to Palatka himself immediately.

Ruth was delighted. "That means St. Augustine for me, doesn't it? Mother and Dolly are still there. Oh, I *am* so glad!"

"Why, Ruthie, do you care so much about it as all that? Why didn't you say so before?" said Chase, looking up from his letters. "Then I could have taken you down there in any case. Whereas now it's only this accident of Patterson's being laid up that has made me decide to go. You must *tell* me what you want, always. It's the only way we can possibly get along," he concluded, with mock severity.

Ruth gazed at the fire; for in New York, at the end of March, it was still cold. "I love St. Augustine. I was *so* happy there this winter," she said, musingly.

"Shall I build you a house near the sea-wall?" inquired her husband, gathering up his letters and telegrams. As he left the room, he paused beside her long enough to pass his hand fondly over her hair.

It was arranged that Walter Willoughby, who had returned with them from California, should also accompany them southward. For there were certain details of the Western enterprise which Patterson understood better than any one else did, as he had devoted his attention to them for six months; it now became important that these details should be explained to the younger man, in the (possible) case of Patterson's being laid up for some time longer. After one day in New York, therefore, Chase and his wife and young Willoughby started for the land of flowers. At Savannah a telegram met them: "Horace Chase, Pulaski House, Savannah. Come alone. Patterson."

"When he's sick, he is always tremendously scared," commented Chase. "I suppose we shall have to humor him. But I'll soon stir him up, and make him feel better, Walter, and then I'll wire for you to come over at once. Probably within twenty-four hours." After taking his wife to St. Augustine, he crossed to Palatka alone. Walter was to wait at St. Augustine for further directions.

The young New-Yorker agreed to everything. He was in excellent spirits; throughout the whole Cali-

16

fornian expedition he had, in truth, been living in a
state of inward excitement, though his face showed
nothing of it. For his uncle had consented, and he
(Walter) had got his foot into the stirrup at last.
The ride might be breakneck, and it might be hard ;
but at least it would not be long, and it would end
at the wished-for goal. Between two such riders as
Patterson and Horace Chase (Horace Chase especially ; best of all, Horace Chase !), he could not fall behind ; they would sweep him along between them ;
he should come in abreast. A closer acquaintance
with Chase had only increased his admiration for
the man's extraordinary mind. "If ever there was
a genius for directing big combinations, here's one
with a vengeance !" he said to himself.

On the second day after Chase's departure for Palatka, Ruth and her mother, in the late afternoon,
drove across the Sebastian River by way of the red
bridge, and thence to the barrens. These great tree-
dotted Florida prairies possess a charm for far-sighted
eyes ; their broad, unfenced, unguarded expanses,
stretching away on all sides, carpeted with flowers
and ferns, and the fans of the dwarf-palmetto, have
an air of freedom that is alluring. Walter Willoughby accompanied the two ladies, perched in the little
seat behind. He had, in fact, nothing else to do, as
Chase had as yet sent no telegram.

They drove first to the Ponce de Leon spring.
And Ruth made them drink: "so that we shall always be young !"

Leaving the spring, they drove to another part of the barren. Here the violets grew so thickly that they made the ground blue. "I must have some," said Ruth, joyously. And leaving her mother comfortably leaning back in the phaeton under her white umbrella, she jumped out and began to gather the flowers with her usual haste and impetuosity. "Why don't you come and help?" she said to Walter. "You're terribly lazy. Tie the ponies to that tree, and set to work."

Walter obeyed. But he only gathered eight violets; then he stopped, and stood fanning himself with his straw hat. "It is very warm," he said. "Won't you let me get pitcher-plants instead? There are ever so many over there. They are so large that eight of them will make a splendid show." Daily companionship for seven weeks had made him feel thoroughly at his ease with her. He had forgiven her for those old delays which she had unknowingly caused in his plans; he now associated her with his good-fortune, with his high hopes. She had been in the gayest spirits throughout their stay in California, and this, too, had chimed in with his mood.

"Pitcher-plants!" said Ruth. "Horrid, murdering things! Let them alone." But they strolled that way to look at them; and then they walked on towards a ridge, where she was sure that they should find calopogon. Beyond the ridge there was a clear pool, whose amber-colored water rested on a bed of silver sand; along one side rose the tall, delicate plumes of the *Osmunda regalis*. "Isn't it lovely?" said Ruth. "I don't believe there is anything more beautiful in all Florida!"

"Yes, one thing," thought Walter, "and that is Ruth Chase." For Ruth's beauty had deepened richly during the past half-year. It was not Walter alone who had noticed the change, every one spoke of it. At present his eyes could not but note it once more, as she stood there in her white dress under the ferns.

Then suddenly his thoughts were diverted in another direction. "I'm sure that's for me!" he exclaimed. For he had discerned in the distance a little negro boy on horseback. "He is bringing me my telegram at last—I mean the one from your husband, Mrs. Chase, which I have been expecting for two days. The stupid is following the road. I wonder if I couldn't make him see me from here, so as to gain time?" And taking off his hat, he waved it high in the air. But the child kept on his course. "Perhaps I can make him hear," said Walter. He shouted, whistled, called. But all to no purpose. "We might as well go back towards the phaeton," he suggested. And they started.

"What will the telegram be?" said Ruth, arranging her violets as she walked on. "Have you any idea?"

"A very clear one; it will tell me to arrive at Palatka as soon as possible."

"And, from Palatka, do you go back to New York?"

"Yes; immediately."

"We shall be in New York, too, by the middle of April. You are to stay in New York, aren't you?"

"Yes. It is to be my post in the game which will end, we trust, in your husband's piling up still higher his great fortune, while *I* shall have laid very solidly the foundation of mine. Good! that boy sees me at last." For the little negro, suddenly leaving the road, was galloping directly towards them over the barren, his bare feet flapping the flanks of his horse to increase its speed. Walter ran forward to meet him, took the telegram, tore open the envelope, and read the message within. Then, after rewarding the messenger (who went back to town in joyful opulence), he returned to Ruth.

"Palatka?" she said, as he came up.

"No. Something entirely different. And very unexpected. I am to go to California; I am to start to-morrow morning. And I am to stay there—live there. It will be for a year or two, I suppose; at any rate, until this new campaign of your husband's planning has been fought out and won—as won it surely will be. For Patterson, it seems, won't be able to go at present, and I am to take his place. Later, he hopes to be on the spot. But even then I am to remain, they tell me. My instructions will be here to-night by letter." He felt, inwardly, a great sense of triumph that he was considered competent

—already considered competent—to take charge of the more important post. And as he put the telegram in his pocket, the anticipation of success came to him like a breeze charged with perfume; his pulses had a firm, quick beat; the future—a future of his own choosing—unrolled itself brightly before him.

Ruth had made no reply. After a moment her silence struck him—struck him even in his preoccupation—and he turned to look at her.

Her face had a strange, stiffened aspect, as though her breathing had suddenly been arrested.

"Are you ill?" he asked, alarmed.

"Oh no; I am only tired. Where is the phaeton? I have lost sight of it."

"Over there; don't you see your mother's white parasol?"

"Let us go back to her. But no—not just yet. I'll wait a moment or two, as I'm so tired." And, turning her back to him, she sat down on a fallen pine-tree, and rested her head on her hand.

"I can bring the phaeton over here?" Walter suggested. "There is no road, but the ground is smooth."

She shook her head.

After a moment he began to talk; partly to fill the pause, partly to give expression to the thoughts that occupied his own mind—occupied it so fully that he did not give close heed to her. She was suddenly tired. Well, that was nothing unusual; it was always something sudden; generally a sudden gayety. At any rate, she could rest there comfortably until she felt able to go on. "It's very odd to me to think that to-morrow I shall be on my way to California again," he began. "That's what I get by being the poor one of the company, Mrs. Chase! Your husband, and Patterson, and my uncle, they sit comfortably at home; but they send *me* from pillar to post without the least scruple. I don't mind the going. But the staying—that's a change indeed. To live in California— I have had a good many ideas in my mind, but I confess I have never had that." He laughed. But it was easy to see that the idea pleased him greatly.

Ruth turned. Her eyes met his. And then, startled, amazed, the young man read in their depths something that was to him an intense surprise.

At the same moment she rose. "I can go now. Mother will be wondering where I am," she said.

He accompanied her in silence, his mind in a whirl. She said a few words on ordinary subjects. Every now and then her voice came near failing entirely, and she paused. But she always began again. Just before she reached the phaeton she took a gray gauze veil from her pocket, and tied it hastily across her face under her broad-brimmed hat. Mrs. Franklin was waiting for them in lazy tranquillity. While Walter untied the ponies, Ruth took the small seat behind. "Just for a change," she explained. Walter, therefore, in her vacant place, drove them back to town. Having taken Mrs. Franklin home, he left Ruth at her own door. "As I'm off early to-morrow morning, Mrs. Chase, I'll bid you good-by now," he said, as the waiting servant came forward to the ponies' heads. She gave him her hand. He could not see her face distinctly through that baffling gray veil.

That evening at eleven o'clock he passed the house again; he was taking a farewell stroll on the sea-wall. As he went by, he saw that there was a light in the drawing-room. "She has not gone to bed," he thought. He jumped down from the wall, crossed the road, and, going up the steps, put his hand on the bell-knob. But a sudden temptation took possession of him, and, instead of ringing, he opened the door. "If her mother is with her, I'll pretend that I found it ajar," he said to himself. But there were no voices, all was still. His step had made no sound on the thick rugs, and, advancing, he drew aside a curtain. On a couch in a corner of the drawing-room was Ruth Chase, alone, her face hidden in her hands.

She started to her feet as he came in. "After all, Mrs. Chase, I found that I wanted more of a good-by—" he began. And then, a second time, in her eyes he read the astonishing, bewildering story. "She is still unconscious of what it is," he thought. "If I go away at once—at once and forever—no harm is done. And that is what I shall do." This was his intention, and he knew that he should follow it. The very certainty, however, made him allow himself a moment or two of delay. For how beautiful she was, and how deeply she loved him! He could not help offering, as it were, a tribute to both; it seemed to him that he would be a boor not to do so. And then, before he knew it, he had gone further. "You see how it is with me," he began. "You see that I love you; I myself did not know it until now." (What was this he was telling her? And somehow, for the moment, it was true!) "Don't think that I do not understand," he went on. "I understand all—all—" While he was uttering these words he met her eyes again. And then he felt that he was losing his head. "What am I doing? I'm not an abject fool!" he managed to say to himself, mutely—mutely but violently. And he left the house.

It took all his strength to do it.

CHAPTER XIII

HORACE CHASE, meanwhile, had arrived at Palatka, and opened the discussion with David Patterson which ended in the decision to despatch young Willoughby to California without delay. Having sent these instructions, he remained at Palatka two days longer, his intention being to cross, on the third day, to St. Augustine, get his wife and go back to New York, stopping on the way at Raleigh in order to see Jared. Always prompt, as soon as the question of the representative in California was settled, his thoughts had turned towards his brother-in-law; the proper moment had now arrived for fulfilling his promises concerning him. But in answer to this note to Ruth, mentioning this plan, there had come a long epistle from Mrs. Franklin. Ruth, she wrote, wanted to go north by sea; it was a sudden fancy that had come to her. Her wish was to go by the *Dictator* to Charleston, and there change for the larger steamer. "As Dolly and I intend to start towards L'Hommedieu next week, Ruth's idea is that we could go together as far as Charleston; for the rest of the way, Félicité could look after her. You need not therefore take the trouble to come to St. Augustine at all, she says; you can go directly from Palatka to Raleigh. All this sounds a little self-willed. But, my dear Mr. Chase, if we spoiled her more or less in the beginning, you must acknowledge that *you* have carried on the process! In the eighteen months that have passed since your marriage, have you ever refused compliance with even one of her whims? I think not. On the contrary, I fear you encourage them; you always seem to me to be waiting, with an inward laugh, to see what on earth she will suggest next!" Thus wrote the mother in a joking strain. Then, turning to the subject which was more important to her, she filled three sheets with her joyful anticipations concerning her son. "Insist upon his resigning his present place on the spot," she urged; "take no denial. Make him go *with* you to New York. *Then* you will be sure of him."

"The old lady seems to think he will be a great acquisition," said Chase to himself, humorously.

Her statement that he had, from the first, allowed his wife to follow her fancies unchecked was a true one. It amused him to do this, amused him to watch an idea dawn, and then, in a few minutes, take such entire possession of her that it shook her hard—only to leave her and vanish with equal suddenness. The element of the unexpected in her was a constant entertainment to him. Her heedlessness, her feminine indifference to logic, to the inevitable sequences of cause and effect—this, too, had given him many a moment of mirth. If her face had been less lovely, these characteristics would have worn, perhaps, an-

other aspect. But in that case Horace Chase would
not have been their judge; for it was this alluring
beauty (unconsciously alluring) which had attracted
him, which had made him fall in love with her. He
was a man whose life, up to the time of his engagement to Ruth, had been irregular. But, though irregular, it had not been uncontrolled; he had always been able to say, " Thus far; no farther !" But
though her beauty had been the first lure, he was now
profoundly attached to his wife; his pride in her
was profound, his greatest pleasure was to make her
happy.

" By sea to New York, is it ?" he said to himself,
as his eyes hastily glanced through the remainder of
Mrs. Franklin's long letter (that is, the three sheets
about Jared). " Well, she is a capital sailor, that's
one comfort. Let's see; which of our steamers will
she hit at Charleston ?"

He was not annoyed because Ruth had not written,
herself; Ruth did not like to write letters. But it
was a surprise to him that she should, of her own
accord, relinquish an opportunity to see her brother.
" I reckon she is counting upon my taking him up to
New York with me, so that she'll see him on the
dock waiting for her when her steamer comes in,"
he thought. " I guess she knows, too, that I'm likely to succeed better with Jared when *she's* out of the
business entirely. Franklin isn't going to be boosted
by his sister—that's been his fixed notion all along.
He doesn't suspect that his sister's nowhere in the

matter compared with his wife; his whole position
of being independent of *me*, and all that, has been so
undermined and honeycombed by Gen, that, in reality, his sticking it out there at Raleigh is a farce!
But he doesn't know it. It's lucky he don't!"

Ruth had her way, as usual. Chase went northward from Palatka to Savannah, where he had business; thence he was to go to Raleigh. His wife,
meanwhile, remained in St. Augustine for one week
longer, and her mother and sister, closing their own
home, spent the time with her.

Their last day came; they were to leave St. Augustine on the morrow. Early in the afternoon, Ruth
disappeared. When they were beginning to wonder
where she was, Félicité brought them a note. Mrs.
Franklin read it, and laughed. " She has gone for a
sail; by herself!"

" She might have told us. We could have gone
with her," said Dolly, irritably. " I don't like her
being alone."

" Oh, she is safe enough, as far as that goes,"
answered the mother, comfortably. " She has taken
old Donato, who, in spite of his seventy years, is an
excellent sailor; and he has, too, a very good boat."

Dolly went to the window. " You are not in the
least thinking of Ruth, mother! You are thinking
of Jared; you are thinking that if he takes that place
in New York, we must somehow get up there to see
him this summer; and you are planning to go to

that boarding-house on Staten Island that the commodore told you about."

Mrs. Franklin, who really was thinking of Staten Island, rolled a lamplighter the wrong way. "It is happening oftener and oftener!" she said to herself. "Is she going to die?" And she glanced towards her invalid daughter with the old pang of loving pity quickened for the moment to trepidation.

Dolly's back was turned; she was gazing down the inlet. The house, which was formerly the residence of General Worth, the Military Governor of Florida, commanded an uninterrupted view of the Matanzas north and south, and, over the low line of Anastasia Island, even the smallest sail going towards the ocean was visible. But in spite of this long expanse of water, Dolly could not see old Donato's boat. "His Grand suspects nothing! Are mothers always so blind?" she thought. "So secure? But she shall never know anything through *me*—dear old Grand! Ruth has of course gone to say good-bye to the places which are associated in her mind with that hateful Willoughby. If I could only have known it, I would have kept her from it at any price. These long hours alone which she covets so—they are the worst things, the worst!"

Ruth's boat was far out of sight; at this moment she was landing on Anastasia at the point where she had disembarked with Walter on the day of the excursion. Telling the old Minorcan to wait for her, she sought for the little Carib trail, and followed it inland to the pool. Here she spent half an hour, seated in the loop of the vine where she had sat before. Then, rising, she slowly retraced their former course along the low ridge.

Since Walter's departure — he had left St. Augustine at dawn after that strange evening visit — Ruth had been the prey of two moods, tossed from one to the other helplessly; for the feelings which these moods by turn excited were so strong that she had had no volition of her own—she had been powerless against them. One of these mental states (the one that possessed her now) was joy. The other was aching pain.

For her fate had come upon her, as it was sure from the first to come. And it found her defenceless; those who should have foreseen it had neither guarded her against it, nor trained her so that she could guard herself. She had no conception of life —no one had ever given her such a conception—as a lesson in self-control; from her childhood all her wishes had been granted. It is true that these wishes had been simple. But that was because she had known no other standard; the degree of indulgence (and of self-indulgence) was as great as if they had been extravagant. If her disposition as a girl had been selfish, it was unconscious selfishness; for her mother, her elder sister, and her brother had never required anything from her save that she should be happy. With her joyous nature, life had always been delightful to her, and her marriage had only made it more delightful. For Horace Chase, unconsciously, had adopted the habit that the family had always had; they never expected Ruth to take responsibility, to be serious, and, in the same way, he never expected it. And he loved to see her contented, just as they had loved it. There was some excuse for them all in the fact that Ruth's contentment was a very charming thing—it was so natural and exuberant.

And, on her side, this girl had married Horace Chase first of all because she liked him. What he had done for her brother, and his wealth—these two influences had come only second, and would not have sufficed without the first; her affection (for it was affection) had been won by his kindness to herself. Since their marriage his lavish generosity had pleased her, and gratified her imagination. But his delicate consideration for her—this girl nineteen years younger than himself — and his unselfishness, these she had not appreciated; she supposed that husbands were, as a matter of course, like that. As it happened, she had not a single girl friend who had married, from whose face (if not from whose words also) she might have divined other ways. Thus she had lived on, accepting everything in her easy, epicurean fashion, until into her life had come love—this love for Walter Willoughby.

Walter devoting himself to Mrs. Chase for his own purposes, had never had the slightest intention of falling in love with her; in truth, such a catastrophe

(it would have seemed to him nothing less) would
have marred all his plans. He had wished only to
amuse her. And, in the beginning, it had been in
truth his gay spirits which had attracted Ruth, for
she possessed gay spirits herself. She had been unaware of the nature of the feeling which was taking
possession of her; her realization went no further
than that life was now much more interesting; and,
with her rich capacity for enjoyment, she had grasped
this new pleasure eagerly. It was this which had
made her beauty so much more rich and vivid. It
was this which had caused her to exclaim, "How
delightful it is to live!" If obstacles had interfered,
the pain of separation might have opened her eyes,
at an earlier period, to the nature of her attachment.
But, owing to the circumstances of the case, the
junior partner had been with Mr. and Mrs. Chase
almost daily ever since their return from Europe.
That announcement, therefore, out on the barrens—
his own announcement—of his departure the next
morning, and for an indefinite stay, had come upon
her like the chill of sudden death. And then in the
evening, while she was still benumbed and pulseless,
had followed his strange, short visit, and the wild
thrill of joy in her heart over his declaration of his
own love for her. For he had said it, he had
said it!

These two conflicting tides — the pain of his
absence and the joy of his love — had held entire
possession of her ever since. But passionate though

17

her nature was, in matters of feeling it was deeply reticent as well, and no one had noticed any change in her save Dolly, Dolly who had divined something from her sister's new desire to be alone. Never before had Ruth wished to be alone ; but now she went off for long walks by herself; and this plan for returning to New York by sea — that was simply the same thing. From the moment of Ruth's engagement, Dolly had been haunted by a terrible fear. Disliking Horace Chase herself, she did not believe that he would be able to keep forever a supreme place in his wife's heart. And then ? Would Ruth be content to live on, as so many wives live, with this supreme place unoccupied ? It was her dread of this, a dread which had suddenly become personified, that had made her form one of almost all the excursions of this Florida winter ; she had gone whenever she was able, and often when she was unable — at least, she would be present, she would mount guard.

But in spite of her guardianship, something had evidently happened. What was it ? Was this desire of Ruth's to be alone a good sign or a bad sign ? Did it come from happiness or unhappiness ? "If it is unhappiness, she will throw it off," Dolly told herself. " She hates suffering. She will manage, somehow, to rid herself of it." Thus she tried to reassure herself.

Ruth gave not only the afternoon but the evening to her pilgrimage ; she visited all the places where she had been with Walter. When the twilight had deepened to night, she came back to town, and, still accompanied by Donato, she went to the old fort, and out the shell road; finally she paid a visit to Andalusia. A bright moon was shining; over the low land blew a perfumed breeze. Andalusia was deserted, Mrs. Kip had gone to North Carolina. Bribing Uncle Jack, the venerable ex-slave who lived in a little cabin under the bananas near the gate, Ruth went in, and leaving her body-guard, the old fisherman, resting on a bench, she wandered alone among the flowers. "You see that I love you. I myself did not know it until now"—this was the talisman which was making her so happy; two brief phrases uttered on the spur of the moment, phrases preceded by nothing, followed by nothing. It was a proof of the simplicity of her nature, its unconsciousness of half-motives, half-meanings, that she should think these few words so conclusive. But to her they were final. Direct herself, she supposed that others were the same. She did not go beyond her talisman; she did not reason about it, or plan. In fact, she did not think at all; she only felt—felt each syllable take a treasure in her heart, and brooded over it happily. And as she wandered to and fro in the moonlight, it was as well that Walter did not see her. He did not love her—no. He had no wish to love her; it would have interfered with all his plans. But if he had beheld her now, he would have succumbed—succumbed, at least, for the moment, as he had done before. He was not there, however. And he had no intention of being there, of being anywhere near Horace Chase's wife for a long time to come. "I'll keep out of *that!*" he had said to himself, determinedly.

It was midnight when at last Ruth returned home, coming into the drawing-room like a vision, in her white dress, with her arms full of flowers.

"Well, have you had enough of prowling?" asked her mother, sleepily. "I must say that it appears to agree with you!"

Even Dolly was reassured by her sister's radiant eyes.

But later, when Félicité had left her mistress, then, if Dolly could have opened the locked door, her comfort would have vanished; for the other mood had now taken possession, and lying prone on a couch, with her face hidden, Ruth was battling with her grief.

Pain was so new to her, sorrow so new! Incapable of enduring (this was what Dolly had hoped), many times during the last ten days she had revolted against her suffering, and to-night she was revolting anew. "I *will* not care for him; it makes me too wretched!" Leaving the couch, she strode angrily to and fro. The three windows of the large room—it was her dressing-room—stood open to the warm sea-air; she had put out the candles, but the moonlight, entering in a flood, reflected her white figure in the long mirrors as she came and went. Félicité had braided her hair for the night, but the strands had become loosened, and the thick, waving mass flowed over her shoulders. "I will not think of him; I will *not!*" And to emphasize it, she struck her clinched hand with all her force on the stone window-seat. "It is cut. I'm glad! It will make me remember that I am *not* to think of him." She was intensely in earnest in her resolve, and, to help herself towards other thoughts, she began to look feverishly at the landscape outside, as though it was absolutely necessary that she should now resee and recount each point and line. "There is the top of the light-house — and there is the ocean — and there are the bushes near the quarry." She leaned out of the window so as to see farther. "There is the North Beach; there is the fort and the lookout tower." Thus for a few minutes her weary mind followed the guidance of her will. "There is the bathing-house. And there is the dock and the club-house; and there is the Basin. Down there on the right is Fish Island. How lovely it all is! I wish I could stay here forever. But even to-morrow night I shall be gone; I shall be on the *Dictator*. And then will come Charleston. And then New York. (Her mind had now escaped again.) "And then the days—and the months—and the *years* without him! Oh, what shall I do? What shall I do?" And the pain descending, sharper than ever, she sank down, and with her arms on the window-seat and her face on her arms, and cried and cried—cried so long that at last her shoulders fell forward stoopingly, and her whole slender frame lost its strength, and drooped against the window-sill like a broken reed. Her despair held no plan for trying to see Walter, her destiny seemed to her fixed ; her revolts had not been against that destiny, but against her pain. But something was upon her now which was stronger than herself, stronger than her love of ease, stronger than her dread of suffering. Dolly knew her well. But there were some depths which even Dolly did not know.

Dawn found her still there, her hands and feet cold, her face white ; she had wept herself out—there were no more tears left. The sun came up; she watched it mechanically. "Félicité mustn't find me here," she thought. She dragged herself to her feet ; all her muscles were stiff. Then going to the bed-room, she fell into a troubled sleep.

It would be too much to say that during the entire night her mind had not once turned towards her husband. She had thought of him now and then, much as she had thought of her mother ; as, for in-stance—would her mother see any change in her face the next morning, after this night of tears ? Would her husband see any at New York when he arrived ? Whenever she remembered either one of them, she felt a sincere desire not to make them unhappy. But this was momentary ; during most of the night the emotions that belonged to her nature swept over her with such force that she had no power, no will, to think of anything save herself.

CHAPTER XIV

HORACE CHASE, following the suggestion of Mrs.
Franklin (a suggestion which had come in reality
from Ruth), travelled northward to Raleigh from
Palatka without crossing to St. Augustine. He went
"straight through," as he called it; when he was
alone he always went straight through. He was no
more particular as to where he slept than he was as
to what he ate. Reaching Raleigh in the evening, he
went in search of his brother-in-law. He had not
sent word that he was coming. " I won't give him
time to trot out all his objections beforehand," he had
said to himself. He intended to make an attempt to
arrange the matter with Jared without calling in the
aid of Genevieve. " If I fail, there'll always be time
to bring her on the scene. If I succeed, it'll take her
down a bit; and that won't hurt her!" he thought,
with an inward smile.

Ruth's " horrid Raleigh " looked very pretty as he
walked through its lighted streets. The boarding-
house where Jared had passed the winter proved to
be an old mansion, which, in its day, had possessed
claims to dignity; it was large, with two wings running backward, and the main building had a high
pointed roof with dormer-windows. The front was

even with the street; but the street itself was rural, with its two long lines of magnificent trees, which formed the divisions (otherwise rather vague) between the sidewalks and the broad expanse of the sandy roadway. Chase's knock was answered by a little negro boy, whose head did not reach the doorknob. "Mas' Franklin? Yassah. He's done gone out. Be in soon, I reckon," he added, hopefully.

Chase, after a moment's reflection, decided to go in and wait.

"Show you in de parlo,' or right up in his own room, boss?" demanded the infant, anxiously. "Dere's a party in de parlo'." This statement was confirmed by the sound of music from within.

"A party, is there? I guess I'll go up, then," said Chase.

The child started up the stairs. His legs were so short that he had to mount to each step with both feet, one after the other, before he could climb to the next. These legs and feet and his arms were bare; the rest of his small, plump person was clad in a little jacket and very short breeches of pink calico. There were two long flights of stairs, and a shorter flight to the attic; the pink breeches had the air of climbing an Alp. Presently Chase took up the little toiler, candle and all.

"You can tell me which way to go," he said. "What's your name?"

"Pliny Abraham, sah."

"Do you like Mr. Franklin?"

"Mas' Franklin is de bes' body in dishyer house!" declared Pliny Abraham, shrilly.

"The best what?"

"De bes' body. We'se got twenty-five bodies now, boss. Sometimes dere's twenty-eight."

"Oh, you mean boarders?"

"Yassah. Bodies."

Jared's room was in the attic. Pliny Abraham, who had been intensely serious, began to grin as his bearer, after putting him down, placed a dime in each of his little pink pockets; then he dashed out of the room, his black legs disappearing so suddenly that Chase had the curiosity to follow to the top of the stairs and look over. Pliny had evidently slid down the banisters; for he was already embarked on the broader rail of the flight below.

Twenty minutes later there was a step on the stair; the door opened, and Jared Franklin came in.

"They didn't tell you I was here?" said Chase, as they shook hands.

"No. Mrs. Nightingale is usually very attentive; too much so, in fact; she's a bother!" Jared answered. "To-night, however, there's a party down below, and she has the supper on her mind."

"Is Pliny Abraham to serve it?"

"You've seen him, have you?" said Jared, who was now lighting a lamp. "Confounded smell—petroleum!" And he threw up the sash of the window.

"I'm on my way up to New York, and I came

across from Goldsborough on purpose to see you, Franklin, on a matter of business," Chase began. "Ruth isn't with me this time; she took a notion to go north by sea. Your mother and sister, I expect, will be seeing her off to-morrow from Charleston; then, after a little rest for Miss Dolly, they're to go to L'Hommedieu."

"They'll stop here, won't they?" asked Jared, who was standing at the window in order to get air which was untainted by the odor of the lamp.

"Perhaps," Chase answered. He knew that Dolly and her mother believed that by the time they should reach Raleigh, Jared would have already left. "Well, the gist of the matter, Franklin, is about this," he went on. And then, tilting his chair back so that his long legs should have more room, and with his thumbs in the pockets of his waistcoat, he began deliberately to lie.

For in the short space of time which had elapsed since his eyes first rested upon Ruth's brother, he had entirely altered his plan. His well-arranged arguments and explanations about the place in New York in connection with his California scheme—all these he had abandoned; something must be invented which would require no argument at all, something which should attract Jared so strongly that he would of his own accord accept it on the spot, and start northward the next morning. "Once in New York, in our big house there, with Gen (for I shall telegraph her to come on) and Ruth and the best doctors, perhaps the poor chap can be persuaded to give up, and take a good long rest," he thought.

For he had been greatly shocked by the change in Jared's appearance. When he had last seen him, the naval officer had been gaunt; but now he was wasted. His eyes had always been sad; but now they were deeply sunken, with dark hollows under them and over them. "He looks *bad*," Chase said to himself, emphatically. "This sort of life's been too much for him, and Gen's got a good deal to answer for!" The only ornament of the whitewashed wall was a large photograph of the wife; her handsome face, with its regular outlines and calm eyes, presided serenely over the attic room of the lonely husband.

To have to contrive something new, plausible, and effective, in two minutes' time, might have baffled most men. But Horace Chase had never had a mind of routine, he had always been a free lance; original conceptions and the boldest daring, accompanied by an extraordinary personal sagacity, had formed his especial sort of genius—a genius which had already made him, at thirty-nine, a millionaire many times over. His invention, therefore, when he unrolled it, had an air of perfect veracity. It had to do with a steamer, which (so he represented) a man whom he knew had bought, in connection with what might be called, perhaps, a branch of his own California scheme, although a branch with which he himself had nothing whatever to do. This man needed an experienced officer to take the steamer immediately from San Francisco to the Sandwich Islands, and thence on a cruise to various other islands in the South Pacific. "The payment, to a navy man like you, ought to be pretty good. But I can't say what the exact figure will be," he went on, warily, "because I'm not in it myself, you see. He's a good deal of a skinflint" (here he coolly borrowed a name for the occasion, the name of a capitalist well known in New York); "but he's sound. It's a *bona fide* operation; I can at least vouch for that. The steamer is first-class, and you can pick out your own crew. There'll be a man aboard to see to the trading part of it; all *you've* got to do is to sail the ship." And in his driest and most practical voice he went on enumerating the details.

Jared knew that his brother-in-law had more than once been engaged in outside speculations on a large scale; his acquaintance, therefore, with kindred spirits, men who bought ocean steamers and sent them on cruises, did not surprise him. The plan attracted him; he turned it over in his mind to see if there were any reasons why he should not accept it. There seemed to be none. To begin with, Horace Chase had nothing to do with it; he should not be indebted to *him* for anything save the chance. In addition, it would not be an easy berth, with plenty to get and little to do, like the place at Charleston; on the contrary, a long voyage of this sort would call out all he knew. And certainly he was sick of his present life —deathly sick!

Chase had said to himself: "Fellows who go down so low—and he's at the end of *his* rope; that's plain—go up again like rockets sometimes, just give 'em a chance."

Jared, however, showed no resemblance to a rocket. He agreed, after a while, to "undertake the job," as Chase called it, and he agreed, also, to start the next morning with his brother-in-law for New York, where the final arrangements were to be made; but his assent was given mechanically, and his voice sounded weak, as though, physically, he had very little strength. Mentally there was more stir. "I shall be deuced glad to be on salt-water again," he said. "I dare say *you* think it's a very limited life," he went on (and in the phrase there lurked something scornful).

"Well," answered Chase, with his slight drawl, "that depends upon what a man wants, what he sets out to do." He put his hands down in the pockets of his trousers, and looked at the lamp reflectively; then he transferred his gaze to Jared. "I guess you've got a notion, Franklin, that I care for nothing but money? And that's where you make a mistake. For 'tain't the money; it's the making it. Making it (that is, in large sums) is the best sort of a game. If you win, there's nothing like it. It's sport, *that* is! It's fun! To get down to the bed-rock of the subject, it's the power. Yes, sir, that's it—the power! The knowing you've got it, and that other men know it too, and feel your hand on the reins! For a big pile is something more than a pile; it's a proof that

a man's got brains. (I mean, of course, if he has
made it himself; I'm not talking now about fortunes
that are inherited, or are simply rolled up by a rise in
real estate.) As to the money taken alone, of course
it's a good thing to have, and I'm going on making
more as long as I can; I like it, and I know how.
But about the disposing of it" (here he took his
hands out of his pockets and folded his arms), "I
don't mind telling you that I've got other ideas.
My family—if I have a family—will be provided for.
After that, I've a notion that I may set aside a certain sum for scientific research (I understand that's
the term). I don't know much about science myself; but I've always felt a sort of general interest in
it, somehow."

"Oh, you intend to be a benefactor, do you?" said
Jared, ironically. "I hope, at least, that your endow-
ment won't be open to everybody. It's only fair to
tell you that, in *my* opinion, one of the worst evils of
our country to-day is this universal education—
education of all classes indiscriminately."

Chase looked at him for a moment in silence.
Then, with a quiet dignity which was new to the
other man, he answered, "I don't think I understand
you."

"Oh yes, you do," responded Jared, with a little
laugh. But he felt somewhat ashamed of his speech,
and he bore it off by saying, "Are you going to
found a new institution? Or leave it in a lump to
Harvard?"

"I haven't got as far as that yet. I thought perhaps Ruth might like to choose," Chase answered, his voice softening a little as he pronounced his wife's name.

"Ruth? Much *she* knows about it!" said the brother, amused. In his heart he was thinking, "Well, at any rate, he isn't one of the blowers, and that's a consolation! He is going to 'plank down' handsomely for 'scientific research.' (I wonder if he thinks they'll research another baking-powder!) But he isn't going to shout about it. The fact is that this is the first time I have ever heard him speak of himself, and his own ideas. What he said just now about making money, that's his credo, evidently. Pretty dry one! But, for such a fellow as he is, natural enough, I suppose."

Chase's credo, if such it was, was ended; he showed no disposition to speak further of himself; on the contrary, he turned the conversation towards his companion. For as the minutes had passed, more and more Jared seemed to him ill — profoundly changed. "I'm afraid, Franklin, that your health isn't altogether first-class nowadays?" he said, tentatively.

"Oh, I'm well enough, except that just now there's some sort of an intermittent fever hanging about me. But it's very slight, and it only appears occasionally; I dare say it will leave me as soon as I'm fairly out of this hole of a place," Jared answered, in a dull tone.

"He must be mighty glad to get away, and yet he

doesn't rally worth a cent," thought Chase, with inward concern. "I say," he went on, aloud, "as there's a party in the house, why not come along down to the hotel and sleep there? I'm going to have some sort of a lunch when I go back; you might keep me company?"

Jared, however, made a gesture of repugnance. "I couldn't eat; I've no appetite. The party doesn't trouble me—I'll go to bed. There'll be plenty to do in the morning, if we are to catch that nine o'clock train."

Chase therefore took leave, and Jared accompanied him down to the street door. Dancing was going on in the parlors on each side of the hall, and the two, as they passed, caught a glimpse of pretty girls in white, with flowers in their hair. After making an early appointment for the next day, Chase said good-night, and turned down the tree-shaded street towards his hotel.

His step was never a hurried one; he had not, therefore, gone far when a person, who had left the house two minutes after his own departure, succeeded in overtaking him. "If you please—will you stop a moment?" said this person. She was panting, for she had been running.

Chase turned; by the light from a street-lamp, which reached them flickeringly through the foliage, he saw a woman. Her face was in the shadow, but a large flower, poised stiffly on the top of her head, caught the light and gleamed whitely.

"I am Mrs. Nightingale," she began. "Mr. Franklin, the gentleman you called awn this evenin', is a member of my family. And I've been right anxious about Mr. Franklin; I'm thankful somebody has come who knows him. For indeed, sir, he's more sick than he likes to acknowledge. I've been watchin' for you to come down; but when I saw *he* was with you, I had to wait until he'd gone up again; then I slipped out and ran after you."

"I've been noticing that he looked bad, ma'am," Chase answered.

"Oh, sir, somebody ought to be with him; he has fever at night, and when it comes awn, he's out of his head. I've sat up myself three nights lately to keep watch. He locks his do'; but there's an empty room next to his where I stay, so that if he comes out I can see that he gets no harm."

"He walks about, then?"

"In his own room — yes, sir; an' he talks, an' raves."

"Couldn't you have managed to have him see a doctor, ma'am?"

"I've done my best, but he won't hear of it. You see, it only comes awn every third night or so, an' he has no idea himself how bad it is. In the mawnin' it's gone, an' then all he says is that the breakfast is bad. He goes to his business every day regular, though he looks so po'ly. And he doesn't eat enough to keep a fly alive."

Chase reflected. "I'll have a doctor go with us on

18

the sly to-morrow," he thought, "and I'll engage a whole sleeper at Weldon to go through to New York. I'll wire to Gen to start at once; she needn't be more than a day behind us if she hurries." Then he went on, aloud: "Do you think he is likely to be feverish to-night, ma'am?"

"I hope not, sir, as last night was bad."

"I guess it will be better, then, not to wake him up and force a doctor upon him now, as he told me he was going to bed. I intend to take him north with me to-morrow morning, ma'am, and in the meantime—that little room you spoke of next to his—*I'll* occupy it to-night, if you'll let me? I'll just go down to the hotel and get my bag, and be back soon. I'm his brother-in-law," Chase continued, shaking hands with her, "and we're all much obliged, ma'am, for what you've done; it was mighty kind—the keeping watch at night."

He went to his hotel, made a hasty supper, and returned, bag in hand, before the half-hour was out. Mrs. Nightingale ushered him down one of the long wings to her own apartment at the end, a comfortless, crowded little chamber, full of relics of the war—her husband's sword and uniform (he was shot at Gettysburg); his portrait; the portrait of her brother, also among the slain; photographs of their graves; funeral wreaths and flags.

"Excuse my bringin' you here, sir; it's the only place I have. Mr. Franklin hasn't gone to bed yet; I slipped up a moment ago to see, and there was a

light under his do'. I'm afraid it would attract his
attention if you should go up now, sir, for he knows
that the next room is unoccupied."

" *You've* occupied it, ma'am. But I guess you
know how to step pretty soft," Chase answered, gallantly. For now that he saw this good Samaritan in
a brighter light, he appreciated the depth of her charity. The mistress of the boarding-house was the
personification of chronic fatigue; her dim eyes, her
worn face, her stooping figure, and the enlarged
knuckles and bones of her hands, all told of hard toil
and care. Her thin hair was re-enforced behind by
huge palpably false braids of another shade, and the
preposterous edifice, carried over the top of the head,
was adorned, in honor of the party, by the large
white camellia, placed exactly in the centre—"like a
locomotive head-light," Chase thought—which had attracted his notice in the street. But in spite of her
grotesque coiffure, no one with a heart could laugh at
her. The goodness in her faded face was so genuine
and beautiful that inwardly he saluted it. "She's
the kind that 'll never be rested *this* side the grave,"
he said to himself.

Left alone in her poor little temple of memories, he
went to the window and looked out. It was midnight,
and the waning moon — the same moon which had
been full when Ruth made her happy pilgrimage at St.
Augustine — was now rising in its diminished form ;
diminished though it was, it gave out light enough to
show the Northerner that the old house had at the

back, across both stories, covered verandas — "galleries," Mrs. Nightingale called them. Above, the pointed roof of the main building towered up dark against the star-decked sky, and from one of its dormer-windows came a broad gleam of light. "That's Jared's room," thought Chase. "He is writing to Gen, telling her all about it; sick as he is, he sat up to do it. Meanwhile *she* was comfortably asleep at ten."

At last, when Jared had finally gone to bed, Mrs. Nightingale (who made no more sound than a mouse) led the way up to the attic. Chase followed her, shoeless, treading as cautiously as he could, and established himself in the empty room with his door open, and a lighted candle in the hall outside. By two o'clock the party down-stairs was over; the house sank into silence.

There had been no sound from Jared. "He's all right; I shall get him safely off to-morrow," thought the watcher, with satisfaction. "At New York, if he's well enough to talk, I shall have to invent another yarn about that steamer. But probably the doctors will tell him on the spot that he isn't able to undertake it. So that 'll be the end of *that*."

His motionless position ended by cramping him; the chair was hard; each muscle of both legs seemed to have a separate twitch. "I might as well lie down on the bed," he thought; "there, at least, I can stretch out."

He was awakened by a sound; startled, he sat up,

listening. Jared, in the next room, was talking. The words could not be distinguished; the tone of the voice was strange. Then the floor vibrated; Jared had risen, and was walking about. His voice grew louder. Chase noiselessly went into the hall, and stood listening at the door. There was no light within, and he ventured to turn the handle. But the bolt was fast. A white figure now stole up the stairs and joined him; it was Mrs. Nightingale, wrapped in a shawl. "Oh, I heard him 'way from my room! He has never been so bad as this before," she whispered.

Chase had always been aware that the naval officer disliked him; that is, that he had greatly disliked the idea of his sister's marriage. "If he sees me now, when he is out of his head, will it make him more violent? Would it be better to have a stranger go in first?—the doctor?"—these were the questions that occupied his mind while Mrs. Nightingale was whispering her frightened remark.

From the room now came a wild cry. That decided him. "I am going to burst in the lock," he said to his companion, hurriedly. "Call up some one to help me hold him, if necessary." His muscular frame was strong; setting his shoulder against the door, after two or three efforts he broke it open.

But the light from the candle outside showed that the room was empty, and, turning, he ran at full speed down the three flights of stairs, passing white-robed, frightened groups (for the whole house was

now astir), and, unlocking the back door, he dashed
into the court-yard behind, his face full of dread.
But there was no lifeless heap on the ground. Then,
hastily, he looked up.

Dawn was well advanced, though the sun had not
yet risen ; the clear, pure light showed that nothing
was lying on the roof of the upper gallery, as he had
feared would be the case. At the same instant, his
eyes caught sight of a moving object above; coming
up the steep slope of the roof from the front side,
at first only the head visible, then the shoulders,
and finally the whole body, outlined against the violet sky, appeared Jared Franklin. He was partly
dressed, and he was talking to himself ; when he
reached the apex of the roof he paused, brandishing
his arms with a wild gesture, and swaying unsteadily.

Several persons were now in the court-yard ; men
had hurried out. Two woman joined them, and
looked up. But when they saw the swaying figure
above, they ran back to the shelter of the hall, veil-
ing their eyes and shuddering. In a few moments
all the women in the house had gathered in this
lower hall, frightened and tearful.

Chase, meanwhile, outside, was pulling off his
socks. "Get ladders," he said, quickly, to the other
men. "I'm going up. I'll try to hold him."

"Oh, how _can_ you get there?" asked Mrs. Nightingale, sobbing.

"The same way he did," Chase answered, as he
ran up the stairs.

The men remonstrated. Two of them hurried after him. But he was ahead, and, mounting to the sill of Jared's window, he stepped outside. Then, not allowing himself to look at anything but the apex directly above him, he walked slowly and evenly towards it up the steep incline, his head and shoulders bent forward, his bare feet clinging to the moss-grown shingles, while at intervals he touched with the tips of his fingers the shingles that faced him, as a means of steadying himself.

Down in the court-yard no word was now spoken. But the gazers drew their breath audibly. Jared appeared to be unaware of any one below; his eyes, though wide open, did not see the man who was approaching. Chase perceived this, as soon as he himself had reached the top, and he instantly took advantage of it; he moved straight towards Jared on his hands and knees along the line of the ridge-pole. When he had come within reach, he let himself slip down a few inches to a chimney that was near; then, putting his left arm round this chimney as a support, he stretched the right upward, and with a sudden grasp seized the other man, throwing him down and pinning him with one and the same motion. Jared fell on his back, half across the ridge, with his head hanging over one slope and his legs and feet over the other; it was this position which enabled Chase to hold him down. The madman (his frenzy came from a violent form of inflammation of the brain) struggled desperately. His strength seemed so prodigious that to the watchers below it appeared impossible that the rescuer could save him, or even save himself. The steep roof had no parapet; and the cruel pavement below was stone; the two bodies, grappled in a death-clutch, must go down together.

"Oh, *pray!* Pray to God!" called a woman's voice from the court below.

She spoke to Chase. But at that moment nothing in him could be spared from his own immense effort; not only all the powers of his body, but of his heart and mind and soul as well, were concentrated upon the one thing he had to do. He accomplished it; feeling his arm growing weak, he made a tremendous and final attempt to jam down still harder the breast he grasped, and the blow (for it amounted to a blow) reduced Jared to unconsciousness; his hands fell back, his ravings ceased. His strength had been merely the fictitious force of fever; in reality he was weak.

The ladders came. Both men were saved.

"Come, now, if the roof had been only three inches above the ground—how then?" Chase said, impatiently, as, after the visit of a doctor and the arrival of two nurses, he came down for a hasty breakfast in Mrs. Nightingale's dining-room, where the boarders began to shake hands with him, enthusiastically. "The thing itself was simple enough; all that was necessary was to act as though it *was* only three inches."

CHAPTER XV

A WEEK later, early in the evening, a four-horse stage was coming slowly down the last mile or two of road above the little North Carolina village of Old Fort at the eastern base of the Blue Ridge. It was a creaking, crazy vehicle, thickly encrusted with red clay. But as it had pounded all the way from Asheville by the abominable mountain-road, no doubt it had cause to be vociferous and tarnished. Above, the stars were shining brightly; and the forest also appeared to be starlit, owing to the myriads of fire-flies that gleamed like sparks against the dark trees.

A man who was coming up the road hailed the stage as it approached. "Hello! Is Mr. Hill inside? The Rev. Mr. Hill of Asheville?"

"Yes," answered a voice from the back seat of the vehicle, and a head appeared at the window. "What—Mr. Chase? Is that you?" And, opening the door, Malachi Hill, with his bag in his hand, jumped out.

"I came up the road, thinking I might meet you," Horace Chase explained. "Let's walk; there's something I want to talk over." They went on together, leaving the stage behind. "I've got a new idea," Chase began. "What do you say to going up to New York to get my wife? I had intended to go for her myself, as you know, starting from here to-night, as soon as I had put the other ladies in your charge, to take back to Asheville. But Mrs. Franklin looks pretty bad; and Dolly—she might have one of her attacks. And, take it altogether, I've begun to feel that it's my business to go with 'em all the way. For it's a long drive over the mountains at best, and though the night's fine so far, there's no moon, and the road is always awful. I have four men from Raleigh along—the undertaker (who is a damn fool, always talking), and his assistants; and so there'll be four teams—a wagon, the two carriages, and the hearse. I guess I know the most about horses, and if you can fix it so as to take my place, I'll see 'em through."

"Certainly. I am anxious to help in any way you think best," answered Malachi. "I wish I could start at once! But the stage is so late to-night that, of course, the train has gone?"

"That's just it—I kept it," Chase answered; "I knew one of us would want to take it. You'll have to wait over at Salisbury in the usual stupid way. But as Ruth can't be here in time for the funeral, it's not of vital importance. The only thing that riles me is that, owing to that confounded useless wait, you can't be on the dock to meet her when her steamer comes in at New York; you won't be able to get there in time. There'll be people, of course—I've telegraphed. But no one she knows as well as she knows you."

Reaching the village, they walked quickly towards the railroad and finished their talk as they stood beside the waiting train. There was no station, the rails simply came to an end in the main street. A small frame structure, which bore the inscription "Blue Ridge Hotel," faced the end of the rails.

"He's in there," said Chase, in a low tone, indicating a lighted window of this house; "that room on the ground-floor. And the old lady—she is sitting there beside him. She is quiet, she doesn't say anything. But she just sits there."

"Mrs. Jared and Miss Dolly are with her, aren't they?" said the young clergyman.

"Well, Dolly is keeping Gen in the other room across the hall as much as she *can*. For Dolly tells me that her mother likes best to sit there alone. Women, you know, about their sons — sometimes they're queer!" remarked Chase.

"The mother's love—yes," Malachi answered, his voice uncertain for a moment. He swallowed. "There isn't a man who doesn't feel, sooner or later, after it has gone, that he hasn't prized it half enough —that it was the best thing he had! It was brain-fever, wasn't it?" he went on, hurriedly, to cover his emotion. For he, too, had been an only son.

"Yes, and bad. He was raving; he knocked down one of the doctors. After the fever left him, it was just possible, they told me, that he might have pulled through, if he had only been stronger. But he was played out to begin with; I discovered that myself as soon as I reached Raleigh. Gen got there in time to see him. But the old lady was too late; and pretty hard lines for her! She kept telegraphing from different stations as she and Dolly hurried up from Charleston; and I did my best to hearten her by messages that met her here and there; but she missed it. By only half an hour. When I saw that it had come—that he was sinking and she wouldn't find him alive—I went out and just cursed, cursed the luck! For Gen had his last words, and everything. And his poor old mother had nothing at all."

Here the conductor came up.

"Ready?" said Chase. "All right, here's your through ticket, Hill — the one I bought for myself. And inside the envelope is a memorandum, with the number and street of our house in New York, and other items. I'm no end obliged to you for going." They shook hands cordially. "When you come back, don't let my wife travel straight through," added the husband. "Make her stop over and sleep."

"I'll do my best," answered Hill, as the train started. In deference to the mourning party which it had brought westward, there was no whistle, no ringing of the bell; the locomotive moved quietly away, and the clergyman, standing on the rear platform, holding on by the handle of the door, watched as long as he could see it the lighted window of the room where lay all that was mortal of Jared Franklin.

An hour later the funeral procession started up the mountain. First, there was a wagon, with the undertaker and his three assistants. Then followed the large, heavy hearse drawn by four horses. Next came a carriage containing Mrs. Franklin and Dolly; and, finally, a second carriage for Genevieve and Horace Chase.

"Poor mamma is sadly changed," commented Genevieve to her companion. "She insisted upon being left alone with the remains at the hotel, you know; and now she wishes her carriage to be as near the hearse as possible. Fortunately, these things are very unimportant to me, Horace. I do not feel, as they do, that Jay is *here*. My husband has gone—gone to a better world. He knew that he was going; he said good-bye to me so tenderly. He was always so—*so* kind." And covering her face, Genevieve gave way to tears.

"Yes, he thought the world and all of you, Gen. There's no doubt about that," Chase answered.

He did full justice to the sobbing woman by his side. He was more just to her than her husband's family had ever been, or ever could be; he had known her as a child, and he comprehended that according to her nature and according to her unyielding beliefs as to what was best, she had tried to be a good wife. In addition (as he was a man himself), he thought that it was to her credit that her husband had always been fond of her, that he had remained devoted to her to the last. "That doesn't go for nothing!" he said to himself.

The ascent began. The carriages plunged into holes and lurched out of them; they jolted across bits of corduroy; now and then, when the track followed a gorge, they forded a brook. The curves were slippery, owing to the red clay. Then, without warning, in the midst of mud would come an unexpected sharp grind of the wheels over an exposed ledge of bare rock. Before midnight clouds had obscured the stars and it grew very dark. But the lamps on the carriages burned brightly, and a negro was sent on in advance carrying a pitch-pine torch.

In the middle of the night, at the top of the pass, there was a halt. Chase had made Genevieve comfortable with cushions and shawls, and soon after their second start she fell asleep. Perceiving this, he drew up the window on her side, and then, opening the carriage-door softly, he got out; it was easy to do it, as all the horses were walking. Making a detour through the underbrush, so that he should not be seen by Mrs. Franklin and Dolly in case they were awake, he appeared by the side of the hearse.

"Don't stop," he said to the driver, in a low tone; "I'm going to get up there beside you." He climbed up and took the reins. "I'll drive the rest of the way, or at least as far as the outskirts of the town.

For between here and there are all the worst places. You go on and join that fellow in front. You might carry a second torch; you'll find some in the wagon."

The driver of the hearse, an Asheville negro, who knew Chase, gave up his seat gladly. There were bad holes ahead, and there was a newly mended place which was a little uncertain; he would not have minded taking the stage over that place (none of the Blue Ridge drivers minded taking the stage anywhere), but he was superstitious about a hearse. " Fo' de Lawd, I'm glad to be red of it!" he confided to the other negro, as they went on together in advance with their flaring torches. " It slips an' slews when dey ain't no 'casion! Sump'n mighty quare 'bout it, I tell you *dat!*"

Presently the plateau came to an end, and the descent began. Rain was now falling. The four vehicles moved slowly on, winding down the zigzags very cautiously in the darkness, slipping and swaying as they went.

After half an hour of this progress, the torch-bearers in front came hurrying back to give warning that the rain had loosened the temporary repairs of the mended place, so that its edge had given away; for about one hundred and forty yards, therefore, the track was dangerously narrow and undefended, with the sheer precipice on one side and the high cliff on the other; in addition, the roadway slanted towards this verge, and the clay was very slippery.

Chase immediately sent word back to the drivers of the carriages behind to advance as slowly as was possible, but not to stop, for that might waken the ladies; then,. jumping down from the hearse, and leaving one of the negroes in charge of his team, he hurried forward to make a personal inspection. The broken shelf, without its parapet, certainly looked precarious; so much so that the driver of the wagon, when he came up, hesitated. Chase, ordering him down, took his place, and drove the wagon across himself. Whereupon the verbose undertaker began to thank him.

"Don't worry; I didn't do it for *you*," answered Chase, grimly. "If you'd gone over, you'd have carried away more of the track; that was all." Going back, he resumed his place on the hearse. Then speaking to his horses, he guided them on to the shelf. Here he stood, in order to see more clearly, the men on the far side watching him breathlessly, and trying meanwhile (at a safe distance) to aid him as much as they could, by holding their torches high. The ponderous hearse began to slip by its own weight towards the verge. Then, with strong hand, Chase sent his team sharply towards the cliff that towered above them, and kept them grinding against it as they advanced, the two on the inside fairly rubbing the rock, until, by main strength, the four together had dragged their load away. But in a minute or two it began over again. It happened not once merely, but four times. And, the last time, the hind wheels slipped so far, in spite of Chase's efforts, that it seemed as if they would inevitably go over, and drag the struggling horses with them. But Chase was as bold a driver as he was speculator. How he inspired them, the horror-stricken watchers could not discover; but the four bays, bounding sharply round together, sprang in a heap, as it were, at the rocky wall on the left, the leaders rearing, the others on top of them; and by this wild leap, the wheels (one of them was already over) were violently jerked away. It was done at last; the dark, ponderous car stood in safety on the other side, and the spectators, breathing again, rubbed down the wet horses. Then Horace Chase went back on foot, and, in turn, drove the two carriages across. Through these last two transits not a word was spoken by any one; he mounted soundlessly, so that Genevieve slept on undisturbed, and Mrs. Franklin and Dolly, unaware of the danger or of the new hand on the reins, continued to gaze vaguely at the darkness outside, their thoughts pursuing their own course. Finally, leaving one of the negroes on guard to warn other travellers of the washout and its perils, Chase resumed his place on the hearse, and the four vehicles continued their slow progress down the mountain.

After a while, the first vague clearness preceding dawn appeared; the rain ceased. Happening to turn his head fifteen minutes later, he was startled to see, in the dim light, the figure of a woman beside the hearse. It was Mrs. Franklin. The road was now

19

smoother, and she walked steadily on, keeping up
with the walk of the horses. As the light grew
clearer, she saw who the driver was, and her eyes
met his with recognition. But her rigid face seemed
to have no power for further expression; it was set
in lines that could not alter. Chase, on his side,
bowed gravely, taking off his hat; and he did not
put it on again, he left it on the seat by his side.
He made no attempt to stop her, to persuade her
to return to her carriage; he recognized the presence of one of those moods which, when they
take possession of a woman, no power on earth can
alter.

As they came to the first outlying houses of Asheville, he gave up his place to the negro driver, and
getting down on the other side of the hearse, away
from Mrs. Franklin, he went back for a moment to
Dolly. "You must let her do it! *Don't* try to prevent her," Dolly said, imperatively, in a low tone, the
instant she saw him at the carriage door.

"I'm not thinking of preventing her," Chase answered. Waiting until the second carriage passed,
he looked in; Genevieve was still asleep. Then, still
bareheaded, he joined Mrs. Franklin, and, without
speaking, walked beside her up the long, gradual ascent which leads into the town.

The sun now appeared above the mountains; early
risers coming to their windows saw the dreary file
pass—the wagon and the two carriages, heavy with
mud; the hearse with four horses, and the mother

walking beside it. As they reached the main street, Chase spoke. " The Cottage ?"

" No ; home," Mrs. Franklin answered. As the hearse turned into the driveway of L'Hommedieu, she passed it, and, going on in advance, opened the house door ; here, waving away old Zoe and Rinda, who came hurrying to meet her, she waited on the threshold until the men had lifted out the coffin ; then, leading the way to the sitting-room, she pointed to the centre of the floor.

" Oh, not to *our* house ?" Genevieve whispered, as she alighted, her eyes full of tears.

But Dolly, to whom she spoke, limped in without answering, and Mrs. Franklin paid no more heed to her daughter-in-law, who had followed her, than as though she did not exist. Genevieve, quivering from her grief, turned to Horace Chase.

He put his arm round her, and led her from the sitting-room. " Give way to her, Gen," he said, in a low tone. " She isn't well—don't you see it ? She isn't herself ; she has been walking beside that hearse for the last hour ! Let her do whatever she likes ; it's her only comfort. And now I am going to take you straight home, and you must go to bed ; if you don't, you won't be able to get through the rest— and you wouldn't like that. I'll come over at noon and arrange with you about the funeral ; to-morrow morning will be the best time, won't it ?" And half leading, half carrying her, for Genevieve was now crying helplessly, he took her home.

When he came back, Dolly was in the hall, waiting for him.

There was no one in the sitting-room save Mrs. Franklin; he could see her through the half-open door. She was sitting beside the coffin, with her head against it, and one arm laid over its top. Her dress was stained with mud; she had not taken off her bonnet; her gloves were still on. Dolly closed the door, and shut out the sight.

"You ought to see to her; she must be worn out," Chase said, expostulatingly.

"I'll do what I can," Dolly answered. "But mother has now no desire to live—that will be the difficulty. She loves Ruth, and she loves me. But not in the same way. Her father, her husband, and her son—these have been mother's life. And now that the last has gone, the last of the three men she adored, she doesn't care to stay. That is what she is thinking now, as she sits there."

"Come, you can't possibly know what she is thinking," Chase answered, impatiently.

"I always know what is in mother's mind; I wish I didn't!" said Dolly, her features working convulsively for a moment. Then she controlled herself. "I am sorry you came all the way back with us, Mr. Chase. It wasn't necessary as far as *we* were concerned. We could have crossed the mountain perfectly well without you. But Ruth—that is another affair, and I wish you had gone for her yourself, instead of sending Mr. Hill! You must be prepared to see Ruth greatly changed. I should not be surprised if she should arrive much broken, and even ill. She was very fond of Jared. She will be overwhelmed—" Here, feeling that she was saying too much, the elder sister abruptly disappeared.

Chase, left alone, went out to see to the horses. The men were waiting at the gate, the carriages and the hearse were drawn up at a little distance ; the undertaker and his assistants were standing in the garden. "Get your breakfast at the hotel; I'll send for you presently," he said to the latter. Then he paid the other men, and dismissed them. "You go and tell whoever has charge, to have that bad bit of road put in order to-day," he directed. "Tell them to send up a hundred hands, if necessary. I'll pay the extra."

CHAPTER XVI

THE morning after the funeral, Chase, upon coming down to breakfast, found Mrs. Franklin already in the sitting-room. She had not taken the trouble to put on the new mourning garb which had been hastily made for her; her attire was a brown dress which she had worn in Florida. She sat motionless in her easy-chair, with her arms folded, her feet on a footstool, and her face had the same stony look which had not varied since she was told, upon her arrival at Raleigh, that her son was dead.

"Well, ma'am, I hope you have slept?" Chase asked, as he extended his hand.

She gave him hers lifelessly.

"Yes; I believe so."

"Ruth will soon be here now," her son-in-law went on, as he seated himself. "I told Hill not to let her travel straight through, for it would only tire her; and she needs to keep well, ma'am, so as to be of use to you. I'm going to drive over to Old Fort to-day, starting late—about six o'clock, I guess. I've calculated that if Ruth spent a night in New York (as she probably did, waiting for Hill to get there), and if she stops over one night on the way, she would reach Old Fort to-morrow noon. Then I'll bring her right on to L'Hommedieu."

"Yes, bring her. And let her stay."

"As long as ever you like, ma'am. I can't hold on long myself just now, but I'll leave her with you, and come for her later. I am thinking of taking a house at Newport for the summer; I hope that you and Miss Dolly will feel like spending some time. there with Ruth? Say August and September?"

"I shall travel no more. Leave her with me; it won't be for long."

"You must cheer up, ma'am—for your daughters' sake."

"Ruth has you," Mrs. Franklin responded. "And *you* are good." Her tone remained lifeless. But it was evident that her words were sincere; that a vague sense of justice had made her rouse herself long enough to utter the commendation.

"That's a mistake. I've never laid claim to anything of *that* sort," Chase answered rather curtly, his face growing red.

"When I say '*good*,' I mean that you will be good to Ruth," said the mother; "it is the only sort of goodness I care for! At present you don't like Dolly. But Dolly is so absolutely devoted to her sister that you will end by accepting her, faults and all; you won't mind her little hostilities. I can therefore trust them both to you — I do so with confidence," she added. And, with her set face unchanged, she made him a little bow.

"Why talk that way, ma'am? We hope to have you with us many years longer," Chase answered.

"A green old age is a very fine thing to see." (He thought rather well of that phrase.) "My grandmother—she stuck it out to ninety-eight, and I hope you'll do the same."

"Probably she wished to live. I have no such desire. As I sat here beside my son the morning we arrived, I knew that I longed to go, too. I want to be with him—and with my husband—and my dear father. My life here has now come to its end, for *they* were my life."

"That queer Dolly knew!" thought Chase. "But perhaps they've talked about it?" He asked this question aloud. "Have you told your daughter that, ma'am?"

"Told my poor Dolly? Of course not. Please go to breakfast, Mr. Chase; I am sure it is ready." Chase went to the dining-room. A moment later Dolly came in to pour out the coffee.

"Is there anything I can do for you this morning?" Chase asked, as he took a piece of Zoe's hot cornbread. "I am going to drive over to Old Fort this afternoon, and wait there for Ruth, for I've calculated the trains, and I reckon that she and Hill will reach there to-morrow."

Dolly looked at him for a moment. Then she said: "You have a great deal of influence with Genevieve; perhaps you could make her understand that for the present it is better that she should not try to see mother. Tell her that mother is much more broken than she was yesterday; tell her that she is very nervous; tell her, in short, anything you please, provided it keeps her away!" Dolly added, suddenly giving up her long effort to hide her bitter dislike.

Chase glanced at her, and said nothing; he ate his corn-bread, and finished his first cup of coffee in silence. Then, as she poured out the second, he said: "Well, she might keep away entirely? She might leave Asheville? She has a brother in St. Louis, and she likes the place, I know; I've heard her say so. If her property here could be taken off her hands—at a good valuation—and if a well-arranged, well-furnished house could be provided for her there, near her brother, I guess she'd go. I even guess she'd go pretty quick," he added; "she'd be a long sight happier there than here." For though he had no especial affection for Genevieve, he at least liked her better than he liked Dolly.

Dolly, however, was indifferent to his liking or his disliking. " *Oh !*" she said, her gaze growing vague in the intensity of her wish, "if it could only be done!" Then her brow contracted, she pushed her plate away. "But we cannot possibly be so much indebted to you—I mean. so much *more* indebted."

" You needn't count yourself in, if it worries you," Chase answered with his deliberate utterance. " For I should be doing it principally for Ruth, you know. When she comes, the first thing she'll want to do, of course, is to make her mother comfortable. And if Gen's clearing out, root and branch, will help that, I rather guess Ruth can fix it."

"You mean that *you* can."

"Well, we're one; I don't think that even *you* can quite break that up yet," Chase answered, ironically. Then he went on in a gentler tone: "I want to do everything I can for your mother. She has always been very kind to me."

And Dolly was perfectly well aware that, as he looked at her (looked at her yellow, scowling face), his feeling for her had become simply pity, pity for the sickly old maid whom no one could possibly please—not even her sweet young sister.

Soon after breakfast Chase went to the Cottage. Genevieve received him gratefully. Her cheeks were pale; her eyes showed the traces of the tears of the previous day, the day of the funeral.

Her visitor remained two hours. Then he rose, saying, "Well, I must see about horses if I am to get to Old Fort to-night. I shall tell Ruth about this new plan of ours, Gen. She'll be sure to like it; she'll enjoy going to St. Louis to see you; we'll both come often. And you'll be glad of a change yourself. The other house, too, is likely to be shut up. For, though they don't say so yet, I guess the old lady and Dolly will end by spending most of their time with Ruth, in New York."

"I must go over and see mamma at once," answered Genevieve. "I must have her opinion, first of all. I shall ask mamma's advice more than ever now, Horace; it will be my pleasure as well as my duty. For Jay was very fond of his mother; he often told me—" Her voice quivered, and she stopped.

"Now, Gen, listen to me," said Chase, taking her hand. "Don't go over there at all to-day. And, when you go to-morrow, and later, don't try to see the old lady; wait till she asks for you. For she is all unhinged; I've just come from there, and I know. She is very nervous, and everything upsets her. It won't do either of you any good to meet at present; it would only be a trial to you both. And Dolly says so, too. Promise me that you'll take care of yourself; promise me especially that you won't leave the house at all to-day, but stay quietly at home and rest."

Genevieve promised. But after he had gone, the sense of duty that was a part of her nature led her to reconsider her determination. That her husband should have been laid in his grave only twenty-four hours before, and that she, the widow, should not see his bereaved mother through the whole day, when their houses stood side by side; that they should not mingle their tears, and their prayers also, while their sorrow was still so new and so poignant —this seemed to her wrong. In addition, it seemed hardly decent. The mother was ill and broken? So much the more, then, was it her duty to go to her. At four o'clock, therefore, she put on her bonnet and its long crape veil, and her black mantle, and crossed the meadow towards L'Hommedieu.

Mrs. Franklin was still sitting in the easy-chair with her arms folded, as she had sat in the morning when Chase came in. The only difference was that now a newspaper lay across her lap; she had hastily taken it from the table, and spread it over her knees, when she recognized her daughter-in-law's step on the veranda.

Genevieve came in. She was startled at first by the sight of the brown dress, which happened to have red tints as well as brown in its fabric. But it was only another cross to bear; her husband's family had always given her so many! "I hope you slept last night, mamma?" she said, bending to kiss Mrs. Franklin's forehead.

"Yes, I believe so," the elder woman answered, mechanically, as she had answered Chase. She was now indefinitely the elder. Between the wife of forty, and the slender, graceful, vivacious mother of fifty-eight, there had been but the difference of one short generation. But now the mother might have been any age; her shoulders were bent, her skin looked withered, and all the outlines of her face were set and sharpened.

Genevieve took off her crape mantle, folding it (with her habitual carefulness) before she laid it on a chair. "You must let me see to your mourning, mamma," she said, as she thus busied herself. "I suppose your new dress doesn't fit you? It was made so hastily. I shall be sitting quietly at home for the present, day after day, and it will occupy me and take my thoughts from myself to have some sewing to do. And I know how to cut crape to advantage also, for I was in mourning so long when I was a girl."

Mrs. Franklin made no reply.

Her daughter - in - law, seating herself beside her, stroked back her gray hair. "You look so tired! And I am afraid Dolly is tired out also, as she isn't with you?"

"I sent her to bed half an hour ago; for I am afraid one of her attacks is coming on," Mrs. Franklin answered, her lips compressing themselves as she endured the caress. Genevieve's touch was gentle. But Mrs. Franklin did not like to have her hair stroked.

"Poor Dolly! But, surely, it is not surprising. I must see her before I go back. But shall I go back, mamma? As you are alone, wouldn't it be better for me to stay with you for the rest of the day? I could read to you; I should love to do it. It seems providential that my dear copy of *Quiet Hours* should have come back from Philadelphia only yesterday; I had sent it to Philadelphia, you know, to be rebound. But there have been greater providences still; for instance, how I was able to get to Raleigh in time to see our dear one. For the stage had gone when Horace's telegram came, and Mr. Bebb's having arranged, by a mere chance, to drive to Old Fort with that pair of fast horses at the very *moment* I wished to start — surely that was providential? But you look so white; do let me get you some tea? Or, better still, won't you go to bed ? I should so love to undress you, and bathe your face with cologne."

Mrs. Franklin shook her head ; through her whole life she had detested cologne. On the top of her dumb despair, on the top of her profound enmity, rose again (a consciousness sickening to herself) all the petty old irritations against this woman ; against her " providential" ; her *Quiet Hours ;* her " surely " ; her " cutting crape to advantage " ; and even her " cologne." She closed her eyes so that at least she need not *see* her.

" I have had a letter from my sister," Genevieve went on. " I brought it with me, thinking that you might like to hear it, for it is so *beautifully* expressed. As you don't care to lie down, I'll read it to you now. My sister reminds me, mamma, that in the midst of my grief I ought to remember that I have had one great blessing — a blessing not granted to all wives ; and that is, that from the first moment of our engagement to his last breath, dear Jay was perfectly devoted to me ; he never looked — he never cared to look — at any one else !"

Mrs. Franklin refolded her arms ; her hands, laid over her elbows, tightened on her sleeves.

Genevieve began to read the letter. But when she came to the passage she had quoted, the tears began to fall. "I won't go on," she said, as she wiped them away. " For we must not dwell upon our griefs—don't you think so, mamma ? Not *purposely* remind ourselves of them ; surely that is unwise.

I have already arranged to give away Jay's clothes, for instance — give them to persons who really need them. For as long as they are in the house I can't help cr-crying whenever I see them." Her voice broke, and she stopped; her effort at self-control, both here and at home, was sincere.

She replaced the letter in her pocket. And as she did so, the crape of her sleeve, catching on the edge of the newspaper which lay over Mrs. Franklin's knees, drew it so far to one side that it fell to the floor. And there, revealed on the mother's lap, lay a little heap: a package of letters in a school-boy hand; a battered top, and one or two other toys; a baby's white robe yellow with age; some curls of soft hair, and a little pair of baby shoes.

"Oh, mamma, are you letting yourself brood over these things? Surely it is not wise? Let me put them away."

But Mrs. Franklin, gathering her poor treasures from Genevieve's touch, placed them herself in her secretary, which she locked. Then she began to walk to and fro across the broad room — to and fro, to and fro, her step feverishly quick.

After a minute, Genevieve followed her. "Mamma, try to be resigned. Try to be calm."

Mrs. Franklin stopped. She faced round upon her daughter-in-law. "You dare to offer advice to me, you barren woman? You tell me to be resigned? What do *you* know of a mother's love for her son — you who have never borne a child? You can comprehend neither my love nor my grief. Providential, is it, that you reached Raleigh in time? Providence is a strange thing if it assists *you*. For you have killed your husband — killed him as certainly as though you had given him slow poison. You broke up his life—the only life he loved; you never rested until you had forced him out of the navy. And then, your greed for money made you urge him incessantly to go into business — into business for himself, which he knew nothing about. You gave him no peace; you drove him on; your determination to have all the things *you* care for — a house of your own and a garden; chairs and tables; handsome clothes; money for *charities*" (impossible to describe the bitterness of this last phrase) — " these have been far more important to you than anything else — than his own happiness, or his own welfare. And, lately, your process of murder has gone on faster. For he has been very ill all winter (I know it *now!*) and you have not been near him; you have stayed here month after month, buying land with Ruth's money, filling your pockets and telling him nothing of it, adding to your house, and saying to yourself comfortably meanwhile that this wise course of yours would in the end bring him round to your views. It *has* brought him round — to his death! His life for years has been wretched, and you were the cause of the misery. For it was his feeling of being out of his place, his gradual discouragement, his sense of failure, that finally broke down his

health. If he had never seen *you*, he might have
lived to be an old man, filling with honor the position he was fitted for. Now, at thirty-nine, he is
dead. He was faithful to you, you say? He was.
And it is my greatest regret! I do not wish ever to
see your face again. For he was the joy of my life,
and you were the curse of his. Go!"

These sentences, poured out in clear, vibrating
tones, had filled Genevieve with horror. And something that was almost fear followed as the mother,
coming nearer, her eyes blazing in her death-like face,
emphasized her last words by stretching out her arm
with a gesture that was fiercely grand—the grandeur
of her bereavement and her despair.

Genevieve escaped to the hall. Then, after waiting
for a moment uncertainly, she hurried home.

When the sound of her footsteps had died away,
Mrs. Franklin went to the secretary and took out
again the dress and the top, the little shoes and the
baby-curls; seating herself, she began to rearrange
them. But her hands only moved for a moment or
two. Then her head sank back, her eyes closed.

20

As it happened, Horace Chase was the next person who entered the parlor. He was touched when he saw the old-looking figure, with the pathetic little heap in its lap. But when he perceived that the figure was unconscious, he was much alarmed; summoning help, he sent hastily for a doctor. After being removed to her own room, Mrs. Franklin was extremely restless; she moved her head incessantly from side to side on the pillow, and she seemed to be half blind; her mind wandered, and her voice, as she spoke incoherently, was very weak. Then suddenly she sank into a lethargic slumber. The doctor waited to see in what condition she would waken; for there were symptoms he did not like. Miss Billy, meanwhile, was installed as nurse.

Mrs. Kip, Maud Muriel, and Miss Billy had visited this house of mourning many times since the arrival of the funeral procession two days before, with the mother walking beside the coffin of her son. And now that this poor mother was stricken down, they all came again, anxious to be of use. Chase, who had always liked her gentle ways, selected Miss Billy.

Dolly knew nothing of her mother's prostration; for her pain (her old enemy), having been deadened by an opiate, she was sleeping. In order that she should not suspect what had happened, Miss Billy did not show herself at all in Dolly's room; Rinda, who was accustomed to this service, was established there on a pallet, ready to answer if called.

Chase had decided that he would wait for the doctor's report before starting on his drive across the mountain; it would be satisfactory to have something definite to tell Ruth. It was uncertain when that report would come. But as he intended to set out, in spite of the darkness, the first moment that it was possible, there was no use in going to bed. Alone in the parlor, therefore, he first read through all the newspapers he could find. Then, opening the window, he smoked a cigar or two. Finally, his mind reverted, as it usually did when he was alone, to business; drawing a chair to the table, he took out some memoranda and sat down. Midnight passed. One o'clock came. Two o'clock. He still sat there, absorbed. Mrs. Franklin's reading-lamp, burning brightly beside him, lighted up his hard, keen face. For it looked hard now, with its three deeply set lines, one on each side of the mouth, and one between the eyes; and the eyes themselves were hard and sharp. But though the business letter he was engaged upon was a masterpiece of shrewdness (as those who received it would not fail to discover sooner or later), and though it dealt with large interests that were important, the faintest sound upstairs would have instantly caught the attention of its

writer. On a chair beside him were railroad time-
tables, and a sheet of commercial note-paper with
two lines of figures jotted down in orderly rows side
by side; these represented the two probabilities regarding the trains which his wife might take—their
hours of departure and their connections. He had
received no telegrams, and this had surprised him.
"What can the little chap be about?" he had more
than once thought. His adjective "little" was not
depreciatory; Malachi Hill was, in fact, short. In
addition, his fresh, pink-tinged complexion and bright
blue eyes gave him a boyish air. To Horace Chase,
who was over six feet in height, and whose dark face
looked ten years older than it really was, the young
missionary (whom he sincerely liked) seemed juve-
nile; his youthful appearance, in fact, combined with
his unmistakable "grit" (as Chase called it), had been
the thing which had first attracted the notice of the
millionaire.

A little before three there was a sound. But it
was not from upstairs, it was outside; steps were
coming up the path from the gate. The man in the
parlor went into the hall; and as he did so, to his
surprise the house-door opened and his wife came
in.

Behind her there was a momentary vision of
Malachi Hill. The clergyman, however, did not
enter; upon seeing Horace Chase, he closed the
door quietly and went away.

Ruth's face, even to the lips, was so white that

her husband hastily put his arm round her; then he drew her into the sitting-room, closing the door behind them.

"Where is he?" Ruth had asked, or rather, her lips formed the words. "Didn't you *wait* for me?"

"My darling, he was buried yesterday," Chase answered, sitting down and drawing her into his arms. "Didn't Hill tell you?"

"Yes, but I didn't believe it. I thought you would wait for me; I thought you would *know* that I wanted to see him."

"No one saw him after we left Raleigh, dear. The coffin was not opened again."

"If I had been here, mother would have — *mother* would have—"

"It was your mother who arranged everything," Chase explained gently, as with careful touch he took off her hat, and then her gloves; her hands were icy, and he held them in his to warm them.

"Where *is* mother? And Dolly? Weren't they expecting me? Didn't they *know* I would come?"

"Your mother is sick upstairs. No, don't get up —you can't see her now; she is asleep, and mustn't be disturbed. But the first moment she wakes up the doctor is to let me know, and then you shall go to her right away. Miss Breeze is up there keeping watch. Dolly has broken down, too. But Dolly's case is no worse than it has often been before, and you'd better let her sleep while she can. And now, will you stay here with me, Ruthie, till the doctor comes? Or would you rather go to bed? If you'll go, I promise to tell you the minute your mother wakes." He put his hand on her head protectingly, and kissed her cheek. Her face was cold. Her whole frame had trembled incessantly from the moment of her entrance. "My darling little girl, how tired you are!"

"Tell me everything — everything about Jared," Ruth demanded, feverishly.

Though she was so white, it was evident that she had not shed tears; her eyes were bright, her lips were parched. Her husband, with his rough-and-ready knowledge of women, knew that it would be better for her to "have her cry out," as he would have phrased it; it would quiet her excitement and subdue her so that she would sleep. As she could not eat, he gave her a spoonful of brandy from his own flask, and wrapped her cold feet in his travelling-shawl; then, putting her on the sofa, he sat down beside her, and, holding her tenderly in his arms, he told her the story of Jared's last hours.

His account was truthful, save that he softened the details. In his narrative Mrs. Nightingale's shabby house became homelike and comfortable, and Jared's bare attic a pleasant place; Mrs. Nightingale herself (here there was no need for exaggeration) was an angel of kindness. He dwelt upon Jared's having agreed to go with him to New York. "I had planned to start at nine o'clock the next morning, Ruthie, having a doctor along without his knowing

it; and I had ordered a private car — a Pullman
sleeper—to go through to New York; once there, I
thought you could make him take a good long rest.
That kind woman had been sitting up at night in the
room next to his. So I fixed that by taking the
same room myself. I didn't undress, but I guess I
fell asleep; and I woke up hearing him talking. And
then he walked about the room, and he even climbed
out on the roof; but we soon got him back all right.
Everything possible was done, dear; the best doctor
in Raleigh, and a nurse—two of 'em. But it was
no use. It was brain-fever, or inflammation of the
brain rather, and after it had left him he was too
weak to rally. They thought everything of him at
Raleigh; your mother wanted him brought here, and
when we went to the depot, everybody who had
ever known him turned out, so that there was a long
procession; and all the ladies of his boarding-house
brought flowers. At Old Fort, I had intended to let
Hill (I had wired to him to meet us there)‘ take
charge of them across the mountains, for I wanted to
go to New York to get *you*. But the night was
dark, and the road is always so bad that I thought,
on the whole, you'd rather have me stay with your
mother. And she has been tolerably well, too, until
this afternoon, when she had an attack of some sort.
But I guess it's only that she is overtired; the doctor will probably come down and tell us so before
long."

"I *wanted* to see him," repeated Ruth, her eyes

still dry and bright. "It was very little to do for me, I think. If I could have just taken his poor hand once—even if it *was* dead! Everybody else got there in time to speak to him, to say good-by."

"No; your mother didn't get there," Chase explained.

"She didn't get there? And Genevieve *did?* I know it by your face. Let me go to mother—poor mother! Let me go to her, and *never* leave her again."

"You shall go the instant she wakes; you shall stay with her as long as you like," Chase answered, drawing her down again, and putting his cheek against her head as it lay on his breast. "There is nothing in the world I wouldn't do for your mother; you have only to choose. And for Dolly, too. You shall stay with them; or they can go with you; or anything you think best, my poor little girl."

Ruth still trembled, and no tears came to her relief.

Her cry, "And Genevieve *did?*" had struck him. "How they all hate her?" he thought.

He had seen Genevieve since Mrs. Franklin's attack; he had gone over for a moment to tell her what had happened.

Genevieve, when driven from L'Hommedieu, had taken refuge in her own room at the Cottage; here, behind her locked door, she had spent a long hour in examining herself searchingly, examining her whole married life. Her hands had trembled as she looked over her diaries, and as she turned the pages of her "Questions for the Conscience." But with all her efforts she could not discern any point where she had failed. Finally, at the end of the examination, she summed the matter up more calmly: "It *was* best for Jared to be out of the navy; he was forming habits there that I understood better than his mother. And I *know* that I am not avaricious. I know that I have always tried to do what was best for him, that I have tried to elevate him and help him in every way. I have worked hard—hard. I have never ceased to work. It is all a falsehood, or, rather, it is a delusion; for she is, she *must* be, insane." Having reached this conclusion (with Genevieve conclusions were final), she put away her diaries and went down-stairs to tea. When Chase came in and told what had happened, she said, with the utmost pity, "I am *not* surprised! When she comes out of it, I fear you will find, Horace, that her mind is affected. But surely it is natural. Mamma's mind— poor, dear mamma!—never was very strong; and, in this great grief which has overwhelmed us all, it has given way. We must make every allowance for her." She told him nothing of her terrible half-hour at L'Hommedieu. She never told any one. Silence was the only proper course—a pitying silence over Jay's poor mother, his crazed mother.

Ruth had paid no heed to her husband's soothing words, his promise to do everything that he possibly could for her mother and Dolly. "What did Jared say? You were with him before he was ill. Tell me everything, everything!"

He tried to satisfy her. Then he attempted to draw her thoughts in another direction. "How did you get here so soon, Ruthie? I told Hill to make you stop over and sleep."

"Sleep!" repeated Ruth. "I only thought of one thing, and that was to get here in time to see him." She left the sofa. "You ought to have waited for me. It would have been better if you had. *Jared* was the one I cared for. One look at his face, even if he *was* dead. Where did they put him when they brought him home? For I know mother had him here, here and not at the Cottage. It was in this room, wasn't it? In the centre of the floor?" She walked to the middle of the room and stood there. "*Jared* could have helped me," she said, miserably. "Why did they take my *brother*—the one person I had!"

The door opened and the doctor entered. "*You* here, Mrs. Chase? I didn't know you had come." He hesitated.

"What is it?" said Ruth, going to him. "Tell me! *Tell* me."

The doctor glanced at Chase.

Chase came up, and took his wife's hand protectingly. "You may as well tell her."

"It is a stroke of paralysis," explained the doctor, gravely.

"But she'll *know* me?" cried Ruth in an agony of tears.

" She *may*.   You can go up if you like."

But the mother saw nothing, heard nothing on earth again.   She might live for years.   But she did not know her own child.

Chase came at last, and took his wife away.

" Oh, be good to me, Horace, or I shall die!   I think I *am* dying now," she added in sudden terror.

She clung to him in alarm.   His immense kindness was now her refuge.

CHAPTER XVIII

In spite of all there was to see that afternoon, Dolly Franklin had chosen to remain at home; she sat alone in the drawing-room, adding silken rows to her stocking of the moment. Wherever Ruth was, that was now Dolly's home; since Mrs. Franklin's death, two years before, Dolly had lived with her sister. The mother had survived her son but a month. Her soul seemed to have departed with the first stroke of the benumbing malady; there was nothing but the breathing left. At the end of a few weeks, even the breathing ceased. Since then, L'Hommedieu had been closed, save for a short time each spring. Horace Chase had bought a cottage at Newport, and his wife and Dolly had divided their time between Newport and New York. This winter, however, Chase had reopened his Florida house, the old Worth place, at St. Augustine; for Ruth's health appeared to be growing delicate; at least she had a dread of the cold, of the icy winds, and the snow.

"Well, we'll go back to the land of the alligators," said Chase; "we'll live on sweet potatoes and the little oysters that grow round loose. You seem to have forgotten that you own a shanty down there, Ruthie?"

At first Ruth opposed this idea. Then suddenly she changed her mind. "No, I'll go. I want to sail, and sail!"

"So do I," said Dolly. "But why shouldn't we try new waters? The Bay of Naples, for instance? Mr. Chase, if you cannot go over at present, you could come for us, you know, whenever it was convenient?" Dolly expended upon her idea all the eloquence she possessed.

But Horace Chase never liked to have his wife beyond the reach of a railroad. He himself often made long, rapid journeys without her. But he was unwilling to have her "on the other side of the ferry," as he called it, unless he could accompany her; and at present there were important business interests which held him at home. As Ruth also paid small heed to Dolly's brilliant (and wholly imaginary) pictures of Capri, Ischia, and Sorrento, the elder sister had been forced (though with deep inward reluctance) to yield; since December, therefore, they had all been occupying the pleasant old mansion that faced the sea-wall.

To-day, four o'clock came, and passed. Five o'clock came, and passed; and Dolly still sat there alone. At last she put down her knitting, and, taking her cane, limped upstairs and peeped into her sister's dressing-room. Ruth, who was lying on the lounge with her face hidden, appeared to be asleep. Dolly, therefore, closed the door noiselessly and limped down again. Outside the weather was ideally lovely. The beautiful floral arch which had been erected in the morning still filled the air with its fragrance, though the tea-roses of which it was composed were now beginning to droop. St. Augustine, or rather the visitors from the North, who at this season filled the little Spanish town, had set up this blossoming greeting in honor of a traveller who was expected by the afternoon train. This traveller had now arrived; he had passed through the floral gateway in the landau which was bringing him from the station. The arch bore as its legend: "The Ancient City welcomes the great Soldier." The quiet-looking man in the landau was named Grant.

At length Dolly had a visitor; Mrs. Kip was shown in. A moment later the Reverend Malachi Hill appeared, his face looking flushed, as though he had been in great haste. Mrs. Kip's eyes had a conscious expression when she saw him. She tried to cover it by saying, enthusiastically, " How *well* you do look, Mr. Hill! You look so fresh; really *classic*."

The outline of the clergyman's features was not the one usually associated with this adjective. But Mrs. Kip was not a purist; it was classic enough, in her opinion, to have bright blue eyes and golden hair; the accidental line of the nose and mouth was less important.

" Yes, my recovery is now complete," Malachi answered; " I must go back to my work in a day or two. But I wish it hadn't been measles, you know. Such a ridiculous malady !"

"Oh, don't say that; measles are so sweet, so domestic. They make one think of dear little children; and lemons," said Mrs. Kip, imaginatively. "And then, when they are getting well, all sorts of toys!"

While she was speaking, Anthony Etheridge entered. And he, too, looked as if he had been making haste. "What, Dolly, neither you nor Ruth out on this great occasion? Are you a bit of a copperhead?"

"No," Dolly answered. "I haven't spirit enough. *My* only spirit is in a lamp; I have been making flaxseed tea and hot lemonade for Ruth, who has a cold."

"Does she swallow your messes?" Etheridge asked.

"Never. But I like to fuss over them, and measure them out, and *stir* them up!"

"Just as I do for Evangeline Taylor," remarked Mrs. Kip, affectionately.

"Lilian, isn't Evangeline long enough without that Taylor?" Dolly suggested. "I have always meant to ask you."

"I do it as a remembrance of her father," replied Lilian, with solemnity "For I myself am a Taylor no longer; *I* am a Kip."

"Oh, is that it? And if you should marry again, what then could you do (as there is no second Evangeline) for your present name?" Dolly inquired, gravely.

"I have thought of that," answered the widow.

" And I have decided that I shall keep it. It shall
precede any new name I may take ; I should make it
a condition."

" You are warned, gentlemen," commented Dolly.

Etheridge for an instant looked alarmed. Then,
as he saw that Malachi had reddened violently, he
grew savage. " Kip-Hill ? Kip-Larue ? Kip-Wil-
loughby ?" he repeated, as if trying them. " Walter
Willoughby, however, is very poor dependence for
you, Mrs. Lilian ; for he is evidently here in the
train of the Barclays. He arrived with them yesterday, and he tells me he is going up the Ocklა-
waha ; I happen to know that the Barclays are taking that trip, also."

Walter Willoughby's name had rendered Mrs.
Kip visibly conscious a second time. The commodore's allusion to " the Barclays," and to Walter's
being " in their train," had made no impression upon
her. They were presumably ladies ; but Lilian's
mind was never troubled by the attractions of other
women, she was never jealous. One reason for this
immunity lay in the fact that she was always so ac-
tively engaged in the occupation of loving that she
had no time for jealousy ; another was that she had
in her heart a soft conviction, modest but fixed, regarding the power of her own charms. As excuse
for her, it may be mentioned that the conviction was
not due to imagination, it was a certainty forced
upon her by actual fact ; from her earliest girlhood
men had been constantly falling in love with her, and

apparently they were going to continue it indefinitely. But though not jealous herself, she sympathized deeply with the pain which this tormenting feeling gave to others, and, on the present occasion, she feared that Malachi might be suffering from the mention of Walter Willoughby's name, and that of Achilles Larue, in connection with her own; she therefore began to talk quickly, as a diversion to another subject. "Oh, do you know, as I came here this afternoon I was reminded of something I have often meant to ask you—ask all of you, and I'll say it now, as it's in my mind. Don't you know that sign one so often sees everywhere—'Job Printing'? There is one in Charlotte Street, and it was seeing it there just now as I passed that made me think of it again. I suppose it must be some especial kind of printing that they have named after Job? But it has always seemed to me so odd, because there was, of course, no printing at all, until some time after Job was dead? Or do you suppose it means that printers have to be so *very* patient (with the bad handwriting that comes to them), that they name *themselves* after Job?"

Dolly put down her knitting. "Lilian, come here and let me kiss you. You are too enchanting!"

Mrs. Kip kissed Dolly with amiability. She already knew—she could not help knowing—that she was too enchanting. But it was not often a woman's voice that mentioned the fact. "It is late, I must go," she said. "Mr. Hill, if you—if you want those roses for Mrs. Chase's bouquet, this is the best time to gather them."

Malachi Hill found his hat with alacrity, and they went out together. And then Etheridge took refuge in general objurgations. "I'm dead sick of Florida, Dolly! It's so monotonous. So flat, and deep in sand. No driving is possible. One of the best drives I ever had in my life was in a sleigh; right up the Green Mountains. The snow was over the tops of the fences, and the air clear as a bell!"

"Do the Green Mountains interest the little turtle-dove who has just gone out?" Dolly inquired.

"Little turtle-fool! She makes eyes at every young idiot who comes along."

"Oh no, she only coos. It's her natural language. I won't answer as to Achilles Larue, commodore, for that is a long-standing passion; she began to admire his fur-lined overcoat, his neat shoes, his 'ish,' and his mystic coldness within a month after the departure of her second dear one. But as to her other flames, I think you could cut them out in her affections if you would give your mind to it seriously; yes, even the contemporary Willoughby. But you'll never give your mind to it, you're a dog in the manger! You have no intention of marrying her yourself. Yet you don't want any one else to marry her. Isn't it tremendously appropriate that she happens to own an orange-grove? Orange-blossoms always ready."

"Contemporary?" Etheridge repeated, going back to the word that had startled him.

"Yes. Haven't you noticed how vividly contemporary young fellows of Walter's type are? They have no fixed habits; for fixed habits are founded in retrospect, and they never indulge in retrospect. Anything that happened last week seems to them old; last year, antediluvian. They live in the moment, with an outlook only towards the future. This makes them very 'actual' wooers. As my brother-in-law would phrase it, they are 'all there!'"

"Nonsense!" said Etheridge. But as he went home to his own quarters (to take a nap so as to be fresh for the evening), he turned over in his thoughts that word "contemporary!" And he made up his mind that from that hour he would mention no event which had occurred more than one year before; he would tell no story which dated back beyond the same period of time; he would read only the younger authors (whom he loathed without exception); he would not permit himself to prefer any particular walking-stick, any especial chair. At the club he would play euchre instead of whist; and if there was any other even more confoundedly modern and vulgar game, he would play that. Habits, indeed? Stuff and nonsense!

Left alone, Dolly went upstairs a second time. But Ruth's door was now locked. The elder sister came back therefore to the drawing-room. Her face was anxious.

She banished the expression, however, when she heard her brother-in-law's step in the hall; a moment later Horace Chase entered, his hands full of letters, and newspapers piled on his arm; he had come from the post-office, where the afternoon mail had just been distributed. "Where is Ruth? Still asleep?" he asked.

"I think not; I heard Félicité's voice speaking to her just now, when I was upstairs," Dolly answered.

"They're taking another look at that new frock," Chase suggested, jocosely, as he seated himself to reread his correspondence (for he had already glanced through each letter in the street). "Where is Hill?" he went on rather vaguely, his attention already attracted by something in the first of these communications.

"He came in, after the welcoming ceremonies, red in the face from chasing Mrs. Kip. And the commodore appeared a moment later, also breathless, and in search of her. But Malachi was selected to walk home with the fair creature. And then the commodore trampled on Florida, and talked of the Green Mountains."

Dolly's tone was good-natured. But beneath this good-nature Chase fancied that there was jealousy. "Eh—what's that you say?" he responded, bringing out his words slowly, while he bestowed one more thought upon the page he was reading before he gave her his full attention. "The little Kip? Well, Dolly, she is a very sweet little woman, isn't she?" he went on, reasonably, as if trying to open her eyes gently to a fact that was undeniable. "But I didn't

know that Hill had a fancy in that quarter. If he
has, we must lend him a hand."

For Chase had a decided liking for Malachi; the
way the young clergyman had carried through that
rapid journey to New York and back, after Jared
Franklin's death, had won his regard and admiration.
Malachi had not stopped at Salisbury; his train went
no farther, but he had succeeded in getting a locomotive, by means of which, travelling on all night, he
had made a connection and reached New York in
time after all to meet Ruth's steamer. As it came in,
there he was on the dock, dishevelled and hungry,
but there.

And then when Ruth, frenzied by the tidings he
brought (for it really seemed to him almost frenzy),
had insisted upon starting on her journey to L'Hommedieu without an instant's delay, he had taken her,
with Félicité, southward again as rapidly as the
trains could carry them. His money was exhausted,
but he did not stop; he travelled on credit, pledging
his watch; it was because he had no money that he
had not telegraphed. At Old Fort he procured a
horse and light wagon, also on trust, and though he
had already spent four nights without sleep, he did
not stop, but drove Ruth across the mountains in the
darkness on a sharp trot, with the utmost skill and
daring, leaving Félicité to follow by stage. The sum
which Chase had placed in the envelope with the
ticket had been intended merely for his own expenses; the additional amount which was now re-

quired for Ruth and her maid soon exhausted it, together with all that he had with him of his own. Ruth's state of tension—for she was dumb, white, and strange—had filled him with the deepest apprehension; she did not think of money, and he could not bear to speak to her of it. Such a contingency had not occurred to Chase, who knew that his wife had with her more money than the cost of half a dozen such journeys; for her purse was always not only full, but over-full; it was one of his pleasures to keep it so. When, afterwards, he learned the facts (from Ruth herself, upon questioning her), he went off, found Malachi, and gave him what he called "a good big grip" of the hand. "You're a trump, Hill, and can be banked on every time!" Since then he had been Malachi's friend and advocate on all occasions, even to the present one of endeavoring to moderate the supposed jealousy of his sister-in-law regarding Lilian Kip.

After this kindly meant attempt of his, Dolly did not again interrupt him; she left him to finish his letters, while she went on with her knitting in silence.

Mrs. Franklin's prophecy, that Chase would end by liking Dolly for herself, had not as yet come true. Ruth's husband accepted the presence of his wife's sister under his roof; as she was an invalid, he would not have been contented to have her elsewhere. Dolly's life now moved on amid ease and comfort; she had her own attendant, who was partly a lady's-maid, partly a nurse; she had her own phaeton, and,

when in New York, her own coupé. If she was to
live with Ruth at all, there was, indeed, no other way;
she could not do her own sister the injustice of remaining a contrast, a jarring note by her side. Chase
was invariably kind to Dolly. Nevertheless Dolly
knew that her especial combination of ill-health and
sarcasm seemed to him incongruous; she could de-
tect in his mind the thought that it was odd that a
woman so sickly, with the added misfortune of a
plain face, should not at least try to be amiable, since
it was the only rôle she could properly fill. Her
little hostilities, as her mother had called them, were
now necessarily quiescent. But she had the conviction that, even if they had remained active, her tall
brother-in-law would not have minded them; he
would have taken, probably, a jocular view of them;
and of herself as well.

When the last letter was finished, and she saw her
companion begin on his newspapers, she spoke again:
"I don't think Ruth ought to go to that reception
to-night; she is not well enough."

" Why, I thought it was nothing but a very slight
cold," Chase said, turning round, surprised. "She
mustn't think of going if she's sick. She *wants* to
go; she telegraphed for that dress."

"Yes; last week. But that was before — before
she felt ill. If she goes now, it will be only because
you care for it."

"Oh, shucks! *I* care for it! What do I care for
that sort of thing? I'll go and tell her to give the

whole right up." He rose, leaving his newspapers
on the floor (Chase always wanted his newspapers
on the floor, and not on a table), and went towards
the door. But, at the same instant, Ruth herself
came in. "I was just going up to tell you, Ruthie,
that I guess we won't turn out to-night after all—I
mean to that show at the Barracks. I reckon they
can manage without us?"

"Oh, but I want to see it," said Ruth. "If you
are tired, I can go with Mrs. Kip."

"Well, who's running this family, anyway?" Chase
demanded, going back to his seat, not ill-pleased,
however, that Dolly should see that her information
concerning her sister was less accurate than his own.
But his care regarding everything that was connected
with his wife made him add, "You'll give it up if I
want you to, Ruthie?"

"You don't. It's Dolly!" Ruth declared. "Dolly-
Dulcinea, I have changed my mind. I did not want
to go this morning; I did not want to go this noon.
But, at half-past five o'clock precisely, I knew that I
must go or perish! Nothing shall keep me away."
And, gayly waving her hand to her sister, she went
into the music-room, which opened from the larger
apartment, and, seating herself at the piano, began
to play.

Chase returned to his reading; his only comment
to Dolly was, "She seems to *look* pretty well." And
it was true that Ruth looked not only well, but brilliant. After a while they heard her begin to sing:

"My short and happy day is done;
The long and dreary night comes on;
And at my door the Pale Horse stands,
To carry me to unknown lands.

"His whinny shrill, his pawing hoof,
Sound dreadful as a gathering storm;
And I must leave this sheltering roof,
And joys of life so soft and warm."

"*Don't* sing that!" called Dolly, sharply.

"Why not let her do as she likes?" suggested Chase, in the conciliatory tone he often adopted with Dolly. To him all songs were the same; he could not tell one from the other.

At this moment Malachi Hill entered, with his arms full of roses. "Long stalks?" said Ruth, hurrying to meet him. "Lovely! Now you shall help me make my posy. What shall I bring home for you in my pocket, Mr. Hill? Ice-cream?"

"Well, the truth is I am thinking of going myself," answered Malachi, coloring a little. "It has been mentioned to me that I ought to go—as a representative of the clergy. It is not in the least a ball, they tell me; it is a reception—a reception to General Grant. The young people may perhaps dance a little; but not until after the general's departure."

"Capital idea," said Chase, adding a fourth to his pile of perused sheets on the floor. "And don't go back on us, Hill, by proposing to escort some one else. Ruth wants to make an impression on the general, and, three abreast, perhaps we can do it."

Suddenly Ruth went to her sister. "Dolly, you must go too. Now don't say a word. You can go early and have a good seat; and as to dress, you can wear your opera-cloak."

"Oh no—" began Dolly.

But Ruth stopped her. "You must. I want you to *see* me there."

"Well, who's conceited, I'd like to know?" commented Chase, as he read on.

But Ruth's face wore no expression of conceit; its expression was that of determination. With infinite relief Dolly saw this. "I'll go," she said, comprehending Ruth's wish.

The reception was given by a West Point comrade of General Grant's, who happened to be spending the winter in Florida. As he had left the army many years before, he was now a civilian, and the participation of St. Francis Barracks in the affair was therefore accidental, not official. For the civilian, being a man of wealth, had erected for the occasion a temporary hall or ball-room, and had connected it by a covered passage with the apartments of his brother, who was an artillery officer, stationed that winter at this old Spanish post. At ten o'clock, this improvised hall presented a gay appearance, owing to the flowers with which it was profusely decorated, to the full dress of the ladies, and to the uniforms; for the army had been reinforced by a contingent from the navy, as two vessels belonging to the Coast Survey were in port.

The reticent personage to whom all this homage was offered looked as if he would like to get rid of it on any terms. He had commanded great armies, he had won great battles, and that seemed to him easy enough. But to stand and have his hand shaken —this was an ordeal!

A lane had been kept open through the centre of the long room in order to facilitate the presentations. At half-past ten, coming in his turn up this avenue, the tall figure of Horace Chase could be seen; his wife was with him, and they were preceded by the Rev. Malachi Hill. Chase, inwardly amused by the ceremony, advanced towards Grant with his face very solemn. But for the moment no one looked at him; all eyes were turned towards the figure by his side.

Half an hour earlier, as he sat alone in his drawing-room, waiting (and reading another newspaper to pass away the time), Ruth had come to him. As he heard her enter, he had looked up with a smile. Then his face altered a little.

"What! no diamonds?" he said.

Ruth wore the new dress about which he had joked, but no ornaments save a string of pearls.

"It shall be just as you like," she answered, in a steady voice.

"Oh no, Ruthie; just as *you* like."

He admired diamonds, and now that she was nearly twenty-three, he had said to himself that even her mother, if she had lived, would no longer have objected to her wearing them. He had therefore bought

for her recently a superb necklace, bracelets, and
other ornaments, and he had pleased himself with the
thought that for this official occasion they would be
entirely appropriate. Ruth, reading his disappoint-
ment in his eyes, went out, and returned a few minutes later adorned with all his gifts to the very last
stone. And now, as she came up the lane in the
centre of the crowded room, the gems gleamed and
flashed, gleamed on her neck, on her arms, in her
hair, and in the filmy lace of her dress. Always tall,
she had grown more womanly, and she could therefore bear the splendor. To-night, in addition, her
own face was striking, for her color had returned,
and her extraordinarily beautiful eyes were at their
best—lustrous and profound. It had always been said
of Ruth that her beauty came and went. To-night it
had certainly come, and to such a degree that it
spurred Etheridge to the exclamation, in an undertone :

"Too many diamonds. But, by George, she
shines them down!"

After the presentation was over Chase stepped
aside, and, with his wife, joined Dolly. Dolly had
a very good place ; draped in her opera-cloak, which
was made of a rich Oriental fabric, she looked odd,
ugly, and distinguished.

"Everybody is here except the Barclays," Etheridge announced. "There can't be a soul left in any
of the hotels. And all the negroes in town are on
the sea-wall outside, ready to hurrah when the great
man drives away."

"Here's Walter. He is coming this way—he is looking for *us*," said Chase. "How are you, Walter?"

"Mrs. Chase! Delighted to meet you again," said Willoughby, shaking hands with Ruth with the utmost cordiality.

"My sister is here also," Ruth answered, moving aside so that he could see Dolly. And then Walter greeted Miss Franklin with the same extreme heartiness.

"Bless my soul, what enthusiasm!" commented Etheridge. "One would suppose that you had not met for years."

"And we haven't," said Ruth, surveying Walter, coolly. "Mr. Willoughby has changed. He has a sort of Chinese air."

"Willoughby has been living in California for two years, commodore; didn't you know that?" Chase explained, inwardly enjoying his wife's sally. "*I've* been to California four times since then. But as he hasn't been east, the ladies have lost sight of him."

"Are you returning to the Pacific?" Etheridge inquired of the younger man, "so as to look more Chinese still?"

"The Celestial air I have already caught will have to do," Walter answered, laughing. "California is a wonderfully fascinating country. But I am not going back; the business which took me there is concluded."

Horace Chase smiled, detecting the triumph under these words. For his Pacific-coast enterprise had been highly successful, and Walter had carried out his part of it with great energy and intelligence, and had profited accordingly. That particular partnership was now dissolved.

When the dancing began, Ruth declined her invitations. "It isn't necessary to stay any longer, is it?" Dolly suggested in a low tone. "The carriage is probably waiting."

Here Chase, who had left them twenty minutes before, came up. "I've been seeing the general off," he said. "Well—he appeared middling glad to go! No dancing, Ruthie?" For he always remembered the things that amused his wife, and dancing, he knew, was high on her list.

And then, with that overtouch which it is so often the fate of an elder sister to bestow, Dolly said, "I really think she had better not try it. She is not thoroughly strong yet—after her cold."

This second assertion of a knowledge superior to his own annoyed Chase. And Ruth perceived it. "I am perfectly well," she answered. And, accepting the next invitation, she began to dance. She danced with everybody. Walter Willoughby had his turn with the rest.

A week later, Chase, coming home at sunset, looked into the drawing-room. His wife was not there, and he went upstairs in search of her. He found her in her dressing-room, with a work-basket by her side. "Well! I've never seen you *sew* before," he declared, amused by this new industry.

"I've had letters that make it necessary for me to go north, Ruthie. You'll be all right here, with Dolly, won't you?" He had seated himself, and was now glancing over a letter.

"Don't go," said Ruth, abruptly. And she went on sewing with her unnecessarily strong stitches; her mother had been wont to say of her that, if she sewed at all, the results were like iron.

Petie Trone, Esq., aged but still pretty, had been reposing on the lounge by her side. But the moment Chase seated himself, the little patriarch had jumped down, gone over, and climbed confidently up to his knees, where, after turning round three times, he had finally settled himself curled up like a black ball, with his nose on his tail.

"Oh, I must," Chase answered. "There's something I've got to attend to." And he continued to study the letter.

"Take me with you, then," said Ruth, going on with her rocklike seam.

"What's that? Take you?" her husband responded, still absorbed. "Not this time, I guess. For I'm going straight through to Chicago. It would tire you."

"No; I should like it; I don't want to stay here." She put down her work; going to one of the tables, she stood there with her back towards him, turning things over, but hardly as though she perceived what they were. Chase finished his letter. Then, as he replaced it in his pocket, he saw that she had risen, and, depositing Mr. Trone on the lounge, he went to her and put his arm round her shoulders.

"I'd take you if I could, Ruthie," he said, indulgently, beginning a reasonable argument with her. "But my getting to Chicago by a certain date is imperative, and to do it I've got to catch to-night's train and go through, and that would be too hard travelling for you. Besides, you would lose all the benefit of your Southern winter if you should hurry north now, while it is still so cold; that is always a mistake—to go north too early. Your winter here has done you lots of good, and that's a great pleasure to me. I want to be proud of you next summer at Newport, you know." And he pinched her cheek.

Ruth turned and looked at him. "*Are* you proud of me?"

"Oh no!" answered Chase, laughing. "Not at.all!" Then, after a moment, he went on, his tone altering. "I like to work a big deal through; I'm more or less proud of that, I reckon. But down below everything else, Ruthie, I guess my biggest pride is just—*you*." He was a man without any grace in speech. But certain tones of his voice had an eloquence of their own.

Ruth straightened herself. "I will do what you wish. I will stay here—as you prefer it. And you must keep on being proud of me. You must be proud of me always, *always*."

This made her husband laugh a second time. "It's a conceit that's come to stay, Mrs. Chase. You may put your money on it!"

CHAPTER XIX

As he walked down the sea-wall to his hotel after the Grant reception, Walter Willoughby said to himself that Mrs. Chase's coldness was the very thing he desired, the thing he had been hoping for, devoutly, for more than two years. The assertion was true. But though he had hoped, he had hardly expected that her indifference would have become so complete. If he did not exactly enjoy it, it had at least the advantage of leaving him perfectly free. For purposes of his own (purposes which had nothing to do with her), he had found it convenient to come to Florida this winter. And now that St. Augustine was reached, these same private purposes made him desire to remain there rather longer than he had at first intended. After the Grant reception he told himself with relief that there was now no reason, "no reason on earth," why he should not stay as long as it suited him to do so. He therefore remained. He joined in the amusements of the little winter-colony, the riding, driving, sailing, walking, and fishing parties that filled the lovely days. Under these conditions two weeks went by. Horace Chase had not as yet returned; he was engaged in one of those bold enterprises of a speculative nature

22

which he called " a little operation ;" occasionally he planned and carried through one of these campaigns alone.

On the last night of this second week Ruth came into her sister's room. It was one o'clock, but Dolly was awake ; the moonlight, penetrating the dark curtains, showed her who it was. " Is that you, Ruth?"

" Yes," Ruth answered. " Dolly, I want to go away."

Dolly raised herself, quickly. " Whenever you like," she answered. " We can go to-morrow morning by the first train ; they can pack one trunk, and the rest can be sent after us. I shall be quite well enough to go." For Dolly had been in bed all day, suffering severely ; it was the only day for two weeks which she had not spent, hour by hour, with her sister. " You will have had a telegram from Mr. Chase," she went on ; " we can say that as explanation."

Ruth turned away. She left the details to her sister.

" Oh, don't go off and shut yourself up. Stay here with me," pleaded Dolly, entreatingly.

" I'd rather be alone," Ruth began. But her voice broke. " No, I'm afraid ! I *will* stay here. But you mustn't talk to me, Dolly."

" Not a word," Dolly responded ; " if you will tell me, first, where you have been ?"

" Oh, only at Andalusia, as you know," Ruth answered, in the same exhausted tone. " It isn't very late ; every one stayed till after twelve. And I came home as I went; that is, with Colonel and Mrs. Atherton ; they left me just now at the door."

" Alone ?"

" No ; with Walter Willoughby. But he did not come in ; he only stood there on the steps with me for a moment ; that's all." While Ruth was saying this, she had taken off her hat and gloves ; then, in the dim light, Dolly saw her sink down on the divan, and lie there, motionless. The elder sister crept towards her on the outside of the bed (for the divan was across its foot), and covered her carefully with a warm shawl ; then, faithful to her promise, she returned to her place in silence. And neither of them spoke again.

On the divan Ruth was not fighting a battle ; she had given up, she was fleeing.

When, two years before, absorbed in her love for Walter, she had insisted upon that long, solitary voyage northward from Charleston, so that she could give herself up uninterruptedly to her own thoughts, alone with them and the blue sea, the tidings which had met her at New York as she landed—the tidings of her brother's death — had come upon her almost like a blinding shaft of lightning. It was as if she, too, had died. And she found her life again only partially, as she went southward in the rushing trains, as she crossed the mountains in the wagon, and arrived by night at dimly lighted L'Hommedieu. Sleepless through both journeys—the voyage north-

ward and the return by land — worn out by the
intense emotions which, in turn, had swept over
her, she had reached her mother's door at last so
exhausted that her vital powers had sunk low.
Then it was that the gentle care of the man who
knew nothing of the truth had saved her — saved
her from the dangerous tension of her own excitement, and, later, from a death-like faintness which, if
prolonged, would have been her end. For when she
beheld the changed, drawn, unconscious face of her
mother, that "mother" who had seemed to her as
much a fixed part of her life as her own breath, her
heart had failed her, failed not merely in the common meaning of the phrase, but actually; its pulsa-
tions grew so weak that a great dread seized her
— the instinctive shrinking of her whole young
being from the touch of death. In her terror, she
had fled to her husband, she had taken refuge in
his boundless kindness. "Oh, I am dying, Horace;
I *must* be dying! Save me!" was her frightened
cry.

For she was essentially feminine. In her character, the womanhood, the sweet, pure, physical womanhood, had a strong part; it had not been refined
away by over-development of the mental powers, or
reduced to a subordinate position by ascetic sur-
roundings. It remained, therefore, what nature had
made it. And it gave her a great charm. But its
presence left small place for the more masculine
qualities, for stoical fortitude and courage; she

could not face fear; she could not stand alone; and she had always, besides, the need to be cherished and protected, to be held dear, very dear.

This return to her husband was sincere as far as it carried her. From one point of view, it might be said that she had never left him. For her love for Walter had contained no plan; and her girlish affection for Horace Chase remained what it always had been, though the deeper feelings were now awake underneath.

Time passed; the days grew slowly to months, and the months at last became a long year, and then two. Little by little she fell back into her old ways; she laughed at Dolly's sallies, she talked and jested with her husband. She sometimes asked herself whether those buried feelings would ever rise and take possession of her again. But Walter remained absent — that was the thing that saved her. A personal presence was with her always a powerful influence. But an absence was equally powerful in its quieting effect; it produced temporarily more or less oblivion. She had never been able to live on memories. And she had a great desire at all times to be happy. And, therefore, to a certain degree, she did become happy again; she amused herself with fair success at Newport and New York.

And then Walter had re-entered the circle of her life. And by a fatality this had come to her at St. Augustine. On the morning of the day of the Grant reception, she had suddenly learned that he was in town. And she knew (it came like a wave over her) that she dreaded the meeting.

There had been no spoken confidences between the sisters. But Dolly had instantly extended all the protection that was in her power, and even more; for she had braved the displeasure of her brother-in-law by maintaining that his wife was ill, and that she (Dolly) knew more of the illness than he did. And then, suddenly, this elder sister was put in the wrong. For Ruth herself appeared, declaring gayly that she was well, perfectly well. The gayety was assumed. But the declaration that she was well was a truthful one; she was not only well, but her heart was beating with excitement. For the idea had taken possession of her that this was the very opportunity she needed to prove to herself (and to Dolly also) that she was changed, that she was calm and indifferent. And it would be a triumph also to show this indifference to Walter. Her acts, her words, her every intonation should make this clear to him; delightfully, coldly, brilliantly clear!

Yet, into this very courage had come, as an opposing force, that vague premonition which had made her suddenly begin to sing "The Stirrup Cup."

But a mood of renewed gayety had followed; she had entered the improvised ball-room with pulses beating high, sure that all was well.

Before the evening was over she knew that all was ill; she knew that at the bottom of everything what had made her go thither was simply the desire to see Walter Willoughby once more.

When, a few days later, her husband told her that he was going north, with one of her sudden impulses she said, "Take me with you." He had not consented. And she knew that she was glad that he had not. Certain tones of his voice, however, when he spoke of his pride in her, had touched her deeply; into her remembrance came the thought of all he had done for her mother, all he had done for Jared, and she strengthened herself anew: she would go through with it and he should know nothing; he should remain proud of her always, always.

But this was not a woman who could go on unmoved seeing daily the man she loved; those buried feelings rose again to the surface, and she was powerless to resist them. All she could do (and this required a constant effort) was to keep her cold manner unaltered.

Walter, meanwhile, was not paying much heed to Mrs. Chase. At the Grant reception, he had been piqued by her sarcasms; he had smarted under the surprise which her laughing coolness and gayety gave him. But this vexation soon faded; it was, after all, nothing compared with the great desire which he had at this particular moment to find himself entirely free from entanglements of that nature. He was therefore glad of her coldness. He continued to see her often; in that small society they could not help but meet. And occasionally he asked himself if there was nothing underneath this glittering frost? No least little scrap left of her feeling of two years before? But, engrossed as he was with his own projects, this curiosity remained dormant until suddenly these projects went astray; they encountered an obstacle which for the time being made it impossible for him to pursue them further. This happened at the end of his second week in St. Augustine. Foiled, and more or less irritated, and having also for the moment nothing else to do, he felt in the mood to solace himself a little with the temporary entertainment of finding out (of course in ways that would be unobserved by others) whether there was or was not anything left of the caprice which the millionaire's pretty wife had certainly felt for him when he was in Florida before.

For that was his idea of it—a caprice. He saw only one side of Ruth's nature; to him she seemed a thoughtless, spoiled young creature, highly impressionable, but all on the surface; no feeling would last long with her or be very deep, though for the moment it might carry her away.

What he did was so little, during this process of finding out, and what he said was so even less, that if related it would not have made a narrative, it would have been nothing to tell. But the woman he was studying was now like a harp: the lightest touch of his hand on the strings drew out the music. And when, therefore, upon that last night, taking advantage of the few moments he had with her alone at her door, after her friends from the Barracks had passed on—when he then said a word or two, to her it was fatal. His phrase meant in reality nothing; it was tentative only. But Ruth had no suspicion of this; her own love was direct, uncomplicated, and overmastering; she supposed that his was the same. She looked at him dumbly; then she turned, entering the house with rapid step and hurrying up the stairs, leaving the sleepy servant who came forward to meet her to close the door. Fatal had his words been to her; fatally sweet!

The two sisters left St. Augustine the next morning; in the evening they were far down the St. John's River on their way to Savannah. They sat together near the bow of the steamer, watching in silence the windings of the magnificent stream; the moonlight was so bright that they could see the silvery long-moss draping the live-oaks on shore, and, in the tops of signal cypresses, bare and gaunt, the huge nests of the fish-hawks, like fortifications.

" Poor Chase! covering her with diamonds, and giving her everything; while *I* can turn her round my finger!" Walter said to himself when he heard they had gone.

On the day of his wife's departure—that sudden departure from St. Augustine of which he as yet knew nothing, Horace Chase, in Chicago, was bringing to a close his " little operation "; by six o'clock, four long-headed men had discovered that they had been tremendously out-generalled. Later in the evening, three of these men happened to be standing together in a corridor of one of the Chicago hotels, when the successful operator, who was staying in the house, came by chance through the same brightly lighted passage-way.

"I guess you think, Chase, that you've got the laugh on us," said one of the group. "But just wait a month or two; we'll make you walk!"

"Oh, the devil!" answered Chase, passing on.

"He's as hard as flint!" said the second of the discomfited trio, who, depressed by his losses (which to him meant ruin), had a lump in his throat. "There isn't such a thing as an ounce of feeling in Horace Chase's *whole* composition, damn him!"

CHAPTER XX

His little campaign over, Horace Chase made his preparations for returning to Florida. These consisted in hastily throwing into a valise the few things which he had brought with him, and ringing the bell to have a carriage called so that he could catch the midnight train. As he was stepping into this carriage, a telegram was handed to him. "Hold on a minute," he called to the driver, as he opened it. "We are on our way to Savannah," he read. "You will find us at the Scriven House. Ruth not well." And the signature was "Dora Franklin." "Drive on," he called a second time, and as the carriage rolled towards the station he said to himself, "That Dolly! Always trying to make out that Ruth's sick. I guess it's only that she's tired of Florida. She wanted to leave when *I* came north; asked me to take her."

But when he reached Savannah, he found his wife if not ill, at least much altered; she was white and silent, she scarcely spoke; she sat hour after hour with her eyes on a book, though the pages were not turned. "She isn't well," Dolly explained again.

"Then we must have in the doctors," Chase answered, decisively. "I'll get the best advice from New York immediately; I'll wire at once."

"Don't; it would only bother her," objected Dolly. "They can do no more for her than we can, for it is nothing but lack of strength. Take her up to L'Hommedieu, and let her stay there all summer; that will be the best thing for her, by far."

"That's the question; will it?" remarked Chase to himself, reflectively.

"Do I know her, or do I not?" urged Dolly. "I have been with her ever since she was born. Trust me, at least where *she* is concerned; for she is all I have left in the world, and I understand her every breath."

"Of course I know you think no end of her," Chase answered. But he was not satisfied; he went to Ruth herself. "Ruthie, you needn't go to Newport this summer, if you're tired of it; you can go anywhere you like, short of Europe (for I can't quite get abroad this year). There are all sorts of first-rate places, I hear, along the coast of Maine."

"I don't care where I go," Ruth answered, dully, "except that I want to be far away from—from the tiresome people we usually see."

"Well, that means far away from Newport, doesn't it? We've been there for two summers," Chase answered, helping her (as he thought) to find out what she really wanted. "Would you like to go up the lakes—to Mackinac and Marquette?"

"No, L'Hommedieu would do, perhaps."

"Yes, Dolly's plan. Are you doing it for *her?*"

"Oh," said Ruth, with weary truthfulness, "don't you know that I never do things for Dolly, but that it's always Dolly who does things for me?"

Her husband took her to L'Hommedieu.

She seemed glad to be there; she wandered about and looked at her mother's things; she opened her mother's secretary and used it; she sat in her mother's easy-chair, and read her books. There was no jarring element at hand; Genevieve, beneficent, much admired, and well off, had been living for two years in St. Louis; her North Carolina cottage was now occupied by Mrs. Kip.

Chase had the inspiration of sending for Kentucky Belle, and after a while Ruth began to ride. This did her more good than anything else; every day she was out for hours among the mountains with her husband, and often with the additional escort of Malachi Hill.

One morning they made an expedition to the wild gorge where the squirrel had received his freedom two years before; Ruth dismounted, and walked about under the trees, looking up into the foliage.

"He's booming; he's got what *he* likes," said Chase—"your Robert the Squirrel; or Robert the Devil, as Dolly called him."

"Oh, I don't want him back," Ruth answered; "I am glad he is free. Every one ought to be free," she went on, musingly, as though stating a new truth which she had just discovered.

" I came out nearly every week, Mrs. Chase, during the first six months, with nuts for him," said Malachi, comfortingly. " I used to bring at least a quart, and I put them in a particular place. Well—they were always gone."

As they came down a flank of the mountain overlooking the village, Chase surveyed the valley with critical eyes. " If we really decide to take this thing up at last—Nick and Richard Willoughby, and myself, and one or two more—my own idea would be to have a grand combine of all the advantages possible," he began. " In the United States we don't do this thing up half so completely as they do abroad. Over there, if they have mountains—as in Switzerland, for instance—they don't trust to that alone, they don't leave people to sit and stare at 'em all day ; they add other attractions. They have boys with horns, where there happen to be echoes ; they illuminate the waterfalls ; girls dressed up in costumes milk cows in arbors ; and men with flowers and other things stuck in their hats, yodel and sing. All sorts of carved things, too, are constantly offered for sale, such as salad-forks, paper-cutters, and cuckoo clocks. Then, if it isn't mountains, but springs, they always have the very best music they can get, to make the water go down. It would be a smart thing to have the sulphur near here brought into town in pipes to a sort of park, where we could have a casino with a hall for dancing, and a restaurant where you could always get a first-class meal. And, outside, a stand for the band.

And then in the park there ought to be, without fail, long rows of bright little stores for the ladies—like those at Baden-Baden, Ruthie? No large articles sold, but a great variety of small things. Ladies always like that; they can drink the water, listen to the music, and yet go shopping too, and buy all sorts of little knick-knacks to take home as presents; it would be extremely popular. The North Carolina garnets and amethysts could be sold; and specimens of the mica and gold and the native pink marble could be exhibited. Then those Cherokee Indians out Qualla way might be encouraged to come to the park with their baskets and bead-work to sell. And there must be, of course, a museum of curiosities, stuffed animals, and mummies, and such things. There's a museum opposite that lion cut in the rock at Lucerne Hill—I guess you've heard of it? It attracts more interest than the lion himself; I've watched, and I know; ten out of twelve of the people who come there, look two minutes at the lion, and give ten at least to the museum. Then it wouldn't be a half-bad idea to get hold of an eminent doctor; we might make him a present of half a mountain as an inducement. Larue, by the way, won't be of much use to our boom, now that he isn't a senator any longer. Did they kick him out, Hill, or freeze him out?"

"Well—he resigned," answered Malachi, diplomatically. "You see, they wanted the present senator—a man who has far more magnetism."

"Larue never *was* 'in it'; I saw that from the

first," Chase commented. "Well, then, in addition, there must, of course, be a hospital in the town, so that the ladies can get up fairs for it each year at the height of the season; they find the *greatest* interest in fairs; I've often noticed it. Then I should give *my* vote for a good race-course. And, finally, all the churches ought to be put in tip-top condition—painted and papered and made more attractive. But that, Hill, we'll leave to you."

Malachi laughed. He admired Horace Chase greatly, but he had long ago despaired of making him pay heed to certain distinctions. "I think I won't meddle with the other churches if you will only help along ours," he answered; "our Church school here, and my mountain missions."

"All right; we'll boom them all," said Chase, liberally. "There might be a statue of Daniel Boom in the park, near the casino," he went on in a considering tone; "he lived near here for some time. Though, come to think of it, his name was Boone, wasn't it?—just missed being appropriate! Well, at any rate, we can have a statue of Colonel David Vance, and of Dr. Mitchell, who is buried on Mitchell's Peak. And of David L. Swain."

"Have you any especial sculptor in view?" inquired Malachi, who was not without a slight knowledge of art.

"No. But we could get a good marble-cutter to take a contract for the lot; that would be the easiest way, I reckon."

Malachi could not help being glad, revengefully glad, that at least there was no mention of Maud Muriel. Only the day before the sculptress had greeted him with her low-breathed "Manikin!" as he came upon her in a narrow winding lane which he had incautiously entered. A man may be as dauntless as possible (so he told himself), but that does not help him when his assailant is a person whom he cannot knock down—"a striding, scornful, sculping spinster!" "She had better look out!" he had thought, angrily, as he passed on.

His morning ride over, Chase took a fresh horse after lunch, and went down to Crumb's. Nicholas Willoughby, struck by the wildness and beauty of these North Carolina mountains, had built a cottage on the high plateau above Crumb's, the plateau which Chase had named "Ruth's Terrace" several years before. During the preceding summer, Nicholas had occupied this house (which he called The Lodge) for a month or more. This year, having lent it to some friends for August and September, he had asked Chase to see that all was in order before their arrival.

While Chase was off upon this errand, Ruth and Dolly were to go for a drive along the Swannanoa. But first Dolly stopped at Miss Mackintosh's barn; her latest work was on exhibition there. This was nothing less than a colossal study in clay of the sculptress's own back from the nape of the neck to the waist; Dolly, who had already had a view of this masterpiece, was now bringing Ruth to see it, with the hope that it would make her laugh. It did. Her old mirth came back for several minutes as she gazed at the rigidly faithful copy of Maud Muriel's shoulder-blades, her broad, gaunt shoulders, and the endless line of conscientiously done vertebræ adorning her spine.

Mrs. Kip was there, also looking. " Maud Muriel, how could you *see* your back ?" she inquired.

" Hand-glass," replied the sculptress, briefly.

" Well, to me it looks hardly proper," commented Mrs. Kip ; " it's so—*exposed*. And then, without any head or arms, it seems so mutilated ; like some awful thing from a battle-field ! I don't think it's necessary for lady artists to study anatomy, Maud Muriel ; it isn't expected of them ; it doesn't seem quite feminine. Why don't you carve angels ? They *have* no anatomy, and, of course, they need none. Angels, little children, and flowers—I think those are the most appropriate subjects for *lady* artists, both in sculpture and in painting." Then, seeing Maud Muriel begin to snort (as Dolly called the dilation of the sculptress's nostrils when she was angry), Mrs. Kip hurried on, changing the subject as she went. " But sculpture certainly agrees with you, Maudie dear. I really think your splendid hair grows thicker and thicker ! You could always earn your living (if you had occasion) by just having yourself photographed, back-view, with your hair down, and a placard — ' Results of Barry's Tricopherus.' Barry would give *anything* to get you."

Maud Muriel was not without humor, after her curt fashion. "Well, Lilian," she answered, "*you* might be 'Results of Packer's Granulated Food,' I'm sure. You look exactly like one of the prize health-babies."

"Oh no!" cried Mrs. Kip, in terror, "I'm not at *all* well, Maud Muriel. Don't tell me so, or I shall be ill directly! Neither Evangeline Taylor nor I are in the *least* robust; we are *both* pulmonic."

At this moment Evangeline herself appeared at the door, accompanied by her inseparable Miss Green, a personage who was the pride of Mrs. Kip's existence. This was not for what she was, but for her title: "Evangeline Taylor and her governess"—this to Mrs. Kip seemed almost royal. She now hurried forward to meet her child, and, taking her arm, led her away from the torso to the far end of the barn, where two new busts were standing on a table, one of them the likeness of a short-nosed, belligerent boy, and the other of a dreary, sickly woman. "Come and look at these *sweet* things, darling."

And then Ruth broke into a second laugh.

"Mrs. Chase," said Maud Muriel, suddenly, "I wish *you* would sit to me."

"No. Ask her husband to sit," suggested Dolly. "You know you like to do men best, Maud Muriel."

"Well, generally speaking, the outlines of a man's face are more distinct," the sculptress admitted. "And yet, Dolly, it doesn't always follow. For, generally speaking, women—"

"Maud Muriel, I am *never* generally speaking, but always particularly," Dolly declared. "Do Mr. Chase. He will come like a shot if you will smoke your pipe; he has been dying to see you do it for three years.

"I have given up the pipe; I have cigars now," explained Maud, gravely. "But I do not smoke here; I take a walk with a cigar on dark nights—"

"Sh! Don't talk about it now," interrupted Mrs. Kip, warningly. For Evangeline Taylor, having extracted all she could from the "sweet things," was coming towards them. There was a good deal to come. Her height was now six feet and an inch. Her long, rigid face wore an expression which she intended to be one of deep interest in the works of art displayed before her; but as she was more shy than ever, her eyes, as she approached the group, had a suppressed nervous gleam which, with her strange facial tension, made her look half-mad.

"Dear child!" said the mother, fondly, as Ruth, to whom the poor young giant was passionately devoted, made her happy by taking her off and talking to her kindly, apart. "She has the true Taylor eyes. So profound! And yet so dove-like!" Here the head of Achilles Larue appeared at the open door, and Lilian abandoned the Taylor eyes to whisper quickly, "Oh, Maud Muriel, do cover that dreadful thing up!"

"Cover it up? Why—it is what he has come to see," answered the intrepid Maud.

The ex-senator inspected the torso. "Most praiseworthy, Miss Mackintosh. And, in execution, quite —quite fairish. Though you have perhaps exaggerated the anatomical effect—the salient appearance of the bones?"

"Not at all. They are an exact reproduction from life," answered Maud, with dignity.

Lilian Kip, still apprehensive as to the influence of the torso upon a young mind, sent her daughter home to play "battledoor and shuttlecock, dear" (Evangeline played "battledoor and shuttlecock, dear," every afternoon for an hour with her governess, to acquire "grace of carriage"); Larue was now talking to Ruth, and Lilian, after some hesitation, walked across the barn and seated herself on a bench at its far end (the only seat in that resolute place); from this point she gazed and gazed at Larue. He was as correct as ever—from his straight nose to his finger-tips; from his smooth, short hair, parted in the middle, to his long, slender foot with its high instep. Dolly, tired of standing, came after a while and sat down on the bench beside the widow. They heard Achilles say, "No; I decided not to go." Then, a few minutes later, came another "No; I decided not to do that."

"All his decisions are *not* to do things," commented Dolly, in an undertone. "When he dies, it can be put on his tombstone: 'He was a verb in the passive voice, conjugated negatively.' Why, what's the matter, Lilian?"

"It's nothing—I am only a little agitated. I will tell you about it some time," answered Mrs. Kip, squeezing Dolly's hand. Ruth, tired of the senator, looked across at Dolly. Dolly joined her, and they took leave.

Maud Muriel followed them to the door. "I *should* like to do your head, Ruth."

"No; you are to do Mr. Chase's," Dolly called back from the phaeton. "She has been in love with your husband from the first," she went on to her sister, as she turned her pony's head towards the Swannanoa. And then Ruth laughed a third time.

But though Dolly thus made sport, in her heart there was a pang. She knew—no one better—that her sister's face had changed greatly during the past three months. Now that his wife was well again, Chase himself noticed nothing. And to the little circle of North Carolina friends Ruth was dear; they were very slow to observe anything that was unfavorable to those they cared for. To-day, however, Maud Muriel's unerring scent for ugliness had put her (though unconsciously) upon the track, and, for the first time in all their acquaintance, she had asked Ruth to sit to her. It was but a scent as yet; Ruth was still lovely. But the elder sister could see, as in a vision, that with several years more, under the blight of hidden suffering, her beauty might disappear entirely; her divine blue eyes alone could not save her if her color should fade, if the sweet expression of her mouth should alter to confirmed unhappiness, if her face should grow so thin that its irregular outlines would become apparent.

Two hours later there was a tap at Miss Billy Breeze's door, at the Old North Hotel.

"Come in," said Miss Billy. "Oh, is it you, Lilian? I am glad to see you. I haven't been out this afternoon, as it seemed a little coolish!"

Mrs. Kip looked excited. "Coolish, Billy?" she repeated, standing still in the centre of the room. "Ish? *Ish?* And I, too, have said it; I don't pretend to deny it. But it is over at last, and I am free! I have been — been different for some time. But I did not know *how* different until this very afternoon. I met him at Maud Muriel's barn, soon after two. And I sat there, and looked at him and *looked* at him. And suddenly it came across me that *perhaps* after all I didn't care *quite* so much for him. I was so nervous that I could scarcely speak, but I did manage to ask him to take a little stroll with me. For you see I wanted to be perfectly *sure.* And as he walked along beside me, putting down his feet in that precise sort of way he does, and every now and then saying 'ish' — like a great light in the dark, like a falling off of *chains,* I knew that it was at last at an end—that he had ceased to be all the world to me. And it was such an *enormous* relief that when I came back, if there had been a circus or a menagerie in town, I give you my word I should certainly have gone to it—as a celebration! And then, Billy, I thought of *you.* And I made up my mind that I

would come right straight over here and ask you—
Is he worth it? What has Achilles Larue ever done
for either of us, Billy, but just snub, snub, snub?
and crush, crush, crush? If you could only feel what
a joy it is to have that tiresome old ache gone! And
to just *know* that he is hateful!" And Lilian, much
agitated, took Billy's hand in hers.

But Billy, dim and pale, drew herself away. "You
do him great injustice, Lilian. But he has never
expected the ordinary mind to comprehend him. Your
intentions, of course, are good, and I am obliged to
you for them. But I am not like you; to me it is a
pleasure, and always will be, as well as a constant
education, to go on admiring the greatest man I have
ever known!"

"Whether he looks at you or not?" demanded
Lilian.

"Whether he looks at me or not," answered Billy,
firmly.

"If you had ever been *married*, Wilhelmina, you
would know that you could not go on forever living
on *shadows!*" declared the widow as she took leave.
"Shadows may be all very well. But we are human, after all, and we need *realities*." Having decided upon a new reality, her step was so joyous that
Horace Chase, coming home from his long ride to
Crumb's, hardly recognized her, as he passed her in
the twilight. At L'Hommedieu he found no one in
the sitting-room but Dolly. "Ruth is resting after
our drive," explained the elder sister. "I took her

first to the barn to see Maud Muriel's torso, and that made her laugh tremendously. Well, is The Lodge in order?"

"Yes, it's all right; Nick's friends can come along as soon as they like," Chase answered.

"And are none of the Willoughbys to be there this summer?" Dolly went on.

"No; Nick has gone to Carlsbad—he isn't well. And Richard is off yachting. Walter has taken a cottage at Newport."

Dolly already knew this latter fact. But she wished to hear it again.

Rinda now appeared, ushering in Malachi Hill. The young clergyman was so unusually erect that he seemed tall; his face was flushed, and his eyes had a triumphant expression. He looked first at Dolly, then at Chase. "I've done it!" he announced, dashing his clerical hat down upon the sofa. "That Miss Mackintosh has called me 'Manikin' once too often. She did it again just now—in the alley behind your house. And I up and kissed her!"

"You didn't," said Chase, breaking into a roaring laugh.

"Yes; I did. For three whole years and more, Mr. Chase, that woman has treated me with perfectly outrageous contempt. She has seemed to think that I was nothing at all, that I wasn't a man; she has walked on me, stamped on me, shoved me right and left, and even kicked me, as it were. I have felt that I couldn't stand it *much* longer. And I have tried to think of a way to take her down. Suddenly, just now, it came to me that nothing on earth would take her down quite so much as that. And so when she came out with her accustomed epithet, I just gave her a hurl, and did it! It is true I'm a clergyman, and I have acted as though I had kept on being only an insurance agent. But a man is a man after all, in spite of the cloth," concluded Malachi, belligerently.

"Oh, don't apologize," said Dolly. "It's too delicious!" And then she and Horace Chase, for once of the same mind, laughed until they were exhausted.

Meanwhile the sculptress had appeared in Miss Billy's sitting-room. She came in without knocking, her footfall much more quiet than usual. "Wilhelmina, how old are you?" she demanded, after she had carefully closed the door.

"Why—you know. I am thirty-nine," Billy answered, putting down with tender touch the book she was reading (*The Blue Ridge in the Glacial Period*).

"And I am forty," pursued Maud, meditatively. "It is never too late to add to one's knowledge, Wilhelmina, if the knowledge is accurate; that is, if it is observed from life. And I have stopped in for a moment, on my way home, to mention something which *is* so observed. You know all the talk and fuss there is in poetry, Wilhelmina, about kisses (I mean when given by a man)? I am now in a position to tell you, from actual experience, what they amount to." She came nearer, and lowered her voice. "They are *very far indeed* from being what is described. There is nothing in them. Nothing whatever!"

CHAPTER XXI

HORACE CHASE spent the whole summer at
L'Hommedieu, without any journeys or absences. His
wife rode with him several times a week; she drove
out with Dolly in the phaeton; she led her usual life.
Usual, that is, to a certain extent; for, personally,
she was listless, and the change in her looks was
growing so much more marked that at last every one,
save her husband, noticed it. When September
came, Chase went to New York on business. He
was absent two weeks. When he returned he found
his wife lying on the sofa. She left the sofa for a
chair when he came in; but, after the first day, she
no longer made this effort; she remained on the
couch, hour after hour, with her eyes closed. Once
or twice, when her husband urged it, she rode out
with him. But her figure drooped so, as she sat in
the saddle, that he did not ask her to go again. He
began to feel vaguely uneasy. She seemed well;
but her silence and her pallor troubled him. As she
herself was impenetrable—sweet, gentle, and dumb—
he was finally driven to speak to Dolly.

"You say she seems well," Dolly answered. "But
that is just the trouble; she seems so, but she is
not. What she needs, in my opinion, is a complete

change—a change of scene and air and associations of all kinds. Take her abroad for five or six years, and arrange your own affairs so that you can stay there with her."

"Five or six years? That's a large order; that's *living* over there," Chase said, surprised.

"Yes," answered Dolly, "that is what I mean. Live there for a while." Then she made what was to her a supreme sacrifice: "*I* will stay here. I won't try to go." This was a bribe. She knew that her brother-in-law found her constant presence irksome.

"Of course I wouldn't hesitate if I thought it would set her up," said Chase. "I'll see what she says about it."

"If you consult her, that will be the end of the whole thing," answered Dolly; "you will never go, and neither will she. For she will feel that you would be sure to dislike it. You ought to arrange it without one syllable to her, and then *do* it. And if I were you, I wouldn't postpone it too long."

"What do you talk that way for?" said Chase, angrily. "You have no right to keep anything from me if you *know* anything. What do you think's the matter with her, that you take that tone?"

"I think she is dying," Dolly answered, stolidly. "Slowly, of course; it might require three or four years more at the present rate of progress. If nothing is done to stop it, by next year it would be called nervous prostration, perhaps. And then, the year after, consumption."

Chase sprang up. "How dare you sit there and talk to me of her dying?" he exclaimed, hotly. "What the hell do you mean?"

Dolly preserved her composure unbroken. "She has never been very strong. Nobody can know with absolute accuracy, Mr. Chase; but at least I am telling you exactly what I think."

"I'll take her abroad at once. I'll live over there forever if it will do any good," Chase answered, turning to go out in order to hide his emotion.

"Remember, if you tell her about it beforehand, she will refuse to go," Dolly called after him.

Always prompt, that same afternoon Chase started northward. He was on his way to New York, with the intention of arranging his affairs so that he could leave them for several years. It would be a heavy piece of work. But work never daunted him. The very first moment that it was possible he intended to return to L'Hommedieu, take his wife, and go abroad by the next steamer, allowing her not one hour for demur. In the meanwhile, she was to know nothing of the project; it was to take her by surprise, according to Dolly's idea.

Dolly spent the time of his absence in trying to amuse her sister, or at least in trying to occupy her and fill the long days. These days, out of doors, were heavenly in their beauty; the atmosphere of paradise, as we imagine paradise, was now lent to earth for a time; a fringe of it lay over the valley of the French Broad. The sunshine was a golden haze; the hue of the mountains was like violet velvet; there was no wind, the air was perfectly still; in all directions the forest was glowing and flaming with the indescribably gorgeous tints of the American autumn. For a time Ruth had seemed a little stronger; she had taken two or three drives in the phaeton. Then her listlessness came back with double force. One afternoon Dolly found her lying with her head on her arm (like a flower half-broken from its stalk, poor Dolly thought). But the elder sister began bravely, with a laugh. "Well, it's out, Ruth. It is announced to-day, and everybody knows it. I mean the engagement of Malachi and the fair Lilian. But somebody ought really to speak to them, it is a public matter; it ought to be in the hands of a Society for the Prevention of Cruelty to the Future. Think of her profile, and then of his, and imagine, if you can, a combination of the two let loose upon an innocent world!"

Ruth smiled a little, but the smile was faint. She lay for some minutes longer with closed eyes, and then, wearily, she sat up. "Oh, I am so tired of this room! I believe I'll go out, after all. Please call Félicité, and order the phaeton."

"A drive? That is a good idea, as it is such a divine afternoon," said Dolly. "I will go with you."

"Oh no—with your lame arm." (For rheumatism had been bothering Dolly all day.) "If you are afraid to have me go alone, I can take Félicité."

"Very well," said Dolly, who thwarted Ruth now in nothing. "May I sit here while you dress?"

"If you like," answered Ruth, her voice dull and languid.

Dolly pretended to knit, and she made jokes about the approaching nuptials. "It is to come off during Christmas week, they say. The bishop is to be here, but he will only pronounce the benediction, for Lilian prefers to have Mr. Arlington perform the ceremony. You see, she is accustomed to Mr. Arlington; she usually has him for her marriages, you know." But in Dolly's heart, as she talked, there were no jokes. For as Félicité dressed Ruth, the elder sister could not help seeing how wasted was the slender figure. And when the skilful hand of the Frenchwoman brushed and braided the thick hair, the hollows at the temples were conspicuous. Félicité, making no remark about it, shaded these hollows with little waving locks. But Ruth, putting up her hands impatiently, pushed the locks all back.

When she returned from her drive two hours later, the sun was setting. She entered the parlor with rapid step, her arms full of branches of bright leaves which she had gathered. Their tints were less bright than her cheeks, and her eyes had a radiance that was startling.

Dolly looked at her, alarmed, though (faithful to her rule) she made no comment. "Can it be fever?" she thought. But this was not fever.

Ruth decorated the room with her branches. She

said nothing of importance, only a vague word or two about the sunshine, and the beauty of the brilliant forest; but she hummed to herself, and finally broke into a song, as with the same rapid step she went upstairs to her room.

A few moments later Miss Billy Breeze was shown in. "I couldn't help stopping for a moment, Dolly, because I am so perfectly delighted to see that dear Ruth is *so* much better; she passed me a little while ago in her phaeton, looking really brilliant! Her old self again. After all, the mountain air *has* done her good. I was so glad that (I don't mind telling you) — I went right home and knelt down and thanked God," said the good little woman, with the tears welling up in her pretty eyes.

Miss Billy stayed nearly half an hour. Just before she went away she said (after twenty minutes of excited talk about Lilian and Malachi), "Oh, I saw Mr. Willoughby in the street this afternoon; he had ridden up from The Lodge, so Mr. Bebb told me. I didn't know he was staying there?"

"Why, has he come back from Carlsbad?" asked Dolly, surprised.

"Oh, I don't mean Mr. Nicholas Willoughby," answered Billy, "I mean Walter; the nephew, you know. The one who was groomsman at Ruth's wedding."

24

Ruth had seen Walter. It was this which had given her that new life. Tired of Félicité's "flapping way of driving," as she called it, she had left the phaeton for a few moments, and was sitting by herself in the forest, with her elbow on her knee and her chin resting on the palm of her hand; her eyes, vaguely fixed on a red bush near by, had an indescribably weary expression. Her figure was out of sight from the place where the phaeton and the maid were waiting; her face was turned in the other direction. In this direction there was at some distance a second road, and along this track she saw presently a man approaching on horseback. Suddenly she recognized him. It was Walter Willoughby. He slackened his speed for a moment to say a word or two to a farmer who was on his way to Asheville with a load of wood; then, touching his horse with his whip, he rode on at a brisk pace, and in a moment more was out of sight.

Ruth had started to her feet. But the distance was too great for her to call to him. Straight as the flight of an arrow she ran towards the wagon, which was pursuing its way, the horses walking slowly, the wheels giving out a regular "scrunch, scrunch."

"The gentleman who spoke to you just now—do you know where he is staying?"

"Down to Crumb's; leastways that new house they've built on the mountain 'bove there. He 'lowed I might bring him down some peaches! But *peaches* is out long ago," replied the man. Ruth returned home. She went through the evening in a dream, listening to Dolly's remarks without much answer; then, earlier than usual, she sought her own room. She fell asleep instantly, and her sleep was so profound that Dolly, who stole softly to the door at midnight and again at one o'clock, to see if all was well, went back to her room greatly cheered. For this was the best night's rest which Ruth had had for months. The elder sister, relieved and comforted, soon sank into slumber herself.

Ruth's tranquil rest came simply from freedom, from the end of the long struggle which had been consuming her strength and her life. The sudden vision of the man she loved, his actual presence before her, had broken down her last barrier; it had given way silently, as a dam against which deep water has long pressed yields sometimes without a sound when the flood rises but one inch higher. She slept because she was going to him, and she knew that she was going.

She had been vaguely aware that she could not see Walter again with any security. It was this which had made her take refuge in her mother's old home in the mountains, far away from him and from all chance of meeting him. She could not trust herself, but she could flee. And she had fled. This, however, was the limit of her force; her will had not the power to sustain her, to keep her from lassitude and despair; and thus she had drooped and faded until to her sister had come that terrible fear that the end would really be death. When Walter appeared, she was powerless to resist further, she went to him as the needle turns to the pole. Her love led her like a despot, and it was sweet to her to be thus led. Her action was utterly uncalculating; the loss of her home was as nothing to her; the loss of her good-repute, nothing; her husband, her sister, the whole world—all were alike forgotten. She had but one thought, one idea—to go to him.

She woke an hour before dawn; it was the time she had fixed upon. She left her bed and dressed herself, using the brilliant moonlight as her candle; with soft, quick steps she stole down the stairs to the kitchen, and taking a key which was hanging from a nail by the fireplace, she let herself out. The big watch-dog, Turk, came to meet her, wagging his tail. She went to the stable, unlocked the door, and leaving it open for the sake of the light, she saddled Kentucky Belle. Then she led the gentle creature down the garden to a gate at its end which opened upon the back street. Closing this gate behind her so that Turk should not follow, she mounted and rode away.

The village was absolutely silent; each moonlit street seemed more still than the last. When the outskirts were left behind, she turned her horse towards the high bridle-path, whose general course was the same as that of the road along the river below, the road which led to the Warm Springs, passing on its way the farm of David Crumb.

As she did these things, one after the other, she neither thought nor reasoned; her action was instinctive. And the ride was a revel of joy; her cheeks were flushed with rose, her eyes were brilliant, her pulses were beating with a force and health which they had not known for months; she sang to herself little snatches of songs, vaguely, but gayly.

The dawn grew golden, the sun came up. The air was perfectly still and softly hazy. Every now and then a red leaf floated gently down from its branch to the ground; the footfalls of Kentucky Belle were muffled in these fallen leaves.

The bridle-path, winding along the flanks of the mountain, was longer than the straighter road below. It was eight o'clock before it brought her in sight of Crumb's. "I must leave Kentucky Belle in good hands," she thought. A steep track led down to the farm. The mare followed it cautiously, and brought her to Portia's door. "Can your husband take care of my horse for an hour or two?" she asked, smiling, as Portia came out. "Is he at home?"

"He's at home. But he ain't workin' to-day," Mrs. Crumb replied; "he's ailin' a little. But *I'll* see to yer mare."

Ruth dismounted; patting Kentucky Belle, she put

her cheek for a moment against the beautiful creature's head. "Good-bye," she whispered. "I am going for a walk," she said to Portia.

"Take a snack of sump'n' nerrer to eat first?"
Portia suggested.

But Ruth shook her head; she was already off.
She went down the river road as though she intended
to take her walk in that direction. But as soon as
the bend concealed her from Portia's view she turned
into the forest. The only footpath to the terrace,
"Ruth's Terrace," where Nicholas Willoughby had
built his cottage, was the one which led up from
Crumb's; Ruth's idea was that she should soon reach
this track. But somehow she missed it; she gave
up the search, and, turning, went straight up the
mountain. This slope also was covered with the
fallen leaves, a carpet of red and gold. She climbed
lightly, joyously, pulling herself up the steepest
places by the trunks of the smaller trees. Her color
brightened. Taking some of the leaves, she twisted
their stalks round the buttons of her habit so as to
make a red-and-gold trimming.

When she reached the summit she knew where
she was, for she could now see the cliffs on the other
side of the French Broad. They told her that she
had gone too far to the left; and, turning, this time
in the right direction, she made her way through the
forest along the plateau, keeping close to its verge as
a guide. As the chimneys of the Lodge came into
view, she reminded herself that she wished to see

Walter first—Walter himself, and not the servants. She had already paid several visits to The Lodge; she knew the place well. A good carriage-road led to it through a ravine which opened three miles below Crumb's; Nicholas Willoughby had constructed this new ascent. But he had not built any fences or walls, and she could therefore approach without being seen by keeping among the trees. At the side there was a thicket, which almost touched one end of the veranda; she stole into this thicket, and noiselessly made her way towards the house. When she reached the nearest point which she could attain unseen, she paused; her idea was to wait here until Walter should come out.

For he would be sure to come before long. The veranda was always the sitting-room; it commanded that wide view of the mountains far and near which had caused Nicholas Willoughby, at the cost of much money and trouble, to perch his cottage just here. The friends to whom he had lent The Lodge had left it ten days before, as Ruth knew. A man and his wife were always in charge, but when they were alone the front of the house was kept closed. To-day the windows were all open, a rising breeze swayed the curtains to and fro, and there were numerous other signs of Walter's presence; on the veranda were several easy-chairs and a lounge, besides a table with books and papers. And wasn't that the hat he had worn when she saw him talking to the farmer the day before? Yes, it was the same. "What time can it be?" she thought. She had not her watch with her—the costly diamond-decked toy which Horace Chase had given her; she had left it with her rings on the toilet-table at L'Hommedieu. Her wedding-ring was there also. But this was not from any plan about it; she always took off her rings at night. She had simply forgotten to put them on.

After ten minutes of waiting her heart gave a leap —she heard Walter's voice within the house. "That is a woman answering. He is talking to the housekeeper," she said to herself.

But presently there seemed to be three voices. "It is another servant," she thought. Then, before she had time to recognize that the intonations were not those of the mountain women (who were the only resource as servants in. this remote spot), Walter Willoughby himself came into view, pushing aside the curtains of one of the long windows that opened on the veranda.

But before Ruth could detach herself from the branches that surrounded her, he had drawn back again to make room for some one else, and a lady came out. He followed this lady; he took his seat familiarly upon the lounge where she had placed herself. It was Marion Barclay, the handsome, inanimate girl who, with her father and mother, had spent some weeks at St. Augustine during the preceding winter.

Marion was no longer inanimate. The fault of her finely chiselled face had been its coldness; but there was no coldness now as Walter Willoughby took her hand and pressed it to his lips.

At this moment Mrs. Barclay, Marion's mother, appeared. "Well, Darby and Joan," she said, smiling, as she established herself in the most comfortable chair.

Mrs. Barclay had favored Walter's suit from the first. It was her husband who had opposed it. Christopher Barclay had, in fact, opposed it so strongly that at St. Augustine he had dismissed young Willoughby with a very decided negative. It was while held at bay by this curt refusal that young Willoughby had entertained himself for a time by a fresh study of Mrs. Horace Chase.

This, however, had been but a brief diversion; he had never had the least intention of giving up Marion, and he had renewed his suit at Newport as soon as the summer opened. This time he had been more successful, and finally he had succeeded in winning Christopher Barclay to the belief that he would know how to manage his daughter's fortune, as, from the first, he had won Mrs. Barclay to the conviction that he would know how to manage her daughter's heart. Marion herself meanwhile had never had the slightest doubt as to either the one or the other. The engagement was still very new. As Mr. Barclay had investments at Chattanooga to look after, the little party of four had taken these beautiful October days for an excursion to Tennessee. Mrs. Barclay had heard that one of the elder Willoughbys had built a

cottage " not far from the Great Smoky Mountains,"
and as the paradisiacal weather continued, with the
forests all aglow and the sky a mixture of blue and
gold, she suggested that they should go over from
Chattanooga and take a look at it. Walter had therefore arranged it. From the Warm Springs he himself had ridden on in advance, in order to have the
house opened; this was the moment when he had
made his brief visit to Asheville for the purpose of
ordering supplies. The Barclays were to come no
farther eastward than The Lodge; they were to return in a day or two to Warm Springs, and thence
back to Chattanooga. Even if he had known that
Ruth Chase was at L'Hommedieu, Walter would not
have been deterred from pleasing Mrs. Barclay by
any thought of her vicinity; but, as it happened, he
supposed that she was in New York. For a recent
letter from Nicholas Willoughby had mentioned that
Chase himself was there, and that he was going
abroad with his wife for several years, sailing by the
next Wednesday's Cunarder.

"Darby and Joan?" Walter had repeated, in answer to Mrs. Barclay's remark. "That is exactly
what I am after, mother. Come, let us settle the
matter now on the spot—the *bona fide* Darby-and-
Joan-ness. When shall it begin?"

"'Mother'!" commented Mrs. Barclay, laughing.
"You have not lost much in your life through timid-
ity, Walter; I venture to say that."

"Nothing whatever," Walter replied, promptly.

"Shall we arrange it for next month? I have always said I should select November for my wedding, to see how my wife bears bad weather."

"No, no. Not quite so soon as that," answered Mrs. Barclay. "But early in the year perhaps," she went on, consentingly, as she looked at her daughter's happy blushing face.

Ruth heard every word; the veranda was not four yards distant; through the crevices in the foliage she could see them all distinctly.

She had immediately recognized the Barclays. Anthony Etheridge's speech about Walter's being in their train came back to her, and other mentions of their name as well. But this was mechanical merely; what held her, what transfixed her, was Walter's own countenance. Marion Barclay, Mrs. Barclay, all the rumors that Etheridge could collect, these would have been nothing to her if it had not been for that—for Walter's face.

And Walter was, in truth, very happy. Marion was everything that he wished his wife to be: she was accomplished and statuesque; to those she liked she could be charming; her features had the distinction which he had always been determined that his wife should possess. He was not marrying her for her fortune, though he was very glad she had that, also. He was much in love with her, and it was this which Ruth had perceived—perceived beyond a doubt.

For ten minutes she stood there motionless, her

eyes resting upon him. Then, feeling a deathlike chill coming, she had just sense enough, just life enough left, to move backward noiselessly through the smooth leaves until she had reached the open forest beyond. As a whole life passes before the eyes of a drowning man, in the same way she saw as in a vision her long mistake, and her one idea was to get to some spot where he could not see her, where he would never find her, before she sank down. She glanced over her shoulder; yes, the thicket concealed her in that direction. Then she looked towards the verge; her hurrying steps took her thither. Sitting down on the edge, she let herself slip over, holding on by a little sapling. It broke and gave way. And then the figure in the dark riding-habit, which was still adorned gayly with the bright leaves, disappeared.

CHAPTER XXIII

DOLLY FRANKLIN woke soon after dawn. A moment later she stole to Ruth's door and listened. There was no sound within, and, hoping that the tranquil slumber still continued, the elder sister turned the door-handle and looked in.

The window-curtains were drawn widely aside, as Ruth had arranged them several hours before, in order to let in the moonlight; the clear sunshine showed that the bed was tenantless, the room empty. Dolly entered quickly, closing the door behind her. But there was no letter bearing her name fastened to the pin-cushion or placed conspicuously on the mantel-piece, as she had feared. The rings, watch, and purse lying on the toilet-table next attracted her attention; she placed them in a drawer and locked it, putting the key in her pocket. Then, with her heart throbbing, she looked to see what clothes had been taken. "The riding-habit and hat. She has gone to The Lodge! She has found out in some way that he is staying there. Probably she is on Kentucky Belle."

After making sure that there were no other betrayals in Ruth's deserted room, the elder sister returned to her own apartment and rang for her English maid, Diana Pollikett. Diana was not yet up. As soon as possible she came hurrying in, afraid that Miss Franklin was ill. "Call Félicité," ordered Dolly. Then when the two returned together, the sallow Frenchwoman muffled in a pink shawl, Dolly said: "Mrs. Chase has gone off for an early ride. I dare say that she thought it would be amusing to take me by surprise." And she laughed. But that there was anger underneath her laugh was very evident. "Félicité, go down and see if I am not right," she went on. "I think you will find that her horse is gone."

Her acting was so perfect — the feigned mirth, with the deep annoyance visible beneath it — that the two maids were secretly much entertained; Mrs. Chase's escapade and her sharp-eyed sister's discomfiture were in three minutes known to everybody in the house. "Your mademoiselle, she tr'ry to keep *my* young madame a *leetle* too tight," commented Félicité in confidence to Miss Pollikett.

Dolly, having set her story going, went through the form of eating her breakfast. Then, as soon as she could, without seeming to be in too great haste, she drove off in her own phaeton, playing to the end her part of suppressed vexation.

She was on her way to The Lodge. It was a long drive, and the road was rough; the gait of her old pony was never more than slow; but she had not dared to take a faster horse, lest the unusual act should excite surprise. "Oh, Prosper, *do* go on!"

she kept saying, pleadingly, to the pony. But with all her effort it was two o'clock before she reached Crumb's, Prosper's jog-trot being hardly faster than a walk.

As the farm-house at last came into sight, she brushed away her tears of despair and summoned a smile. "My sister is here, or she has been here, hasn't she?" she said, confidently, to Mrs. Crumb, who, at the sound of the wheels, had come to the door.

"Yes, she's been yere. She's gone for a walk," Portia answered. "She left her mare; but she wouldn't stop to eat anything, though she must have quit town mortial early."

"Oh, she had breakfast before she started," lied Dolly, carelessly. "And I have brought lunch with me; we are to eat it together. But I am very late in getting here, my fat old pony is so slow! Which way has she gone?"

"Straight down the road," replied Portia. "An' when you find her, I reckon you'd both better be thinkin' of gettin' todes home befo' long. For the fine weather's about broke; there's a change comin'."

"Down the road—yes," thought Dolly. "But as soon as she was out of sight she went straight up the mountain! Oh, if I could only do it too! It is *so* much shorter." But as she feared her weak ankle might fail, all she could do was to drive up by the new road, the road which Nicholas Willoughby had built through the ravine below. She went on, therefore; there were still three miles to cover before this new road turned off.

It was the only well-made carriage-track in the county. First it followed the ravine, crossing and recrossing the brook at its bottom; then, leaving the gorge behind, it wound up the remainder of the ascent in long zigzags like those of the Alpine passes. The breeze, which had stirred the curtains of The Lodge when Ruth was standing in the thicket, had now grown into a wind, and clouds were gathering. But Dolly noticed nothing. Reaching the new road at last, she began the ascent.

When about a third of the way up, she thought she heard the sound of wheels coming down. The zigzag next above hers was fringed with trees, so that she could see nothing, but presently she distinguished the trot of two horses. Was it Ruth with Walter Willoughby? Were they already taking flight? Fiercely Dolly turned her phaeton straight across the road to block the way. "She shall never pass me. I will drag her from him!" The bend of the zigzag was at some distance; she waited, motionless, listening to the wheels above as they came nearer and nearer. Then round the curve into view swept a pair of horses and a light carriage. The top of the carriage was down; she could see that it held four persons; on the back seat was a portly man with gray hair, and with him a comfortable-looking elderly lady; in front was a tall, fair-haired girl, and by her side—Walter Willoughby.

In the first glance Dolly had recognized Walter's
companions. And the radiant face of Marion Barclay, so changed, so happy, told her all. She drew
her pony straight, and, turning out a little so as to
make room, she passed them with a bow, and even
with a smile.

Walter seemed astonished to see her there. But
he had time to do no more than return her salutation,
for he was driving at a sharp pace, and the descent
was steep. He looked back. But her pony was
going steadily up the zigzag, and presently turning
the bend the phaeton disappeared.

"This road leads only to The Lodge; I cannot
imagine why Miss Franklin is going there now," he
commented. "Or what she is doing here in any
case, so far from L'Hommedieu."

"L'Hommedieu? What is that? Oh yes, I remember; Anthony Etheridge told me that the Franklins had a place with that name (Huguenot, isn't it?)
in the North Carolina mountains somewhere," remarked Mrs. Barclay. "What has become, by-the-
way, of the pretty sister who married your uncle's
partner, Horace Chase? She wasn't in Newport this
summer. Is she abroad?"

"No. But she is going soon," Walter answered.
"My last letter from my uncle mentioned that Chase
was in New York, and that he had taken passage for
himself and his wife in the Cunarder of next Wednesday."

"Dear me! those clouds certainly look threaten-

25

ing," commented Mrs. Barclay, forgetting the Chases, as a treeless space in front gave her for a moment a wider view of the sky.

It was this change in the weather which had altered their plans. Nicholas Willoughby's mountain perch, though an ideal spot when the sky was blue, would be dreary enough in a long autumn storm; the Barclays and their prospective son-in-law were therefore hastening back to the lowlands.

Dolly reached the summit. And as the road brought her nearer to The Lodge, she was assailed by sinister forebodings. The first enormous relief which had filled her heart as she read the story told by the carriage, was now darkened by dread of another sort. If Ruth too had seen Marion, if Ruth too had comprehended all—where was she? From the untroubled countenances of the descending party, Dolly was certain that they, at least, had had no glimpse of Ruth; no, not even Walter. Dolly believed that men were capable of every brutality. But Walter's expression, when he returned her bow, had not been that of assumed unconsciousness, or assumed anything; there was no mistaking it — he was happy and contented; he looked as though he were enjoying the rapid motion and his own skilful driving, but very decidedly also as though all the rest of his attention was given to the girl by his side. "He has not even seen her! And he cares nothing for her; it is all a mistake! Now let me only find her and get her home, and no one shall *ever* know!" Dolly had said to herself with inexpressible relief. But then had followed fear: *could* she find her?

When the chimneys of The Lodge came into sight she drove her pony into the woods and tied him to a tree. Then she approached the house cautiously, going through the forest and searching the carpet of fallen leaves, trying to discover the imprint of footsteps. "If she came here (and I *know* she did), is there any place from which, herself concealed, she could have had a glimpse of Marion? That thicket, perhaps? It stretches almost to the veranda." And limping to this copse, Dolly examined its outer edge closely, inch by inch. She found two places where there was a track; evidently some one had entered at one of the points, and penetrated to a certain distance; then had come out in a straight line, backward. Dolly entered the thicket herself and followed this track. It brought her to a spot whence she had a clear view of the veranda. All signs of occupation were already gone; the chairs and tables had been carried in, the windows had been closed and barred. "If she stood here and saw them, and then if she moved backward and got herself out," thought Dolly, "where did she go next?" When freed from the thicket, she knelt down and looked along the surface of the ground, her eyes on a level with it; she had seen the negroes find small articles in that way—a button, or even a pin. After changing her place two or three times, she thought she discerned a faint indication of footsteps, and she followed this possible trail, keeping at some distance from it at one side so that it should not be effaced, and every now and then stooping to get another view of it, horizontally. For the signs were so slight that it was difficult to see them—nothing but a few leaves pressed down a little more than the others, here and there. The trail led her to the edge of the plateau. And here at last was something more definite—flattened herbage, and a small sapling bent over the verge and broken, as though some one had borne a weight upon it. "She let herself slip over the edge," thought Dolly. "She is down there in the woods somewhere. Oh, how shall I find her!"

The October afternoon would be drawing to its close before long, and this evening there would be no twilight, for black clouds were covering the sky, and the wind was beginning to sway the boughs of the trees above. In spite of her lameness, Dolly let herself down over the edge. There was no time to lose; she must find her sister before dark.

The slope below was steep; she tried to check her sliding descent, but she did not succeed in stopping herself until her clothes had been torn and her body a good deal bruised. When at last her slide was arrested, she began to search the ground for a second trail. But if there had been one, the leaves obscured it; not only were they coming down in showers from above, but the wind every now and then scooped up armfuls of those already fallen, and whirled them round and round in eddying spirals.

Keeping the peeled sapling above her as her guide, Dolly began to descend, going first to the right for several yards, then to the left, and pausing at the end of each zigzag to examine the forest beyond. With her crippled ankle her progress was slow. She lost sight, after a while, of the sapling. But as she had what is called the sense of locality, she was still able to keep pretty near the imaginary line which she was trying to follow. For her theory was that Ruth had gone straight down; that, once out of sight from that house, she had let herself go. Light though she was on her feet, she must have ended by falling, and then, if there was a second ledge below— "But I won't think of that!" Dolly said to herself, desperately.

She was now so far from the house that she knew she could not be heard. She therefore began to call "Ruth! Ruth!" But there was no reply. "I will count, and every time I reach a hundred I will call. Oh why, just this one day, should it grow dark so early, after weeks of the clearest twilight?" Drops began to fall, and finally the rain came down in torrents. She crouched beside a large tree, using its trunk as a protection as much as she could. Her hat and jacket were soon wet through, but she did not think of herself, she thought only of Ruth—Ruth, who had been fading for months— Ruth, out in this storm. "But I'll find her and take her back. And no one shall ever know," thought the elder sister, determinedly.

After what seemed a long time the rain grew less dense. The instant she could see her way Dolly resumed her search. The ground was now wet, and her skirts were soon stained as she moved haltingly back and forth, holding on by the trees. "Ruth! Ruth?" At the end of half an hour, when it was quite dark, she came to a hollow lined with bushes. She hesitated, but her determination to make her search thorough over every inch of the ground caused her to let herself down into it by sense of feeling, holding on as well as she could by the bushes.

And there at the bottom was the body of her sister.

"O God, *don't* let her be dead!" she cried, aloud. Drying the palm of her hand, she unbuttoned the soaked riding-habit and felt for the heart. At first there seemed to be no beating. Then she thought she perceived a faint throb, but she could not be sure; perhaps it was only her intense wish transferred to the place. Ruth's hat was gone, her hair and her cold face were soaked. "If I could only *see* her! Poor, poor little girl!" said Dolly, sobbing aloud.

Presently it began to rain again with great violence; and then Dolly, in a rage, seated herself on the soaked ground at the bottom of the hollow, took her sister's lifeless form in her arms, and held it close. "She is *not* dead, for she isn't heavy; she is light. If she had been dead I *couldn't* have lifted her." She dried Ruth's face. She began to chafe her temples and breast. After half an hour she thought she perceived more warmth, and her cramped arm redoubled its effort. The rain was coming down in sheets, but she did not mind it now, for she felt a breath, a sigh. "Ruth, do you know me? It is Dolly; no one but Dolly."

Ruth's eyes opened, though Dolly could not see them. Then she said, "Dolly, he loves some one else." That was all; she did not speak again.

The storm kept on, and they sat there together, motionless. Ruth's clothes were so wet that they were like lead. At length the black cloud from which that especial deluge had come moved away, and fitful moonlight shone out. Now came the anxious moment: would Ruth be able to walk?

At first it seemed as if she could not even rise, her whole body was so stiff. She was also extremely weak; she had eaten nothing since the night before, and the new life which had inspired her was utterly gone. But Dolly, somehow, made herself firm as iron; standing, she lifted her sister to her feet and held her upright until, little by little, she regained breath enough to take one or two steps. Then slowly they climbed from the hollow. With many pauses they went down the mountain; from this point, fortunately, its slope was not quite so steep. How she did it Dolly never knew, but the moment came at last when she saw a lighted window, and made her way towards it. And the final moment also came when she arrived at a door. Her arm was still supporting her pale young sister, who leaned against her. Ruth had not spoken; she had moved automatically; her senses were half torpid.

The lighted window was that of Portia Crumb. Portia had not gone to bed. But she was not sitting up on their account; she supposed that they had found shelter at one of several small houses that were scattered along the river road in the direction which they had taken. She was sitting up in order to minister to her "Dave." David Crumb's fits of drunkenness generally lasted through two days. When he came to himself, his first demand was for coffee, and his wife, who never could resist secretly sympathizing a little with the relief which her surly husband was able to obtain for a time from the grief which gnawed incessantly at her own poor heart—his wife always remained within call to give him whatever he needed. And, oddly enough, these vigils had become almost precious to Portia. For occasionally at these moments David of his own accord would talk of his lost boys—the only times he ever mentioned them or permitted his wife to do so. And now and then he would allow her to read her Bible to him, and even to sing a hymn perhaps, to which he would contribute in snatches a growling repentant bass.

Portia's coffee-pot now stood on the hot coals of her kitchen fireplace; she had been occupying the

time in spinning, and in chanting softly to herself,
as the rain poured down outside:

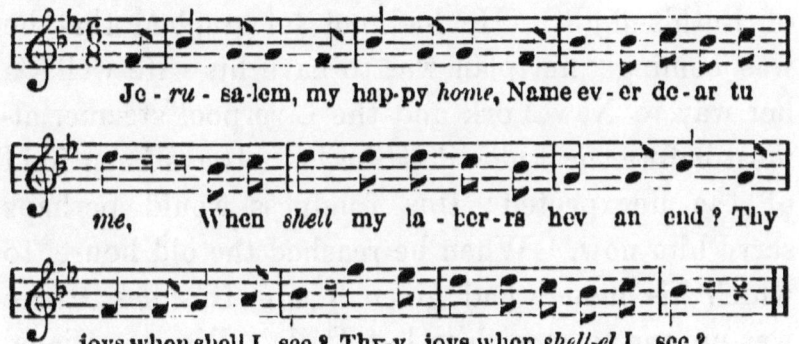

Je - ru - sa-lem, my hap-py *home,* Name ev - er de - ar tu

me,   When *shell* my la - ber-rs hev an end ? Thy

joys when shell I see ? Thy-y joys when *shell-el* I see ?

Then, hearing some one at the outer door, she had
come to open it.

"Good Lors! Miss Dolly! Here!—lemme help
you! Bring her right into the kitchen, an' put her
down on the mat clost to the fire till I get her wet
close off!"

CHAPTER XXIV

HORACE CHASE, having by hard work arranged his far-stretching affairs so that he could leave them, reached L'Hommedieu late in the evening of the day of Ruth's flight. He had not telegraphed that he was coming; his plan was to have his wife well on her way to New York and the Liverpool steamer almost before she knew it. She had always been fond of the unexpected; this fondness would perhaps serve him now. When he reached the old house, to which his money had given a new freshness, there was no one to meet him but Dolly's Diana. Diana, in her moderate, unexcited way, began to tell him what had happened. But she was soon re-enforced by Félicité, whose ideas (regarding the same events) were far more theoretic.

"Miss Franklin had a lunch prepared, and took it with her," Diana went on.

"Eet ended in a peekneek," interrupted Félicité. "The leaf was so red, and the time so beautiful, monsieur; no clouds, and the sky of a blue! Then suddenlee the rain ees come. No doubt they have entered in a house to wait till morning."

"Which road did my wife take?" inquired Chase, his tone anxious.

"Ah, monsieur, no one *see* herr, she go so early. Eet was herr joke—to escape a leetle from herr sistare, if eet is permit to say eet; pardon."

"Which way, then, did Miss Franklin go?" continued Chase, impatiently.

Both women pointed towards the left. "She went *down* the street. *That* way."

"Down the street? That's no good. What I want to know is which road she took after leaving town?"

But naturally neither Félicité nor Miss Pollikett could answer this question; they had not followed the phaeton.

Chase rang the bell, and sent for one of the stablemen. "Let Pompey and Zip go and ask at all the last houses (where the three roads that can be reached from the end of this street turn off) whether any one noticed Miss Franklin drive past this morning? They all know her pony and trap. Tell Pompey to step lively, and if the people have gone to bed, he must knock 'em up."

The two negroes returned in less than fifteen minutes; they had found the trace without trouble: Miss Franklin had taken the river road towards Warm Springs.

"Saddle my horse," said Chase; "and you, Jeff, as soon as I have started, put the pair in the light carriage and drive down to Crumb's. Have the lamps in good order and burning brightly, and see that the curtains are buttoned down so as to keep the inside dry. Felicity, put in shawls and whatever's necessary; the ladies are no doubt under cover somewhere; but they may have got wet before reaching it. Perhaps one of you had better go along?" he added, looking at the two women reflectively, as if deciding which one would be best.

"Yes, sir; I can be ready in a moment," said Diana, going out.

"Ah! for *two* there is not enough place," murmured Félicité, relieved.

Chase ate a few mouthfuls of something while his horse was being saddled; then, less than half an hour after his arrival, he was off again. It was very dark, but he did not slacken his speed for that, nor for the rough, stony ascents and descents, nor for the places where the now swollen river had overflowed the track. The distance which Dolly's slow old pony had taken five hours to traverse, this hard rider covered in less than half the time. At one o'clock he reached Crumb's. It was the first house in that direction after the village and its outskirts had been left behind. Along the mile or two beyond it, farther towards the west, were three smaller houses, and at one of the four he hoped to find his wife. As he drew near Crumb's, he saw that the windows were lighted. "They're here!" he said to himself, with a long breath of relief. As he rode up to the porch, Portia, who had heard his horse's footsteps, looked out.

"They're here?" he asked.

" Yes," answered Portia, " they be."

" And all right ?"

" I reckon so, by this time. Mis' Chase, she was pretty well beat when she first come ; but she's asleep now, an' restin' well. And Miss Dolly, she's asleep too."

Chase dismounted. " Can my horse be put up? Just call some one, will you ?"

" Well, Isrul Porter, who works here, has gone home," answered Mrs. Crumb. " Arter Mis' Chase and Miss Dolly got yere, I sent Isrul arter their pony, what they'd lef' in the woods more'n two miles off, an' he 'lowed, Isrul did, that he'd take him home with him for the night when he found him, bekase the Porters's house is nearer than our'n to the place where he was lef'. An' Dave, he ain't workin' ter-day; he's ailin' a little. But *I* kin see to yer hoss."

" Show a light and I'll do it myself," Chase answered, amused at the idea of his leaving such work to a woman.

Portia returned to the kitchen, and came back with a burning brand of pitch-pine, which gave out a bright flare. Carrying this as a torch, she led the way to the stable, Chase following with the horse. " Your mare, she's in yere errcady," said the farmer's wife, pointing to Kentucky Belle.

Then, as they went back to the house by the light of the flaring brand, she asked whether she should go up and wake Ruth.

"Yes, and I'll go along; which room is it? Hold on, though; are you sure my wife's asleep?"

"When I went up the minute before you come, she was, an' Miss Dolly too."

"Well, then, I guess I won't disturb 'em just yet," said Chase, and he went with Portia to her kitchen, where she brought forward her rocking-chair for his use. "What time did they get here?" he inquired.

Portia, seating herself on a three-legged stool, told what she knew. As she was finishing her story there came a growl from the dark end of the long room, the end where the loom stood. "It's only Dave wakin' up," she explained, and she hastened towards her husband. But as she did so he roared "Coffee!" in impatient tones, and, hurrying back, she knelt down and blew up the fire. "I'm comin', Dave; it's all ready," she called. Then as she continued to work the bellows quickly she went on in a low voice to Chase: "He'll stay awake now for an hour or two. An' he'll be talkin', an' takin' on, p'raps. Mebbe you'd ruther set in the best room for a whilst? There's a fire; an' the stairs mount right up from there to the room where yer wife's asleep, so you kin go up whenever you like. Relse you might lay down yourself, without disturbin' 'em at all till mawnin'. There's a good bed in the best room; none better."

"Coffee!" demanded the farmer a second time, and Portia quickly took the cup, which stood waiting with sugar and cream already in it, and lifting her pot

from the coals, poured out the odorous beverage, the
strong coffee of Rio. Though she had an intense desire to be left alone with "Dave," now that his precious waking-time had come, her inborn sense of hos-
pitality would never have permitted her to suggest
that her guest should leave her, if she had not believed with all her heart that her best room was really a bower of beauty; she even had the feeling that
she ought to urge it a little, lest he should be unwilling to "use it common." Chase, perceiving that she
wished him to go, went softly out, and, entering the
bower, closed the door behind him. The fire was low.
He put on some pitch-pine splinters, and added wood;
for, in spite of his water-proof coat (which was now
hanging before the fireplace in the kitchen), his
clothes were damp. He lifted the logs carefully, so
as not to waken the sleepers above; then he sat down
and stretched out his legs to the blaze. In spite of
Portia's assertion that his wife was "all right," he
was very uneasy; he could scarcely keep himself
from stealing up to get a look at her. But sleepless-
ness had been for so long one of her troubles that he
knew it was far wiser to let her rest as long as she
could. One thought pleased him; it had pleased him
since the moment he heard it: her stealing off for a
ride at dawn simply to tease Dolly. That certainly
looked as if she must be much stronger than she had
been when he left her. It was an escapade worthy
of the days when she had been the frolicking Ruth
Franklin. On the other hand loomed up the results

of this freak of hers, namely, her having been out so
long in the storm. Portia's expression, " pretty well
beat when she first come "—that was not encourag-
ing. Thus he weighed the possibilities, sitting there
with his chair tilted back, his eyes fixed on the re-
viving flame. He knew that he could not sleep until
he had seen her. Portia's " best bed," therefore, did
not tempt him. In addition, he wished to wait for
the carriage, in order to contrive some sort of shelter
for it, and to assist in putting up the horses, since
there was no one else to do it. After a while, with
his hands clasped behind his head, he moved his
chair a little and looked vaguely round the room.
Everything was the same as when he had paid his
former visit there during the excursion which he had
made over the Great Smoky Mountains with the
Franklins and poor Jared. The red patch-work quilt
was spread smoothly over the bed; the accordion
was on the mantel-piece, flanked by the vase whose
design was a pudgy hand holding a cornucopia; on
the wall was the long row of smirking fashion-plates.
This means of entertainment, however, was soon exhausted, and after a while he took some memoranda
from his pocket, and, bending forward towards the
fire, began to look them over.

He had been thus engaged for nearly half an hour
when a door opened behind him, and Dolly Franklin
came in.

She had no idea that he was there. The bedroom
above, whose flight of steep stairs she had just de-

scended, possessed windows only towards the river; and the second-story floors of the old house were so thick that no sound from below could penetrate them. She had not therefore heard Chase ride up on the other side; she had not distinguished any sounds in the kitchen.

He jumped up when he saw her. "I'm *mighty* glad you've come down, Dolly. I've been afraid to disturb her. Is she awake?"

Dolly closed the door behind her. "No; she is sleeping soundly. I wouldn't go up just now if I were you. A good sleep is what she needs most of all."

"All right; I'll wait. But how in the world came she to be out so long in the rain, and you too? That's the part I don't understand."

Dolly's heart had stood still when she saw her brother-in-law. "I'll sit here for a while," she suggested, in order to gain time. "Will you please pull forward that chair—the one in the corner? I had no idea you were here. I only came down for the pillows from this bed; they are better than those upstairs." While she was getting out these words her quick mind had flown back to L'Hommedieu, and to the impression which she had left behind her there, carefully arranged and left as explanation of their absence. The explanation had been intended for any of their friends who might happen to come to the house during the day. But it would do equally well for Horace Chase, and Félicité could be safely trusted to have repeated it to him within five minutes after his unexpected arrival! For Félicité was not fond of Miss Dora Franklin. The idea that her young mistress had gone off for a ride at daylight would be an immense delight to the Frenchwoman, not for the expedition itself (such amusements in a country so "sauvage" being beyond her comprehension), but for the annoyance to mademoiselle — mademoiselle whose watchfulness over everything that concerned her sister (even her sister's maid) was so insupportably oppressive. Their start, therefore, Dolly reflected, both Ruth's at dawn and her own a little later, was probably in a measure accounted for in Horace Chase's mind. But as regarded the hours in the rain, what could she invent about that? For Portia had evidently described Ruth's exhaustion and their wet clothes. She had seated herself by the fire; arrayed in one of the shapeless dresses of her hostess, with her hair braided and hanging down her back, her plain face looked plainer than ever. Worn out though she was, she had not been asleep even for a moment; she had been sitting by the bedside watching her sister. Ruth had lain motionless, with her head thrown back lifelessly, her breathing scarcely perceptible. Whenever Portia had peeped in (and the farmer's wife had stolen softly up the stairs three times) Dolly had pretended to be asleep; and she knew that Portia would think that Ruth also was sleeping. But Ruth was not asleep. And Dolly's mind was filled

with apprehension.   What would follow this ap-
athy?

"As I understand it, Ruthie took a notion to go
off for a ride at daybreak," Horace Chase began,
"and then, after breakfast, you followed her.   How
did you know which way she went?   I suppose you
asked.   But she left her mare here as early as half-
past eight this morning, the woman of the house tells
me, and you yourself got here at two; what happened afterwards?   How came you to stay out in the
rain?   Unless you got lost, I don't see what you
were about."

"We *were* lost for a while," answered Dolly, who
had now arranged her legend.   "But that was afterwards.   Our staying out was my fault, or, rather, my
misfortune."   She put out her feet and warmed them
calmly.   "After I drove on from here, I didn't find
Ruth for some time.   When at last I came upon her,
we took our lunch together, and then I tied the pony
to a tree and we strolled off through the woods, picking up the colored leaves.   Suddenly I had one of my
attacks.   And it must have been a pretty bad one, for
it lasted a long time.   How long I don't know; but
when I came to myself it was dark.   Ruth, of course,
couldn't carry me, poor child.   And she wouldn't
leave me.   So there we stayed in the rain.   And when
finally I was able to move, it took us ages to get here,
for not only was I obliged to walk slowly, but it was
so dark that we couldn't find the road.   I am all right
now.   But meanwhile *she* is dreadfully used up."

Here, from the kitchen, came the sound of Portia's gentle voice:

> "When *shell* these eyes thy heavenly walls
>   An' peerly gates behold?
> Thy buildin's with salvation strong,
>   An' streets of shinin' gold?
>   An'-an' streets of shi-*i-nin*' gold!"

"Crumb has arrived at his religious stage, and his wife is celebrating," commented Dolly. "He goes through them all in regular succession every time he is drunk. Obstinacy. Savagery. Lethargy. And then, finally, Repentance, for he isn't one of those unimportant just persons who need none."

Chase glanced at her with inward disfavor; cynicism in a woman was extremely unpleasant to him. His mental comment, after she had explained their adventures, had been: "Well, if *Dolly* had let the whole job alone, none of this would have happened; Ruth would have had her lark out and come home all right, and that would have been the end of it. But Dolly must needs have *her* finger in the pie, and out she goes. Then of course she gets sick, and the end is that instead of her seeing to Ruth, Ruth has to see to her." But he kept these reflections to himself. He brought forward instead the idea that was important to him: "Isn't it a pretty good sign she's better, that she *wanted* to go off for a ride in that way? It's like the things she used to do when I first knew her. Don't you remember how she stayed out so long that

cold, windy night without her hat, talking with Malachi Hill over the back fence about his Big Moose
masquerade? And how she even went on, bareheaded and in the dark, half across the village to find
Achilles Larue and get him to come, so that she could
tease Miss Billy?" He gave a short laugh over the
remembrance. "I cannot help thinking, Dolly, that
she isn't half as sick as you made out; in fact, I've
never thought she was, though I've more or less
fallen in with your idea of giving her a change. I
had made arrangements to start for New York to-
morrow morning, so as to hit the Cunarder of Wednesday. But, as things have turned out, I don't know
that we need pull up stakes so completely, after all.
She's evidently better."

For one instant Dolly thought. Then she spoke:
"No, carry out your plan. Take her away to-morrow morning just as you intended. Even if she *is*
somewhat stronger (though I think you'll find that
she isn't), she needs a change." She said this
decidedly. But the decision was for her own sake;
it was an effort to make herself believe, by the
sound of the spoken words, that this course would
still be possible. "It *shall* be possible," she resolved
in her own mind.

"Well, I guess I won't decide till I see her," Chase
answered. "Perhaps she's awake by this time?"

Dolly got up quickly. "I will go and see; my
step is lighter than yours. If I do not come back,
that will mean that she is still asleep, and that I think

it best not to disturb her. The moment she does wake, however, I will come and call you. Will that do ?"

" All right," said Chase, briefly, a second time. He did not especially enjoy the prospect of several years in Europe. But at least it would be agreeable to have his wife to himself, with no Dolly to meddle and dictate.

After she had gone, he sat expectant for nearly fifteen minutes. But she did not return ; Ruth evidently had not wakened. He rose, gave a stretch, and, going to the window, raised the curtain and looked out. The rain was pouring down ; there was no sign of the carriage ; it was so dark that he could not see even the nearest trees. Dropping the curtain again, he walked about the room for a while. Then he started to go to the kitchen, to see how his wet coat was coming on ; but remembering Portia's vigil (which nothing could have induced him to break in upon, now that he understood its nature), he stopped. He looked at all the simpering ladies of the fashion - plates, ladies whose bodies were formed on the model which seems to be peculiar to such publications, and to exist only for them ; he lifted the vase and inspected it a third time ; he even tried the accordion softly. Finally he sat down by the fire, and, taking out his memoranda again, he went back to business calculations.

Dolly had gone swiftly up the stairs and along the entry which led to the bedroom. Ruth was lying just as she had left her, with her eyes shut, her head thrown back. Dolly closed the door and locked it; then she came and leaned over her.

"Ruth, do you hear me?"

"Yes," answered Ruth, mechanically.

Dolly sat down by the side of the bed and drew her sister towards her.

"I have something to tell you," she whispered. "Your husband is down-stairs."

Ruth did not start. After a moment she opened her eyes and turned them slowly towards her sister.

"He came home unexpectedly," Dolly went on, in the same low tone. "He reached L'Hommedieu this evening, and when they told him that we had not returned he had inquiries made as to the road we had taken, and came down here himself on horseback. At L'Hommedieu, Ruth, they think that you slipped out at dawn for a ride, just to play me a trick, because I have watched you so closely about your health lately that you were out of all patience. I let them think this; or, rather, I made them think it. And they have repeated it to your husband, who accepts it just as they did. The only thing he could not understand was why we stayed out so long in the storm, for Portia had evidently told him how late it was when we came in, and how exhausted you looked. So I have just said that after I found you we had our lunch together, and then, after tying the pony to a tree, we strolled through the woods, picking up the colored leaves. Suddenly one of my attacks came on, and it was a bad attack; I was unconscious for a long time. You wouldn't leave me; and so there we had to stay in the rain. When at last I could walk I had to come slowly. And we couldn't find the road for a long while—it was so dark. All this seems to him perfectly natural, Ruth; he suspects nothing. The only point he is troubled about is your health—how that will come out after the exposure. He is sitting by the fire down-stairs waiting for you to wake, for I told him you were asleep. And here is something supremely fortunate: his plan is to take you off to New York to-morrow morning, to hit the Wednesday's Cunard steamer for Liverpool. He has had this idea for some weeks—the idea of going abroad. That was the reason he went away—to make ready. He didn't tell you about it, because he thought he would take you by surprise. And he still hopes to sail on Wednesday, provided you are well enough. it isn't to be a flying trip this time; he is willing to stay over there for years if you like. Now, Ruth, listen to me. You *must go*. You need make no effort of any kind; just let yourself slip on from day to day, passively. There is nothing difficult about that. If there were, I should not ask you to do it, for I know you could never play a part. But here there is no part; you need do no more than you always have done. That has never been much, for from the first the devotion has been on his side, not on yours, and he will expect no more. Now try to sleep a little, and then at sunrise I will let him come up. When he comes you needn't talk; you can say

you are too tired to talk. He is so uneasy about
your health that he will fall in with anything. Don't
think about it any more. The whole thing's settled."

Suiting her actions to her words, Dolly rearranged
the coverlet over her sister, and then, rising, she began to make a screen before the fire with two chairs
and a blanket, so that its light should not fall across
the bed. While she was thus engaged she heard a
sound, and, turning her head, she saw that Ruth was
getting up.

"What is it?" she said, going to her. "Do you
want anything?"

"Where are my clothes?" Ruth asked. She was
sitting on the edge of the bed, her bare feet resting
on the rag mat by its side.

"Portia is drying them. She left some of her
things on that chair for you. But don't get up now;
the night isn't anywhere near over."

Ruth went to the chair where lay the garments,
coarse but clean; she unbuttoned her night-gown
(also one of Portia's). Then her strength failed, and
she sank down on the chair. "Come back to bed,"
said Dolly, urgently.

Ruth let her head rest on the chair-back for a moment or two. Then she said: "I won't try to dress;
I don't feel strong enough. But please get me some
stockings and shoes, and a shawl. That will be
enough."

"Are you tired of the bed? I can make you comfortable in that chair by the fire, then," Dolly an-

swered. " Here are stockings. And shoes, too — Portia's. But I'm afraid they will drop off !" Kneeling down, she drew on the stockings, and then Ruth, rising, stepped into the shoes. Dolly went to spread a blanket over the chair, and while she was thus engaged Ruth, seeing a homespun dress of Portia's hanging from a peg, took it and put it on over her night-gown.

" You need not have done that," commented Dolly ; " here is a second blanket to wrap you up in."

But Ruth was going towards the door. Dolly hurried after her and caught her arm. " You are not going down ? What for ?"

" I don't know," answered Ruth, vaguely. Then, with quickened breath, she added, " Yes, I *do* know ; I am going to tell—tell what I did." She was panting a little ; Dolly could hear the sound.

The elder sister held her tightly. But Ruth did not struggle, she stood passive. " What are you going to tell ?" Dolly asked, sternly. " What *is* there to tell ? You took a ride ; you walked in the forest ; you stood in a thicket ; you came back. That is all. No one saw you ; no one on earth knows anything more. And there *was* nothing more, save in thought. Your thoughts are your own affair, you are not required to tell them ; it would be a strange world indeed if we had to tell all our thoughts ! In your *acts* as it has turned out, there has been nothing wrong. Leave it so, then. Let it rest."

Ruth did not reply. But in her clouded eyes

Dolly thought she read refusal. "Ruth, let me judge for you," she pleaded. "Could I possibly advise you to do anything that was not your best course? Your very best? If you force an account of your inward feelings upon your husband—who does not ask for them or want them—you destroy his happiness, you make him wretched. Don't you care for that? If I have never liked him—and I may as well confess that I never have—at least I know his devotion to you. If you tell, therefore, tell so unnecessarily, it will be a great cruelty. Think of all he did for mother! Of all he did and tried to do for Jared!"

Two tears welled up in Ruth's eyes. But she did not speak.

"And then there is another thing," Dolly went on. "If he knows the truth, all the good in him will be changed to bitterness. And, besides, he will be very harsh to you, Ruth; he will be brutal; and he will even think that it is right that he should be so. For those are the ideas of—of some people about wives who go wrong." To the woman who had married Horace Chase Dolly could say no more. But if she had spoken out all that was in her heart, her phrase would have been, "For those are the ideas of common people about wives who go wrong." (For to Dolly, Horace Chase's commonness—or what seemed to her commonness—had always been the insupportable thing.) But what she was saying now about her dread of his possible brutality was not in the least a fiction invented to influence Ruth; she had in reality the greatest possible dread of it.

Ruth, however, seemed either to have no fears at all, or else she was all fear — fear that had reached the stage of torpor.

"Think of *this*, too," urged Dolly, finally. "If you tell, have you the slightest idea that your husband will be able to keep himself from breaking off instantly all relations with the Willoughbys — with the uncles as well as the nephew? And do you want Walter Willoughby to suspect—as he certainly would suspect—the cause? Do you wish this young fellow who has merely played with you, who from the beginning has amused himself at your expense, and, no doubt, laughed at you over and over again—do you wish him to have a fresh joke at the sight of your imbittered husband's jealousy? Is he to tell the whole story to Marion Barclay? And have *her* laughing also at your hopeless passion for him?—at the way you have thrown yourself at his head? If you are silent, not only will your husband be saved from all his wretchedness, but Walter Willoughby will have no story to tell!"

For answer, Ruth gave a moan of physical weakness; she did not try to free herself from her sister's hold; she stood motionless, her figure drooping, her eyes closed. "Dolly," she murmured, "if you keep on opposing me — and my strength won't hold out very long—you will end by preventing it, preventing my telling. But there is something you won't be able to prevent: I am so tired that I want to die! And I shouldn't be afraid of *that;* I mean, finding a way."

Dolly's hands dropped.

And then Ruth, after a moment more of delay, pushed back the bolt, passed along the entry, and began to go down the dark stairs. She went slowly, a step at a time. A step; then a hesitation; then another step. Finally she reached the bottom, and opened the door.

Her descent had been noiseless; it was not until her hand touched the latch that Chase turned his head. When he saw her, he sprang up. "*You,* Ruthie!" he exclaimed, delightedly, as she entered, followed, after a moment, by the frightened, wretched Dolly. "Are you well enough to be up?" He put his arm round her and kissed her. "Come to the fire."

But Ruth drew herself away; she moved off to a little distance. "Wait; I have something to tell you," she answered.

"At any rate, sit down," Chase responded, bringing the best arm-chair and placing it before her. He had had a long experience regarding her changing caprices; he never disputed them.

But she did not seat herself; she only leaned on the back of the chair, her hands grasping its top. "I did not take that ride this morning for the reason you think," she began. "I was going to Walter Willoughby; I knew he was at The Lodge."

"Well, then, I wish you hadn't," replied Chase. He looked annoyed, but not angry. "Fellows like Walter are conceited enough without that sort of thing. If you wanted to see him, you could have sent a note, asking him to come to L'Hommedieu. Or Dolly could have written it for you; that would have been the best way. But don't stand there; sit down."

Ruth took a fresh grasp of the chair. "You do not comprehend," she said, her voice showing how little strength she had. But though she was weak physically, there was no nervousness; she was perfectly calm. "You do not comprehend. I was going to him because I loved him, Horace. I have loved him for a long time. I loved him so that I *had* to go!"

As she said this her husband's face changed—changed in a way that was pitiful to see. He looked stunned, stricken.

"I did not mean to," Ruth went on. "I did not know what it was at first. And then—it was too late. I thought he loved me; I was sure of it. And so—I went to him."

Dolly, hurrying forward, laid her hand restrainingly on Chase's wrist. "He didn't see her, no one saw her. And she did no harm, no harm whatever."

But Chase shook Dolly off with a motion of his shoulder. Ruth, too, paid no heed to her sister; she looked straight at her husband, not defiantly, but drearily; she went on with her tale almost mechanically, and with the same desperate calmness as before. "So I went to him; I left my horse here, and went up through the woods. But he had Marion Barclay there; I saw her. And I saw his face, the expression of his face, as he talked to her; it is Marion he loves!"

"I could have told you that. At least I could have told you that he has been trying to get that girl for a long time," said Chase, bitterly. "But there was nothing in that to hold him back as regards *you*. And it hasn't held him back; it hasn't prevented him from— But he shall answer for this! Answer to *me*." The rage in his face was deep; his eyes gleamed; his hands were clinched. Dolly turned cold. "He will *kill* Walter," she thought. "Oh, what will he do to Ruth?"

Ruth had left her chair; she came and stood before her husband. "He isn't to blame, Horace. I would tell you if he were; I should like to see Marion Barclay suffer! But if you go to him, he will only laugh at you, and with reason; for he has never cared for me, and he has never even pretended to care; I see that now. It is *I* who have been in love with *him*. It began that first winter we spent in Florida," she went on. She had returned to her place behind the chair, and her eyes were again fixed upon her husband's face. "And when he told me, suddenly, that he was going to California, going for years, I could not breathe. Then, when Jared died, and mother died, and you were so good to me, I tried to forget him. But as soon as I saw him again I knew that it was of no use—no sort of use!"

"You'll never make me believe that *he* did nothing all this time," said Chase, savagely. "That he didn't profit—that he didn't take advantage—"

But Ruth shook her head. "No. Perhaps he amused himself a little. Once or twice he said a few words. But that was all. And even this was called out by me — by *my* love. Left to himself, he always drew back, he always stopped. But *I*— I never did! You must believe me about this—I mean about its having been *my* doing. How can I make you believe it? If I say that by my mother's memory, by Jared's, what I have told you is true, will you believe it then? Very well; I *do* say so." Exhausted, she put her face down upon her hands on the top of the chair-back.

The firelight, which was now brilliant, had revealed her clearly. Her figure in the homespun dress looked wasted; in her face there was now no beauty, the irregularity of its outlines was conspicuous, the bright color was gone, the eyes were dull and dead.

Something in her bowed head touched Chase keenly. A memory of her as she was when he married her came before him, the radiant young creature who had given herself to him so willingly and so joyously.

"Ruthie, we'll forget it," he said, in a changed voice. "I was too old for you, I am afraid. I ought not to have asked you to marry me. But it's done now, past mending, and we must make the best of it. But we'll begin all over again, my poor little girl." For his wife had always seemed to him a child, an impulsive, lovely child; a little spoiled, no doubt, but enchantingly sweet and dear. Her affection for him, as far as it went, had been sincere; he had comprehended that from the beginning. And alluring though she was to him in her young beauty, he would not have married her without it; her consent, even her willing consent, would not have been enough. And now it seemed to him that he could go back to that girlish liking, that he could foster it and draw it out. He had not protected her from her own fancies, he had not guarded her or guided her. Now he would make her more a part of his life; he would no longer think of her as a child.

He had come to her as he spoke. This time she did not draw herself away; but, looking at him with the same fixed gaze, she went on. She had been speaking slowly, but now her words came pouring forth in a flood as though she felt that it was the only way in which she could get them spoken at all; each brief phrase was hurried out with a quick pant.

"Oh, you don't understand. You think it was a fancy. But it wasn't, it wasn't; I *loved* him! I was going to stay with him forever. I would have gone to the ends of the earth with him. I would never have asked a question. I hadn't the least hesitation; you mustn't think that I had. I sang to myself as I rode out here, I was so happy and glad. I didn't care what became of you; I didn't even

27

think of you. If he had been alone at The Lodge, I should have gone straight into his arms. And you might have come in, and I shouldn't have minded; I shouldn't even have known you were there! From the moment I started, you were nothing to me—nothing; you didn't exist! I am as guilty as a woman can be. I had every intention, every inclination. What was lacking was *his* will; but never mine! It was only twelve hours ago. I haven't changed in that time. The only change is that now I know he doesn't care for *me*. I would have accepted anything—yes, anything. It was only twelve hours ago, and if he *had* been alone at The Lodge, whether he really loved me or not, he would not have—turned me out."

"No; damn him!" answered Chase.

"And *I* should have been glad to stay," Ruth concluded, inflexibly.

Her husband turned away. It was a strong man's anguish. He sat down by the fire, his face covered by his hands.

Into the pause there now came again the strains of Portia's hymn in the kitchen—that verse about "the pearly gates" which she was hopefully singing a second time to Dave. Then, in the silence that followed, the room seemed filled with the rushing sound of the rain.

Ruth had remained motionless. "I shall never be any better," she went on with the same desperation; "I wish you to understand me just as I really am.

I might even do it a second time; I don't know. You may make whatever arrangements you like about me; I agree to all in advance. And now—I'll go." Turning, she went towards the door of the stairway, the pale Dolly joining her in silence.

Then Horace Chase got up. His face showed how profoundly he had suffered; it was changed, changed for life. "After all this that you've told me, Ruth, I don't press myself upon you—I never shall again; I *couldn't;* that's ended. You haven't got any father or mother, and you're very young yet; so I shall have to see to you for the present. But it can be done from a distance, and that's the way I'll fix it. You mustn't think I don't feel this thing because I don't say much. It just about kills me! But as to condemning, coming down on you out and out, I don't do it, I haven't got the check! Who am I that I should dare to? Have I been so faultless myself that I have any right to judge *you?*" And as he said this, his rugged face had, for the moment, an expression that was striking in its beauty; its mixture of sorrow, honesty, and grandeur.

Ruth gazed at him. Then she gave an inarticulate entreating cry, and ran to him.

But she was so weak that she fell, and Dolly rushed forward.

Horace Chase put Dolly aside—put her aside forever. He lifted his wife in his arms, and silently bent his head over hers as it lay on his breast.

THE END

THE PRINCE OF INDIA;

Or, Why Constantinople Fell. By LEW. WALLACE, Author of "Ben-Hur," "The Boyhood of Christ," etc. Two Volumes. 16mo, Cloth, Ornamental, $2 50; Half Leather, $4 00; Three-quarter Leather, $5 00; Three-quarter Calf, $6 00; Three-quarter Crushed Levant, $8 00. (*In a Box.*)

General Wallace has achieved the (literary) impossible. He has struck the bull's-eye twice in succession. After his phenomenal hit with "Ben-Hur" he has given us, in "The Prince of India," another book which no man will say shows the least falling off. . . . It is a great book.—*N. Y. Tribune.*

A great story. It has power and fire. We believe that it will be read and re-read.—*N. Y. Sun.*

For boldness of conception this romance is unique of its kind. The amount of research shown is immense. The mere *mise en scène* necessary for the proper presentation of the Byzantine period alone involves a life-long study. . . . There are incidents innumerable in this romance, and all are worked up with dramatic effect.—*N. Y. Times.*

Its human interest is so vivid that it is one of those historical novels laid down reluctantly, only with the last page, with the feeling that one turns away from men and women with whom for a while he lived and moved. . . . A masterly and great and absorbing work of fiction. . . . Dignity, a superb conjunction of historical and imaginative material, the movement of a strong river of fancy, an unfailing quality of human interest, fill it overflowingly.—*N. Y. Mail and Express.*

In invention, in the power to make mind-impressions, in thrilling interest, "The Prince of India" is not inferior to "Ben-Hur." The visit to the grave of Hiram, King of Tyre, with which the story opens, at once arouses the reader's keenest interest, which culminates in the closing pages of the second volume with the downfall of Constantinople. — *Philadelphia Inquirer.*

PUBLISHED BY HARPER & BROTHERS, NEW YORK.

☞ *For sale by all booksellers, or will be sent by mail, postage prepaid, to any part of the United States, Canada, or Mexico, on receipt of the price.*